I0770648

BORN ON MONDAY

Richard R. Becker

Copywrite, Ink.

*For Sandy, and all trauma survivors.
You are not alone.*

CHAPTER 1

TIME CAPSULE

Billy resisted the urge to pull his wool jacket closed, walking between his truck and the front door of the Bear Paw. It was a chilly fall night with some brisk weather blowing off the Kennebec River, but the bar manager, Charlie, liked to run the local pub hot for out-of-towners even if most of his customers were Mainers. It had something to do with tips, he said. The farther away, the better the tips.

So instead of pulling his jacket tighter, Billy picked up the pace and took off his coat as he crashed through the front door. He tossed it on one of the coatracks and headed toward a small opening at the bar.

"Hey, Charlie, give me a Geary's, will you?"

"Yeah, I'll need a minute on the pour," he said.

Placing an order at the Paw, as they called it, was an unofficial announcement that you'd arrived. It also allowed people an opportunity to finish part of their conversation before giving you a proper greeting as a newcomer. They welcomed him with a chorus of how-do-you-dos and raised highballs. He obliged them all, hugging a few and nodding to others. By the time they finished, Charlie was back with a glass of beer.

"Hey, um, let me be the one to tell you before someone else does," Charlie said. "Look who's set up at the table."

Billy gave him a shrug, indicating he wouldn't care. But then Charlie gave an insistent head bob. Billy would have never shrugged it off had he known. His eyes moved quickly past Ed Mailer and toward the woman who was readying a shot.

Her hair was shorter and framed her face, but there was no mistaking who it was. Jessica Michaud — the girl who gave him up for New York City five years ago — was shooting the seven ball in the corner pocket and lining up the nine. He fished two quarters out of his pocket as he walked over to them.

"Winner, if it's open," he said, slipping the quarters under the opposite bumper as she sunk the nine ball.

"Yeah, Billy, of course," Ed said. "I need to eat something anyway."

Jessica didn't greet him right away. She leaned into the table with a sigh before turning around.

"Hey, Billy," she said, brushing some stray hairs off her forehead and out of her eyes.

"Hey, Billy?" He echoed her observation as a question and asked one of his own. "What are you doing here?"

"Honestly, I didn't bank on you being here," she said. "I figured you'd be at Skeeters, if anywhere."

"Preemptive avoidance," he acknowledged. "Good one."

"It's not that," she said. "I just ... what did you expect? That I would come back, unchanged, and call up Billy Stevens as if maybe time stood still?"

"Why are you back?"

"My mom needs my help," she said. "She was diagnosed with small-cell lung cancer."

"I'm sorry, Jess," he said. "I didn't know."

"It's surprising you don't," she said. "It's a small town in a small state."

Billy put the quarters in the slot and pushed. The balls tumbled down unseen chutes, punctuating the end of her statement.

"Anyway, I'm back for the duration, however long that is," Jessica said. "I've been back for about a week and came out tonight to get some air, if you know what I mean. I needed to decompress and not think about it."

"I get it," Billy said. "I won't push anymore. Let's just play. You can tell me about big-city life."

"Okay," she said. "But that might not be my favorite subject, either. And New York City isn't big. It's only about three hundred square miles."

As they played, she began to describe a world unlike any he had ever experienced. She talked about the boroughs and neighborhoods, how hard it is to set priorities in a city that wants to dictate them, how many pairs of walking shoes she blew out, and what it's like to get stuck in the subway. She complained a bit about the noise, the smells, the less-than-friendly people. But he could tell she found some beauty in that concrete jungle.

When she started describing Grand Central Station, he was taken in by her love of it. To her, there was something magical about the dirt and grit. The same could be said about the bridges or the brownstones or the skyscrapers or the ferries or the dizzying amount of choices all stacked upon each other in a city that doesn't think about sleep until the bars close at 4 a.m.

"I had every intention of scaling the big corporate ladder of New York City advertising and earning a corner office like everybody covets there," she said. "But after my boyfriend — yeah, sorry ... I've had several — dumped me in a blaze of glory and left me wondering how to pay for the apartment, all of the anxiety of New York finally got to me, and all I wanted to do was come home. So I called my mom, and instead of offering comfort or words of wisdom, she sent me screenshots of her X-rays."

"Harsh," he said, attempting to look like he was at least trying to focus on a shot.

"That's me," she said. "For better or worse, not the girl who left here five years ago. You?"

"Nothing so exotic," he said. "I graduated like you, felt lost after we broke up, and took a job with Cutter's Stoneworks, mining granite, so all those home chefs have something nice to cut their vegetables on. It's not a bad gig. I've advanced to running the saw mostly."

She smiled at him, and he could feel it cut all the way to his heart. When she smiled for real, her cheeks rose and lit up her eyes. For as long as they held you, he remembered, it felt like you were the only person in the world who mattered.

"Don't take this the wrong way," she said. "But you look the same. I mean, aside from the scruff under your chin, I feel like I've unearthed the past."

"I get it," he said, shaking his head as the spell was broken.

"What about your stone carvings?" she asked. "Still do anything like that?"

"No, well, not really," he said and then reconsidered and started pulling at a piece of rawhide around his neck. "I have this one piece."

He took it off and handed it to her. Dangling from the leather was a granite dragonfly. While her collection of dragonflies was packed away somewhere, the meaning of this one wasn't lost on her.

"It's beautiful," she said, tracing the wings before trying to hand it back.

"You can keep it," he said. "I kind of made it for you anyway."

She set it on the edge of the pool table.

"This is what I meant," she said, still smiling but pressing her lips together. "Coming back is like opening a time capsule. Augusta is the same. The Paw is the same. Charlie is the same. You're the same. Everything here is preserved like the granite that you dig up every day. But I'm not the same girl I was five years ago, and you know, maybe I better go."

"Come on, Jess," said Billy, looking over the unfinished game. "Give me a bone here, and let me welcome you home. There's got to be something I can do, even if it's as friends."

"Yeah, you can walk me out," she said, heading to the door. "Thanks for everything, Charlie. Have a good night."

"Hey, he's not running you out of here, is he?" Charlie mused.

"No, I just got to get home," she said. "That's why I came back, mostly."

"Yeah, sorry about your mom," Charlie said. "Let me know if there's anything I can do."

"Thanks, Charlie," she said.

When they reached the coatracks, Billy grabbed his jacket and started to size up which one might be hers. She pointed.

"The blue one from L.L.Bean," she said.

"Really?" Billy raised an eyebrow. "You know they only make the boots and tote bags in Maine."

"So?" she said, crinkling her face.

"So, the coats aren't as good," he said.

She slipped the coat on as they exited together. As soon as they were outside, she gulped in the clean air, then spun on her heels to face him.

"Maybe we can try again," he said. "I don't know, maybe some Sunday baked beans."

"Billy, look." She paused, putting a hand on his chest, partly to push him back and partly as a gesture of endearment. "I'm going to be too busy taking care of my mom, you know? And what we had was really special. I don't want to change that, okay?"

"Ayuh, I hear you," he said. "Like Charlie said. Your mom is a good person. Let me know if I can do anything."

She didn't say anything else. She patted his chest, gave him a downward-cast smile, and turned toward her Jeep Cherokee. He stood there and watched her drive away for the second time in his life. Only this time, he had an urge to let her go.

CHAPTER 2

FALLEN IDOLS

Jessica almost felt guilty dropping the granite dragonfly in the Jeep Cherokee's cup holder, but she didn't know what else to do with it. The carving was beautiful, a fossil from when her high school boyfriend stood with her in the doorway of opportunity but refused to walk through it.

"Come with me to New York City." She had pleaded with him. "This is our chance to escape together. You can get into an art program there. I know it."

"Nah, carving is just a hobby. Besides, I'm a Mainer through and through," he said, thumping his chest with exaggerated enthusiasm. "Whatever would I do in New York?"

She scoffed. "Whatever will you do here?"

He enrolled in classes at a community college. He only attended a few of them, picking up hours at the granite quarry during the day and picking fights at the same tired parties they used to attend together in high school at night. She fled to New York City, landed a receptionist job at an advertising agency, and took classes at a university until earning her spot as a junior account executive.

There was never any chance of a long-distance relationship. She broke it off with Billy a week after graduation. He never saw it coming, which only reinforced her resolve.

"You're like a loadstone to me," she said. "You know what a loadstone is, Billy?"

"Yeah. It's a naturally magnetized mineral," he said with a grin. "We're connected. You and me."

"No, not a lodestone. A loadstone, l-o-a-d. It's a weighty object and hard to get rid of," she said. "That's you."

"You're serious?"

"So I've decided. If you won't come with me, I can't let you keep me here."

"Keep you here? What are you even talking about?"

"I don't want anything or anybody tying me to Augusta," she said. "I'm leaving and not looking back."

"Your mom lives here," he said flatly.

"That's different."

"Your mom is here. Your home is here. Your history is here. Your friends are here."

"I'm not the only one looking for a way out, you know," she said. "Izzy has a scholarship. Justice is leaving. Dustin has a full ride."

"Don't talk to me about Dustin," Billy said. "Who cares about him?"

"You used to," she said.

"Now you're just trying to start a fight."

She was trying to start a fight. She had been working up to it for weeks, finding tiny fractures she could chip into fissures. What did he like that she didn't like? What didn't he like that she liked? How often did he call, and was that too much or not enough? What did he talk about when they were together? What did he talk about when they were apart? When was the last time he had taken her on an actual date instead of out with friends?

Everything, even his favorite flannel shirt, became another badge of contempt.

She didn't need a shrink to tell her that this kind of thinking wasn't good for a healthy relationship. She wasn't looking for one. She was looking to feel better about their imminent breakup, and quiet disdain seemed like the quickest, least painful way to do it.

She never shared what became a mountain of criticisms about him. She just filed them away like footnotes to her more extensive thesis. He loved her, but not enough to leave. And while he never asked her to stay, he did expect her to come back someday.

She wasn't planning on coming back, and somehow, that made the years they were together in high school a waste of time. She tried to make herself hate him for it, just enough to shake off how she felt a few hours before she dropped it on him.

The last thing she wanted was to leave him with a puffy face and runny mascara. She'd had enough of that alone, shuffling through old pictures. So she worked her tears into anger, justified because he didn't understand how she felt.

He didn't cry when she told him. He turned himself off too, looking more dazed than damaged. It wasn't much different from how he looked in the parking lot at the pub a few minutes ago. Billy hadn't changed, but she had.

She'd even lied to him in the bar. While everyone knew her mother had cancer, nobody knew the truth about her last boyfriend. He didn't dump her in a blaze of glory. She was running from him and didn't have any place to go but home. Had she told him the truth, the irony wouldn't have been lost on Billy. She had pretended he wanted to control her when they graduated from high school, only to fall for someone who literally tried to control her.

It was easy to do in a big city. There were so many people packed together that the urge to be anything but alone was addictive. It clouded her judgment. Instead of sticking with immature college classmates or office romances with closet creatives after graduation, she hooked up with a corrections officer named Kyle on a dating app.

The warning signs should have been as bright as the glow of the taillights up ahead, but she didn't see them then. In less than six months, she climbed into a cage of comfort with more entrances than exits. Then she gradually eased into his abuse and didn't question much until she came home from work to find a bone saw on the kitchen table. Kyle didn't hunt, but he had asked if she could fit in a chest freezer.

Looking back, she couldn't fathom why it took so long to snap out of her trance. Her mom always told her to pay attention to the butterflies in her stomach. She didn't feel anything then, but she felt something now. She was gaining on the taillights ahead of her. They weren't moving.

It didn't take that long to see the car ahead of her had careened off the road and into a ditch. She slowed, surveying the accident as she passed. The driver-side door of a dark blue Challenger stood open; a figure slumped in the seat.

She put on her hazard lights and pulled over a few dozen feet in front of it. She popped the glove compartment to look for a flashlight but came up empty. Emergency kits aren't as top of mind in New York City as they are in Maine. She shook her head. She would have to use the flashlight on her phone right after she called 911.

When she opened her door, the rush of cold air reined in her wandering mind. She dialed as she walked toward the car.

"Nine one one. Where's your emergency?"

"Hello?"

"Yes, miss. Where's your emergency?"

"Granite Hill Road, north of Kerns fork," she said. "There's been an accident."

"Do you know if anyone is injured?"

"Um, it looks like the driver tried to get out of the car. I think he's hurt, maybe unconscious."

"Are there any obvious broken bones or bleeding that you can see? What can you see without moving him?"

"I have to get closer," she said. "I just drove past it and was walking back to the car when I called. It doesn't look too bad, maybe."

"What kind of car?"

"It's a Challenger, dark blue."

"And the other vehicle?"

"There's just one. It looks like he drove off the road, hit a barrier, and went into the trees."

She never understood why anyone would want a muscle car in Maine. There were too many snow days, which is why she drove a Jeep. This Challenger might have been one of the new all-wheel-drive models, but it still didn't make sense to her. All it took was a light cold rain to make some of these roads dangerous, let alone the snowfall they expected in a few weeks.

"Let me know if the driver is the only one in the vehicle when you get a better look. What's your name?"

"My name is Jessica Michaud."

"I'm sending some help your way," the dispatcher said. "Your vehicle is safely out of the way?"

"Yes, I pulled off to the side of the road and put on my hazards."

"Good. If you see anyone else in the vehicle, call us back right away so we can send another ambulance. Thank you."

"Okay, you want me to hold?"

"No, but please call back if something changes."

"I will. Thank you."

She almost called back as soon as she had a better view of the accident. The hood had buckled like a half-crushed beer can. The entire front of the car had wrapped itself around one of the trees on the other side of the ditch in a deadly embrace. Steam rose from the broken engine as its heat met the cold night air.

The man in the driver's seat was slumped forward into the steering wheel and deflated airbag. His left arm hung limp by his side. He had apparently opened the door before losing consciousness.

"Heya," she said. "Are you hurt?"

She bent down to get a better look at him, using her phone as a flashlight. He was dressed for the weather, and she guessed he was about her age based on his build and thick black hair.

"Heya," she said again. "Can you hear me?"

She didn't want to move him, not knowing if he had hurt his back or neck. So she tried to push the airbag away from his face without moving his head. As she did, recognition started to sink in. Despite his goatee, blood, and abrasions, she knew him.

"Oh my God, Dustin?"

The calm she had managed began to slip toward a growing panic. This wasn't a stranger anymore but a classmate she never expected to see again and certainly not in Maine. He had gotten out, just like she had.

Dustin Fields was their high school's star running back for all four years they attended high school together and one of Billy's best friends until a falling out during their junior year. Before that, Dustin had felt like another brother to Jessica by default. Even after the fallout, she tracked his success — offers from Baylor,

Michigan State, and Connecticut College. He eventually picked Baylor after one of its mechanical engineering professors received a national award for building an area of research around polymer composites.

Dustin wanted to be an engineer and was especially interested in using alternative materials for construction. He loved football but always considered it a means to an end. He was the first to say success was about living in the moment while planning for the future. If there was anyone she would never expect to see here and now, it would be him. But then again, if their roles were reversed, he might think the same thing of her.

Seeing him now, in this state, was startling. She wanted to do something for him but didn't know what to do. She eventually took her coat off and draped it over him. The sting of the cold air hit her hard, but it felt like a do-or-die moment. He was losing too much body heat.

"Hang in there, Dustin," she whispered, gently touching his cheek before pulling the coat around the exposed skin. "Just a little longer."

She cupped her free hand and blew hot air into it, wishing she had left home with a pair of gloves or a hat. She hadn't, never expecting to be outside for more than a hundred paces from the parking lot to the pub or even less from the driveway to her home.

Now, every second felt like a punishment for her previous malevolence for Maine, and every minute, a compounded sentence drawn out even longer after she heard the first faint siren in the distance. She would die here along with Dustin if they didn't hurry, she thought, forgotten fossils like the trilobites they dug up in Maine instead of dinosaurs.

The first one on the scene wasn't the ambulance but a young police officer who exchanged her coat for a thick wool blanket retrieved from his trunk. He was surprisingly amiable, as if they were meeting under more casual circumstances. She didn't understand why until after the paramedics arrived and safely extracted Dustin.

"You don't remember me, do you?" asked the officer.

She shook her head. "Should I?"

"Maybe not." He frowned. "I was a year behind, so we only had one class together."

She looked at him, straining to place him.

"Biology? Miss Allen?"

The words were meaningless to her, but she played along. "Oh, right."

"I know, right? Who would even imagine I'd be rescuing Dustin Fields, and Jessica Michaud would be the one to call it in? Ain't that something."

"It's something."

"Yeah, I wouldn't have taken odds on it," he mused. "Well, you better get on home and warm up. You look a little pale from the exposure."

"Yeah, I'll do that."

"I'll follow up with you tomorrow if I have any questions."

"Questions?"

"Well, yeah. A follow-up to your statement. You know, the usual stuff, like the smell of alcohol on the victim."

She hadn't smelled any alcohol on Dustin. Had she? She hadn't given it much thought in the moment and the cold, but the officer was right. The stink of it wasn't coming from her.

"I don't know if I can help you there," she lied.

"I'm sorry?"

"He wasn't drinking and driving, if that's what you mean," she said. "At least, I wouldn't know it if he was."

"Ms. Michaud." He looked puzzled. "We both know he was drinking. He reeked of it."

She shrugged.

"Suit yourself. We'll get it from the blood sample. Drive safe now."

"Okay, thanks. Do you think they'll take him to MaineGeneral?"

"It's the only place open."

"Some things never change."

"Thank goodness for that," he said, touching the brim of his hat before a second thought. "Oh, and sorry about your coat."

"What?"

"Your coat."

She looked down at the sleeve he was pointing to. Dustin's blood was on it. The sight of it made her anxious, but she tried not to show it, even as the thought she had earlier crept into her mind. They were all going to get stuck in Augusta and die here.

She squinted at the name above his badge. "Goodnight … Officer Ouellette."

"Call me Danny," he said with a cautious smile, realizing for the first time that she hadn't remembered him. He pressed his lips together and turned toward the flashing red and blue lights of his squad car.

The smile unsettled her. It reminded her of an old quote by that French novelist she studied in school. When you stay too long in the same place, things and people go to pot on you; they rot and start stinking for your special benefit. Isn't that what they were all doing? Her mom. Billy. Dustin. And now Danny.

She returned to the Jeep, picked the dragonfly out of the cup holder, and looked at it again. Maybe Billy was one of the few people who understood her back then after all. She had wings and wanted to fly away while the rest of them stayed behind to relive the same lessons over and over again. She had come back to Augusta, hoping the sameness would help settle her. Now she felt more unsettled than ever.

When she got home, she found her mom asleep on the couch and covered her with the afghan they kept draped over the back of it. She would wake her for bed in another hour. Her mom looked too peaceful to move right away.

The answering machine had four messages. Three hang-ups, probably solicitors, but she didn't know for sure because her mother's answering machine was ancient and didn't display caller ID. The fourth one was from the agency where she worked. She had given them her mom's landline if they couldn't reach her cell, service being what it was in parts of Maine and her mom living in a dead zone.

Her supervisor, Keiko, checked in to let her know how much the agency was behind her during this difficult time. Keiko didn't ask, but Jessica knew they wanted to know how long she would be gone. She would call her back on Monday after taking her mom to her next appointment at the hospital tomorrow.

She could check on Dustin when she was there. If he was conscious, they could catch up on lost time. Maybe he would tell her the truth too. Why had he come back to Maine, of all places? And why, more importantly, had he risked his life, let alone a DUI, by getting behind the wheel of his car? It didn't make sense. But that wasn't the only thing.

She didn't understand why she had lied for Dustin. Maybe that's what fallen idols do, she decided. They lie for one another to keep their myths alive. At least she hoped that's what they did. She and Dustin had gotten out. They were exempt from small-town gossip.

CHAPTER 3

MISERY'S COMPANY

The urge to let her go only lasted a few seconds. Then, the hollow feeling that had haunted Billy for years returned. He still loved her and hated himself for it.

He kicked at the parking lot, scuffing the heel of one boot where the concrete had eroded from long winters and freezing rain. Jessica had said everything looked the same, but she was wrong. Everything was in a state of decay.

Isn't that what had happened to them? They were the perfect couple until the start of their senior year. She said he was becoming too bitter because he couldn't play football anymore, and she was partly right. He was angry, but not for any reason she conjured up.

He was angry because he lost almost everything after the injury, except her. And then, eventually, he lost her, too. She blamed him for the breakup because she wanted to fly away to parts unknown, and he wanted to stagnate.

"You have to pick yourself up and brush yourself off, Billy," she told him after the cast came off. "The injury broke your leg. Don't let it break your heart."

No, he thought, she was the one who broke his heart. She broke it because she didn't even try to understand the magnitude of what he lost. It wasn't just the bright lights of being a high school football star but everything else that went with it. His college prospects and athletic scholarships. His hopes and dreams.

His identity and sense of purpose. Everything, including the best friend who caused it, was gone.

Dustin Fields attended Baylor on a full-ride scholarship he didn't even need. He would have gone to college regardless because he came from the right family. Billy didn't have that luxury. Although his parents could escape to a mobile home retirement community in Florida and leave him the house he grew up in, they couldn't afford the out-of-state tuition that top art schools were asking.

Billy was the one who needed it. He had been so dedicated to the sport that it hadn't left much room for anything else. So he managed most of his high school career with mediocre grades, a few friends, and the best-looking girl in school on his arm. She was brilliant, too, not only in the classes she took but in her social circles.

In some ways, she had more in common with his then best friend Dustin than he did. Her family wasn't wealthy, but they were affluent. Even after her father died of a heart attack during her freshman year of high school, she and her mom were financially secure. Edward Michaud had bought the largest life insurance policy a power system dispatcher for Central Maine Power could afford. The policy paid off, ensuring the family had security despite sacrificing the stability her dad brought to the household.

Billy had only met him a few times before he died. He was well respected, especially after a snowstorm when he coordinated crews to get the power back up, going so far as driving out to the location himself. Ed used to shrug off the compliments people gave him for doing it, saying it was the right thing to do. He had worked his way up from being a power lineman and knew the job.

When he died, Jessica was grateful Billy wasn't like her dad. She didn't want a persistent, tough guy who grew up in the backwoods of southern Missouri and then moved to Maine after retiring from the army. As the story went, it was one of the reasons they started their family late. Ed needed time to recover from Vietnam.

No, she wanted someone she could lean into for a while. Billy's shoulder was just what she needed, something strong but not smothering. But when Billy was injured, lying in a hospital bed with a compound fracture of his tibia, she wanted him to be exactly like her dad and somehow shake it off.

She couldn't seem to understand it wasn't something he could shake off. It took six months to heal, much of it spent in a drug-infused daze with slipping grades and high school standing. The first casualty was the cause. Dustin had ended Billy's career during one of the dumbest practices Coach Dawson had ever devised — flipping the field for a day and having most of the defense play offense.

"The biggest clue to knowing what the offense is up to — a pass play or run — is to look at the lineman after the snap," he said, addressing the team as it took a knee. "If they back up, it's a pass. If they fire across the line, it's a run. If they are looking for a draw, they'll sucker you into believing it's a pass by making the lineman back up anyway. So how are you going to learn that?"

"Films?"

"Wrong."

"You, Coach?" Twitch Miley laughed. "You'll tell us."

"Maybe you, Miley. God knows I have to tell you everything else."

Everybody laughed.

"Experience," Billy said.

"That's right, Stevens," he said. "Experience. As I always tell you lug heads, the offense is proactive, and the defense is reactive, but it doesn't always have to be that way. The defense can learn to be proactive by reading the play early and pressing the offense. And the offense can be reactive in looking for deceptions or false coverages. The best way to learn it is experience."

And just like that, Coach Dawson flipped them, making Billy Stevens a running back and Dustin Fields a strong safety. The flip allowed Dustin to end the two-week feud that started with him breaking it off with Stacy Brenner. Billy knew the reason why, even if nobody else did, and Dustin wanted to keep it that way.

Billy kicked at the crumbling asphalt again. This wasn't the way his life was supposed to turn out. He was ready to leave Maine once upon a time but on a football scholarship. Without football, he didn't know how to do it.

The wind was picking up again, so he retreated into the warmth of the Bear Paw. The crowd had thinned out while he and Jessica had caught up. He hadn't even noticed until now. He looked as lost as he felt, surveying the landscape for someone who didn't exist anymore.

Charlie stopped cleaning out a glass, gave him a long look, and leaned into the bar. He had seen Billy like this before, and it always meant trouble.

"Another Geary's, Charlie."

"There's not going to be any trouble tonight, is there, Billy?" Charlie said. "Because if there is, I might as well run you off right now."

"Nah, no trouble."

"Somehow, I'm not believing you."

Billy shrugged and tapped the bar top.

"Look," Charlie said. "I'm not trying to be that guy, but…"

"I'll buy the round," said a stranger two stools over. He was a tank of a man whom Billy hadn't noticed before. He tried to make eye contact, but the man didn't turn his head. A cap covered a military haircut, and he was hunched over a two-finger pour of whiskey.

"Nah, you don't have to do that," Billy said. "I'm not a charity case."

"I know," he said, slowly turning to face Billy. "I also know the look. She broke your heart."

"Again," he huffed.

"Yeah, I get it," said the man. "Get him a Geary's and Kings County double."

Charlie narrowed his eyes and set the glass he was polishing down.

"Just because you're buying doesn't mean I'm selling," Charlie said. "We have some history here. Billy's like family."

The man shrugged and tossed a twenty on the bar top. Then he reached into his windbreaker and flashed Charlie the inside of his wallet.

"It'll be all right," he said. "I'll take responsibility."

"It doesn't work that way," Charlie said, leaning into the bar again.

"Sure it does," said the man. "Take the twenty and keep my tab open."

"Let it go, Charlie," Billy said before turning to the man. "Why would you do that?"

"I dunno," he said. "Let's just say I had my heart broken, too, recently. Misery loves company."

Charlie pushed the whiskey and freshly tapped beer in front of Billy. But then he held out his hand. Billy knew what that meant. He pulled out his car keys and pressed them into Charlie's palm.

"For the record," Charlie said, rapping his knuckles on the bar top to get Billy's attention. "I don't like this. But you can have them back if there's no trouble and when I know you have a ride home."

"Yeah, don't worry about it," the man said. "I'll get him home."

"Thanks," Billy said, lifting the rock glass to the stranger and knocking back the whiskey in one gulp.

It burned the back of his throat when it went down, reviving his spirits. Five years is a long time, he told himself. Jessica wasn't even the same girl anymore.

"So what's the story?"

"The story?" Billy squinted. "There's no story."

"There's always a story," the man said with a chuckle.

Billy didn't want to sound like he felt — pathetic, sad, a failure. So, he kept it short.

"Boy meets girl. Boy plays football. Football breaks boy. Girl takes off."

He brought his hands together like a bird, flapping his fingers and exaggerating flight. When they extended beyond his head, he pulled them apart into an open-handed shrug.

"They do that," he said, extending a fist. "Name's Dale, by the way."

"Billy."

"High school football, huh? So I take it the breakup isn't fresh."

"Nah. Years ago."

"Could have fooled me."

"How so?"

"I saw you two shooting a game," said Dale. "You moved around each other like you really fit."

"You're right," Billy said, putting a finger to his nose. "Exactly right. It's always been like that. We fit like a hand and glove."

"Coffee and donuts."

"What?"

"It's a cop joke," he said. "Coffee and donuts."

"You're a cop?"

"New York's boldest," Dale said.

"Well, that explains it," Billy said, pointing under Dale's arm.

He could see the butt of a gun. The walnut grip of a .38 Special was inconspicuous but not invisible.

"Don't leave home without it." Dale winked.

"I guess not," Billy said. "So what is New York's boldest doing here in Augusta?"

"Came up for a little hunting," Dale said. "Thought that might be the best way to get my mind off things."

"Well, I hope you have some PTO coming to you," Billy said. "You're a week too early for deer."

"Oh, I know," he said. "I came up for the extra legwork. I understand there's a lot of room to roam up here, with more deer than hunters. I'm looking for whitetail, mostly."

"You might want to try more north or the coastal islands instead," Billy said. "I dunno. Maybe even scout a few places before the season starts and pick out a trophy."

"Maybe," Dale said. "But I'm not interested in just any deer. I'm looking for something special, and I have a ton of time banked to find it."

"What are you shooting?"

"Winchester 30-30," said Dale.

"Fair enough," said Billy. "That's the one that gets the most loyalty. I'm a little more partial to a Marlin lever-action in .35 Remington. It's the perfect brush gun up here. And if not that, I like the challenge of a Ruger No. 1. You only get one shot."

"Ain't that the truth."

Billy looked at Dale and considered him. He was a 30-30 man, which meant he was mostly interested in shot placement. Shot placement is what brings home the venison. It also reminded Billy that it had been a while since he had been hunting. Two years, at least.

"So what's your story?"

"My story?"

"Misery loves company."

"Oh, that," he said, pulling a pack of cigarettes from an inside coat pocket.

As soon as he did, Charlie swooped over again.

"Badge or no badge, you can't do that here," Charlie said.

"No? Sorry," Dale said, putting the pack away. "Some of the private bars still allow it in New York. You know. They're grandfathered."

"This is Maine," Charlie said. "You can't even smoke in a car with a minor."

"Yeah, got it," he said.

"Come on," Billy said. "We can take it outside for a minute. Charlie has an ash can out there, around to the right."

Dale slipped off the barstool and reached for his drink.

"The glasses stay inside," Charlie said.

Dale put his hands up in surrender and then followed Billy outside to the unofficial smoking section of the Bear Paw. Every night, Charlie put out an old lobby ash can on what they called the far side of the building. He originally did it for the cooks because most of them smoked, but a few of the regulars liked to light up, too.

Dale took the pack out again and offered one to Billy. Billy shook him off.

"Right," he said. "I'm a minority nowadays. I can't help it, though. It calms the nerves, and I'm not interested in vaping."

"I'm not one to judge," Billy said.

"So, to answer your question," he said before taking a drag. "I met this girl at the gym last year. Young thing. Five years younger than me anyway. And it turned out she lived only a few blocks away. Not all that strange, I suppose, being most people want a gym they can walk to in New York. But I don't know, I kind of thought it was fate, like she met me at just the right time so I could show her the way."

"Show her the way?" Billy wondered if the alcohol was getting to him.

"To grow up ... to be an adult," he said, taking another long drag. "She was just a college kid when we met and had to learn how to be a woman. I was opening a whole new world to her. She hadn't even been to a restaurant where they pulled the chair out for you or placed a napkin on your lap. Yeah, the waiter picked it up off the table, and she said, 'Oh, I'm going to need that.' It was the funniest damn thing."

Billy tried to laugh along, but he had never been to a restaurant that did that, either. It wasn't a thing in Maine. Chef Melissa Kelly wasn't moving Primo to Augusta anytime soon. They had excellent restaurants, sure, but he supposed someone from New York City would consider them mid at best.

"I took her to clubs. The good ones are only open to fat cats, models, movers, and a few boys in blue," he said. "You probably don't have anything like that around here, but there are a few in the city that will shake up your libido. They make you feel alive. And man, did she feel alive. The things she was willing to do."

Billy looked down at the ground as Dale pursed his lips. Billy tried to force another smile, but he avoided eye contact. He wasn't interested if this guy was taking his talk in that direction. Dale was precisely the kind of guy he picked fights with when he drank too much.

"Hey, you okay?" Dale said, giving his shoulder a shove.

"Yeah, fine," he said. "It's colder out here than I thought. That's all."

"Hold on. I'm almost done, and we can go back in," he said. "So she moved in with me after about six months or so, and that's when I realized she was still a kid in a lot of ways. She wasn't always contributing like I thought she would, keeping the place clean and whatnot. Groceries needed to be shopped, laundry done, kitchens cleaned. The cat isn't taking out its own litter. It's not even like I'm a neatness freak or anything, but there comes a point when you live with someone who isn't your mom, and you have to start picking up the slack. It can't always be me when I'm the one working the long shifts. So I was torn, you know. I mean, on the one hand, she had to learn. On the other hand, I loved her and would do anything for her, you understand. So I thought, I know, a pinch and twist. That would do it."

"A pinch and twist?"

"You never did that? You're lying together on the couch and watching a movie or something, and you need a beer. But you don't want to get up because you're more on the bottom, and she's on the top. So you ask her to get it, and she laughs at you like it's a joke. You say, 'Hey, I really mean it, baby.' And she laughs again and tells you to get it yourself. You can't let that stand if you're a man. So you take your thumb and index finger like this, reach around to that soft fleshy part of their inner thigh, and give it a good pinch. I mean a good one, something hard that will leave a mark to remember. If they still don't get it, there are other places to give them a good pinch and twist."

As the guy kept talking and getting more vivid, Billy pulled out his phone and looked at the screen as if he had just felt the low buzz of a notification. He needed an escape route, but he didn't find any there. Maybe he could finish his beer and call someone else to pick him up.

"Anyway, after everything I did for her, she up and left me," said Dale. "No note. No text. No message. No phone call. Poof. Gone. She didn't even take all of her junk. Hey, you hearing me?"

Billy slipped the phone back into his pocket and put a hand on the cold bricks of the tavern to steady himself. He clenched his other hand into a fist.

"Yeah, yeah," Billy said. "That whiskey just started to hit me."

He wasn't lying. He was already drunk before downing the double. But what was making him more unsteady was the conversation. He knew guys like Dale. They spent too much time making self-aggrandizing dick jokes, calling women chicks, and giving them outlandish compliments like they look rape-able.

He didn't need to go to college to understand that guys like this were looking to dehumanize and objectify women. So he did his best to avoid them because if he didn't, then he was obliged to set them straight.

"All right, I'm done with this anyway." Dale pinched the filter from his burning cigarette and tossed it into the ashtray. He dropped the smoldering tobacco on the ground and crushed it out. "Let's go back inside."

"Good timing," Billy said. "I have to hit the head."

His friend Andrea would also complain about guys like this, saying how exhausting they could be. Half of the time, she didn't know how to respond to the relentless misogyny from attractive men who turned out to be not-so-closet chauvinists. Billy didn't know what to tell her. He spent his sober life being afraid someone would label him among the more pathetic macho majority, even though those were the same guys who got the girls. And he spent much of his intoxicated life picking fights with them over women, usually intervening on an insult, innuendo, or uninvited touch.

There were only a couple of people left by the time they reentered, and Charlie was already closing out their tabs. The Bear Paw was the only bar along the river that stayed open past midnight. The rest had closed hours ago.

Billy didn't know either of the lonely souls who were left and figured they were guests at one of the inns or hotels down the road. Six were clustered around the small state airport less than two miles away.

Since they were randoms, Billy bypassed the bar altogether and headed to the bathroom, taking long, stiff, deliberate strides to keep his balance. When he put his hand on the back of the chair to steady himself, he knew it didn't matter. There was no way Charlie was going to give his car keys back.

As soon as he crashed through the bathroom door, he fished his phone out of his pocket again and wondered if it was too late to text Andrea. Maybe that's why she had come to mind. She could give him a ride home instead of the cop.

He tried to do the math in his head. The numbers were a jumble. How long would it take Andrea to get here? How long would Charlie let him hang around for a new ride after closing? Would she even come if last night's fog rolled in again? He couldn't figure out any of it, so he texted her.

Hey, you awake?

He hoped she would respond before he finished tapping off in the urinal, but she didn't. So he washed his hands, splashed some water on his face, and headed back out. He could stall a few minutes by finishing the beer he had left behind, and hopefully, she would see the text before Charlie closed up.

He immediately felt better having some kind of plan to cut this guy out, enough that he reevaluated his feelings. Maybe he was the problem and not this out-of-towner. Jessica really did shake him up earlier, and alcohol consistently amplified his anger. The guy might not have even been telling the truth. And even if the cop was telling the truth, it's not like Billy was at risk of getting a pinch and twist. Billy could take care of himself.

Half a beer and then I'm out, he told himself before seeing the fresh one waiting for him when he returned to the bar. Charlie said something about it being the last round and that he had already given Billy's keys to the officer. Billy feigned another smile and shook his head in disbelief. Andrea hadn't responded yet.

"So, I was meaning to ask you," Dale said with a grin. "What was that thing you gave her?"

"Gave who?"

"Your old girlfriend," he said. "You took something off your neck and gave it to her. What? Was it a charm or something?"

"A dragonfly," Billy said.

"A dragonfly?"

"Yeah, she has always liked dragonflies," said Billy. "Ever since she was a kid, even before I had the nerve to ask her out."

"Huh," Dale said absently. "I didn't know that."

"Why would you?"

"No, I mean in general," he said. "I didn't know women would like something like that."

"I'm not sure she did," Billy said. "I made it."

"You don't say."

"Yeah, I'm a stone carver," said Billy, taking another drink. "Granite cutter, actually. But I carve a few pieces here and there on the side. I even have a business card nowadays."

"Oh, I get it," Dale said. "That's why she didn't like it."

"Yeah, maybe."

"That's cold," Dale said. "Women are bitches."

"Sometimes I guess they are," he said, trying to reflect on the conversation outside again. Was it something Dale had said that really triggered him or how he said it? Billy couldn't remember anymore. It was more about what Dale wasn't saying, but that didn't make sense. He was just some typical guy, a big-city cop with a chip on his shoulder.

They talked for another twenty minutes, with Billy glancing at his phone from time to time to see if Andrea had responded until, eventually, he didn't look anymore.

The last call hit him unusually hard, and he was suddenly grateful to get his mind off Jessica and have a ride home. That wasn't always the case when he tried to drink the pain away. *Be grateful* was the last thought he had before he finished his beer and the world spun away from him.

CHAPTER 4

DEAD ECHOES

J essica was scrolling through her Twitter feed on her phone, randomly liking every third tweet served up by friends and the few thousand people she followed, in the waiting room of GeneralMaine Health's Radiology and Imaging Department. She was happy to have Wi-Fi again and felt obligated to check in with her tribe, most of them a mix of friends from college, advertising insiders, celebrities she admired but never met, and a few semi-interesting people who followed her back when she was starting out and desperate for followers.

Her mom, Muriel Michaud, sat next to her. She was flipping through the pages of her third magazine, handling them noisily enough that Jessica couldn't lose herself on the small screen. Muriel, or El, as most people called her, didn't understand why anyone would want to scan over the endless waves of uninformed opinions about whatever caught their eye. So whenever it looked like Jessica would respond to someone with anything more than a like or repost, El interrupted her by calling out whatever caught her eye in the magazine.

"Do you think she's pretty?"

"Who?"

Her mom opened the magazine to the center spread. "Wild About Harry," screamed the *Vanity Fair* headline above the barefoot brunette in a black dress.

"Mom." Jessica sighed and shook her head. "She's kind of fake."

"Is that your opinion or those people on your phone? What do you call them? Tweeters? Tweets? Twits?"

Jessica laughed and shook her head. "They're followers."

"Oh, well," El said. "What do they think? Will she marry Prince Harry or not?"

"She loves the attention." Jessica said it as if it was a foregone conclusion. "But I don't know why you're asking me. You're not even reading the articles."

"It's not my fault. There aren't any good ones."

"You're lucky they have any magazines here at all," Jessica said. "They're disappearing from waiting rooms altogether."

"You're the reason," El said, pointing an accusatory finger at Jessica's phone. "Nobody wants to read the news anymore. They just want to share the headlines."

Jessica knew El wasn't wrong. She had seen studies circulate around her agency claiming that less than one in four people read what they shared. Photos, headlines, and memes shape the entirety of some people's realities.

"It's the future, Mom," Jessica said. "You can't fight it."

"Well, no. I can't. But you can. You and all your twits."

"Followers."

"You say followers. I say twits."

"Mom," Jessica said sternly before changing her tone and trying to soothe her mother. "You're going to be okay."

El shook her head. "I'm not going to be okay."

"Sure you are," Jessica said, then patted her mom's knee. "It's just a biopsy."

"Two to four months without treatment and seven to eleven months with treatment," El said. "That's what my phone told me anyway. I can't even look at the screen anymore."

Jessica tried to reassure her mom despite her own faith being shaken. She knew the odds and they weren't good. The symptoms had started several months ago with labored breathing during a short walk around the block and grocery shopping. Then, one day, El bent down to pick up her hairbrush off the bathroom floor, and the pressure she felt in her chest scared her. They took a liter of fluid out of her lungs, ran a scan, and found the first mass.

The CT-guided biopsy she was getting today was a formality. Some pathologist her mother would never meet would look at it under a microscope to determine the size and shape of the cells. Then, they would confirm what everybody already knew. Muriel Whitney Michaud, age fifty-six, born in Fort Wayne, Indiana, to two young textile workers from Aachen, Germany, who had migrated to the United States to pursue the American dream for their family, would be lucky to see her next birthday.

After El was gone, Jessica would be the last in a short branch of Webers who surrendered their lives protecting the American dream for others but never had time to realize it for themselves. Both of El's older brothers were killed in the same war that eventually brought her and her husband, Edward Michaud, together.

The two of them met at the University of Maine at Augusta. Ed was taking advantage of a newly amended GI Bill to get his life back after Vietnam. El had two years in toward a degree in library administration, eventually settling with an associate's. El always said she intended to return to school but never did. The two of them, El and Ed, enjoyed a quiet life together until convincing themselves they would never have children.

When the news of her pregnancy hit them, it was such a surprise that El considered terminating the pregnancy. It was one of the hardest choices she ever had to make, given they had already settled into being an empty-nest couple without any close family connections other than Ed's younger sister who lived clear across the country in Washington.

Living alone felt comfortable, and adding a tiny screaming and kicking person into the mix would do more than disrupt their routine. There was an exhaustive list of questions: risks of maternal mortality, gestational diabetes, premature birth, chromosomal disorders, and pregnancy loss. And even if those things did work out, they weren't sure they had the time and energy for an infant at their age.

The story always unsettled Jessica despite the happy ending. El always insisted they loved her even more than those parents who never had to think of it as a difficult choice. Besides, all their fears disappeared when the doctor proclaimed they had a beautiful baby girl with ten fingers and ten toes.

Jessica always said it sounded more like a coin toss, an analogy she couldn't shake when her father died. He had been right about one of his fears after all. He was too old and would never see any grandchildren. And now, the two of them faced an uglier reality. El would never see any grandchildren, either. Not even her dad had seen that one coming.

"Ms. Muriel Michaud?"

"Yes," her mom managed.

The technician smiled at her before stating the obvious.

"We're ready for you now."

Jessica and her mom stood up.

"Oh, I'm sorry," the technician said, putting up a hand to stop Jessica. "You'll have to wait out here."

Her mother gave her a panicked glance. Jessica patted her hand.

"It will be all right, Mom," Jessica said.

"Are you sure?"

El looked to Jessica and then to the technician.

"This is all very routine, Ms. Michaud," the girl said, trying to soothe her. "We'll have you back out here in about an hour or so."

"That long?"

"Mom, it's all right," said Jessica. "I'll be fine. In fact, you know what? I have a friend who was admitted last night, and this will give me a chance to check in on him."

"A friend?"

"I'll tell you all about it when you're done," Jessica said. "Promise."

Her mom considered and accepted it. Jessica gave her a final thumbs-up as the last gentle push her mom needed. El gave her one in return and followed the technician through the door.

When the door shut, she left the waiting area and asked the information desk for the room number for Dustin Fields. She was happy to learn the hospital had admitted him to a semiprivate room in the west wing after being cleared by critical care. The west wing was close by.

The staff volunteer didn't hesitate to give her his room number. GeneralMaine always considered visitors vital to recovery after an injury or surgery, even if staff cut off visiting hours early at 8 p.m., with a few exceptions that seemed to revolve around beginnings and endings.

She poked her head in to find an older man in the bed closest to the door. He had matted gray hair and an oxygen tube running up to his nose. He stopped thumbing the bedside remote to look at her. She gave him a hesitant wave and quickly tiptoed across the room to the other side of the curtain. Dustin was looking at his phone and then noticed her.

"Well, you're too pretty to be a nurse," he said, setting his phone down.

"Ayuh," she said, reverting to an expression she hadn't used since move-in day at college in New York more than five years ago. "I'm not a nurse."

"My lucky day," he said, waiting for an explanation before squinting at her. "Jessica?"

"Hey, it's me," she said, drawing her shoulders in and rolling her eyes like a blushing schoolgirl. "Thought I'd surprise you."

"No crap," he said. "I thought you lived — where again? New York?"

"That's right," she said. "I'm up visiting my mom."

"Oh yeah? She's all right?"

"Yeah, well, no," she said with a frown. "Lung cancer."

"No," he said, drawing it out. "Sorry to hear it. Ms. M was always good to me."

"Except when she caught you talking in the library," Jessica said with a laugh.

"There was that, yeah," said Dustin. "Books weren't my thing as much as pigskins and pucks. So how did you know I was here anyway?"

"Oh, long story," she said. "Well, not really. I'm the one who found you on the side of the road."

"No kidding?" He considered. "How was the Challenger? Nobody around here wants to talk to me."

"Banged up a bit worse than you, I'm afraid," she said, gesturing to the cast on his left wrist and butterfly bandages on his face. "You ran off the road around Granite Hill Road and Kerns fork."

He shrugged and looked down, as if he were trying to pluck a memory from the depths of his subconscious but couldn't reach it. Then he shook his head in disgust.

"Any other vehicles?"

"None that I saw."

"I guess that's good unless somebody ran me off the road, hit and run," he said. "I honestly don't remember."

"The officer on scene thought you might be, um, impaired."

"Did he now? And who was that?"

"Officer Ouellette."

"Danny boy?" Dustin smirked. "Now if that don't beat all. Danny has had a grudge against me ever since the coach cut him from the football team."

"Funny, I don't remember him," she said.

"I don't think you would have remembered," Dustin said. "Billy wasn't playing football the year Danny was cut, and nobody paid much attention to him when he was an underclassman."

"I think he wants you to pay attention to him now," she said, leaning in to whisper. "He kept asking if I smelled alcohol on you."

"Did you?"

"None worth mentioning," Jessica said.

"Attagirl," he said with a wink and held out his fist.

It was corny, but she touched his fist with one of her own before laughing.

"Heya, you laughing with me or at me?"

"At you," she said with an eye roll.

"Don't make me laugh," he said with a chuckle and a wince. "It hurts when I laugh."

She laughed again and felt her face flush. Dustin was spoon-feeding her shallow clichés, and she was eating them up like they were still in junior high. She didn't remember Dustin as overly charming or vulnerable. Yet, here he was.

There was something rugged about this iteration of the boy she knew from high school. Texas had been good for him like New York had mostly been good for her.

"I don't think what I said or didn't say will make a bit of difference," she said. "I'm sure they took a blood test."

He waved her concern away. "That's for the lawyers to figure out. I'm more interested in what you think."

"Stop it already," she said, not wanting him to stop.

She hadn't felt safe around men since she left Kyle in New York. Even playing pool last night with Billy wasn't comfortable. She felt under pressure because he wanted her to be someone or something she would never be again. Billy wasn't as interested in what she thought as much as how he felt about her.

"No, really, I want to know what kind of big shot you've become in New York City," he said. "What do you do down there in the Empire State?"

"I'm an account executive for an advertising agency," she said. "Well, junior advertising executive, really. But a promotion isn't too far off if things keep going well."

"Account executive? Sounds important," Dustin said. "But I have no idea what that means."

"Oh, right. We meet with clients and then meet with creatives, ah, artists and writers, who make all those ads and commercials you see," she said. "If it's a production, like something for television, we help coordinate everything and make sure everybody knows what's going on, especially if a campaign has more than one element, like magazine ads or radio commercials or stuff on social networks."

She was twirling her hair. As soon as she realized it, she stopped.

"So you're like a project manager," said Dustin, relating her job to the construction industry. "I get it. What kind of campaigns have you worked on? Anything I would know?"

"Um, have you ever heard of Brandon Maxwell?"

"Should I have?"

"Probably not," Jessica said before searching for a memory she could share with him. "So, earlier this summer, we worked on a transformation fashion campaign kicked off by this beautiful fashion model in a cinema verité style. There's this one part when her mom is in the video and says that the only thing that can stop her is her own self. Then the model goes on to talk about how she isn't afraid to be herself anymore. How she isn't afraid of her past. How when she dances, she dances out of her past and into her future because all those things, not just one part of it, make her who she is. It's powerful. Sorry, I'm rambling."

"No, it's all right," he said. "I like listening to you. You're passionate about it."

"Yeah, I guess I am," she said. "People like to complain about advertising, but when it's done right, it's a like a snapshot of the soul of our culture."

"Oh, I wasn't talking about advertising as much as the message," Dustin said. "It sounds like you really know who you are or who you are about to be."

"Yeah, I was or maybe I am," Jessica said. "I don't know. There was a moment when I almost lost myself in the city, and coming back here is like finding myself again. Not who I was, really, but who I am because of who I was. Does that make any sense?"

"I get it," Dustin said. "We've all grown up a bit since high school."

"We have," Jessica said. "So what about you? What happened to the big football star after graduating from Baylor?"

"Oh, I didn't graduate from Baylor."

"Wait, what? Why?"

"Don't be sorry for me. I'm not," he said. "Texas is a big place with a lot of big distractions. I got caught up in some of them, so I thought, what difference will a piece of paper make when I build an empire?"

"And did you build one?"

"I did."

"I sense a 'but' in there somewhere," Jessica said. "Is there?"

"Let's just say I think we're in the same place," Dustin said. "I came back up here to find myself again."

"Fair enough. You don't have to tell me," Jessica said. "We all have boundaries."

"It's not like that. I'm just not interested in talking about myself as much as hearing more about you."

"Uh-huh, right."

"No, I'm serious. Tell me again why we never got together?"

"Well, Billy for one," said Jessica. "And then you went on a ... I don't even know what to call it ... a spree of conquests after breaking up with Stacy. Our orbits were clearly not aligned."

"And yet, here we are."

"Here we are."

"Some people think when two people keep crossing paths, then they are bonded together like a soul contract or karmic bond," said Dustin. "It might even be the reflection of a relationship echo from an alternate timeline or two entwined souls weaving in and out of past lives."

"Wow."

"Wow, what?"

"Who would have ever thought Dustin Fields would be so corny," Jessica said, teasing him. "Do you actually use this in bars, or do you save your best material for hospital rooms?"

"You got me." Dustin laughed, holding up his hands in surrender.

"There are easier ways to ask someone out."

She surprised herself by saying it. She did want him to ask her out.

"Oh, really?" Dustin said. "What about Thursday?"

"You're asking me out on a date this Thursday?"

"We don't have to call it a date," he said. "Let's call it a reunion, another chance to catch up when I'm not wearing a disposable smock with my ass hanging out."

"All right, Mr. Dustin Fields," she said. "You're on, but I get to pick the place."

"Shoot."

"If it's going to be a proper reunion, then it has to be the Red Barn."

She could tell by the expression on his face that it was her turn to surprise him. The Red Barn was a mainstay in Augusta, a family-owned quick-service restaurant that served fried chicken, seafood, and homemade whoopie pies. Somehow, the old place had managed to be one of the family owned places to weather an influx of national chain restaurants.

As high school sophomores, the four of them, when there were four of them, used to camp out every other Thursday night at one of the picnic tables that framed the parking lot. It didn't matter which one, but they did have their favorite — the one farthest away from the main barn and collection of expansion buildings and sheds that made up the landmark eatery, affording them a little more privacy while they took turns sneaking behind the tree line marking the corner edge of the lot.

"Remember when Izzy dared Peter Cotella to dress up in a chicken costume and order a hamburger? They had a new kid behind the register that night, and he tried to calmly explain that they didn't serve hamburgers; Pete started flapping his arms and chanting, 'Where's the beef? Where's the beef?'"

"And then the kid made the mistake of trying to explain that they only served chicken and seafood!"

"So Pete stops chanting 'Where's the beef' and starts screaming 'Chicken? How dare you! Free my people! Free my people!'"

They were both laughing again. She couldn't even remember the last time she had laughed so hard. Life had taken such a serious turn during her senior year in high school that there never seemed to be enough time to laugh or have fun unless everybody had already kicked back more alcohol than their body weight could handle.

"Hey, have you seen Izzy?" Jessica asked.

"I haven't seen him in a while, no," Dustin said. "But we've kept in touch now and again. You know, Facebook and whatnot."

"Huh, I didn't know he was still on there," she said. "Most people seem to be moving on to Insta or Twitter."

"It's these new kids. Anywhere their parents aren't," he said. "But I don't have to tell you. You work with all that stuff, don't you?"

"Every day. Brands want a presence on social networks, but they don't want to pay for a copywriter, so it sometimes falls to the account executives, and by that, I mean junior account executives, to manage the network accounts. So we made this system based on Dr Pepper. You check at ten, two, and four and make sure everything is all right. Oh, sorry, I'm doing it again."

"It's fine," he said. "I wish my employees were as excited about their jobs as you are about yours."

"Yeah, well, enough about work," Jessica said. "It seems like we'll have no shortage of things not to talk about on Thursday."

"I'm sure we'll manage," said Dustin.

"Well, I better get back to my mom. I would hate for her to be released and find that I'm not waiting for her. Let me give you my number."

Dustin started to hand her his cell phone but she reached into her purse to retrieve a Sharpie. Then she leaned over him to reach his left wrist, being careful not to put any weight on him in case there were other injuries she didn't know about. She wrote her cell number and circled it with a heart. Dustin grinned, his eyes lighting up like a man who was just handed a victory wreath.

"Hey, it really is good to see you, Jess," Dustin said.

"Shush now, or I'll never get out of here," Jessica said. "This town seems to have it in for us so we have to stick together. Besides, I'll see you Thursday."

"It's a date," he said.

"A reunion," Jessica said, squeezing his toes as she corrected him on the way out.

"Kismet," he whispered, but she pretended not to hear him.

As corny as she said it was, she didn't want the moment to end, and now she felt a little lighter on her feet as she made her way back to radiology. She didn't know how to label it or explain it. It could have been something simple like running into a long-lost friend, which is what Dustin was to her.

She never felt like it was entirely fair that when Dustin and Stacy broke up or when Billy and Dustin had a falling out, she had to go along for the ride. Billy might have blamed Dustin for the accident on the field, but that is ultimately what it was determined to be: two best friends and top athletes giving it everything they had at practice.

At the end of the investigation, the school blamed the coach for running an unorthodox practice. Blame meant a slap on the wrist and a hastily written note that nobody would ever read as it yellowed in the back of an unopened employment folder. The only ones punished were Billy and, indirectly, herself, as some friends took sides.

In some ways, Jessica supposed, Stacy was indirectly punished, too. She seemed to drop off the map after breaking up with Dustin, and everybody quickly forgot Stacy and Dustin were even a thing when Billy's accident took center stage.

Thinking about it again made her cringe. The first two and a half years before the accident were nearly perfect and endless. The last year and a half felt like a whirlwind of regret and trying to hang on to her popularity. Most of it, she decided, was forgettable, especially after being buried under her first couple of years of college.

But that was then, and this was now. She didn't let her last year of high school define her then, and it certainly wouldn't hold her back now. That life sentence was better hung around the necks of those who never ventured forth out of their safe havens and unchanging neighborhoods.

She was home now, and being here would give her another chance to dance out of the past and into the future. When she eventually returned to New York City, it would be on her terms as someone strong enough to let go and brave enough to find what she deserved. And for whatever reason, she was certain that this reunion with Dustin was the next chapter she needed.

CHAPTER 5

EARLY BIRDS

The pounding in Billy's head was louder than the banging on the front door, but it needed to stop. When wishing it away didn't work, he tried to get up as the room swayed away from him like a tide.

"I'm up, I'm up," he muttered, trying to bide some time by willing whoever was at the front door to disappear. He had no such luck. They were persistent.

He tumbled off the couch while trying to remember how he got there, mouth dry and stomach in knots. The hammer at the door leveled off as he did, replaced by an occasional rap meant to prod him out of his slow-motion stupor.

He would have taken a drink from any of the water bottles decorating the coffee table, something to sweep away the cotton in his mouth, but his stomach flipped at the thought. It didn't sympathize with what had become an all-too-familiar condition. Hangovers are the sentences of trials lost the night before, his boss at the quarry liked to say.

Even so, Billy couldn't understand having one this morning. He didn't remember drinking enough for a hangover as horrible as the one he had now, unless what they said was true: there is no justice in getting older.

He was down again, crawling on hands and knees toward the sound. He squeezed his eyes shut, hoping to blink the pain away, along with the bright light of morning that crept in around every corner of the covered windows. His eyes burned as he opened them again.

"Give me a minute," he gasped, forcing himself up on a knee and then onto his feet, mechanically placing one foot in front of the other until he could reach the door. He pulled it open without looking through the peephole his dad installed when he was ten, one hand on the frame to steady himself. The other gripped the knob.

Andrea greeted him with a smile, tight mousy curls bobbing on her head as she peeked around his frame to survey the damage. She was the yin to his yang as the sun streamed into the artificially dark living room, curtains drawn to hide the crime scene.

She immediately played at having the upper hand with a smugness he didn't appreciate. Her eyes were bright behind wire rims. Her mouth curled into a mischievous grin.

"Oh, so you are home," Andrea said through the screen door. "I was starting to wonder."

"Yeah, I guess I am," he said. "Sorry."

"Blackout?"

"I don't know, I guess so," he said, trying to recollect anything from the night before. There were too many holes. "I don't remember much."

"I'm not surprised," she said, holding her phone up. "You only texted me forty, fifty times."

"Sorry," Billy said again, shrugging it off. "I must have had a good reason, but I can't tell you what it was."

"You wanted a ride from me so some cop wouldn't take you home," Andrea said, tired of waiting for an invitation, pulling open the screen door, and pushing her way into the house. "Does that jog anything in that thick head of yours?"

He had no explanation, so he shut the door and watched her move around the room like a whirlwind, tidying up as she went.

"I half expected that by 'home,' you meant a jail cell or drunk tank," said Andrea. "Do we even have a drunk tank in this town, or do they just check you in at the county jail? Note to self: ask Public Information Officer Julie Ross."

"It depends on whether you resist arrest," Billy said. "But it wasn't like that last night. He was just some random knickerbocker with a badge."

"Billy, it was a rhetorical question," she said, glancing at the plants in the window. "Just because Autumn moved out doesn't mean you should kill her plants. It wouldn't hurt you to water the poor things."

"Come on, Andrea. I don't know a thing about plants."

"You don't know a thing about a lot of things," she said. "But I love you anyway."

"Ayuh, cut me a break. I saw Jessica last night."

"You saw Jessica?"

"Yeah, she was at the Paw."

"What was she doing there?"

"Playing a game of pool," he said before grimacing. "She's home because her mom has cancer."

"No kidding," Andrea said. "The way her mom used to smoke, I'm surprised the doctors didn't diagnose her sooner."

"I see you are as sympathetic as always," he said.

"The word you're looking for is empathetic and, no, I'm not," she said. "I'm sorry her mom has cancer, but Jessica has been nothing but bad news for you. Face it. She's the reason Autumn left you. She's the reason they all leave you."

"Jessica didn't have anything to do with Autumn moving out," Billy called after her as she breezed out of the room and toward the kitchen. "She wasn't even here."

Andrea came back with two water bottles and tossed one to him.

"Here, drink this," she said while uncapping the other. "And you're wrong. Jessica was here. Not in person but as a presence. She's always here."

She wasn't wrong. Even after Autumn moved in, he could never shake the feeling that Jessica was his person. He always suspected that she would dash back into his life and right the relationship she had scuttled. It didn't even matter when she did it. He would shake off whomever he was with and pick up where he and Jessica had left off. Never mind what happened last night. Destiny doesn't always come easy.

He took a drink and pressed the bottle to his forehead while Andrea watered the plants with the other bottle. He didn't say anything more about Jessica because he already knew how Andrea felt. He tried to change the subject instead.

"You shouldn't bother," he said. "If she wanted to keep them alive, she would have taken them with her."

"You're such a dolt sometimes," Andrea said. "She left them because she plans to give you another chance."

He threw his hands in the air. "Whatever."

Andrea stopped watering the plants and looked at him as if she could read his thoughts. In a way, she probably could. Andrea always had a way of sizing up her allies and opponents before baiting them.

"Let me guess," she said at last, peering at him over her glasses. "Jessica threw herself at your feet and begged for you to take her back. You were so smitten by her unconditional affection, you called for every bottle of champagne in the Paw to be uncorked, which probably meant two leftover bottles from last New Year's Eve, and then you celebrated yourself into a fuzzy, bubbly bliss until some cop popped in to be a spoiler."

"You can be a real bitch sometimes," he said.

"Maybe, but I'm also the bitch who's going to buy you breakfast and retrieve your truck," she said. "So go wash off your hurt feelings and put on your big-boy britches. I don't have all day."

He knew where she was taking them. Andrea was a creature of habit like much of Augusta. The breakfast-only fare at the Early Bird Restaurant drew in generations of Mainers five days a week.

The menu was straightforward: eggs and toast, eggs and bacon, eggs and sausage, eggs and ham, eggs and corned beef hash, three-egg omelets, eggs Benedict, eggs slid between toast to make a sandwich, eggs wrapped in a tortilla. And on those days someone didn't want eggs, pancakes or French toast would have to do.

Nobody cared. The coffee was strong, and the cinnamon rolls were fresh. Whatever else someone needed, like crispy hash browns or home fries, could be called up as a side. The Early Bird served lunch too, but only after 10:30 a.m. — a menu that some family owners wanted to abolish because breakfast kept the doors open. Lunch had become a liability as more competition from chains had crept into town.

Andrea had written a freelance editorial story about it when she was still in college. Chains took advantage of more extensive selections, cheaper prices, and longer hours while family-owned businesses faltered. The trade was always the same. As moms and pops shuttered their businesses, the community's character eroded. Eventually, every town would resemble every other town that neighbored it, an empty shell filled with cookie-cutter options that meant fewer choices and inflated prices after the competition was choked off.

Walmart was the first superstore that didn't appreciate the pushback and pulled their advertising for a few weeks. They came back after learning the local daily supported their reporters, even those still in college, to be objective. Besides, her commentary was more critical of the town's citizens than its corporations. She focused on the mass hypnosis and hysteria around commercialization. When people were allowed to vote with their dollars, they inevitably voted for their own annihilation.

Andrea felt the same could be said about most things. People moved to escape stifling political policies only to vote for the same policies wherever they landed. Then they would try to escape again, never realizing they carried their problems with them. It wasn't a story people wanted to hear, but she would continue to pound the drum as long as the *Kennebec Journal* defended objective journalism, which is how she had become friends with Billy.

A few weeks after Billy's football-career-ending injury, Andrea capitalized on the nation's attention on high school football concussion rates during football practices and ballooned her high school newspaper story to include every manner of sports injuries under the tutelage of Coach Erik Dawson. Concussions led the way in high school sports, just as they did in college and the National Football League, but Andrea cobbled them together to suggest negligence among the coaching staff.

In addition to an uptick in concussions attributed to so-called accidental helmet-to-helmet collisions during games, the Windsor High Wildcats sustained eighteen serious injuries during the season, which accounted for more than half the team, and ten more injuries than their nearby rivals, the Cony High Rams.

Andrea attributed it to the coach teaching head-down football, a rule violation when it was intentional.

The problem, as Andrea called it out, was twofold. First, the word *unintentional* was being used to mask head-down contact. Second, the coaching staff ignored head-down contact during practices, which is how Billy Stevens had suffered a catastrophic injury. Dustin Fields didn't receive so much as a verbal reprimand for the incident, despite driving his face mask six inches below Billy's knee and breaking the shin, bone piercing the skin. The sound of it still haunted him.

"It was an accident, pure and simple," Coach Dawson had said after the incident. "There's no need to end the college career of two players instead of one. Those boys were friends, for heaven's sake."

Except they weren't friends when it happened. They had been until something came between them. Andrea had always suspected it had something to do with Dustin's girlfriend Stacy, but Billy never told her. It was his secret; he and his family had paid too much to keep it. So Andrea relinquished any deeper insight into what really happened between Billy and Dustin and settled on a story that garnered enough attention for her to string for the Journal while pursuing her journalism degree at the University of Maine at Augusta.

She could have gone anywhere, and Billy knew it. But like him, Andrea wasn't interested in escaping Augusta like so many of their other college-bound peers. Even when she received letters of interest from Columbia University and Northwestern University, she told Billy that journalism wasn't a profession that required an Ivy League or Little Ivy League education.

"The job is straightforward," she told him. "Tell the truth and shame the devil. I don't need someone from Columbia to tell me that. All I need is the right mentor, and her name is Edith Mayer."

Her name could have been Marie Curie for all Billy knew about women in journalism. But he didn't have to know anything about her. Andrea lit up every time she spoke about her. Mayer won this award. Mayer received that recognition. This year, she was up for the Judith Vance Weld Brown Spirit of Journalism Award from the New England Society of News Editors. Billy knew it because Andrea always talked about it with stars in her eyes.

"Think of it as the Heisman Trophy for New England women in journalism," Andrea told him. "It's for trailblazers in a traditionally male-dominated field, something I fully intend to earn one day."

Mayer was the editor who first noticed Andrea's indictment of Coach Dawson on the front page of the school newspaper after one of the faculty members sent her a copy. The Journal followed up with its own story, citing Andrea as a contributor. Coach Dawson wasn't dismissed, but he was reprimanded, and the era of accidental head-down football at Windsor High School came to an end. He might have even been fired over the scandal if it hadn't been for the school's winning season. The team took second at state, mostly attributed to Dustin Fields setting a state rushing record.

The other winner, of course, was Andrea. Mayer invited Andrea to lunch, offered her a position as a stringer, and gave her a scholarship to stay close to home. Billy was glad she did. There was some additional fallout with the rest of the football team after he spoke to Andrea about his injury and the unorthodox practice that led to it. She was among the first to fill in one of the many friendship vacancies in the wake of his speaking out.

It would be two more years before Coach Dawson's forced retirement, and many of his old teammates and the town forgave Billy. There were some, like Dakota Tarbox, who became openly critical of Coach Dawson after moving on to play college ball and then in the National Football League. Then there were others like Conner McGrath, who took a job at the same company where Billy worked.

The rest came to their senses because that's what small communities do. They were cautious of Billy because he was a hothead when he drank too much rather than because of anything that was quoted in a high school newspaper seven years earlier, especially after Andrea Kearney had been proven right. She would be right about a great number of subjects over the next seven years, time and time again.

Andrea may have been right about Autumn, Billy conceded on the drive over to the Early Bird. Autumn had left more than her plants in his childhood home. She left her winter clothes, kitchenware, and an obsolete collection of music CDs — stuff he had thought to box up when her absence drifted into the fourth week. He tried to do it once and surprised himself when he could not.

But he couldn't call her and apologize, either. She needed to apologize to him, pressing him for a commitment he wasn't ready to make just because they had lived together for six months, which was twice as long as any previous relationship he had been in since high school. In fairness to her, it wasn't his unwillingness to make a deeper commitment that prompted their tequila-infused fight. It was the reason.

"If you want to live in the past, Billy, then live in the past," Autumn had said. "Just don't ask me to live there with you when I'm standing right here in the present."

She wasn't the only one to have said it. There had been a dozen before her. The only difference was that most said it within the first three months of dating, not the tenth month. They wanted him to let Jessica go, and he could never articulate that it wasn't just about her. It was the last time in his life when everything felt familiar, safe, and certain.

"Hey, wake up, sleepyhead," Andrea said, pushing him into the window he had leaned against during the drive over to the diner. "We're here."

Billy spilled out of the truck, hands in his pockets and baseball cap brim pulled down to shield his eyes. Andrea waited for him, but only so that she could grab his elbow and tug him inside, under the weathered Early Bird sign, white and brown with its comic strip chicken mascot sporting a gaping smile, wattles, and a snow cap.

Andrea grabbed the only open booth despite Billy protesting against any window seating. The light spilling into the place seemed to amplify the volume, a chorus of regulars and families singing about their weekend plans over the constant percussion of clinking plates and glasses.

"Coffee first," Billy said as soon as he sensed the presence of a server. "Two eggs, over easy, hash, and toast after that."

"Sourdough like always and a side of home fries?"

"Yeah, sure."

Billy felt bad, barely acknowledging the server without much more than a mumble and a nod, but Sally knew the score. She was a Windsor High student who only worked weekends, but she had served Billy several dozen times over the last two years. Sometimes, he was a ray of sunshine who asked questions about his old teachers and her college prospects, and other times, Billy was like he was today or worse, which usually meant a face full of abrasions and a black eye.

"The usual, Sally," Andrea said. "And some grilled blueberry muffins. Party boy could use some sugar to offset last night's libations."

"Of course, Ms. Kearney," she said. "I'll get your coffees and put your order in."

"Appreciate you," said Andrea.

Billy was busy unfolding his silverware from a paper napkin when Andrea reached across the table and grabbed one of his hands. She did it in a way his mom had once done before telling him they had to put his dog down, a twelve-year-old German shepherd named Captain. Andrea wanted to tell him something, and it was bad.

He looked up, squinting at her.

"I didn't want to say anything until we were out," she said. "Jessica's not the only one back in town. Dustin is home, too."

Billy felt his chest tighten and his throat constrict, but he didn't want to give Andrea the satisfaction. He didn't say anything. He looked into her green eyes and then past them, as if he were waiting for something she said to bother him.

"Did you hear what I said?"

He didn't break eye contact until Sally turned over his coffee cup and filled it.

"Thank you," he said, acknowledging the girl for the first time before returning to Andrea. "And this is supposed to bother me how?"

"It doesn't bother you?"

The coffee was too hot, but he sipped at it anyway, hoping the smell of it would begin to make him feel better. It wasn't going to. Nothing could make him feel better. Dustin had destroyed his life.

"What do you want me to say?"

"I don't know. That you can't believe it? That it pisses you off? That you want to know how I know?"

"How do you know?"

"He was picked up for a DUI after driving his Challenger off the road."

"That sounds like Dustin."

"I pulled it off the weekly public records report this morning before coming to check up on you."

"So you decided to share the news with me before breakfast because you want me to lose the little appetite I have anyway?" Billy looked at her. "You should have told me before ordering if you wanted to save a few dollars."

"This really doesn't bother you?"

Billy frowned and shook his head. He took another sip of coffee to mask any involuntary signs of malcontent. His hands trembled as he did, but he assumed she would attribute it to his hangover.

"I suppose everybody comes home now and again, even wonder boys from Baylor."

"That's the thing, Billy. He didn't graduate from Baylor."

"What?"

"Dustin was cut from the team before finishing his third season and dropped out of school shortly after," she said. "This was despite rushing over eleven hundred yards on eighty-two carries that year. He should have been an All-American, but Baylor dumped him instead."

"Why'd they do that?"

"He raped a student."

"I don't know," Billy said, clenching his teeth because he did know. "I think we would have heard something about that. And even if it did happen, plenty of schools give players a pass if it stays out of the paper."

"Unless it happened more than once," Andrea said, clenching her own teeth but for a different reason. "What if two Baylor students were willing to accept cash settlements in exchange for keeping their complaints from becoming public? There would have been other incentives, too, like the university and law enforcement agreeing not to investigate the plaintiffs. We've come a long way from whitewashing rape to date rape, but women who are sexually assaulted still have an uphill battle. It's not good enough to object to a boy's advances if you are dumb enough to leave the bar with him and go to his apartment."

"Come on, Andrea," said Billy. "You're talking about a national news story."

"Unless your daddy is William Fields," said Andrea. "If he's your daddy, then everything disappears pretty easily, last night's DUI included. You know what I'm talking about, Billy. Don't you? Crimes disappear. Careers disappear. People disappear. Families disappear."

"What is that supposed to mean?"

Andrea stopped talking as Sally brought their plates over and set them on the table. She could sense the tension but kept smiling anyway. It was something she had learned as a waitress. It was all too easy to lose a tip at a volatile table if whatever issue they were having spilled over onto the service.

"Here you go," she sang, setting down Billy's plate. "Can I get you two something else?"

The question was obligatory. She knew neither of them would ask for ketchup or any other condiment besides the salt and pepper on the table.

"No, we're good, Sally. Thank you."

Andrea picked up on a defeated lilt in his voice. She steeled herself to ask what she had wanted to ask all morning.

"Why did you and Dustin Fields have a falling out anyway?"

Billy stabbed at his hash and then set his fork down. He took another drink of coffee instead and set the cup down, shaking his head.

"I thought you came over as a friend this morning," Billy said. "I would have never guessed you came over to ambush me and ruin breakfast."

Andrea knew he was right. It hadn't been her intent to ambush him. She let herself get carried away with the conversation, a lioness encircling her prey. But she wasn't supposed to pounce on her friend. She wanted to pounce on the truth.

"You're right, I'm sorry," she said. "Let's drop it."

"Sure," he said, dragging his plate closer to the edge. "The eggs are already getting cold."

Andrea tried to rekindle the conversation, sharing some details from the police report. He hardly acknowledged any of it while they ate, losing himself in thought and wondering if any of this story she had told him was his fault. He would mull this idea over and over again for the rest of the day, long after she dropped him at his truck and he headed over to urgent care because he still couldn't shake the feeling that there was something wrong with him, much worse than a hangover.

He might have come to a different conclusion about what happened in high school had she not omitted one detail from the police report. Andrea wouldn't tell Billy who called in the crash until she checked something out. It wasn't like Andrea to keep secrets from him, but he couldn't fault her. He had secrets, too.

CHAPTER 6

SOLOMON GRUNDY

Jessica rounded the front of her Jeep Cherokee to help her mom out of the passenger seat. El had been quiet most of the ride home.

The procedure had taken over an hour, twice as long as El had been told. And while her mom had anticipated feeling pressure and sharp pain when the needle entered her lung, she didn't know the technicians would repeat the process several times.

Jessica knew her mom had underestimated the soreness she would feel after the procedure every time she took a breath. The doctor's office had warned her, but El expected to be an exception. Her mom wasn't an exception. El told her the entire experience was horrible, and now she had to consciously remind herself to take shallow breaths.

As soon as Jessica opened the door, she noticed the old white handkerchief her mom had brought was streaked with phlegm and blood. She would have to scrub it out with dish soap and peroxide, and even then, there weren't any guarantees. It had once belonged to her dad. Her mom was exhausted.

"You okay, Mom?" she asked, and it rolled out flat.

Jessica offered a hand, but her mom didn't take it. She set her jaw instead and looked out the windshield toward the porch, handkerchief clutched to her mouth.

"Take all the time you need," said Jessica, managing a weak smile. "I'll unlock the front door."

Jessica's smile faded as soon as she turned toward the house. This would be her life for the next few months or as long as it took. She didn't know if she could do it, but she told herself she had no choice. She had to do it. There was no one else.

She embraced the deception that she was strong enough like a security blanket. As she bounded up the steps, a vibrant bouquet of flowers greeted her at the top of the porch with a burst of spring colors, a sharp contrast to the dulling browns and reds of autumn.

She reached for the card poking out from between the flowers. The only inscription was an ink stamp of a dragonfly. It infuriated her. Nothing had sunk into his thick head last night.

"Billy," she exhaled in disgust, fighting the urge to pick them up and hurl them into the bushes.

"Who are they from?" Her mother had caught up to her.

"Oh, Mom," Jessica said, folding the card into her palm and slipping it into her pocket. "Um, I don't know. I didn't see a card, but I bet they are for you."

"For me?"

"I'm sure some of your friends knew you were going in today," said Jessica. "Didn't they?"

"I may have mentioned it, but I didn't think they would go to all this trouble."

"I think you underestimate them," Jessica said. "Unless you have a secret admirer I don't know about. Do you?"

"Don't be silly," El laughed and winced with pain.

"You all right?"

"I'll manage," she said. "Here, let me hold them while you get the door."

As Jessica stood between the storm door and worked the lock, she caught a glimpse of her reflection in the small panes of glass that decorated their door. She looked tired, and it made her feel self-conscious. She wondered if this was how she looked when she visited Dustin in the hospital. Or maybe the haggardness was more immediate, a toll taken by her mom's less-than-positive experience, all told on the ride home.

As the door swung open, she felt the burst of warm air greet her. It was one of the many changes her mom had made when Jessica left for college five years ago. Almost all her life, her family had kept the thermostat at a chilly sixty-two degrees. Nowadays, her mom preferred it warmer at seventy-two.

"You might want to get a heat pump when the oil furnace needs to be replaced," said Jessica, opening the door for her mom. "They're all the rage in New York now."

"Why would I want to do that?"

"Well, you could reduce your carbon footprint, for one thing."

El shook her head, chuckling, as she made her way past Jessica to temporarily set the vase down on the small entry table so that she could take off her shoes and coat at the door. Old habits die hard.

"My carbon footprint? Honey, I think you've been in New York too long. This is Maine, and we use oil."

"Ayuh, but the heat pump heat is more comfortable."

"How so?"

"I don't know, but they say it circulates the air better, and you'll save money."

"That's what they said when we switched to kerosene, then again when they started using blends," El said. "You know how it is. Somebody's always selling a better bill of goods."

"It's called innovation, Mom," Jessica said.

"Don't be so naive. It's called profit. Now help me get these beauties into some fresh water."

An abrupt change of subject could only mean one thing. Her mom was done with the conversation. Jessica might have been annoyed had it been some other topic, but she didn't care this time. She had only brought up the idea of a heat pump as small talk, something to help them move beyond the immediacy of the lung biopsy.

So Jessica followed her mom into the kitchen, where El quickly delegated the stem trimming so that she could make a cup of tea. Jessica offered to make it to let her mom rest, but it became clear that El wanted to do something despite her exhaustion.

"The secret is to keep them in a cool part of the room and away from direct sunlight," El said, sprucing the flowers with her hands after Jessica had finished. "Did you know that?"

"No, I didn't."

"Somebody needs to meet more gentlemen," said El. "I don't know what kind of boys you've run into lately, but Billy was the only gentleman you've ever brought home."

"Really, Mom?" Her sarcasm was pronounced.

"He was," she said. "You know it's true."

"I haven't thought about Billy since high school," Jessica said, floating a white lie. "I've been with dozens of guys since then."

"Oh, I don't think that's anything to brag about. Besides, the real question is, how many of them have been gentlemen?"

None of them, Jessica thought. She didn't think gentlemen existed anymore.

"All right. Let's hold that thought," Jessica said. "How about I check messages while you finish the tea?"

"Suit yourself. As long as we both know I'm right."

"Sure, Mom. I'll agree there aren't many gentlemen out there."

Jessica's tone said it all. She was unconvinced and making a concession, but it unnerved her that Billy was brought up. There was no way for her mom to know the flowers were from him. Was there?

She looked at the machine. It had five messages since they had left in the morning. Three of them were more hang-ups. Two of them were from the agency where she worked, both from Keiko.

The first message was a follow-up from the night before. Jessica was certain Keiko would understand that she had planned to call in on Monday after the test results came back. But a second message from Keiko seemed more urgent. Keiko said she wanted to talk to Jessica about something but was reluctant to leave whatever it was on an answering machine.

Jessica's first thought was that it had to do with a client. She immediately revisited the mental checklist she had made before she left for Maine. She was sure she had taken care of everything she could think of before coming home. It had to be something else. But what?

She picked up the phone and dialed. As it rang, her mom came out with tea.

"Mom, I could have helped you carry it out afterward."

"Everything all right?" El asked, nodding at the phone as she navigated into the family room toward the coffee table with a shaky tea tray.

"Yes, Mom, just a work call," Jessica said, holding up a hand to quiet her mother.

"Kennedy Sloane. How may I assist you?" It was Keiko and not a receptionist.

"Hey, Keiko. It's Jessica."

"Oh, Jessica, I'm so glad you called."

"Yeah, I was going to call on Monday, but your message this morning seemed urgent. I'm surprised you're working the weekend."

"Well, it's all hands on deck for a Monday pitch. But that's not why I called you. So it's not urgent per se, but it is disturbing."

"What?"

"I don't know how to describe it, so I'll just go ahead and say it. Somebody's been leaving strange messages for you."

"Strange messages?"

"At first, I thought it had something to do with your mom, but that doesn't make sense anymore."

"What didn't make sense?"

"Then I thought it was a prank or something, but he's called six or seven more times since the first few."

"Who?"

"Jessica, you can tell me. Did you break up with somebody?"

"Yes, sort of," Jessica said and swallowed.

"Is there any way you can contact him and tell him to stop calling the agency?"

"Why, what is he saying?"

"That's just it. Sometimes, he doesn't say anything. Other times, he asks for you and says, 'Tell her it took ill on Thursday."

Jessica felt a lump rise in her throat. She immediately knew who left the messages.

"Was that it?"

"'It'll be worse on Friday,'" Keiko said.

Jessica didn't say a word, but she could feel her back go rigid.

"Honey, are you okay?" El asked, picking up on the tension.

"Are you there?" Keiko asked on the other end of the line.

She couldn't find the words as the memories flooded back. Kyle liked to singsong those lines from behind a white death mask. He was a baritone.

"You're so weird," she had said to him. "What does that even mean?"

"It's part of an old English nursery rhyme, Solomon Grundy," he said, moving close to her. "You never heard it before?"

"No, I don't think so." Jessica laughed. "And why are you singing it to me?"

"It's about life," Kyle said. "When we first met, our relationship was 'Born on Monday,' and last night, it was 'Christened on Tuesday.'"

"And what comes next?"

"Married on Wednesday," he said with enthusiasm.

"Are you sure you weren't a theater geek in high school or something?"

"Nah," he said, leaning into her with the mask. "Come on, give me a kiss."

"Whatever," Jessica said. "I'm not kissing you with that thing on."

So he took it off, and then he kissed her. It wasn't like the kiss the night before, wild and passionate. It was from somewhere deeper inside him as if he meant what he was saying: she belonged to him now. They had made love for the first time the night before, but he was already laying a claim. What had he said to her? Christened on Tuesday. Married on Wednesday. Took ill on Thursday. And so on, the nursery rhyme went. It wasn't the only one he had sung to her, but she knew what this one meant and why he left the messages. Kyle wasn't done with her yet.

She squeezed her eyes shut and let the memory of his voice fall away until other voices replaced it. Her mother had set the tea down and touched her shoulder. Keiko was raising her voice on the other end of the line.

"Jessica?" El asked.

"Jessica?" Keiko repeated.

"I'm sorry," Jessica said. "It's fine. It's nothing."

"Jessica? Is someone sick or something? I mean, besides your mom?"

"No, no. He's not ill," Jessica said. "It was just something stupid he used to say from time to time. It's about accepting life how it comes, no matter what."

"Well, can you call him and tell him to stop?" Keiko asked. "He's spooking some of the staff."

"I wouldn't know where to begin."

"What?"

"Yes, I'll try to get ahold of him," Jessica said, reminding herself that she was a relative newcomer at Kennedy Sloane and their patience had already been taxed by her request for an undefined leave of absence with the possibility of remote work once the initial dust settled. "I'm sorry he's causing trouble."

"It's all right," said Keiko. "Look, we get it. You have your hands full with your mom. But whoever this guy is, he can't call here every day."

"Yeah, no, you're right," she said. "I get it."

"Okay, then. Thank you, Jessica. You take care and call me as early as you can next week when you have a handle on things ... an idea of whether you can work remotely or an ETA on when you'll return ... something, anything, really. I'm the one in your corner here."

"Yeah, of course. I got it," Jessica said. "Good luck on the pitch this Monday."

"Thanks," Keiko said with an upbeat sigh. "We're going to need it."

"I really do wish I was there."

"Bye-bye, Jessica. Talk to you soon."

"Bye," Jessica said, but Keiko had already hung up.

"Everything at work all right?"

Her mother didn't understand much of the call but could surmise enough to know she should be concerned.

"It's fine," Jessica said.

"Oh, honey," El said. "You know you don't have to stay with me during all this. I can look into home health care like a nurse or something."

"Mom," Jessica said, putting up a hand. "Mom, don't."

She didn't want to cry, so she sucked in some air and fanned her face with her hand. The job. The ex. Her mom's cancer. She had to get through it.

She forced a smile and picked up a cup of tea. She sipped. It was too hot.

"I think I'm going to get some air," Jessica said. "Maybe I'll pick up your prescription before it gets too late."

"What about the tea?"

"Save me some, and I'll reheat it," Jessica said. "I don't think it will take me too long anyway. In and out."

"Can't it wait?"

"If I do it now, we can spend the rest of the afternoon together," she said. "Do you need anything from the store?"

"A pack of cigarettes?"

"That's not even funny."

"What does it matter?"

"Mom, don't."

"Fine. Surprise me."

"Challenge accepted," said Jessica. "Maybe you should get some rest while I'm gone?"

"Not likely, but thank you," El said, pulling out the ruined handkerchief again.

Jessica rolled her eyes and headed toward the door. She knew enough to expect some tension. It wasn't uncommon for seniors to take out their frustrations on caregivers. She didn't expect it to seep in so soon. Or maybe she should have.

She had always gotten along with El. After her father died, her mom made it a mission, reinforcing that it was the two of them against the world. Jessica was grateful because it could have easily gone the opposite direction, with her mom just giving up and abandoning her daughter during her teenage years.

The closeness didn't become problematic until Jessica became a high school senior. While her mother was willing to give her daughter enough space to shore up an injured boyfriend, El had become reliant on Jessica to fill the void left behind by her husband. Her dependence on Jessica became increasingly apparent with each college application that she sent off without a Maine address.

Jessica argued that it would be good for her mother to take on more social activities and even entertain a new man in her life. El wasn't interested. While she had a friend group, she didn't want any of them to know her business and be a lifeline, which left Jessica to take care of those everyday things Ed used to do but was never acknowledged for doing. The easy parts were things like mowing the lawn, taking out the trash, or cleaning the rain gutters. The harder parts were being her emotional dumping ground and listening to a lifetime full of regrets and insecurities that would have been better shared with a therapist. Jessica even asked her to consider going to one once, which El brushed off as a waste of money. She preferred talking to her daughter, she said.

Jessica had never considered it before then, but her father, Ed, had served as a secret buffer between her and her mother's anxieties. Growing up, all Jessica had ever known was that her mother was a superhero. El would change lives by managing recommended reading lists for kids at school and changing the bed sheets as part of her chore list at home. She did it all without complaint while nurturing her daughter to be a strong, independent woman. Except El wasn't. She leaned into her husband to soothe a tortured soul and then into her daughter when her rock eroded.

Knowing Jessica was planning to dash off to parts unknown only made it worse. El didn't have anything other than nicotine to quiet her nerves, and even that seemed to grow less effective with each passing year. A half a pack became two packs until she abruptly quit the first year Jessica said she wouldn't make it home for Thanksgiving, half expecting her daughter would change her mind and come home to help her. Jessica didn't change her mind, but El quit anyway. If only her mother had had the foresight to quit sooner.

As Jessica opened the front door, she heard her mom turn on the television and flip through the channels to find a football game. Jessica laughed to herself. Watching football had become one of El's favorite pastimes since she attended her first high school game nine years ago. El originally went to see her daughter cheer from the sidelines, but that quickly morphed into her cheering for Billy, the boy she not-so-secretly fantasized would marry Jessica and chain her to Augusta.

El was wrong, and it wouldn't be the last time. After she broke Billy's heart and El said Jessica was too headstrong for her own good, Jessica broke her mother's heart. It wasn't her and her mother against the world. She was in it to win it alone, like her father would have wanted. And for the entirety of her college career, she lived it.

She might have even gone on living it had it not been for being blindsided by the first person she met since her father who was strong enough to push back when she tried to call the shots. Except *blindsided* wasn't the right word. The physical and mental abuse were gradual, barely noticeable, as their relationship played out over months. She might even still be with Kyle had it not been for an unexpected discovery that snapped her out of the spell.

Her face flushed even thinking about it. She shoved against the storm door and let it slam behind her. Would Kyle be doing the same thing to her that he was doing to the other girl? Did he really have no intention of letting her go without a fight? If that was the case, she would have to be ready for him.

She stormed to her Jeep, climbed inside, and turned the key in the ignition. She didn't even notice anything wrong until she pulled out of the driveway. Then an unexpected vibration and pulling sensation became obvious. She had a flat tire.

She stopped and slammed the steering with her hands, wondering how it was possible. She turned off the car and jumped out to inspect the damage. Sure enough, the front passenger tire sagged.

Jessica shook her head in disgust. There had been no warning light.

"Can this day get any worse?" she said, kicking the tire. She couldn't believe it after such a promising start. She had reunited with Dustin Fields as a friend, which turned into a date. Everything else that followed was one punch after another. Her mother's disastrous lung biopsy. The ridiculous flowers. The idiotic phone messages. The useless bickering. And now a flat.

She bit her lip in defiance. She wasn't going to let this get the better of her. One of the reasons she had bought a Jeep was because it came with a full-size spare. She was going to do what her father had taught her to do. She would change it, just like she had changed everything else in her life that hadn't worked out.

CHAPTER 7

QUICK CARE

Billy slid off the Quick Care exam table, ripping the thin white paper as he dropped down and moved to the chair on the opposite side of the room. He had been waiting in the exam room for twenty minutes and was tired of sitting there with his legs hanging down, forced to read the same poster over and over again.

It was a picture of a smiling family, representing three generations — grandparents and parents framing a ten-year-old girl with bangs. The headline ran contrary to the image. *Cancer: Does it run in your family?*

Billy chuckled at the absurdity of it, wondering who in their right mind would pair a perfect family with the possibility of cancer. But then he started thinking of Jessica's mom. Muriel Michaud, everybody's favorite librarian for as long as he could remember, had lung cancer.

It would be easy to blame the cigarettes, he thought. Who wouldn't? Muriel had always smoked. It was one of her trademarks. She was a beautiful, independent woman marred only by the hole her husband left behind when he died, and the tiny tells that came with her one vice. Wrinkles had set in around her lips, nicotine had stained her fingertips, and the soles of her shoes bore the brunt of crushing out butts on the asphalt.

Of course, there was always the chance that her cancer wasn't from smoking, which meant Jessica could one day inherit the curse, even if it chose to manifest itself in some different and unexpected way. And it was then he envisioned the people in the picture as the family that would never be, with him and Jessica framing an imaginary daughter and the Michauds filling the background, Ed long dead and El now dying. *Cancer: Does it run in your family?* Nobody would be smiling.

From his new vantage point, he could poke fun at the staff-made sign on the door: *Some patients like to have a chaperone (another staff member) present during their physical exam. If you would like a chaperone, please let us know.*

"Too late to ask," he said with a whistle and slid down in the chair, trying to find a comfortable position.

Quick Care was his first stop after Andrea dropped him off at the Bear Paw to retrieve his truck. An exam room was the last place Billy wanted to spend his Saturday afternoon, but Andrea had made him promise he would after a few cups of coffee and breakfast didn't seem to snap him out of his stupor. He resisted, having been raised that medical visits were best left for emergencies.

Andrea and his throbbing head eventually convinced him otherwise. Having a blackout here and there over the years wasn't out of the ordinary, but he had never felt like this before. Andrea had argued they would set him up with an IV drip that would ease the hangover and nausea, if nothing else.

The idea to run a blood and urine test before administering a drip had come from the physician's assistant. Delores said she had a hunch after Billy described some of his symptoms. He asked her what the hunch might be, but she just smiled and said she'd surprise him.

It was one of the reasons he sometimes thought Jessica had the right idea about leaving Augusta for good. Everybody knows everybody in a small town, and the first quip Delores made when she saw him check in at reception was about whether or not he needed stitches again.

Billy felt his phone vibrate and looked down at the screen. It was Autumn. The day couldn't get any better.

Hey.

He watched the blinking ellipsis. She was still typing, so he didn't respond. Then she stopped before starting again. Whatever she wanted to say, she had changed her mind.

How've you been doing?

"Pretty crappy, actually," he said aloud before typing Okay.

I've been thinking a lot about us and what happened. Do you want to grab a cup of coffee?

He wanted to ask if Andrea had called her to check up on him, but he knew it would only piss Autumn off. It was a fair question, all things considered, but he couldn't bring himself to type it and start a fight. Maybe her texts were the opening lines of the apology he expected if he didn't preemptively blow it.

I'm all coffeed out today. It was true, but he didn't know why he sent a nonstarter.

Okay. It was her turn to search for words. A blinking ellipsis, then nothing, and finally the words appeared on his screen. I'm really trying here, Billy.

His shoulders slumped in defeat. He asked himself why it was so painful?

He knew why. It wasn't that he didn't love Autumn. He did love Autumn. That wasn't the problem. The problem was how much he loved her. No matter how good things were, there was always this nagging sensation that he was somehow settling, and he didn't want to ask for anything more while he felt that way.

I know. I want to meet up too.

When?

I'm tied up right now. I'll get back to you.

Okay.

Okay.

I do love you, Billy.

I know. He wrote it and then relented. Me too.

She texted a heart in response. If there was ever a girl he didn't deserve, it wasn't Jessica. It was Autumn. He hadn't even tried to reach out to her for four weeks, yet here she was, being the first to offer an olive branch. It should have been him.

Her name was Autumn, but she looked like spring, he used to say when they first started dating. She was fair-skinned and dark blonde, with a soft chin and light brown eyes, almost amber within their rings and swirls.

Billy had met her in Kennebunk on New Year's Eve. He had driven down with two friends. Then, for fear of feeling like a third wheel, he gave them some distance before the wild blueberry drop at First Parish Church. The drop was a micro version of the ball drop in New York City, with a crowd of maybe fifty people, mostly locals. It was a small wire frame ball lit with a thousand blue and green lights — an upgrade from an old lawn ornament two friends had dropped from the church two years prior.

Ironically, it was Autumn's cousin, whom she had been visiting in Kennebunk for the holidays, who became the third wheel when Billy, better than buzzed, asked who would be the first girl to kiss him in the new year. Autumn took him up on it before the twelfth chime of the church bell.

She stood on her toes to kiss him, and the expectant peck on the cheek turned into something deeper and more meaningful.

The two of them stood there in the midst of cheering strangers and the stars blazing above them. The moon, a waxing crescent, had set several hours before, but Billy remembered noticing it at that moment, a symbol of intention and hope, like a silver lifeline. And for a time, Autumn was that lifeline.

She carried herself with a feminine mystique that seemed unusual to him, inviting him to pull out her chair, put on her coat, and open the door. Most women didn't pause long enough to let men do that anymore, but she seemed content to let him take the lead.

It made him feel stronger than he had ever felt before, with her hands slipping into his pockets to keep warm. She was always content, allowing him to move at his own pace. While some people questioned his ambition after he settled into the job of drilling holes and extracting stone, she didn't care. Her man would get around to being as strong as the stuff he sometimes carved on the weekends when he got around to it.

That wasn't to say Autumn was demure or a pushover. She could be sarcastic at times, especially when she was drinking, matching him one drink for every two because she suspected him of protecting her when she had too much. But this unexpected roughness to her personality was part of her charm.

Billy noticed by the second date that Autumn wasn't like the popular crowd he knew in high school. When Autumn talked about something, she spoke of the thing itself. When the popular crowd talked about something, they always talked about themselves and how they related to it.

He first noticed it when they kicked him to the curb after his injury, but it sunk in after he met Autumn. If you asked most people about a song, they would talk about how it made them feel or how their musical interests evolved. If you asked Autumn, she would talk about the lyrics or melody. If you asked someone about their favorite film, they would talk about when they saw it and whom they saw it with. If you asked Autumn, she would pull out some obscure scene where an actress looks at her reflection in a store window while the two other characters chat.

"Did you see that? She wasn't even part of the scene but became part of it by sharing something about her character," Autumn had said. "So many other actors just stand around like they are waiting to say a line that isn't even in the script."

Her observation of the tiniest details made even some of their smallest moments together charming and memorable. She noticed things. She noticed him. Nobody else had for a very long time.

It was also this attention to detail that derailed them when she came across a shoebox filled with photos, notes, and letters from Jessica Michaud, talismans that Billy could never bring himself to let go or toss out. As much as Autumn felt like the lifeline to his present, Jessica remained the lifeline to his past.

"Do you really need these anymore?" Autumn had mused one weekend afternoon when the pair was cleaning the house.

"What?"

"These old photos and love notes?"

"Yeah, they're from another time, but it's my other time."

"Back when you were a high school superstar?"

She said it with a wink and a smile, but Billy didn't find it funny.

"Strong safety."

"I know what a strong safety is, Billy. I grew up with three brothers, remember?"

He pressed his lips together.

"I was mostly joking," she said. "But now you're making me wonder."

She put her hands on her hips. He shook his head.

"You weren't joking," he said. "Tell you what. Why don't you focus on clearing out your clutter and leave my stuff alone because, you know, it's my house."

"Oh, your house. I see now. You're really going there?"

"Drop it," he said, taking the box from her and putting it back in the closet.

They did drop it, until later that evening when they met up with their friends Conner and Hope at the Bear Paw for drinks. Autumn first reintroduced the topic as a hypothetical, asking Conner and Hope how long they held on to photos of old flames on social networks like Facebook and Instagram. Hope laughed at her.

"Who cares? Dump them all."

"Right?"

"Yeah," said Conner. "I've always found it just complicates things for the next person you meet."

"I mean, I suppose there is no black-and-white answer to this, but any reluctance might be tied to something ridiculous like divine intervention to rekindle lost love," Hope said. "Why? Who are we talking about anyway? Kevin doesn't still have photos of you on his Instagram, does he?"

Billy rolled his eyes at the mention of Autumn's last boyfriend, with the emphasis being on boy. Kevin was two years younger than Autumn, which is primarily why they broke up. He was too immature for a serious relationship.

"She's not talking about Kevin or Instagram," Billy said before taking a long pull on his beer. "She's talking about me."

His words landed between them like a sledgehammer, with Conner taking an equally long drink and then looking away. Conner didn't have to guess. He knew exactly who this was about.

"What am I missing?" Hope asked, looking for a punch line and then trying to provide one. "Some guy doesn't still have pictures of you up on Facebook now, do they, Billy?"

"Hey," Conner said, gently squeezing her leg. "Maybe we should head out."

"I don't want to go yet," Hope said. "Wait, did I say something wrong?"

"No," Billy said, forcing a laugh. "You're the only one who said something right."

"About the guy thing?"

"About not wanting to leave yet," Billy said, standing up and drawing a lasso above the table with his free hand at their waitress. "Let's get some tequila shots over here."

The real fight started later, a few hours after Conner and Hope made their escape. And it was Charlie, tending bar that night, who almost became the next casualty of the evening when he tried to cut Billy and Autumn off.

Things escalated quickly, and Billy gave Charlie a shove. Autumn intervened almost immediately and agreed to get him home before Charlie had to reach for the phone and call Augusta PD or the sheriff's office. The subsequent car ride home was silent, but Billy found some more fight when they got home and he poured a nightcap.

But now, Billy didn't have any fight in him. He leaned his head back and looked up at an old water stain on the ceiling of the exam room and wondered how much drama he could trace to having one too many drinks. How much could anyone?

It always started out well enough, helping everybody unwind. What did his dad like to say? *It takes the past and the future off the table and lubricates the present.* Billy felt another wave of nausea and pulled the trash can a little closer to him with his foot.

He rubbed his temples and hummed some hangover wisdom in his head. What booze really does is open doors while you feel like your best self, and then it slams those same doors closed without warning. That's what it did last night, and that's what it did when Autumn slammed the door on her way out of his life.

He looked down at the garbage can and contemplated throwing up, fending it off with another deep breath. He was grateful for the reprieve because just as he got himself under control, Delores opened the door like she had won a lottery.

"My hunch was right," she said. "You've tested positive for Rohypnol."

"What's that?"

"You were roofied."

"The date rape drug?"

"The one and only," she said. "So I'd like to start an IV drip with some flumazenil to counteract what's left in your system. Mostly, we do this for overdoses, but the doctor thinks it will help clear your head enough to put the pieces together."

"Yeah, sure."

"And I need to ask if you'd like to file a police report."

"For what?"

"Do you think you were assaulted?"

"No," Billy said, trying to wrap his head around her diagnosis. "I don't think so."

"I think you would know so," she said. "Any discomfort besides the nausea and headache?"

"No, not really." He hadn't felt so confused since he woke up in a hospital with a compound fracture in high school.

"Okay, Billy, relax," Delores said, forcing a smile. "I can see you're getting agitated. Look, I get it. But right now you have to figure out why you were dosed. If it wasn't for date rape in the classic sense, I suggest you take a long look around your house when you get home and see if anything looks out of place or missing."

"Why would I do that, Dee?"

"Rohypnol isn't only used for date rape, Billy. We've seen it used for robberies, vehicle theft, and home invasion."

Billy tried to remember if anything looked out of the ordinary when Andrea had picked him up, but he couldn't remember. A murky blackness spanned the time Jessica left the Bear Paw and the time Andrea took him to breakfast, with only fragments of memories spiraling around a black hole like erratic streaks of light. None of it made any sense.

"He was a cop."

"What?"

"The guy who took me home from the Paw was a cop," Billy said. "Nobody we know. He was from out of town."

"I don't know. Maybe you got lucky. Maybe someone else drugged you, and this cop intervened before something bad happened. Do you remember his name?"

"No, but Charlie might. The cop had a tab just like I did."

"You might want to find out," she said. "And even if you weren't assaulted, you should still consider filling out a report. Rohypnol is easy enough to come by, but it is illegal."

"Yeah, tell that to half the high school football players in this town," said Billy, remembering the last time he talked about roofies.

"You make a good point," she said. "Any of your old high school buddies at the bar last night?"

"It's all water under the bridge."

"Is it? Andrea might have written the story, but some folks are still upset you were a willing contributor. The Wildcats are having a rough season."

"It's not because they lack that hack Dawson. They lack talent," said Billy. "You've heard the rumors. Windsor is on the school district's chopping block, and parents are pulling their kids before the axe falls."

"Maybe they blame you for that, too."

"Oh, please. My family has paid the price, twice over."

"Oh yeah, how are your parents doing?"

She asked to change the subject, and Billy didn't blame her. Most people thought his dad closed up shop because of the stories in the newspaper. The truth was much more sinister than any investigation. They were pushed out by what was never investigated.

"They love Florida," Billy said. "My dad can't get enough of it. Every time we talk, it's all about the miles of orange groves and how easy it is to grow a garden. And my mother loves it even more than he does. I guess she joined a bridge club and works at a fruit stand on the weekends."

"No kidding? Well, you send them my love when you visit. Ayuh, maybe you could put in a few good words for me, and I'll pay them a visit in person."

"Yeah, sure. So how long is this IV thing going to take anyway?"

"Oh, right, the drip. Sorry about that. It typically takes around thirty minutes. Why don't you hop back up on the table, and I'll go prep it."

"Anything to make the throbbing stop."

"So what are we doing about the police report? Do you want to file one or not?"

"Let's forget about it. I'm sure the fine officers of the APD have better things to do than chase down the culprit who pranked Billy Stevens. Heck, if they did find out who did it, they'd be just as likely to pin a medal on him as arrest him."

"Suit yourself, but I should warn you. Sometimes, the best defense is a good paper trail."

"I appreciate you looking out for me, but what I really need right now is a reset," said Billy. "Shoot me up with the good stuff, and I promise the first thing I'll do when I get home is inventory the entire place."

"All right," she said. "Give me two shakes."

As soon as she left, Billy moved back to the table and lay down. It took a minute to get comfortable, but then he closed his eyes and tried to make sense of it. Someone had drugged him, and he couldn't for the life of him figure out why.

Other than unexpectedly running into Jessica, it wasn't an eventful night. He had mostly stuck to Geary's on tap, from the time he arrived to the time he left. At some point, he might have had a shot with Jessica when things seemed like they were warming up, but then they cooled off just as quickly.

Jessica was initially playing pool with Ed Mailer, but Ed wouldn't do anything like that. He was one of those good-hearted locals people hoisted up as an example of why you shouldn't believe all the bad stuff people said about the town. He used to be a machinist with Bath Iron Works in Brunswick but now managed a big-box department store.

Most people would have taken the downgrade as a hit, but Ed only said he hated the commute, especially in winter. He donated all the extra time he reclaimed after the shipyard shakeup, which was more political than profit driven, and got involved with planning local events with the city. If someone wanted to know about the festivals and farmers markets, they asked Ed.

There were plenty of other people he knew at the bar when he first arrived. He just lost track of them while playing pool with Jessica. She had his undivided attention, right up until the time she left. And even after, he spent most of the time talking about her when the crowd had thinned down to him, the cop, and a couple of stragglers.

Of course, there always was a chance that the roofie wasn't intended for him. He and Jessica had mostly traded off trips to the bathroom between catching up. Maybe some of the lowlifes who planted quarters under the bumper were tired of waiting their turn and spiked what they thought was her drink. It didn't seem likely, but it was possible. He would have to ask Delores how long it takes for Rohypnol to kick in, but something told him it would not take long.

He remembered how quick it had hit Stacy the night that Dustin slipped it into her red cup at a high school party. She was dizzy before she even finished the drink, giving Dustin every excuse to whisk her away upstairs. Billy was supposed to follow suit with Jessica but chickened out. Instead, he flushed the dose Dustin had given him down the toilet and then climbed the stairs to check on Stacy.

The memory of it made his eyes well up. So this was how Stacy felt the next day, like someone had taken her head and chest and gut and put it all through a blender. Only it was a million times worse for her. Billy hadn't been raped while he stumbled around in a fog last night, but Stacy had been. He had seen them go up.

Later, Dustin would claim it couldn't be rape because it wasn't his first drug-infused encounter with Stacy. They had dropped Molly together a few times. But that excuse never sat well with Billy. The operative word Billy pushed back on Dustin was *together*. And then Dustin told Billy to screw off and let Stacy come to her senses. She never did.

Billy shook his head. Maybe she would have had Billy kept his promise to himself. But he didn't. He went around and around with Dustin for a couple of weeks before finding himself in the hospital with a life-changing, career-ending injury. By the time he had half a mind to come forward again, someone had already gotten to his parents, and Stacy became a ghost, like most of the people he knew before the fracture.

After high school, she fell off the map until Billy ran into her on the street two years ago. Her story was bleak in comparison to his. She had bounced in and out of rehabs before moving in with a guy who owned a trailer a few miles out of town. Billy said he would check in on her at the park sometime, but he never did. She didn't expect him to anyway. He could see it in her eyes when he gave her the two twenties he had in his pocket.

"Thanks for the cash," she said before the sarcasm. "You're a real lifesaver."

CHAPTER 8

GONE FISHING

Andrea sat down on the memorial bench overlooking the Kennebec River. The view from this vantage point was one of many reasons she never subscribed to the "Augusta-disgusta" sentiment shared by her classmates when she was in high school.

Sure, she understood their reasons. Most of them looked at going to an out-of-state college as an escape plan. Augusta sometimes felt more like a rust-belt town than a small New England city.

There were many reasons for the struggling roads and homes in need of renovation. Despite being the state capital, Augusta's population had leveled off in the 1970s and was in free fall by the time Andrea was born for the same reason her college article about small-town commercialization hit a nerve.

As big-box stores and malls were built on the vacant real estate between downtown and the interstate, smaller family-owned downtown businesses that were the lifeblood of the area were forced to shutter, leaving behind boarded windows and urban blight that knocked neighboring stores down like dominoes. In the wake of this exodus to the periphery, high school kids were left with even less to do in what was already described as a sleepy small town, unless they were willing to pile into cars and drive an hour north to the slightly less boring Bangor or an hour south to the slightly more vibrant Portland.

Many of them tried to do that, except in winter. While the plows did a good job getting snow off the road within a few hours or maybe a day after a big storm, nobody liked driving when it was actively snowing. But even when these kids did escape for a day, cruising better downtowns or attending rival college games, most of them did so on a shoestring budget. There were too many adults vying for what used to be teen jobs, like bagging groceries at Shaw's or building burgers at Burger King.

The whole of it seemed like an endless cycle. At the heart of it all, as far as Andrea was concerned, was Dustin's father, William Fields, and men like him. The Fields family was one of the wealthiest in the area. They made a fortune building the strip malls that destroyed downtown, only to be awarded a contract by the Augusta City Council to fix what they had broken.

The plan had started right where Andrea sat overlooking the river. The Kennebec River Rail Trail was a six-and-a-half-mile, ten-foot-wide asphalt and stone dust trail, framed by stones on the riverbank side and manicured access points along the street side. Once constructed, it was turned over to a nonprofit organization with a board representing the four communities it connected.

Along with the trail, Fields Construction renovated Market Square Park, added colorful sturgeon statues up and down Water Street, and were fixing up many historic buildings, including the Colonial Theater. Collectively, the investments and improvements were responsible for the first sustainable economic uptick in three generations.

Yet none of it sat well with Andrea. In her mind, Fields Construction was the reason Augusta needed an "Opportunity Zone" in the first place. Just like in every town in New England, certain families were making fortunes by saving towns they had helped destroy a few decades earlier.

The memorial bench Andrea sat on punctuated her point. Fields Construction had come up with the idea, then advised the city to price out working families from being able to install any for their loved ones. Then again, this was precisely why sitting on it now felt like poetic justice.

The city had cleaned up decades of river damage done by Edwards Dam and the area's old paper mills after removing them, and now it was from this overlook that Andrea would do her part in cleaning up the corruption that still plagued Augusta under the surface. She had appointed herself to this job because she knew that the city manager who helped remove the dam couldn't be expected to do it on his own.

The city manager would need like-minded politicians and city officials to help him, and she could provide the buffer they needed to get the job done. By leaking information to the newspaper, her sources were spared from any agonizing political pushback that could be levied by big party donors like William Fields.

County District Attorney David Mahoney, whom she was meeting with today, was one of her sources. Mahoney was sympathetic to the work Andrea did for the newspaper because he grew up in a low-income housing project south of Augusta. Like many fellow Mainers, he looked at college as an escape route, earning a scholarship to Bowdoin College and then being accepted to Harvard Law School.

After graduation, he worked as a prosecutor in Denver, starting in a trial unit before being promoted to tackle organized crime. He might have stayed there for a few more years, but he unexpectedly earned a fellowship to pursue his doctorate abroad. Upon earning it, he had a change of heart and returned to Maine.

He quickly landed a job as a prosecutor in Augusta until being appointed to his current position, vacated by a predecessor elected to serve in the Maine legislature. One year later, Mahoney was later reelected to the position by the people, with the unsolicited help of none other than Andrea Kearney, whose investigative work all but destroyed his opponent.

"Do you want to take a walk or admire the view?" Mahoney asked as he approached her.

"It's up to you."

He was wearing slacks and a sweater instead of the gray pressed suit she considered one of his trademarks. The casual dress made him look more like a Mainer and less like the big city lawyer he portrayed five days out of seven. It made him look more approachable, especially with the scruff outlining his jaw. He may even be growing a winter beard, Andrea noted. Maybe this meant he was finally embracing Augusta as a place to put down permanent roots.

"Come on, Andrea. You called me. On a Saturday, no less, I might add. What's so important?"

"I want to know what you're doing with the Fields case."

"The accident? It's still under investigation."

"Don't kid, Dave. I already have a copy of the officer's report. The blood sample clinches it. What was the blood alcohol content?"

Mahoney drew in a long breath and exhaled. He sat down next to her.

"There was a complication. He was so banged up that they rushed the draw."

"It's a blood draw, Dave."

"His attorney is already questioning whether the site was sterilized with alcohol to prevent contamination. They've asked to review the handling of the blood after it was drawn and the equipment used. And it doesn't help that the one witness we have refused to corroborate the officer's assessment that he smelled alcohol."

"So, your office is going to bury it?"

His face flushed, and he looked out along the Kennebec River.

"You know this trail follows the railroad right-of-way that once connected Portland to Augusta?"

"I passed Maine state history in high school, too," she said. "What does that have to do with anything?"

"I'm saying history matters here, so see it from my perspective," he said. "There were no witnesses to the accident and nobody else was involved or injured. It makes more sense to let him plea out with the wet reckless charge, which is more than fair, given his family's long history in the area."

"And what about Stacy Brenner's family history?" Andrea asked, tossing out a suspicion she could never seem to pin down.

"Okay," he said, throwing up his hands. He knew what came next.

"She might have been the first girl raped by Dustin, but she wasn't the last," Andrea said, rushing it out before he could shake her off. "There were at least two more at Baylor University."

"Look, you're a good kid," he said, standing up. "You really are, but pressing a DUI on a serial rapist, if that is what he is, is like flicking a mosquito off your arm after it's already drawn blood. But more than that, I shouldn't have to remind you that there is no Brenner case. Sure, it was before my time, but I looked into it like you asked. One complaint was filed and then retracted. No charges were ever pressed. In effect, there is no case. It doesn't exist. As for Baylor University, what am I supposed to do about that? Why don't you press the district attorney in Waco, Texas, instead? Oh, that's right. There were complaints made, then retracted, but no charges. And even if there were, Texas is ten states away."

She knew he wasn't wrong, just like he knew she wasn't after Dustin as much as his father. Dustin seemed like the easiest way to draw first blood, given his father frequently went out on a limb to cover up the boy's crimes. It was his one weakness.

"Did you know Billy Stevens was roofied at the Bear Paw last night?"

Billy had called her from the parking lot of the Quick Care and said she was going to have a field day with the news he had been roofied. She did, giving him more than an earful for fifteen minutes before offering to help him examine his house. He said he could handle it, which may or may not have been true.

Andrea told Billy that she would catch up with him later and immediately put in a call to Mahoney for the meeting. She didn't know why she wanted to meet, but her gut told her there was a connection somewhere. If nothing else, she could fish for information and satisfy her other hunch. Dustin would be given a pass.

He looked at her, waiting. "And?"

"Don't you think it's odd? The same night Dustin Fields pops up on the radar, Billy Stevens is drugged at a bar. The same Billy Stevens that Dustin Fields plowed into the ground seven years ago?"

"Was Dustin at the bar?" He didn't look amused.

"No."

"Was someone Dustin associates with at the bar?"

She opened her mouth but didn't answer. She needed to try another tack, but he didn't give her time to frame a question.

"Did Billy Stevens file a police report? Better yet, did he file one seven years ago? We both know the answer. Between these two boys, Billy Stevens is the one with a questionable reputation and a record. He might be a friend of yours and liked by most of the town on better days, but everybody knows Billy and booze don't mix. He invites bad things into his life when he drinks, enough so that he took a court-ordered anger management course two years ago."

Mahoney wasn't wrong. While things had been better since Billy started dating Autumn, he was a potential hothead anywhere alcohol was served. All anybody had to do was push one of two buttons, and everybody knew what those two buttons were. Disrespect a woman within earshot, on purpose or by accident, and Billy would demand a public apology. Or say anything remotely derogatory about Jessica Michaud, or mention that he still pined away for her, and an apology wouldn't be enough. Some things he could only settle with his fists.

Ironically, it didn't have anything to do with whatever insult or offense was made. Andrea was convinced it was how Billy punished himself. He blamed himself for whatever happened to Stacy. He blamed himself for the injury he sustained on the field. He blamed himself for losing Jessica. He blamed himself for his parents being all but forced out of town.

"Want my advice?"

"What?"

"Find Stacy Brenner and tell her to file a complaint, or press your friend Billy to give up whatever demons he carries around with him," Mahoney said, bending down to pick up a rock from the side of the trail. "And if you can't? Stop trying to catch a minnow when you're obviously casting a lure made for a bigger fish."

"Maybe," Andrea said. "But the way I see it, I have thirteen more years to figure out what really happened. You and I both know the statute of limitations on unlawful sexual contact or gross sexual assault is twenty. And I don't know about you, but my dad, rest his soul, taught me to drop a line in the water with a minnow and keep casting with the other. You double your chances with half the work."

Mahoney skipped the rock he had picked up, and it hopped across the water.

"You, Ms. Kearney, are a real shark with teeth just as big as the reporters I met in Denver. I'll give you that," he said. "But next time you want to go fishing, do me a favor and pick a weekday. Some of us regular folks appreciate our family time. We do our job to see justice done, but we're not trying to trailblaze a career."

"So you think that's what I'm doing?"

"Aren't you?"

"No," she said. "I'm just in it because I'm angry. I thought you knew that about me."

"Angry." He laughed. "What do you have to be angry about?"

"I'm angry that there are only two ways to bring people like Fields and his son down a peg. You either litigate them, making their crimes more expensive than whatever their negligence saves them and malice earns them. Or you expose them in a public forum, although I sometimes wonder if that even has any impact anymore. Newspapers are on the ropes these days, as you know."

He shrugged. "Swim with the sharks too long, and you know what happens."

She huffed. "A district attorney with a sense of humor. Now I can die knowing I've seen everything. Go home, Mr. Mahoney. Enjoy your family. As for me, I'm going to get to work doing your job so that other families have the option."

It was a blow below the belt, and she knew he didn't deserve it. They were on the same side, but she couldn't help it. She was always angry at men like William Fields, who took advantage of the world. She was angry at boys like Dustin, who intended to follow in their daddies' footsteps. She was angry at women like Stacy for not coming forward and at Stacy's parents for not pressing her to do the right thing. And mostly, she was angry at herself because for every story she wrote, there were ten more she would never have a chance to cover.

"I'm glad we're friends because it's clear your enemies will never have a chance," he said. "Enjoy the rest of your day."

She didn't extend a hand but gave him a wave. He forced a smile and started to walk away before unexpectedly turning around. He stroked his chin and tilted his head.

"I do have one question for you," he said. "I wasn't going to ask, but since we're concerned with each other's jobs and all."

"What's that?"

"How could Billy's parents afford to move to Florida without selling their house? Any ideas?"

"His dad sold the garage."

"Right, the garage," Mahoney said. "I heard about it, but never saw it. It was before my time in Augusta. Any idea who he sold it to?"

"I never asked."

"Maybe you should. Good day, Ms. Kearney."

He had turned around before the heat returned to her cheeks. She wasn't mad because he threw a counterpunch. She deserved it.

She was mad because he knew something and didn't tell her. More than that, she was mad because this last-minute jab before the bell made her realize she'd lost the entire round. Even a novice journalist knows that the person asking the questions is in the power position. He had beat her two, maybe three to one.

She could see every mistake she made along the way, too. She was too busy trying to guilt him into giving her something. In the process, he had taken control of the entire conversation. It shouldn't have surprised her because he was a smart man, smarter than most who squeeze their salaries from tax-paying families who make significantly less money. But he wasn't lazy, and it was wrong of her to imply it.

Who bought Stevens Garage? It was a question she never thought to ask Billy, and she didn't have to look it up to know she wouldn't like the answer, whatever it might be. There was no other reason for Mahoney to hit her with it, other than to remind her that she was a twenty-something kid.

But she wasn't such a kid that she had to surrender. Mahoney might be satisfied with a wet reckless charge, but she didn't have to be. There were other people she could interview, starting with Officer Ouellette. After Danny, she would find out which paramedics arrived on the scene, which emergency room doctor was on duty that night, which nurse drew the blood, and which lab technicians analyzed the sample.

Once she built a case with their stories, it would be easy enough to rattle the truth out of Jessica. She would set the trap by asking Jessica to tell her hero story about finding Dustin and then spring the trap by asking why she lied about smelling alcohol when law enforcement and the entire medical community all agreed Dustin was drunk.

Run this story in the newspaper and the district attorney would have little choice but to take the case to trial, forcing Dustin to either tell the truth or compound his guilt by perjuring himself. Forget all the fishing-line analogies Mahoney tossed about: this kind of story was like trolling with a net of moral responsibility. Nobody knew what kind of fish she might catch in it. It challenged people to come forward because it was the right thing to do, to exonerate whatever misdeeds they might have been party to or help them overcome any fear of repercussion.

As for who bought Stevens Garage, it was light work. She wouldn't even have to ask Billy, which is what Mahoney expected.

The sale was a public record. She would look it up. It was the better play, especially if she was going to put a screw to Jessica. She would have a hard enough time asking Billy to forgive her for that.

Andrea smiled. It wasn't going to be a bad day after all.

CHAPTER 9
TRAILER PARKS

Siri offered up an alternate route to save two minutes with its monotone pleasantries, but Billy chose to ignore it. He knew how to get to the trailer park from his home. What he didn't know was whether Stacy still lived there.

He had decided to find out after coming across their friend Izzy's Polaroids. Izzy had bought a vintage camera shortly after Facebook acquired Instagram, fearing that Facebook would shutter the app with a flair for 1970s nostalgia. They were all in middle school when Izzy bought it, but this photo was taken when they were sophomores.

In the photo, the four of them — he and Jessica and Dustin and Stacy — were standing in the parking lot of the Red Barn, arms draped over one another during a munchie run. They looked so young, drunk, and stupid with blissful smiles and squinty flash-burned eyes. Stacy looked the most wasted, one hand slipped between the buttons of Dustin's untucked shirt.

Billy hadn't thought of Stacy for months, but then she had come up again for the third time that day, haunting him like a ghost. He didn't look at the photo for too long, just pushed it into the box where it belonged, along with a half dozen more that had fallen out of a box that had apparently tumbled off the shelf in the closet. At least that was one theory.

It could have fallen off the closet shelf. Or he might have dropped it last night in a drug-induced haze. Or it could be counted among the dozens of inconsistencies he found in his family home after the fourth sweep.

On any other day, most of them could have been explained away by the blackout gaps in his memory or a careless house guest. But being roofied the night before made every unexplained peculiarity part of a bigger picture. It was almost as if someone had been looking for something in his home or, more exactly, looking at everything.

As he found things out of place with each successive inspection, Billy felt unsettled. What had started with the number of empty water bottles on the front table, as if the cop who dropped him off hadn't been alone or maybe stuck around long after Billy passed out, led to discoveries of increasingly invasive tells.

The towels in the guest bathroom had been left on the counter, which is something Billy would never knowingly do. The medicine cabinet was left ajar, something he hadn't even noticed before leaving with Andrea for breakfast. There was dirt on the floor of the kitchen, as if someone had gone out to the garage and back.

Then there were the opened bills on an office desk. Billy never opened bills until he intended to pay them. There was dust disturbed on bookshelves he hadn't gotten around to dusting and clothes sticking out from the drawers of the bedroom dresser he shared with Autumn.

The closet door in the hallway was left ajar, and the coats inside were pushed away from the center, making room for the box of photos that had fallen off its shelf. The first stray he had picked up was one of Jessica's senior photos from high school, a few weeks before she would turn his life upside down. She was wearing a green sundress and standing in a meadow, looking out toward the horizon, past the white picket fences and trees framing a horse stable. She loved to ride. He had almost forgotten that she did. He wondered if she had forgotten, too, now that she was a self-proclaimed city girl.

While it wasn't out of the realm of possibility he had knocked the box off the shelf in the closet, it was the most obvious disturbance beyond the dresser. It eventually prompted him to reach out to Autumn. He didn't think she had come over last night and then neglected to mention it, maybe embarrassed by seeing him in some oddly inebriated state, but part of him would be mildly comforted if she had.

Did you drop by the house after reaching out earlier?

The blinking ellipsis was almost immediate and then stopped. Why would I do that?

I dunno. To pick up some stuff maybe?

You said you'd get back to me, she wrote, and then: Something wrong?

I guess not. The place just felt off.

Off?

It felt like somebody came by. I dunno. Never mind.

Should I be worried? Was anything taken?

He hadn't noticed anything missing, but who could tell? He knew none of the valuables were taken, which is what he had checked on the first pass. None of those things were missing, unless Autumn had left something valuable behind that he didn't know about. It was all much more subtle than that, as if the entire house had been lightly rummaged. But did he really want to tell her that? The few things she had left in his care, her clothes and personal items, had been given a light toss.

No. Nothing. Sorry I bothered you.

If something is wrong, you'd tell me, right?

Was something wrong or was it all in his imagination? He could have just as easily messed up the house and not remembered it. He didn't even remember if the cop was the one who took him home.

For sure. He decided to change the subject. How about Tuesday after work?

Tuesday?

Meet for a drink?

No, not drinks.

As soon as he read her response, he felt stupid. A few drinks had caused the separation in the first place from her perspective.

A bite?

Okay.

Two Guys?

Two Guys was a go-to spot for locals on Mount Vernon Avenue. It originally started as a food truck until the two friends who owned it decided to take a bigger chance on the baseball field patrons who packed their business on game days, college art students, and an odd assortment of small business employees. It was one of four restaurants along an artery that connected Sand Hill and North Augusta, a safe choice and Autumn liked the haddock they served.

I'd like that.

6, okay?

You can make it that early?

The question underscored how long it had been since they had seen each other. He had taken an earlier shift two weeks ago, and she didn't know.

I'm off at 3.

Do you want to meet earlier then?

It made sense. She worked ten minutes away from the restaurant; from his job, it was about thirty. But he didn't want to meet up too early. He wanted to pick something up before he saw her. He wasn't sure what, maybe a bracelet or flowers to show he was willing to accept an apology, whether she intended to offer one up or not.

Okay. We'll make it 5 in case I get hung up.

It's a date, she texted, punctuating it with a heart. He thumbed a heart back.

The conversation wasn't what he had hoped for, but at least some things had been settled. They would meet up and see where the relationship was headed. And now, he knew the closet had borne the brunt of either someone else's nosiness or his intoxication.

He might have even fixated on that fact had the second photo he picked up not been Izzy's Polaroid. The gelatinous layer of film had stirred an urge in him to see Stacy, even if he couldn't pinpoint why.

The therapist he had once been assigned called it rumination. Some people were forced to relive traumatic events over and over again, perpetuating feelings of anxiety, depression, and posttraumatic stress. She had given him some techniques to cope with it, believing it to be related to an injury, like most people. The accident and subsequent loss of identity were part of it for sure, but so was the catalyst he never talked about.

He'd realized he wanted to talk about it now. So he pushed the box back onto the shelf and grabbed a flannel jacket off the hanger. He had to know if Stacy still lived in the trailer park she mentioned, but he had no idea what would come after that.

He could check in on her, tell her it wasn't her fault, and say how sorry he was that there wasn't anything he could do. He had tried. He had confronted Dustin. He had also been injured, another life irreparably altered. But was this punishment enough?

There was a good chance she wouldn't want to hear it. He might even find that reaching out was the worst thing he could do. And yet, at the very least, he could tell her Dustin was back in town and save her from the shock of running into him by accident. She deserved to know, didn't she? And she deserved to know she wasn't alone.

Andrea's words were still haunting him from breakfast as he turned off the main road. *"You know what I'm talking about, Billy. Don't you? Crimes disappear. Careers disappear. People disappear. Families disappear."*

It was the closest Andrea had ever come to asking him straight out: Did Dustin rape Stacy? He was glad she didn't ask. It was like a healing wound the two of them shared, but with Andrea being the one who picked the scab.

What would he have said had she asked? He didn't know. It was one thing to keep secrets but another to lie to her. Andrea had a knack for digging them out.

Sometimes he thought the only reason Andrea didn't press the idea that Stacy had something to do with the fallout between him and Dustin was because it made her culpable. Her hunger to take down Coach Dawson detracted from the circumstances that led up to it, making Dustin look to be as much of a victim as Billy had been. Dustin, after all, was taught head-down contact just like the rest of the team.

Coach Dawson's neglect made for an easy story and helped Billy's family win a small settlement from the school district. If the rape had become public while his family pressed the lawsuit, all eyes would have been on Dustin, likely leading to an outcome nobody wanted.

Dustin Fields was the most promising Windsor High football recruit in the state since Mike Buck had been drafted by the New Orleans Saints in 1990. And like many predicted, Baylor recruiting Dustin put Maine back on the map for football, leading to several more players being drafted, many by way of the University of Maine's Black Bears.

It didn't even matter that Dustin never finished his college career. He still reopened doors. And maybe that made everybody in Augusta culpable. Or maybe it was just Billy's fault for not falling on his sword a second time — the same thought he had played over in his mind a million times in the forty minutes it had taken to get there and across the seven years he had lived with this unconfessed truth.

The handful of others who thought they knew something only had a version of it from the periphery, while everyone else could only entertain an endless array of rumors. That's how small towns operated. It wasn't that small towns kept secrets as much as they pretended to keep them while whispering in the weeds about bullying, shoplifting, domestic violence, alcoholism, drug use, and rape.

Everybody always knew something, even if nobody knew anything, doomed to gossip about the shadows that made up the forever-changing and indefinitely fading past until not even those who were there could see it clearly anymore, if they ever had. Dustin had been plastered, yanking his high school sweetheart up the stairs between boisterous bouts of laughter. Stacy had been drugged, flopping back and forth like a rag doll while simultaneously helping her abductor and hindering his climb to the upstairs bedroom. Billy had been in a legless panic, wobbling up the stairs to stop his best friend from doing what Dustin had dared them both to do.

None of it seemed real, even if the consequences were. This was the thought he kept turning over in his mind as he exited off the highway and turned into the trailer park. He knew the place.

Pine Bluff Village was a land-lease community built in the late 1960s. Most people wouldn't even know it was a trailer park if not for the weathered blue and beige sign standing guard at the street entrance, which was paved but pockmarked and crumbling into the dense thicket of brush and trees, clinging to their last few more days of rust and brown.

An RV was parked another twenty feet in on the opposite side of the road, but the community itself didn't begin for another hundred yards, with aging gray and white mobile homes of various sizes spread along a forking road. He took the bend on the right.

There was a girl playing in the front yard of the one he thought might be Stacy's residence, assuming she still lived there. It was graying white with light-blue trim and an aged tar-shingled flat roof that looked like it was overdue for repair.

The girl stopped to look at him. She clutched the plastic ball she had been rolling to a doll set up on the lawn a few feet away. She must have been five or so. He thought she was too old to be Stacy's child.

"Hi," Billy said, smiling as he got out of his truck. "What's your name?"

She clutched her ball tighter, uncertain of what to do. It was clear she wasn't going to answer him.

"Hey, it's okay. I'm just looking for an old friend of mine. Maybe you know her?"

He crouched down to look less intimidating but then turned his attention toward the creak of a screen door, glass storm windows already inserted ahead of winter. A woman exited the home with a laundry basket and quietly said something to the girl, who quickly gathered up her ball and doll and ran next door.

"Her name is Mable," she said, jutting her chin in the direction the girl ran. "Her family lives next door, but I let her play in this yard too. They're Wabanaki, mostly berry pickers during the season, odd jobs the rest of the year."

It was Stacy, but she didn't look like she had two years ago. She had lost more weight, giving her a gaunt, almost skeletal look, reinforced by dark circles under her eyes and a grayish hue to her skin, which seemed to have given up on adhering to her bones.

"Hey, Stacy."

"Two years." She shook her head. "It took you two years to take me up on that invitation to visit. Well, don't mind me not inviting you in now. I've got this wash to hang."

"A little cold to be putting clothes out, don't you think?"

"Sheets," she said, as if that explained everything. "Some of us poorer folks can't always get to the fancy Laundromat for luxuries like a dryer. Besides, I like the snap they have when I take them down, lightly frozen."

She took a couple of steps down from a tired porch and headed over to a line she had set to the back of the yard. It wasn't much. Two pairs of poles with ropes tied high and tight, making a square if she wanted to use them all.

"So, since I'm not inviting you in, I'd say you have about three minutes to tell me why I am due the honor of your unexpected company."

"I don't know, really." He shrugged. "You ever had an experience where someone from your past just kept coming up for no apparent reason? People mention them or a memory pops in your head, or you find an old photo?"

"What, Billy? You crushing on me?" She dropped the basket and swayed her hips, running her hands up to her breasts. "You saying you came out all this way for a peep show? A Little Bo-Peep show?"

"No," he said, taking a step back and shaking her off. "I kind of wanted to … no, I needed to know if you were all right."

She laughed, moving her hands up into the air and twinkling her fingers, a jazz-hand gesture before she posed with two V signs and stuck her tongue out. Before he said anything, she relaxed into a scowl and rolled her eyes.

"Well, here I am, honey. What do you think?"

"I'm sorry," he said. "I shouldn't have come."

"But you did. So the least you can do is give me an explanation."

"I told you. I wanted to see if you were all right."

She shook her head and returned to hanging the sheets, fishing little clothespins out of her pockets like the ones his grandmother used twenty years ago. Watching her was like looking into a time machine. The whole world had moved on, but Stacy had somehow teleported herself to the way things were when they were preschoolers. Except in this alternative reality, she was a withering fortysomething apparition.

"You're running out of time so let me help you out," she said.

"How's that?"

"The reason you're here, stupid. My guess is the guilt finally got to you."

He didn't say anything. There was nothing to say. He slipped his hands into his pockets as she continued.

"First you felt guilty because you never said anything and then you felt guilty because your parents took the payout to keep quiet."

"That's not fair," Billy said.

"Oh, here it comes." She smirked at him. "'But Stacy, I was a victim too. I couldn't play football anymore.' Whatever."

"No, not that. You never got that my parents never had a choice. Dustin's dad came right at them after my leg was nearly torn off. He told them to accept his offer on the garage or he would build his own just to bury them. So I admit that I should have shaken off the pain of a compound fracture and the drug haze that followed, but don't blame my parents. They were run out of town."

"Run out to Florida," she said with a huff. "Look around. I ain't crying for your mom and pop."

He wanted to say he was sorry and acknowledge that he shouldn't have given Dustin a chance to come clean on his own, but the attack on his parents made him angry. The settlement money and lowball buyout of the garage that his father had worked all his life to build hadn't netted the family much. It paid for his medical bills, a second mortgage on the family house, and a small mobile home in a senior trailer park in central Florida.

"I came here to say I was sorry," he said. "What happened to you shouldn't have happened, but I couldn't stop it."

"So do it already."

"What?"

"Apologize! If you came here to say you were sorry, then say it and get off my lawn."

"I am," he said, his face growing hot. "I'm sorry he raped you. I tried to stop him. I tried to force his hand after. I tried to find a way to make it right. But you have to understand, I was lost, too."

"Would have, could have, should have," she sneered. "It's all too little too late. Fine, you said you were sorry. I don't accept it. Go live with it."

"Damn it, Stacy," he said. "Nobody was going to believe me. We were all wasted. I don't think any of us knew what we were doing. I even tried to stop you from going up the stairs with him, and you pushed me away."

"I was drugged! I was drugged! Don't you get it? He drugged me, and you knew he was going to do it!"

The words hit him in the face like a series of jabs. He hadn't come out here for what was now unfolding. He hadn't come to hurt her but to help her, and maybe get a handle on what was happening in his own life.

"And you know what made it worse?" she asked, continuing on in the wake of his silence. "I was raped, and then everybody dumped me because I broke up with my rapist. You. Jessica. Izzy. Everybody. I was a ghost to everyone and everybody, like I didn't exist."

Billy had never seen it that way. He remembered Stacy pulling away, along with everyone else, after he had been injured. She was one of the few people who had never even come to see him in the hospital. He kicked at the dirt.

"I'm sorry," he said, torn between reaching out to comfort her and wanting to push her away. "I guess I just don't understand why you never came to see me in the hospital. Maybe if you had come by, we could've figured out what was next."

She rubbed at her eyes and started pulling herself together, sniffling to clear the congestion that came with her tears. Then she wiped the wetness off her hands onto her jeans and picked up the last sheet from the basket, as if nothing had happened.

"Maybe your parents weren't the only ones forced to take an offer."

He blinked. "What does that mean?"

"How do you think I could afford all those drugs that helped me cope? My parents weren't rich. I didn't have a job. I didn't have any friends to loan me money. And I didn't have a case because I wasn't a reliable witness. That was you. It didn't matter much that you were drunk that night. It was still you, right up until you had a personal vendetta against the perp."

His head spun with the revelation. Stacy had been paid off, too.

"Mr. Fields?"

"An associate of Mr. Fields. Dustin's dad didn't have the guts to look into my eyes because he knew what he would find there — unequivocal proof that his son was a rapist."

"I didn't know," Billy said.

"You weren't supposed to know," she said. "That was sort of the point. If I filed a complaint, then Dustin would have been seen as culpable for your injury, not some stupid football tactic or whatever they called it."

This is how entitled men do it, he thought. *They divide people against their own interests.*

"Now you're wondering why I won't accept your apology? Pretty simple. I don't accept my apology, either. This. All this. Is a prison of my choosing."

Her words stunned him. He had carried the weight of everything that had happened that night for years, a load he let define him, only to find out that the person he tried to help had turned her back on him.

"Yeah," she said. "I'm a pretty shitty person."

Billy didn't say anything. He stood there, unable to move as he tried to reconcile the last seven years. He would have stood there for hours, head down and unable to look at her again, had the storm door on the mobile home Mable retreated to not opened.

"Sarah? You okay there?"

The man behind it was formidable, six foot three and with the strength of a field worker, long black hair tied back. His dark-brown eyes were narrowed, meaning to pierce Billy's soul.

"It's okay, Luey," Stacy said. "He's an old friend passing by."

"Yeah, I was just leaving," Billy said, the memory of Stacy changing her name to Sarah broke his trance. Then he looked at her. "You should know he's back in town."

"Dustin?"

"Yeah, wouldn't want you to be startled to see him wandering around."

She shrugged. "It's not the first time he's come home. I steer clear."

"You know, he did it again."

"Did what?"

"Raped some girls in college. You were only the first."

She shook her head.

"Is that supposed to make me feel something?"

"I don't know. Maybe it's time for the truth to come out."

She huffed. "You've been hanging around that do-gooder reporter too long."

"Maybe," Billy said, starting to move toward his truck.

As he did, she picked up the empty clothes basket and headed toward the steps of her mobile home.

"Maybe we see it differently," she said.

"How so?"

"We all have our crosses to bear."

Then she stepped inside, letting the storm door slam behind her. As it did, everything fell eerily silent, until Billy climbed into his truck, shut the door, and turned the ignition. He turned the truck around, much like his entire life had been turned around, and, he headed toward home. In the rearview mirror, he could see the neighbor crossing their shared lawns to see if Stacy was all right. Small comfort.

CHAPTER 10

BLOCKED CALLER

As the Dressbarn cashier tucked the black button top with a three-quarter ruffle sleeve into the bag, Jessica knew downtown Augusta would never stand a chance. Instead of supporting local boutiques down by the Kennebec, Augustans saved dollars at Dressbarn and Old Navy at the strip mall about a block from the University of Maine at Augusta. Go, Moose.

Dressbarn had been her second stop of the day. The first was the Maine Veterans' Memorial Cemetery to visit her dad. Despite her shame as she confessed her darkest secrets, Jessica would have given anything to see him again. He was the only person in the world who could have helped her navigate what was shaping up to be a very bad day.

Jessica knew it was the wrong thing to do, but she'd left the house early, unable to sit around and wait for the call from her mother's doctor. They both knew it would be bad news but kept pretending otherwise. They even went to church on Sunday to fill out a prayer request, which the minister somberly recited along with several dozen others. Jessica found the number of prayers for cancer patients startling, as if God had abandoned all of them.

She spent the rest of the day cleaning the house and listening to her mom complain about the phantom smell of smoke in the living room. Jessica tried to explain how nicotine seeps into everything, especially fabrics and books; she knew there was no way to escape the smell completely, short of moving into a nonsmoking college dorm room as Jessica had years ago. It worked right up until she shacked up with a smoker, of all things.

"This is different," her mom complained. "It's like someone lit up right next to me. Come here and smell it. Come on, now."

"Mom, I love you," Jessica said for the twelfth time. "But it's all in your head."

"Why won't you believe me?"

"We've been over this before. One of your medications can affect your sense of smell. It's called parosmia."

"I'm not paranoid."

"Parosmia."

It went on like that for hours, until Jessica threw up her hands and went outside to clear her head. There was no peace in the house, and she couldn't escape into her phone by scrolling social networks. There was no hope of that in her mother's house. It was the ultimate dead spot.

That was the second reason Jessica had to leave. There wasn't a reliable connection. She had promised Keiko she would tell Kyle to stop leaving messages at the office, but doing that required two things: a clear signal and unblocking his number.

She couldn't explain any of this to her mother. The humiliation she felt was bad enough when she shared those indiscretions with her dad's tombstone. The games Kyle had groomed her to play and giving up all control had gone too far for too long.

On the front end of the relationship, the thought of a dominant partner treating her as irresistible was exciting and sexy. But then the games changed as Kyle tried to break down boundaries in and out of the bedroom. She pushed back, but eventually, pushing back only earned her a punishment. As her punishments grew in severity, it was harder to contemplate an escape.

It was like living a double life. At work, she was a confident and competent junior advertising executive. At home in their apartment and sometimes when they went out, she had become a slave to his increasingly abusive misogyny, except she couldn't even see it for what it was. He had cast a spell on her so complete that she'd still be there today, but one call from his bookie had snapped her out of it.

Now, standing in the light of day at the checkout counter of Dressbarn, it almost seemed improbable that any of it had happened. And it felt even more impossible that this top, her excuse to leave the house after an early breakfast, made her feel a little less alone. She bought it for her meetup with Dustin. It would be her first date since she escaped Kyle, a milestone in earning back her independence.

"All set," the cashier said as she slipped the folded garment into a bag.

Jessica smiled and tapped her phone to the reader, surprised by how liberating it was to purchase without asking for permission or approval. Kyle always wanted to interject his opinion, and he wouldn't have liked this one. Too much fabric, he would complain.

Jessica had heard about this kind of thing before, but not in the way Kyle objected. Most men told women to dress more modestly because they might get sexually harassed or assaulted. Kyle relished the idea of other men looking at her.

"You look hot," he would say. "They think you do, too."

The first time it came up, it made her blush. She had even felt impishly liberated, having read so many articles about men telling women their tops were too revealing or skirts too short. He was a man who encouraged her to dress dangerously because he wasn't intimidated. But over time, the smallest suggestions became the biggest demands.

"I like the black top over the light-blue top" eroded into "You don't look good in Barbie blue." Jessica tried to take it in stride. Then helpful became insistent, and annoyance became anger as he wanted shorter skirts and more revealing tops, sometimes with nothing underneath, as if the entire world were teed up as an endless game of truth or dare. It wasn't until later she would learn that he wasn't just trying to tempt them. He was marketing his masculinity through her.

The memory made her shudder, so she tried to shake it off by rushing outside into the parking lot. It was a cool Maine morning, but the sun felt warm on a cloudless day. The Jeep would feel even warmer when she called from the parking lot. Never mind the ominous street named after Stephen King that tied the Marketplace at Augusta together. Bad omen aside, she needed to make the call around people.

Once inside her Jeep, she turned the ignition for some extra heat and stared at her phone. Her thumb navigated the long list of blocked callers. There were thousands of numbers and emails listed, mostly spammers and scammers who were relentless in reaching out to hundreds of people a day to find a few dozen suckers. And yet, today they felt like minor inconveniences compared to the caller she blocked before returning home.

She could not find his name but recognized the number. It had been burned into her memory because Kyle had always insisted she call him back within a five- or ten-minute window. She could already hear his calm, smug voice on the other end, an echo from the hundreds of other calls she tried to forget.

One swipe to the left, and the "Unblock" button appeared. She hesitated, touched it, and made the call. There was no going back now.

Kyle picked up on the first ring with a laugh.

"I knew you would call."

"You didn't give me any choice. Stop calling my work."

"Don't block my number, and I won't have to."

"Kyle, it's over."

"It's only Thursday. It ends on Sunday."

He was referring to the nursery rhyme again. Originally written to teach children the days of the week, it took on a more ominous tone as the person in the poem lived out his entire life in seven days. Kyle likened it to his relationships.

"This isn't a game, Kyle. Stop calling my work."

"Don't block my number."

"Fine," she said. "I won't block your number."

"That's good, Jess. Now, when can I see you again?"

"You're not going to see me again. I'm not even in New York."

"No? Where are you? I'll come right now."

"You're not hearing me. Whatever we had is over. It's dead and buried."

"Impossible."

"What's so impossible about it?"

"We had a perfect life together."

"That's not even funny."

"I'm not laughing, Jess. You know what we had was something special. I showed you how to really live. You might not think so now, but you will when you come back to me. What would you do without me? Wear cheap, mopey clothes? Yeah, I know you better than you know yourself."

Jessica shook her head. There was a time she would have agreed with him, but not here or now. She felt grounded in Maine.

"This is why I blocked your number."

"You blocked my number because you were jealous. Val doesn't mean anything to me."

"They arrested you for stalking her."

"She needed to learn a lesson."

"What lesson was that?"

He didn't say anything, but she could hear him suck in a long controlled breath. This was a conversation he didn't want to have. She didn't want to have it, either, but knew bringing it up would get under his skin. It did, but maybe more than she had bargained for. His voice was harsher the next time he spoke.

"Your icebox isn't empty anymore, Jess."

"What?"

"The icebox. Your icebox. It isn't empty."

She didn't know what he was saying but understood the reference. He had bought a small freezer under the guise of wanting to become a hunter. He never followed through with it.

When she questioned the amount of space an empty freezer was taking up in the apartment, he jokingly said she could climb inside anytime. She had laughed it off, saying there was no way she could fit in a freezer so small.

"I can make you fit, babe," he had said, beaming. It was referred to as her icebox forever after. A few weeks later, he bought a bone saw.

"What did you do?"

"You weren't here to clean up after Buttons. So, you know. In he went."

She gasped, pulling the phone away from her ear and looking down at it in disbelief. She told herself it couldn't be true, but her hands were shaking. Kyle was a liar, and liars lied. It wasn't like Buttons was her cat. Buttons was his cat.

"You're lying," she said as she put him on speakerphone, unable to bring it back to her ear.

"Am I?"

"Why would you kill your cat?"

"Kill him? It's more like a Schrödinger's cat thing. You know, the cat goes in the box. You close the lid. Is it alive, or is it dead? Nobody knows unless you open it."

Jessica pressed "End" and threw the phone on the passenger seat beside her. She didn't know if Kyle was lying, but she was crying. Her hands shook, gripping the wheel, and for a moment, she was back in their apartment, the smell of his cigarettes and a metallic tang of fear stuck in her throat.

She clutched the steering wheel and pushed herself hard into the seat until she could feel the coils under the foam. Her eyes squeezed tight as she tried to focus on shallow breaths to control the sobs.

Her phone buzzed, and she couldn't resist looking. It was him.

It was a bad joke. Buttons is fine. We miss you, babe.

The words set her body on fire. He was always good at twisting the knife and playing it off like a joke. Anger swept over her in a wave, and she started shaking the steering wheel and kicking her feet into the floorboard. It would never stop. He would never stop.

There was a light rap against the glass. There was a man.

At a glance, she thought it was Kyle until she saw the familiar orange Home Depot vest. She rolled down the window to hear him.

"Miss, are you okay?" His voice was gruff but soft. He was an older man with a graying goatee, and tugging one of the six-wheel carts that had strayed too far from the Home Depot lot and the one shared with Dressbarn. He had a limp that favored his left leg, temporarily distracting her from the anguish she felt.

"I'm sorry, yes, yes," she muttered. "I just … I just received some bad news."

"Do you need some help? Should I call someone?"

"No, I … I think I'll be fine. Thank you."

She managed a weak nod and put the Jeep in reverse.

"Thank you again," she said.

He backed off from the Jeep to give her room, the expression of concern never fading from his soft, kind face. She wiped at her eyes with her left hand and slowly backed up.

By the time she was on the highway, she had started to compose herself. She still needed to clear her head and freshen up before heading home, but the anvil had lifted off her chest as she kept telling herself there was nothing wrong with Buttons. He was trying to push her buttons. Kyle liked to do that, and he would keep pushing hers as long as he could.

Isn't that what she learned about Val? Kyle hadn't dated the Long Island nurse for over two years but still hadn't let her go. Worse, Jessica didn't even know she existed until Kyle's bookie had called her.

Kyle had been absent all day and not returning her phone calls. She was worried, but she half expected him to stroll in with a shrug and tell her to relax. He never did. Instead, she got the call that changed everything.

"Hey, Jessica," Jimmy had said when he called. "Your boy is in jail, and I need you to bail him out."

"What?"

"He's been arrested, and he called me to bail him out. I can't make it down there, so you need to pick up the cash and do it for me."

She did her best to keep up as Jimmy barked the details at her. She needed to meet him, pick up the cash, and then drive to the precinct and bail him out.

"Yeah, all right," Jessica said; her head spun as she searched frantically for her keys. "I can do that."

The drive to the local precinct filled her with a blur of dread and disbelief. She couldn't imagine what he could have done.

Bail had already been set at $10,000, which seemed high to Jessica since Kyle worked in law enforcement as a corrections officer. One would think they would take care of their own, prompting her to ask the cashier why it was so high.

"Do you want to look?"

"What do you mean?"

"You're allowed to see the charges if you're posting bail."

Jessica almost passed on the offer, feeling like it would invade his privacy. Then she thought better about it, given his increasingly violent behavior toward her. What if she was living with someone who wasn't just rough but criminally violent?

The cashier eventually convinced Jessica to look. The cashier said she would want to know if she had to post bail for her boyfriend before he was shipped off to Rikers Island. By the time Jessica finished the file, she needed to sit down.

Valerie Knowles was a young, attractive nurse working at North Shore University Hospital until about six months prior. She was terminated after Kyle unceremoniously started to destroy and dismantle her life by releasing sex tapes to everyone she knew — her employers, family members, friends, and even former faculty advisors at the college where she earned her degree. The reputation damage was irreparable.

Inconceivably, releasing revenge porn wasn't why Kyle was in so much trouble. New York still hadn't effectively criminalized nonconsensual pornography beyond being another form of harassment. He was in trouble because he had already violated an order of protection to stay away from the victim.

Based on the reports she read, Kyle had done much worse than release sex tapes. He had repeatedly and intentionally harassed Valerie and people close to her for months, even while Jessica was living with him. The release of the revenge porn was merely another escalation of his enmity toward her.

When Jessica read the file, she almost fled the waiting room for fear of losing her lunch. What made her sick wasn't even what he had done as much as the realization that he had done it while sharing a bed with her. And what made Jessica even more upset now was that Kyle was on the phone. Initially, the first emotion she felt was jealousy. Then common sense slapped her upside the head.

If he could do all that to this girl, what can he do to you?

And then, before she could even answer, common sense asked another question: *If you already know what he can do to you now, what do you think it might be like in another three months?*

What Kyle continually couched as ongoing and often vicious jokes suddenly seemed plausible. The bone saw on the kitchen table said it all. He was never, ever going to let her go unless he stuffed her inside three-and-a-half cubic feet of cold space.

As soon as she paid the bail, she rushed out of the precinct and headed home. She had somewhere between two and twelve hours to put as much distance between her and Kyle as possible. She didn't wait. She raced home, blocked his number, packed a bag with as many clothes and essentials as possible, and called her mom.

Jessica tried to make it sound like she had planned an impromptu visit, even though she was terrified by the image of Kyle becoming unhinged. He would walk out with a smug swagger and look for her. But she wouldn't be there. She would be somewhere between Hartford and home, maybe even unpacked and waking up to her mom making breakfast if she was lucky.

Except she wasn't so charmed. Her mother's diagnosis trumped her surprise visit. By the time she stepped onto the porch of her childhood home, Jessica was exhausted from a seven-and-a-half-hour roller-coaster ride of tears, anger, and anxiety. She couldn't even open the door, which made no sense to her until her mom opened it.

"Oh, honey," her mom said, smiling. "I had the locks changed months ago. You can never be too safe. Are you okay?"

Jessica had collapsed into her mother's arms a few weeks ago, and now she felt like she might do so again as she raced home from the marketplace, Kyle's dead-calm baritone rattling around in her head for the first time since she had fled.

Hearing his voice again triggered a new wave of emotions inside her, but not all were fear. The man she had fallen for was in there somewhere, and part of her wanted to try to appeal to him, just like he used to appeal to her early in the relationship, when accidental hurts were healed with tender apologies. The other part, however, chastised herself for even thinking it.

Her resilience had not been a strength but a prison warden. It had convinced her to endure and hope that they could find a balance between the exhilaration of exploration and crossing the boundary into exploitation, where uttering the safe word could earn a split lip or worse. Ultimately, the lies she had told herself only added another hour, another day, and another week to her sentence.

Even then, it took seeing another woman, one who had the courage to leave, to make her realize how far Kyle would go to control and manipulate anyone who crossed his path. Even in his profession as a corrections officer, he used to tell her how he would purposely invade an inmate's space to demonstrate his superiority, daring them or taunting them to react or resist. Put it all together, and the picture became clear. He didn't love her or Val. He loved bending people to his will.

By the time Jessica got home, she was exhausted. She had taken a roundabout route, giving herself additional time to clear her head, and even stopped by a corner store to pick up some no-guilt snacks for her and her mother. No guilt because Needhams and Humpty Dumpty chips were reminders of the home they once had together — the one she thought she had to escape from but now needed to heal.

"Mom," Jessica said, pushing her way in the front door with her bags. "I have a little surprise for you."

"Oh, isn't that something," El called from the kitchen. "I have a surprise for you, too."

"What? Good news?"

"No call from the doctor yet, but still good news," she said, coming out of the kitchen with a vase of fresh flowers. "More flowers! And this time, I think they are for you."

"For me?"

"Yes," El said, setting the bouquet down and plucking a card. "It's stamped with a dragonfly. You know what I think? I think somebody knows you're in town because nobody knows you love dragonflies more than ..."

"...Billy Stevens," Jessica said, finishing her mother's sentence between bared teeth before dropping the bags on the floor. "Another jerk."

CHAPTER 11

DEAD PETALS

Billy squinted through the dust as the wire saw rig ground away at a granite block, water jets keeping the diamond-studded cable cool. He had been at it the better part of Tuesday morning after the initial setup had taken an hour.

This was his life. Every morning, he would drill pilot holes, thread the wire, and rig it through pulleys. To the untrained eye, slicing useable granite slabs off a multiple-ton block might look easy, even meditative as the saw hummed a slow, steady song and the machine provided percussion. The work was methodical, with the gray-tinged slurry pooling at the base of the stone providing the only proof that progress was made.

As the work continued, Billy adjusted the tension knob on the machine, careful to keep his eyes fixed on the thin line creeping through the rock. He was the conductor as the quarry became an amphitheater of stepped cliffs, co-workers prepping to free another monstrous slab from the earth.

He would have been lost in the work but noticed Conner McGrath picking his way down a dirt path and heading in his direction. Billy cursed under his breath. If Conner interrupted him now, he would fall an hour behind.

There was no way to cut the power without risking a snag. It had to be eased down properly, or it would overheat the machine and ruin it.

"Hold on!" Billy shouted as he put a hand up to Conner and slowed the machine's speed. The whine dipped to a low drone and then a sputter before he turned the power off. The water was next, dripping to a stop, leaving the half-cut granite block glistening, a scar running partway through its face.

Billy straightened up, brushed his hands on his jeans, and then turned to Conner. "Well, this better be something good."

"Hey, Billy," he said with a crooked smile. "I don't know about good, but it is something."

"Get on with it," said Billy, unsure but irritated at Conner's game.

"There's someone to see you up top," said Conner. "And she doesn't look happy."

Billy pulled down his goggles as Conner put his hands behind his back like a kid caught with a cookie. He fidgeted, like he didn't know how to say it.

"Am I in trouble or something?" Billy asked.

"Don't kill the messenger, but Jessica Michaud is standing in the office with a bad attitude and an armful of flowers. Can you believe it, Billy? Jessica, from high school."

Billy could not believe it. He had no idea why Jessica would want to see him, but he didn't like it. She had interrupted him on a job where each inch feels earned, and there were no second chances to get it right.

"What's it about?"

"I don't know, man. She told Russell she wanted to see you and wouldn't take no for an answer."

Billy couldn't imagine what Russell Early might think. Since Russ had an informal agreement with the owner of the quarry to extract what they bought, he was always sensitive to time delays on the job. One day, if the owner finally agreed to sell the site, they might run operations differently. For now, nothing was taken for granted.

"All right," he finally said, pushing past Conner. "I'll figure it out."

Except Billy couldn't figure it out. He originally thought seeing Jessica at the Bear Paw a few nights ago was the universe trying to right the ship, but now it was starting to feel more like a curse. It was as if she had rattled the past loose from where he had grown comfortable keeping it.

Billy trudged up the path to the parking lot portable, the gravel scuffing his boots as his mind churned. The timing could not be worse, and he felt the pain of it in his bones. Today was supposed to be a clean slate. He had planned to shake off the noise of the last few days, lose himself in his work, and pick up something nice for Autumn before meeting her at Two Guys.

Now, Jessica was reinserting her chaos into his life for who knew why, and his plan to leave it all behind for a day was shattered. He wasn't sure what to do, but he knew what Andrea would do. She would tell him to meet Jessica head-on and hard, regardless of the reason. As he trudged up the hill, her words from lunch were as sharp as when she said them a few weeks ago.

"It's all about serotonin," she told him. "They've seen this in lobsters. Lobsters that act dominant experience higher levels of serotonin, which means they are dominant. But once they are defeated, they produce less serotonin and walk around defeated. Get it?"

"You're saying people are just like lunch." Billy chuckled and waved his lobster roll at her. "They're people."

"Stop it," she said, pushing him hard enough he almost fell off the stool. "You know what I mean."

"You're saying I'm like a defeated lobster. Some friend you turned out to be."

"Except when you drink."

"How's that?"

"Booze boosts testosterone and shuts down your prefrontal cortex, unleashing all that unconscious anger you carry around with you."

"Jesus."

"What?"

"You read too much," he said and took a bite.

"You don't read enough," she said. "All I'm saying is you need to stand your ground when you're sober instead of waiting until you're drunk. Stop letting something that happened in the past define your entire life."

The irony of this moment wasn't lost on him. Jessica was the second half of what had defined his life all those years ago, and she was standing at the top of the quarry. She was waiting in the parking lot, too impatient to stay in the warmth of the office.

Russ was standing on the steps leading up to the portable's front door, leaning over a makeshift pipe rail they'd installed to resemble some effort of ADA compliance. He gave Billy a shrug and then muttered something about deadlines.

"Your mom okay?" He didn't know what else to say to her.

"My mom?" Her glaring face reddened, and her lips tightened.

"Yeah, you said you were taking care of her."

She threw the flowers at him, petals and stems fluttering off his face. It didn't hurt, but his hands instinctively flew up to brush them away.

"You can remember that, but you can't remember I told you to leave me alone?"

Billy didn't know what to say, still trying to process what had happened.

"I don't want your flowers. I don't need your attention. And I certainly don't need your pity."

"You're going to have to catch me up," he said. "Because I have no clue what you are talking about."

"The flowers? You've sent two bouquets over to the house since you ran into me at the Bear Paw."

"I didn't send you any flowers," Billy said.

"Oh, no? Then explain this," she said, reaching down to retrieve a card from the pile of dead petals surrounding his feet.

She plucked it off the ground and held it up for him to see. There was a dragonfly stamp in the middle of the note.

"That supposed to mean something?" Billy asked.

"A dragonfly? You know, like the carved necklace you gave me. Who else would have sent flowers with the image of a dragonfly?"

"Somebody who knows you like dragonflies?"

"Are you really going to stand there and tell me you don't know anything about this?"

Back straight and shoulders back, Billy thought. *Be the winning lobster. Don't cave into her.*

"Look, Jess, I didn't send the flowers. You made it clear we're done, and I've respected that. My offer to help stands, but you don't get to storm my job over whatever this is. Respect goes both ways."

"I don't know what game you're playing here, but it's got to stop," she said. "Keep your nostalgic crap out of my life, and I won't have to storm your precious quarry."

Billy shook his head in disbelief. She was standing there calling him a liar, as if he were the one who had the truth twisted up. He crossed his arms and glared back at her, digging for something to say, when her cell phone rang.

She pulled it out of her pocket and held it up to her ear, all the tension and color fading from her face in an instant. The card from the flowers she had crumpled as they talked fell from her hand. She wasn't angry anymore. She was vulnerable in a way Billy only knew from the time when Jessica had lost her father.

"Mom? What's wrong? The doctor's office called. Oh my God. I'll be right there. I'll be right home."

"Everything good?"

"No," she said, spinning around toward her Jeep. "Everything is not good. Everything is a disaster."

"What is it?" Billy asked, taking an instinctive step toward her.

"Six months," she said, her voice trailing off. "They're giving her six months."

She started walking to her Jeep, quickening her pace toward the driver's side door. Then she stopped short and slammed her hand on the back of it. Her arms went stiff, fists clenched at her side.

Everyone within earshot froze and looked in her direction. For a minute, Billy thought she might be having a mental breakdown.

"I can't believe this is happening," she said. "I had to put on the spare tire the other day and was supposed to fill it with air. I didn't do it, and now it's flat from riding up here. I'm so stupid."

"Need some help? I'm sure a couple of us could change it pretty quick."

"Didn't you hear me? I said this is the spare!" She kicked the tire.

"All right, I could give you a ride," Billy said, looking quickly to Russ. "If it's okay with Russ."

"Yeah, yeah, Billy. Whatever you need."

She turned around to look at him, her temples pulsing. She smacked her phone against her thigh, and he thought she might throw it at him for suggesting it.

"What don't you get? I don't want anything from you," she said. "I'll call Dustin and see if he can give me a ride."

While being hit with flowers didn't hurt, Dustin's name did. It rocked him back on his heels.

"Dustin? Why on earth would you call him?"

"Unlike you, Billy, some of us can leave the past in the past and move on."

"What the hell does that mean?"

"It means Dustin and I are friends," she said, enjoying his reaction. "Who knows? Maybe something else."

"This is unbelievable," Billy said. "Of all the guys in Augusta, you're going to lean on Dustin Fields? The same guy who ended my football career? The same guy who..."

"Who, who, who what, Billy? Left the past behind him like I did? Yeah, maybe we've got that in common."

"He's not who you think he is."

"Nobody's who you think they are."

Billy resisted the urge to hit back. He could have called her out for trying to flex her New York smarts, but he hadn't lost his grip on what really mattered. Her mom was just given six months to live.

"You know," she said, gesturing toward the ruined flowers before turning back to her phone. "Maybe we could have been friends or something had you just laid off, but you couldn't help yourself. What is it with men that you all just can't let us go?"

Billy chewed on the thought. If she didn't believe him about the flowers, she would never believe anything he had to say about

Dustin. There may have been a time she would have believed him, but she couldn't hear him through her desperation.

He watched her dial up Dustin and in less than a minute, she had secured a ride. Dustin said he would swing by in about twenty minutes, apparently still driving around as if he wasn't under investigation for a DUI.

"Look, I don't know anything about these flowers," Billy said and bent down to retrieve the card. "But maybe I can find out."

Jessica rolled her eyes and crossed her arms. She was done with the conversation in a way that opened his eyes. He wasn't in love with whoever this woman was standing in front of him. He was in love with a memory of her, a ghost that didn't exist anymore. And maybe even that didn't exist.

"It wasn't easy letting you go. I'll admit it," he said. "But I'm not stalking you, Jess. I have a life here in Augusta, a home, friends, a girlfriend. You might not value it now that you're a big-city girl, but it's not any less important than what you have."

Her face softened, as if she was seeing him for the first time. She may have been wrong. He was seeing a different version of himself for the first time.

"Yeah, well," she said, kicking at the asphalt. "If you say you didn't send the flowers to harass me, then let me know who did."

"Deal."

"And for the record," she said, biting her lip. "It wasn't so easy letting you go, either. Sure, I pretended it was, but it was the hardest thing I ever did. It just had to be done."

It was the last thing he wanted to hear as he was finding his resolve to let her go again. So he leaned on Andrea's advice. He had to be a dominant lobster and remain unaffected by her words even if they sent a shiver up his spine.

"I get it," he said. "Just do me one favor."

"What?"

"Be careful."

"Whatever," she said.

"Yeah, whatever," said Billy. "I'm about to get back to work. Next time you think I did something, find me at home. You know where I live. Same place."

She didn't say goodbye or offer any apologies, so he turned to head back down, still unsure of what had happened. Somehow, she got it in her head that he was dangerous and Dustin was safe. It didn't make sense.

He also wasn't sure how he would find out who sent Jessica the flowers, but he was confident Andrea might have some ideas. He would give her a call tomorrow. She wanted to know how things went with him and Autumn anyway.

Between the two of them, they could figure it out. They could add it to their growing pile of puzzles. Andrea was already chasing leads on Dustin's court dodge and puzzling over who'd snooped through Billy's place after they drugged him at the Bear Paw that night. Eventually, something had to give. Even granite has a breaking point.

CHAPTER 12

CHASING SHADOWS

Andrea arrived at the Augusta Police Station to interview Officer Danny Ouellette ten minutes early. The department's public information officer had given her the green light without a second thought. Trust was a different kind of currency in a small town like Augusta, and Andrea had banked plenty by giving them leads that cracked a few tough cases wide open.

Her arrival was part of a long-practiced routine. She would park at the Augusta parking garage on Dickman Street to avoid paying on-street parking meter fees and then enjoy a four-minute walk in the cool late-morning air to a building that looked more like a dated elementary school than the hub of law enforcement. The department's mission was to partner with the community to provide a safe environment.

In this case, a partner is what she wanted. She had gone to school with Danny, though she had been a year ahead. Back then, he had been a lanky kid with a mop of brown hair and a quiet demeanor. He tended to blend into the background even more after being cut from the football team.

Now, years later, he was Officer Ouellette, a stronger version of himself but still amiable. Andrea had to give him credit for the transformation. Once cut from his dream sport, he set his sights on the Augusta Police Academy, where he earned high marks before putting on his badge and gun. He was a fair cop, but she knew he wouldn't appreciate seeing the case against Dustin dropped on technicalities even though the district attorney seemed resigned to it.

Inside the low-slung building, the lobby smelled of disinfectant and old coffee. The civilian staff member sitting behind the reinforced glass of the reception desk waved her through without a second glance. Andrea was a familiar face, and she didn't need anyone to help her find the break room, where Danny was waiting with a Styrofoam cup pressed into his hand.

He was in uniform, ready to start his shift, but his cap was off. His previously unruly mop of hair was tamed with a short military cut. He smiled when he saw her, a greeting that made it feel more like a class reunion than an interview.

"Andrea Kearney, ace reporter," he said, authentically pleased to see her. "I feel singularly special to get attention from the likes of you. Should I ask someone to take our picture for some misquotes on page two?"

"Very funny, Danny," she said, cutting off his pleasantries. "I'm here about Granite Hill Road. Specifically, the crash involving our old schoolmate Dustin Fields. What's your take?"

"Straight to business," he said and gave her a wink. "All right, have a seat. My shift starts in twenty minutes, and I'm cleared to be a backgrounder. If you want to quote something, run it back up to Linda if you don't mind."

She joined him at the table he had picked out, adjacent to the vending machine tucked in the far corner. She didn't think he picked it by accident. The hum of the machine helped create space between themselves and another officer, one she didn't know. He was flipping through a newspaper, hopefully too engrossed to care about their conversation.

"Okay, shoot," he said, leaning back. "He's guilty. What else do you want to know?"

Andrea resisted the urge to pull out her notebook. It was more of a habit than a need. She would remember every word anyway. The only time it was a necessity was for new names and phone numbers. Every reporter had their weaknesses.

"You're saying that because Dustin reeked of alcohol," she said. "I read that in your report. The only problem is that Jessica Michaud won't corroborate it."

His smile faded as soon as she said it, and he set his cup down. He leaned back in his chair again, arms crossed.

"If you're here to tell me what you know, let's start with that," he said. "Who have you talked to besides me?"

She had tracked down the paramedics first and met them yesterday. They didn't hesitate. Dustin exhibited all the telltale signs, even slurring his speech when he briefly came to in the ambulance, with sluggish pupils that went beyond head trauma. The real giveaway, they insisted, was the smell before they even loaded him up. There was no question he was drunk.

"They said he was lit," Andrea said. "Smelled like a brewery, and that might only account for the chasers. So, my question for you is, why did Jessica lie?"

"You knew her better than I did in school, so maybe you can tell me? I mean, she was pretty shaken up when I got there. She had taken her coat off and draped it over Dustin to keep him warm. I don't know. Maybe she didn't notice the smell because of the cold. Also, I suspected she had knocked back a couple. Not enough to cross the legal limit, but enough that I noticed."

Now that was something Andrea wanted to scribble in her notepad. Jessica wasn't naive when she lived in Maine, and she worked as an advertising executive in New York City. Between the college parties and two-martini lunches or whatever they had, Andrea was sure Jessica could smell vodka in a snowstorm.

"I called her out about the smell, sure. She shrugged it off and said she didn't know what I meant. So, yeah, I knew she was dodging me or covering for him, or maybe she was just scared I might ask her to walk and turn. Who knows? At the time, her dismissiveness didn't bother me much. I've pulled over enough DUIs to know what drunk smells like, and I knew a blood test would nail him. She was the hero of the hour, and I cut her some slack. I messed up."

"How did that work out for you?" she asked, leaning forward.

Danny glanced over at the other officer. He was engrossed in the newspaper, ignoring them.

"Come on, Andrea. You're not running with that story, are you?"

"No." She smiled. "I'm busting your chops. I'm just trying to figure out why she lied. We all know they go way back to when she was dating Billy Stevens. But then the whole crew broke apart after Billy's injury."

"Yeah, I remember," he said. "Look, I don't know why she would lie for him. They were tight before, so it could be high school loyalties, but why now? I mean, they all split up that year. Then Dustin went to Baylor, she bolted to New York, Stacy dropped off the face of the earth, and Billy became a hothead. Sorry. I know you and him are friends, but I've picked him up a few times. Everybody has."

"You're getting ahead of me," Andrea said, trying to brush off his dig and rein him back in. "We're not talking about a bleeding heart. When Billy didn't want to dash off to New York with her, she dumped him cold."

Danny shifted in his seat and tilted his head. She triggered something, forgetting he had decent instincts as a cop.

"Hey, you gunning for Dustin, or you gunning for her?"

"Neither," she said and then tried to soften her voice. "I'm gunning for his dad. William Fields. And I think Dustin might be the right thread to pull."

"What? You think this crash ties back to him?"

"Not directly," she said. "But I'd bet your next coffee that he's behind the cover-up. I mean, think about it. You caught Dustin cold, and suddenly there is so much wrong with the case that Mahoney's leaning toward a wet reckless plea? I don't buy it."

"I don't know, Andrea. I don't want to see the case buried, either, but Mahoney's got a point. No other vehicles involved. No other injuries. The blood draw is botched. And Dustin has family money. You talk to anyone else?"

Andrea nodded. She had cornered the emergency room nurse who had done the draw at MaineGeneral shortly after talking to the paramedics. Nurse Brown became immediately defensive when Andrea brought up the blood draw, quickly mentioning she was a single mother and couldn't afford to be found negligent or guilty of misconduct.

"I followed protocol. Needle was sterile; site was prepped," she said, clipping her answers. "If the BAC was off, then it's on the lab and not me."

Andrea wasn't sure what to believe. Maybe Nurse Brown was truly worried about her job, or perhaps she was holding something back. She decided not to cast any judgment until talking to the lab tech and, if need be, finding out if this was a one-time error or part of a pattern if she did turn out to be at fault.

"She blames the lab," Andrea said. "Could be true. It could also be crap. I'll get a better feel for it once I talk to the ER doc and the lab."

"You might start with the doc," Danny offered. "The lab has a staffing issue. They've been backed up for a couple of days. But I'm glad you got me and the medics singing the same tune. Dustin was drunk. If the blood's compromised, that's on the hospital."

"So again, that leaves Jessica as an outlier."

"Look, like I said, I didn't expect this to turn into a circus. She gave a statement, and I let her go."

"No offense, but this is one time you should have pressed," she said, then regretted it. "I'm not saying it's your fault. You're a good cop. I've seen your work, like that meth bust last year. My tip. Your collar. We're all friends."

He smirked, giving her a glimmer of the same guy he was when she first came into the break room. She was tough. He knew it. Who cares when you're on the same side?

"I'll say it again. I didn't grill her because she was the hero of the hour," he said. "I didn't care for her demeanor, but she was cold and freaked out. You know, like normal people."

"That's fair," she said. "Don't worry. I'm going to do what you should have done and talk to her. Once I have what I need from the doctor and the lab, she'll be hard-pressed to stick with her story."

"Wouldn't hurt."

"You got anything else from that night?"

"Not much more than that. There were no skid marks, so he didn't brake. He probably didn't see the fork until it was too late. He was lucky to have a seat belt and an airbag. He would have been dead without them. The Challenger was totaled, but he walked away with a concussion, cracked ribs, maybe a fractured arm."

"What about the scene? Anything weird?"

"Just the vibe, like I said. I arrived on the scene. There was steam coming off the engine, and the driver's side door was open. Not sure if she opened it or he did before passing out. She had draped her coat over him, which was the smart thing to do. I pointed out some blood on the sleeve, and she just stared at it. Shock and awe."

It occurred to Andrea that she might file for a public records request. If Jessica were a shaken bystander, her call to 911 would paint a different picture than what Andrea saw. She envisioned Jessica as calm under pressure. She pulled over safely, called 911, and then deliberately lied about the alcohol.

"Bottles? Cans?" She was running out of time and needed details.

"Clean. He could have tossed something out, but I doubt it. We didn't sweep the woods because the smell was enough, and I don't think he was in any condition to cover his own mess up."

She let the pieces settle in her mind. Either the nurse or the lab blew the blood draw. Everyone else, except Jessica, agreed Dustin was drunk. Those were the two most important aspects of the case.

"Thanks, Danny," she said. "This helps a ton."

Danny rose, draining the last of his coffee and throwing the cup in the trash.

"Anytime, Kearney. Just don't quote me unless the PIO signs off. Last thing I need is my name splashed around in your paper. But if you splash it around, try to spell it wrong, okay?"

She returned his laugh with a smile, almost wanting to give him a hug. Like Billy, he was the kind of person who made you want to stick to a small town.

"Oh, hey, one more thing," she said before it slipped her mind.

"Yeah?"

"You didn't find any Rohypnol on him, did you?"

"Rohypnol? No." He said with a frown. "Why do you ask?"

"It just occurred to me. Rohypnol could explain the discrepancies in the BAC results."

"I guess," he said. "That's a question for the lab techs or the doctor. What made you think of that?"

"I don't know," Andrea said like she had surprised herself, not wanting to share her suspicion that Billy being drugged and Dustin's crash could be related. "Just a wild hunch."

"Hey, you're the pit bull. Go get 'em. And if you do get her to spill, do me a favor and let me know."

"Will do, Danny. Stay safe out there," she said as she plotted her next move.

By the time the cold hit her again, a little sharper with the wind kicking up off the Kennebec, Andrea knew what she would do. Short-staffed or not, the lab could help her get a handle on what happened. Then Jessica would be next.

Andrea would corner her at home. She would paint it as a random reunion with the prospect of doing a local hero story. Then Andrea would spring the trap, needling Jessica with the facts. Everybody, except her, was certain Dustin was drunk. And if she were fortunate, maybe Jessica's lie would somehow lead back to William Fields, manipulating people with power, money, or whatever else he wanted to hide.

She wouldn't stop there. She fully intended to follow up on Mahoney's jab at her and hit the county records office. If Fields Construction was somehow tied to the unexpected sale of Stevens Garage and Billy's parents fleeing to Florida, she would find out. Either way, she had a full two or three days ahead of her.

CHAPTER 13

BURNT OFFERINGS

On the ride home, Jessica brought Dustin up to speed on how she had found herself stranded at the quarry with a flat tire. She admitted it was impulsive to drive there and confront Billy about sending her flowers after being rebuffed by her at the bar a few nights ago, but she was emotionally charged, given everything in her mom's life.

She was relieved when Dustin didn't judge her, even agreeing that sending flowers to someone who wasn't interested was a high school ploy, not something a real man would do. Other than that, he couldn't explain it. He didn't know what kind of guy Billy Stevens turned out to be. They hadn't been friends for years.

"We never even spoke after his injury," Dustin said. "I wanted to talk to him, but he blamed me for it, like I would intentionally do something to end his football career."

"He told me you were fighting about something but never told me what it was," Jessica said, resting her head on the passenger-side window of the pickup truck he had borrowed from his dad. "I'm just glad you were able to pick me up. I haven't been home long enough to reconnect with anyone. You were the first person I thought to call."

"Hey, I'm just glad I was able to do it," he said, lifting his hand with the cast. "They released me yesterday, and I wasn't sure how I would get on driving with a cast. Thank goodness for automatic transmissions."

"Thank goodness," Jessica parroted, appreciating his attempt to lighten the mood.

She was surprised at how good it felt to have somebody on her side, given the dire circumstances. It was almost like air being let out of a balloon before it popped, making her wonder if everything that had happened was meant to be.

As much as Jessica wished she would have been home when her mom got the call or that the second flat hadn't surprised her, the ride with Dustin had given her space to process everything that had happened and would happen over the next six months. Instead of being caught in the moment like she was in the quarry, she was better prepared to be the calm, nurturing daughter her mom needed. Instead of focusing on the pain and sense of loss she was experiencing, she could concentrate on what mattered most.

First, she would talk to her mom about exploring her options, asking the doctors about targeted therapies or immunotherapies that would match her cancer profile. With all the advances in health care, especially cancer treatments, maybe there was some outlying hope.

Second, she would help her mom focus on the quality of the next six months instead of the quantity of time left. Her mom didn't have to surrender herself to pain meds, sleep, and disposable underpants. They could talk about Christmas shopping, taking a train ride, peppermint foot massages, or indulging in French pastries.

Neither of these thoughts would have taken hold had events not played out exactly as they had. If she would have been at home, the two of them might have fallen into a shared depression. If she hadn't noticed the flat when she did, she might not have made it home in one piece. Most of all, she wouldn't have had the benefit of a strong, comforting presence next to her for twenty minutes, helping her climb back out of the panic and personal hell she had slipped into at the quarry.

"Hey," Jessica said, her voice soft as she emerged from her thoughts as he turned into the driveway. "I just want to thank you again. You really are a lifesaver in more ways than one."

"No trouble, Jess," he said. "I kind of owe you one anyway. You saved my life out there."

"I know it might be rough, so feel free to say no if you don't feel comfortable, but would you mind poking your head in for a minute?"

"I don't know. Are you sure? This seems like such a personal moment with your mom and all. I don't want to intrude."

"Trust me," she said. "If it doesn't feel right, you can always scramble outside, and I'll owe you an apology. But right now, I think you're exactly what we need to keep from falling apart."

"On one condition," he said. "Any more favors and you'll have to pick up the tab at the Barn this Thursday."

Jessica laughed. It was soft and barely audible, but it proved her point. Thirty minutes ago, a smile or a laugh didn't even seem possible. Something right was happening for a change. It felt like the first right thing in a million years.

She took the lead once they got out of the truck, the wood on the front porch groaning under their weight as they climbed the stairs together. The sound gave a fleeting flashback of Billy bringing her home late after a high school party or double feature at the drive-in. It was awkward, given she was climbing the steps with Dustin this time, so she rushed him through the door and into the living room.

The strong scent of lavender from a burning candle greeted them. Her mom must have lit it. The candle undercut the musty warmth of a house that could use another airing before winter.

El was sitting in the living room recliner with a faded quilt draped over her lap. She looked more worn than ever, with lines set deeper into her face and dark circles under her eyes. She immediately started to sit up when she saw Jessica wasn't alone, Dustin taking up the doorframe behind her.

"If I knew you were bringing company home, I would have cleaned up," El said from the chair, unsure if she should rush to her room or remain sitting.

"Mom, it's okay," Jessica said, stepping deeper inside to let Dustin in the house. "You remember Dustin Fields."

El took him in for a minute, looking past the tousled hair, butterfly stitches on his cheek, cast on his left hand, and the broad shoulders of a former football player. Recognition softened her expression.

"Dustin Fields," she said, her voice strained from having recently cried. "Number forty-two, as I live and breathe. Now I know I should have cleaned up."

"Good to see you, Ms. M," he said, rubbing the back of his neck with his good hand. "It's been a long time."

"Too long," El said and gestured to the couch. "Why don't you sit down, the both of you, and tell me where she found you this morning."

"It was the other way around, I'm afraid," Jessica said. "The spare on the Jeep went flat at the quarry, so I needed a ride. He was my rescue."

"What's that? All the way from Texas?"

"I'm home on break, you might say," he said, taking El up on her offer and sitting down on the far side of the couch.

"Oh, I see. So, when you aren't out on an injury, are you still racking up offensive yards and touchdowns?"

Jessica sat on the couch on the opposite side of Dustin and reached out, resting her hand on her mother's knee. She gave it a squeeze.

"Dustin doesn't play anymore, Mom," Jessica said. "But I think I'd really like to know what the doctor had to say."

"He doesn't play anymore? Then how did he get hurt?"

"Oh, don't worry, Ms. M," Dustin said. "I was in a car accident the other night. Don't let the cast fool you. My car and pride took the brunt of it."

"What happened? Somebody hit you?"

"No, no, nothing like that. It was actually kind of a dumb mistake. It was late, and I missed the curve on Granite Hill Road, north of Kerns fork. Just me, thank goodness. Nobody else was involved. I'm surprised Jessica didn't tell you. She's the one who saved me."

"What now?" El was all ears.

"I was going to tell you," Jessica said. "I just couldn't find the right time. Things have been pretty stressful, and you would have just worried. But as you can see, he's fine enough to save a damsel in distress. In fact, Dustin was the friend I went to see when we were at the hospital."

"And you didn't tell me?"

"Yeah, sorry," Jessica said. "I would have told you later today. We have plans to go out to dinner on Thursday."

El tensed, taking another look at Dustin. He tried to smile again, but it melted away.

"That explains it," El said, tightening her fingers on the quilt. "I didn't understand why you were so upset that Billy sent those beautiful flowers, but now it makes sense. You have a date with the boy who ended Billy's dreams. He was a good kid, too. Never did forgive Dustin for that hit on the field."

"Mom!"

"No, it's fine," Dustin said, cutting in to meet El's gaze with a sudden firmness. "I don't blame you for holding on to that. I carry it around with me, too. I don't know how much you know about football, but the coach flipped the field. I should have held back, but I didn't, and we all lost something. Billy was my best friend."

"He was. That is true," said El. "He had a steadiness about him, so I'm not surprised. Maybe that's why you made a good pair while it lasted. He was the ground to all your flash and fire, fun to watch but hard to trust."

Dustin winced, but Jessica knew he wouldn't argue. Her mom had been given the worst news of her life, and Dustin was the kind of guy who could suck it up. Maybe she would have to pick up the tab for dinner after all. Her mom was never one to mince words. They all knew she wasn't wrong. Billy was known for his steadiness, and Dustin for his recklessness. Times change. People change.

The silence stretched, heavy with the ghosts of high school. El was the one to finally break the silence.

"The truth is, I used to fantasize the four of you would stick together back then," said El. "Jessica and Billy. You and Stacy. Whatever happened to her?"

"We all just drifted apart after the accident, Mom. Some of us quicker than others. You know that," Jessica said. "I'm starting to think you're stalling."

"Right. The prognosis. That is what you want to talk about," El said. "I was upset when I called you, but I'm starting to wear it well. There is no sugarcoating it. It's stage four small-cell lung cancer, which is a fancy way of saying my lungs are done."

"What if we slow it down with something like chemo or immunotherapy? There is that new drug. What's it called? Pembrolizumab?"

"Pembrolizumab. Yes, he mentioned that. He said it was a good option for cancer with high PD-L1 expression. Mine isn't that. So I would have to try it in combination with chemo. It would be a lot of pain, misery, and discomfort. I'd get another four months for the trouble."

"Maybe there are other options," Jessica said, her hands trembling as she tried to stick to her plan. "We can figure it out together. You're tougher than anybody I know."

Jessica's frailty must have been obvious because she could feel Dustin put his good hand on her shoulder. He gave it a squeeze so that she'd know she wasn't alone right now. She had a friend who was there to help her be strong for her mom.

"I don't want to fight it," El said. "Your dad, my brothers, none of them got six months. I'm resigned to just making them the best six months I can get, and if it gets too hard for you or you need to go back to your fancy job in New York, I'm prepared for that, too."

"I'm sorry," Dustin said, standing up. "I really am. This is hard news, and I'm intruding. If there is anything I can do, tell me."

El looked at him and seemed to reconsider his intentions.

"This is why I hoped the four of you would stick together. I used to imagine I'd be invited to a backyard barbecue at Billy and Jessica's house, all your kids playing hide-and-seek around the neighborhood. But that's what happens when you stay in one place for so long. You build sandcastles in your head, and life knocks them down."

Jessica struggled to blink back her tears. She had come home to escape Kyle's cage and anchor herself to something familiar, but now the ground was crumbling out from under her. She glanced at Dustin, hoping to keep his comfort a little longer.

"Mom, I'm sorry I pressed," Jessica said. "We shouldn't have talked about it now."

"No, it's fine. Six months isn't long, and I've got things to say before I can't say them. So don't run off yet, Dustin. You're part of this, now, whether you like it or not."

"Ms. M?"

"I don't know why you came back from Texas when you did, but the timing can't be all coincidence. Jessica is going to need someone who gets it. I used to think that would be someone like Billy, but maybe I was wrong. It's you and Jessica who couldn't wait to fly away. And now you both came home to reconsider what you ran away from."

The room fell quiet again as they took in her words. They landed heavy, like a layer of dust on loved furniture. El was right. Jessica had spent the last few years chasing something that she thought Augusta couldn't give her. It could have been freedom, success, or a bigger life than small towns offer, but Jessica had never considered what she might have to trade away to get it. Maybe Dustin felt the same in his own way.

"You're not wrong, Ms. M," Dustin said. "Texas was supposed to be my big break, and I had it all for a while — football, engineering, scholarships, opportunities. Sometimes, you get so caught up in the rush that you take these giant leaps of faith that you would never take in a town where you feel safe. You even convince yourself that you're winning, untouchable, right up until the moment you're not. That's why I came back. I still might be able to salvage the mess I have in Texas, but right now, I need to feel something firmer beneath my feet."

"You're a Mainer, Dustin," said El. "Sooner or later, you have to accept it."

She was talking to Dustin, but Jessica knew she said it for her benefit. Never once did her mom ask what was going wrong in New York, but deep down, she must have known something wasn't going right. It was just like Dustin said. You get so wrapped up in taking leaps of faith that you never realize that you missed the stepping stone you were trying to land on.

"Dustin, let me ask you something," El said and wrinkled her nose. "Do you smell it?"

"Come on, Mom. Not this again," Jessica said before turning to Dustin. "She's taking this medication that messes with her sense of smell."

"What's that now?"

"Cigarette smoke," El said. "Can you smell it? I lit a candle to cover it up, but now it's back."

Jessica waved at the air as if to exorcise a phantom, but Dustin wasn't so quick to dismiss it. He inhaled deeply, and his expression changed from somber to alert.

"She's right," Dustin said. "I smell it, too. There's a faint smell of cigarette smoke in here."

Jessica watched him, puzzled, as he started smelling the air around the room. After circling it twice, he returned to the center of the room and kneeled on the living room floor in front of the coffee table. Then, he lifted the corner of a rug and started tracing the edges of the floorboard.

"Right here," he said, pointing to a gap with a width no bigger than a pencil lead. "It's coming up through this."

"What's that?" Jessica asked.

"I don't know," Dustin said, pulling out his phone.

He turned on the flashlight and tried to angle it to see into the hole, squinting as he peered into the narrow gap. Jessica leaned over his shoulder to see, but the beam was lost between the grain of the wood and the space that swallowed up the light below.

"I can't see anything from here," said Dustin. "What's under the floor? The basement?"

"No, the basement starts back there toward the kitchen," said El. "This part of the house is level with the porch. Ed told me it had something to do with the fact that the original house didn't have a basement. So when the previous owners added one, they didn't excavate the entire basement. I forget why."

"The house was probably built on an uneven lot, or maybe you're sitting on a small bedrock outcropping," Dustin said. "So what's directly under the living room?"

"The same crawl space that's under the porch," said El.

Jessica leaned closer to the gap and breathed in deeply. There was no mistaking it now. There was an acrid whiff of cigarette smoke. It wasn't the stale, musty smell that had soaked into the walls. It was fresh and sharp, like someone had exhaled a drag not that long ago. She would know. She had constantly pestered Kyle to quit.

"Could it be from a neighbor?" Jessica asked. "Maybe the wind is blowing it in here?"

"Maybe," Dustin said, sitting back on his heels. "It's pretty strong, like it's right under us. If you have some putty, I can patch it."

"The porch has been a mess since Ed died," El said. "He used to smoke down there when he cleaned it out. No way was I going to let Jess or myself go under there."

"If you have something, I can patch it right now," Dustin said to Jessica. "But I think it needs to be checked out. I'll have my dad send a guy over later this week to rule out a wiring issue or whatever. Happy to make the ask."

The sudden offer took Jessica aback. She appreciated his presence but never liked how men tried to take charge. Sending someone over was fine, but she was more than capable of patching a hole.

"There's the Fields charm I remember," El said. "Your dad has it, too."

"Like I said earlier, Ms. M," he said. "Anything I can do to help."

"Right," Jessica said. "I think I can manage to put some putty in there, but I can't thank you enough for sending someone over."

"Are you sure? No trouble."

"Yeah, I'm sure," said Jessica.

Dustin squinted at her, and she could see his brain working overtime. He was wondering if he had said something wrong.

"Don't mind her, Dustin," El said. "She's been telling me it's all in my head for days now."

"That's not it. I'm just starting to feel like I broke my original promise to him."

"All right, sure," he said, conceding. "Are we still on for Thursday?"

"Right," she said, managing a smile despite the new mystery forming beneath her feet. "A reunion. Here, I'll walk you out."

"You two go on," El said. "I'm going to take a nap. But Jess, if the smoke gets worse, then don't hesitate to call the fire department. I don't want to go up in a blaze of glory. Bye, Dustin."

Dustin gave El a wave as she headed toward the stairs and then stopped Jessica short as she was about to motion him to the front door. He pushed a lock of hair off her forehead.

"You okay? I mean, really okay?"

"I don't know. Coming home was supposed to be a little simpler than all this," she said, waving at the room. "I wanted to help my mom and clear my head."

"I get it. Coming home is never simple. You should hear some of the conversations my dad and I get caught up in. Trust me, telling him to send over someone to find out why cigarette smoke is coming up through your floor will be a welcome surprise for him."

"Yeah, I guess it is for me, too," she said with a nervous laugh. "My mom is dying. Billy is a stalker. New York is a nightmare. My Jeep needs new shoes. And now my house is haunted by Marlboros."

"I wouldn't say haunted," Dustin said. "We'll figure it out. If not tomorrow, then by the end of the week. It could be nothing. Sometimes these older homes have weird drafts and whatnot."

"Whatnot?"

"I don't know. If you see someone snooping around your porch, don't hesitate to call the police. You can call me, too, if you want."

The thought of a snooper sent a shiver down her spine, colder than anything she had felt since she returned to Augusta. It never occurred to her that the smoke could come from someone and not something.

"Thanks. That's going to make me sleep better tonight."

"Sorry," he said. "It's probably nothing, really. We'll know more when the crew checks it out."

Jessica nodded, but the unease that started with Dustin taking charge was now morphing into something else. There was no question her mom was right. It had been cigarette smoke all along, a ghost of a habit that didn't belong here. It was a warning, and she wouldn't take it lightly.

She walked Dustin out the door and onto the porch. It creaked under her feet in a way she had never noticed before. She watched him go, driving into the distance of an otherwise beautiful afternoon day, before rushing inside and toward the basement. She had a hole to patch.

CHAPTER 14

SECOND CHANCES

Billy sat at the window table farthest from the door inside Two Guys, choosing the alloy chair that faced the entrance so that he could flag Autumn over when she arrived. He slid a white bracelet box back and forth like a hockey puck between his hands, spinning it to calm his mind.

The diner buzzed around him, every table taken inside now that the picnic tables outside were no longer an option in the cooler evening air. Forks clinked, platters clattered, and the burgers sizzled in the kitchen, but he didn't hear any of it. His thoughts snagged on Jessica's Jeep.

He tried to shift his focus to Autumn, given his revelation at the quarry that the high school sweetheart he pined away for didn't exist anymore, if she ever did. But he couldn't shake what had caught his eye at the quarry.

Jessica had blamed herself for the spare tire going flat, claiming to have forgotten to put air in the tire. But that wasn't the case. The tire looked lopsided, and the rim sat close to the ground, the telltale sign of a puncture instead of a tire that was underinflated, sagging, and bulging outward. It was a detail not everyone would notice, but all those summers helping his dad at the garage had a lasting impact.

Billy couldn't help himself. He inspected the tire and proved his hunch right. The was a small, ragged hole with frayed fabric edges in the sidewall. It was about the size of a plasterboard punch, easy to miss unless someone was looking for it.

There was no doubt it was intentional. Somebody was messing with her. But how could he bring this to Jessica's attention after she waved away his warning about Dustin?

He'd have to wait until he could produce a sales receipt for the flowers with someone else's name on it. There was no other way. Even then, with new evidence staring her right in the face, she might not believe him about the tire.

The bracelet box slid across the table again, from his right hand to his left, as the waitress who had greeted him at the door earlier and told him to "pick whatever" came up to the table. He glanced at his watch and told her he would wait to order food. She seemed mildly distressed by the idea, now that no other tables were open and there was more pressure to turn them. He almost ordered a beer to appease the waitress and then thought better of it. Drinking had almost done Autumn and him in.

"I'll go with a Moxie," he said, deciding the caffeine might give him the kick he needed.

Autumn walked in as Billy said it, so he added a lemonade and wished he would have spent more time thinking about her instead of Jessica. This wasn't just dinner. He needed to be present, steady, and ready, with the chaos of the day put as far away as he could manage.

"Hey," she said, sliding into the chair across from him and setting her purse down.

"Hey," he said, echoing her greeting with a smile. "I ordered you a lemonade. I hope that's okay."

"Perfect," she said tentatively. "I'm not late, am I?"

He looked at his watch again and shook his head.

"When are you ever late?"

"True," she said with a little laugh. "You on the other hand. Fifty-fifty."

He leaned back in his chair again and took in the springtime vibe he always loved about her. As far as he could tell, the only difference was her eyes. They carried a slight weariness, a shadow from the past four weeks apart. He hated that he played a part in putting it there.

Before he could say anything else, the waitress returned with their drinks. Without missing a beat, she tapped the order book with a pen and asked what they wanted.

"Fried haddock and fries," said Autumn before squinting at Billy with a guess. "Hot Mess pork sandwich?"

"Oh, you're good," he said. "But I think I'm going to change it up today. Smokehouse burger with the works."

"Apps?"

"Fried pickles," they said in unison and laughed.

"All right," the waitress said, rolling her eyes. "Be right up."

Autumn brushed her hair back behind her ears and gave Billy a smirk. He already knew what she was going to say.

"Well, she's a little clipped," Autumn said.

"Ayuh, cut her some slack. The place has been packed since I came in and took up a table. She's stressed out."

"Fair enough," she said and pointed to the box in front of him. "What's this?"

"Just something Russ asked me to drop off somewhere after dinner."

"You're a terrible liar," she said. "You'd be a terrible poker player with so many tells."

He laughed and slid the box over to her. She didn't waste any time lifting the cover and peeling back the delicate tissue inside.

"Billy, I love it," she said, picking the bangle out of the box to admire the charm.

The bangle itself was gold with an antique finish, softening it with a muted, earthy depth. The charm was a tiny crescent moon and a single star dangling from an attachment opposite the clasp. Unlike the band, the charm didn't have an antique finish, a striking brilliance in contrast to the rest of the piece.

"It's beautiful," Autumn said, holding it up before slipping it on.

"The night we met? New Year's Eve in Kennebunk. There was a crescent moon up there, not long before we found each other. That night felt like a fresh start, and I want tonight to feel that way, too."

"You didn't have to do this, Billy."

"Yes, I did," he said, reaching across the table and taking her hand. "And it's important for me to let you know how important you are in my life. I'm not always good at communicating how I feel. I've known this since second grade when I tried to impress this girl by giving her the best Valentine's Day card out of the box my mom bought from the drugstore. I scribbled my feelings so fast that she couldn't read them. It was just a big jumbled mess."

"What? You never told me this story."

"Not my proudest moment. Anyway, she grabbed up my Valentine and loved it right up until she had to decipher my sloppy scrawl. Her friend asked her what it said, and she tossed it aside because it was too scribbly. I was so embarrassed I couldn't even breathe. And yeah, I could have walked over and said it was mine, but the moment was gone. I clammed up. I couldn't look at her the rest of the day, though she probably forgot about it by recess."

"That's so..." Autumn said, searching for the words.

"Sad and pathetic?"

"Yes." She laughed, joining him.

"I know," Billy said, squeezing her hand. "That's why I picked this up on the way over."

"And probably why you didn't write a note," she said, laughing again.

He held up his hand in mock surrender, face flush with the best kind of embarrassment. But he wasn't embarrassed about his handwriting as much as how stupid he had been to cling to Jessica's memory when Autumn was right here.

The contrast between the two of them was startling. Both were strong, independent women. Still, Jessica could be cynical and demanding, with high expectations, whereas Autumn seemed to have a light shining from within, inviting the people around her to be the best they could be. He had been a fool.

"I didn't bring a gift, but I did bring an apology. I had no right to tell you to throw out that shoebox." She squeezed his hand. "It just hit me in a weird way that day when I was feeling vulnerable. We were shedding things, and I pushed you to erase a part of your past that always scared me."

"Scared you?" His voice was soft under the restaurant's chatter.

"You have to know. It wasn't just you. When we started dating, all your friends, other than Andrea, measured what you and I had against what you and she had. Do you have any idea what that was like? Sometimes, it was terrifying to think that I was losing to a girl who was four years in the past. How does one compete with a memory? After a while, you start to wonder. If you win, maybe it's not earned. That you're second best or worse."

"I never even considered it," he said, knowing it was a lie, not to her but to himself.

He knew the score. His high school romance had wrecked every relationship he ever had. Part of him always wanted Jessica to come back into his life, even after she shot him down at the Bear Paw. Even now, if he was being honest, he was still tied to her in his worry for her safety.

"Look, you're not second best," he said, starting over. "I may have seemed unsure or uncertain at times, but that had nothing to do with you and everything to do with me. There was a time in high school, before my leg, that I had it all figured out. I knew who I was, where I was going, and what my life would look like. I was the best strong safety in the state. College ball was on the table. Scholarships solved the problem that my folks couldn't afford it. And yeah, I was with a girl who I thought was meant to be. But that shoebox doesn't represent Jessica. It represents me when I knew who I was, and I've been trying to figure out who I am without all that ever since."

He could see she understood because her eyes softened, and she squeezed his hand again. It wasn't sympathy. She seemed to be telling him that everything would be okay. He could trust her.

"I didn't get it before, but I get it now," she said. "I always thought she was holding you back. But what I'm hearing now tells me that nothing was holding you back. That's not it. You don't know where to go from the place you are."

Her words hit him like a lightning bolt. Maybe she knew him better than he knew himself.

"Yeah, I don't know where I'm going," he said. "I admit it. It's a scary feeling for someone like me. People always see me as solid, like the rocks I carve out of the ground, but I haven't found my purpose."

"Billy, it's okay," she said. "We can find that out together. Maybe you could invest more time in your art."

"I would love that, Autumn," he said. "You've stuck with me through the best and the worst. I don't know if I deserve it, but I'll try to earn it."

"The fact that you are willing to try means everything to me," she said. "After all these weeks, I wasn't sure we'd get a second chance. I missed you so much."

"So, you're ready? Will you move back in?"

"Yes, yes, yes. A thousand times yes," she said, paraphrasing Jane Bennet from *Pride and Prejudice* with a dramatic flair. "I work late tomorrow, but how about Thursday after work? We can make a home-cooked meal together."

"It sounds perfect," he said. "I'll even water your plants."

"They're still alive?" Autumn asked, laughing. "I wasn't sure but kind of hoping."

"Andrea had your back."

The waitress returned with fried pickles, promising their order would up be up next. They picked at the pickles, rekindling their casual comfort with each other as they caught up. She asked about his parents in Florida. He wondered if her cousin in Kennebunk found a new job. It was easy and familiar, as if nothing had ever happened between them.

When they were finishing the meal, she asked about work and Billy decided to tell her about Jessica showing up at the quarry. It wasn't easy to bring up, but the right thing to do. If this was a fresh start, there couldn't be anything between them.

"Wait, what? She called Dustin, the boy who broke your leg and ended your football career, to pick her up?"

"It was like being in an episode of *The Twilight Zone*," Billy said. "I almost didn't tell you, but you need to know. For whatever stupid reason, she's tied up in my life again. I want you to know there's nothing to it. Somebody is messing with her, and I have to get to the bottom of it."

"I believe you, Billy," she said. "I'll do whatever I can to help, too, even if that just means standing beside you. I'm here, and I'm not going anywhere this time."

He felt the weight of the last few days ease off his shoulders. There was no question in his mind that they belonged together. Things didn't have to be perfect, even though they felt perfect now that the plates were cleared, the bill paid, and Billy had thanked the waitress for her patience.

By the time they stepped into the parking lot, the sky had deepened to plum, with the brightest stars peeking through low clouds. He walked Autumn to her car, just two spaces away from his truck.

"I wish it could be tonight," he said.

"Thursday," she said, stepping in close. "We can wait two more days, and then we'll have all the time in the world together."

"Thursday," he echoed, pulling her in as she looped her arms around his neck.

He kissed her long and steadily, ignoring the patrons waiting outside for the next available seat. They could have been on the fifty-yard line of a Patriots game for all Billy cared.

"Get a room," a bear of a man grumbled from somewhere in the throng of people inside. The voice sounded familiar, tugging at a hazy memory, but Billy was too enthralled to give up anything more than a glance. When they parted, she took a breath and gave him a hopeful smile. Things were going to be all right.

"See you then, Billy Stevens," she said, flashing the bracelet.

"Drive safe," he said as she turned her key in the ignition, the door still open.

He didn't want it to end, and neither did she, but another car pulled into the lot and turned on its blinker, claiming the space. Feeling pressured to be brief, Autumn blew him another kiss and shut the door.

After she pulled away, he headed to his truck, feeling lighter. The day had plenty of loose ends, but he didn't care. The chaos, tire, and dragonfly stamped onto the card that came with the flowers were mysteries better saved for another day. Tonight was about the past making space for the man he wanted to be.

He climbed inside, reflecting on the first night he met Autumn, and drove toward home. He would find a renewed sense of hope when he could wake up in the morning and see her lying next to him again.

CHAPTER 15

BEAR TRAP

Andrea pulled out a stool at the end of the bar and sat down. She felt defeated. The day had started with real promise when Officer Ouellette fired her up about Dustin's case. Then, everything had taken a turn at MaineGeneral.

The emergency room doctor wasn't any help. He had prioritized Dustin as urgent but not critical, leaving the nurse to triage the injuries while he signed off on the usual tests. It was all standard. They took X-rays of his wrist and ribs and a CT scan of his head to rule out a concussion.

"There were other life-threatening cases I had to attend to, but we did our job," the doctor had said. "We noted his condition and the smell of alcohol on his clothes for law enforcement and ordered a blood test. Implied consent, as you know. Frankly, I'm wasting more time with you right now than I did with the patient on the night of the accident."

When she pressed a little harder, the doctor pushed right back. He offered her directory information so that she could find the lab technician she wanted to speak with and then said he was barred by HIPAA restrictions from saying anything else, even if she argued that Fields warranted public interest. If she didn't like it, he was confident she could find the public relations team in there as well, probably faster than he could, given how new he was to MaineGeneral.

"Yes, I know you are allowed to ask," he said. "I'm just not inclined to answer, on or off the record."

By the end of the inquiry, Andrea did find one thing they could agree on: It was a waste of time. The lab technician responsible for the blood draw had clocked out before she could even talk to him, which led to her next disappointment at the county records office, three miles away from the hospital.

It was easy. She walked in with the address in hand, paid one dollar, and a freckle-faced intern gave her a copy of the deed. The grantor was Billy's dad. The grantee was Fields Construction. The next call she made was to a friend in real estate.

"Hey, Darlene," Andrea said, trying to mask the irritation in her voice. "Can you pull a real estate comp for me on an address zoned commercial or mixed use?"

"Of course, love," Darlene said. "Knocking down doors again, are we?"

"Something like that," she said.

"Well, when you're free some evening, why don't you convince me to give Steve and the kid the slip, and we'll get some manicures or something," she said before breaking into a big, hearty laugh that ended in a coughing fit.

Andrea laughed, too, but for a different reason. The people in this town knew her too well, and most of the time, she knew them too well. The only problem was, when the comp came back, Andrea learned that she might not know Billy as well as she thought. Fields Construction bought Stevens Garage for almost twice what it was worth.

"Oh no," Charlie said, snapping her out of a spell. "I know that look."

Andrea made a face she would describe as one of those squiggles cartoon characters like Charlie Brown made when other characters like Lucy left him flummoxed.

"It's that obvious?" Andrea asked, and Charlie nodded, a sly smile creeping across his face. "Good, give me a Maine mule, but swap the vodka with bourbon. Double it up and keep the ginger beer and lime light."

"You know that's four ounces of bourbon, right?" Charlie asked. "Let me know if I should put hazard cones on the seats next to you."

"The night is young, Charlie," she said.

When she saw the sales price of the garage, she had another hunch and asked about a mortgage discharge document on Billy's parents' home. Nobody would have given this a second thought because the money made from the sale of the garage could have covered the house, except for one small discrepancy. The release of the residential lien occurred two days before the sale of the garage. She would bet a month's pay that even District Attorney Mahoney didn't know that one.

Looking back, it all made more sense now. The Stevens family had never been well-off. Billy's dad, Bobby Stevens, owned a two-pump garage that could be described as weathered at best. What it lacked in size, Bobby tried to make up with personality. He would fix anything with a motor, even a lawnmower, if it meant keeping the lights on or swapping stories over cigarettes when everybody smoked.

Billy's mom, Mary Jean, called MJ by friends and family, worked for one of the granite operations off Route 3. She was the one who introduced Billy to Russ a few months before she and Bobby headed off to the Sunshine State. The point that gnawed at Andrea was plain enough. A seasonal quarry clerk doesn't make a mint, either.

Andrea also knew some of Billy's stories about growing up with second-hand coats, patched sneakers, and plenty of room to get into trouble. Even his entrance into sports was haphazard. He played pickup basketball games at the YMCA and two-hand touch football at Capital Park when they weren't building snow forts. But his play seemed to pay off when he discovered football. And now, it seemed like it had paid off after he lost football, too, which is what her gut was telling her.

In addition to the underwhelming settlement from the school, the Stevenses seemed to be the benefactors of another undisclosed settlement from the Fields family, which ran contrary to the deep resentment the two families had for each other after the injury. However, a secret settlement made sense. It made even more sense if it wasn't tied to what happened on the field but to a closet or back room of a high school party house.

"Here you go," Charlie said, slipping the concoction in front of her and crossing his arms. "And this is the part where I ask what's got you down in the dumps."

Andrea took a drink and was hit by the bold warmth of the bourbon. She winced at its strength, with the ginger beer delivering a spicy but muted bite. It caught her by surprise, but she knew she would settle into it as a counterpoint to today's frustrations.

She didn't want to talk about Billy, so she turned her attention to Dustin, narrowing her eyes as she cradled the glass in front of her. She looked at Charlie and pursed her lips before speaking.

"When's the last time you saw Dustin Fields?"

"Dustin? I don't know, maybe three years or so ago when he came home for the holidays. He tried to pass me a fake ID, so I ran him out of here. He's probably still mad at me because I haven't seen him since. Is that what this is? Fields family crap?"

"You don't know the half of it," she said, answering Charlie but also talking about Billy.

"Want my advice?"

"No."

Charlie rubbed his whiskered chin and laughed for the benefit of the early arrivals on the other end of the bar. He made a show of it, then leaned in and wiped at the bar around Andrea.

"I'm going to give it to you anyway," he said, not much more than a mutter. "Whatever it is, leave it alone."

"What the heck, Charlie?" Andrea said, taking another drink and letting the warmth of it spread across her chest. "Why would you say that to me? It's like telling a bear to skip the honey."

"I'm telling a reporter to stop digging like an overeager coonhound," he said. "You know how Fields made his money, don't you?"

"Sure, construction and political clout," she said. "Everybody knows that."

"No, before that," Charlie said, pressing his lips together. "Of course you don't. You were running around in diapers at the time, maybe not even born yet."

"Okay, I'm all ears," she said. "Hit me before I order another one of these."

"Have you ever heard of the Patriarca crime family?"

Of all the things he could have said, she didn't expect that. She knew who the Patriarca crime family was. Everybody in New England knew. They were one of the most visible crime families in the history of the Boston Mob. They swept across New England between the 1960s and 1980s. Nowadays, surviving members of that golden era were struggling to maintain local rackets as the crime shifted from gambling and extortion to the opioid crisis hitting Maine hard.

"Bullshit," Andrea said, taking another drink. "Big William Fields isn't part of the Mob."

"I didn't say he was," said Charlie. "I said that was how he made his early money. That's how a lot of people made their money."

"I don't see any vending machines in the Bear Paw, Charlie," Andrea said, a dismissive swipe referring to one of the Patriarca family's outlets. "So you must be exempt."

"Come on, Andrea," he said, a hint of hurt in his voice. "Don't brush me off like I'm your boyfriend, Billy."

"Not my boyfriend," she said flatly, twirling her glass.

"He might as well be," he said. "You have the same temperament when you drink."

"Noted." She took a drink.

"Anyway, all I was saying is that you don't have to be a part of the Mob to be connected. Some families, like the Fields family, weren't in the Mob. They were just friends."

"How does that work?" Andrea asked, suddenly more interested.

"All sorts of ways," Charlie said. "When the Patriarca family needed legit businesses to wash some cash, Augustans would let them haul a little more lumber than their trucks could carry. If you have extra room for someone on the lam, maybe you get an introduction to someone on the zoning commission. Or if you have a little extra room on a construction site and don't mind a suspicious semi parked outside overnight, maybe you get an insider tip on an investment."

"Or if you need to ruin a blood test before the district attorney can file DUI charges?"

"Hey, there are all sorts of ways to play 'rub my back, and I'll rub yours,'" Charlie said. "This is a small town. We do it all the time."

Andrea considered. It answered every question but sounded too convenient. She didn't like things so neat. She also didn't like what that might say about her friend.

"I have something else," she said. "It's a small town back-rub kind of thing."

"What's up?"

"Do you remember a cop drinking with Billy the other night?"

"Yeah, sure," he said. "He walked Billy out. I think he was going to give him a ride home, but I don't know if Billy called an Uber. Billy was a wreck. He had just run into Jessica."

"What was the cop's name? Do you remember?"

"It was Dale. I only remember because I didn't like him much."

"Did he run a tab?" Charlie said.

"He did," Charlie said.

"Can I see a record of the transaction?"

"That's not a back rub," he said. "I could get in a lot of trouble."

"Come on, I'll give you a heads-up the next time the health inspector wants to breeze by your kitchen," Andrea said before changing her tack. "Or, I could not tell you and write up the results in fifteen hundred words or less."

"That's not funny, even from you," Charlie said. "Hold on. Let me serve those folks at the end of the bar."

He shuffled away, leaving Andrea with a little less in her glass and a little more buzz in her brain. How did it all connect? Dustin was back in town, and his dad was pulling strings again? Did they pay off a lab tech to bury a DUI? Were they afraid Billy might go back on past promises? Where did Jessica fit into all this? Where did Stacy Brenner disappear to?

She had to remember that the four of them — Billy, Dustin, Jessica, and Stacy — were all friends long before she and Billy were friends. Loyalty was better left to a dog of a different breed, as far as she was concerned, but they might feel differently.

She shook her head. The idea was possible but not plausible. She had known Billy too long. Once he made up his mind, it was hard to change it.

"Here you go," Charlie said, handing her a printout. She glanced at the record and frowned.

"Hey, I think you gave me the wrong one. You said his name was Dale, but this says Kyle Brondi."

"No, that's the one," Charlie said, pointing at the time, date, and order. Then he shrugged. "He said 'Dale.'"

"Do you know this zip code?"

"I don't know. New York somewhere?"

"That's what I was thinking."

"He might have said something about that too. He said 'New York's boldest.' He sat right over there and lit up at the bar, if you can believe it."

"What about Billy? Do you remember anything about him?"

"I was going to cut him off until the big guy intervened."

"Intervened?"

"He said he would take care of him and flexed his badge. I didn't like that, either, because we all know Billy drinks too much when he is in a mood. Man, was he in a mood. I tried to warn him that Jessica was here when he walked in, but he didn't take it that way. He made a beeline right for her at the pool table."

"Did you know somebody drugged Billy that night?"

"Drugged? How would I know that? The kid was drinking Kings County with the cop after he was already too drunk to drive home."

"He was roofied."

Charlie's face soured. "You think it was the cop?"

"We don't know," Andrea said. "Was there anyone else who might have done it?"

"It was a busy night," he said. "He spent most of it at the pool table with Jessica. He okay?"

"Yeah, he's all right," she said before redirecting him. "This cop. You think you would recognize him again?"

"I'll never forget him. He was built like a Mack truck. All shoulders and no neck. Scruff, like he was growing a goatee, but everything else was trimmed clean. I just figured he was on vacation or something. Hunting."

"Did you catch anything else, like what they talked about?"

"They started on about women and football, typical Billy, and then drifted into hunting," Charlie said. "They spent some time outside, too. You know, for the smoking. Hey, Billy's not in any sort of trouble, is he? He's about as close as it gets to family."

"He'll be fine," Andrea said. "Out on a date with Autumn."

"Yeah? Good for him," he said. "I always liked those two as a couple. She'd do him right. Hey, I hate to cut this short, but I have a hundred things to do before it picks up."

"No worries, Charlie," Andrea said. "I think I'm going to head out anyway. Another one of these, and you would be peeling me off the floor."

"Okay, good enough," he said. "Tell you what. That one is on the house. Have a good night."

"Thanks, Charlie, you too," Andrea said, but she tossed a twenty on the bartender's well when he turned his back.

She headed to the door and braced herself for the brisk fall air, every day a little colder than the last. As she walked to the car, she fought the urge to call Billy. She wanted to tell him they had a suspect, and then she wanted to confront him.

"So, this is what it feels like to be a mother," she said to herself, pulling her coat tighter against a breeze. It was time to go home, order Chinese, and rehash her notes. She had plenty to do tomorrow. She still needed to listen to the 911 call Jessica made that night, talk to the lab technician, and talk to Billy. Maybe she could catch him at lunch.

CHAPTER 16

SMOKE PROOF

After Dustin's discovery the night before, Jessica smelled cigarette smoke whenever she entered the living room. The smell had lingered, even after patching the sliver of a hole with wood filler. She knew it had to be in her head, a symptom she had accused her mom of having, but she couldn't help it. It had become a fixation.

After waking to the gray light of an overcast morning and walking downstairs, she stopped and stared at the spot. Then she headed into the kitchen, made coffee, and tried to ignore it. It worked as long as she stayed out of the living room.

She made a quick call to Dustin, then busied herself by calling Pine Hollow's Garage to tow her Jeep. She chose Pine Hollow because it was close to the quarry. Dustin had offered to send someone from his family's garage, once better known as Stevens Garage. She declined the offer because his family was already sending two men over to look under the porch and she wasn't looking for any more handouts.

Dustin wasn't coming. While he wanted to be with her during the investigation, he and his dad had planned a last-minute trip to New Hampshire. It was his dad's idea. They used to frequent a pub called Crabby's in Nashua because it had the best fish and chips in New England. Jessica doubted it was better than Lil Chippy in Portland, but she was all for it if it helped Dustin reconnect with his dad.

There wasn't any reason to share her revelation about his family relations during the call. She was too tired after a restless sleep, disrupted by her mom's occasional coughs and her growing obsession with the hole.

Deep down, she felt Kyle had something to do with it, even if it didn't make sense. El had been smelling smoke since a few days after Jessica arrived. The last time she texted Kyle, he was in New York. She'd told him to stay there.

It was nearly ten when the doorbell finally cut through the quiet of the house, her mom still sleeping. She was so lost in her thoughts that the bell made her jump.

Two men were on the porch, dressed in jeans, flannels, and work boots. Looking past them, she could see their pickup truck, Fields Construction stamped on the door in blue. The leaner of the two, Remi, made the introduction with an up-north French accent.

"I'm Remi, eh, and this is Dave," he said, pointing at the broader man with a beard. "Dustin says to check under your porch. You smelled smoke?"

"Yes. It was coming through a hole in the floor," she said. "It's this odd cigarette smell, but Dustin wanted to rule out an electrical issue under the porch."

"Okay, I check the crawlspace. Eh, it won't take long," he said. "You need Dave to patch the hole, *oui*?"

"No, I did it last night," she said, coming out onto the porch and shutting the front door behind her. "Here, I'll show you where the entrance is."

Dave followed her while Remi went to the truck to fetch a flashlight. She led him to a spot where the lattice skirting abutted the half-basement wall on the east side of the house. Her dad used to climb under there to clean it out when she was a kid. As soon as she showed him, Dave didn't waste any time. He pried the lattice free as Remi returned.

"This won't take long," Remi said, shining his flashlight into the crawlspace, the beam floating across the joists, dirt, and debris. "Old place like this need to be clean out better, *oui*? Junk piles up."

"Yeah, I don't think my mom ever got around to it," she said. "It was one of my dad's jobs. He hasn't been with us for a while now."

"Sorry to hear it," Dave said as Remi gave her a glance and slid inside. "We'll get it figured. The good news is your boards look fine. The porch is a little weathered, which explains the creaking, but there aren't any signs of anything burning from here."

"I hope you're right," Jessica said, looking up to see El at the window. The doorbell must have woken her up.

"There's leaves and crap everywhere," Remi said, muffled under the house and straining to be heard. "Somebody make a little path, pushin' stuff around. Whoa. What's that now?"

"You okay?" Dave asked, looking into the opening. "Should I get another light?"

"Somet'ing snagged me," Remi said. "*Tabarnak! Ouais*, there can tie up in 'ere. Spook me."

"Cans?" Jessica asked Dave, her frown deepening.

"Critters drag stuff in places like this all the time," Dave said with a shrug. "Kids, too, sometimes. You'd be surprised."

She shook her head and braced for something worse. Cans were the sort of thing Kyle might think up. He was always reading magazines like *Soldier of Fortune* and *Tactical Edge*.

"Stink in 'ere, too," said Remi. "There's a fishy smell. And I scrape my arm. You want me to keep goin'?"

"Yeah, Remi," Dave said. "Mr. Fields was pretty clear. His son wants answers."

They waited for the next report, wind picking up in the trees. Dave was vested now, squatting by the opening with his hands on his hips. Jessica crouched down beside him, peering into the darkness and half expecting to see Kyle's face or that stupid death mask he sometimes wore.

"Whoa. I find somet'ing," Remi said. "This is weird. There is a bunch of stuff in 'ere. A sleepin' bag. Some camera and stuff like wires. Whoa. Somebody been diggin' down 'ere, too."

"Digging?" Dave called to Remi and then stood up and looked at Jessica.

Jessica's stomach lurched. There was no denying it now. Kyle wasn't in New York. He had to be here.

"I see more than one. Two hole drilled up," said Remi. "Diggin' at the basement concrete. Somebody want in, maybe?"

"Remi, this isn't right," Dave said with some urgency. "Get out of there."

"Okay, comin' out," Remi said, anxious to leave the tight space. They could see his light angle toward the entrance at them.

As Remi made his way back to the entrance, a loud creak came from behind him, and he yelled. Jessica jumped, heart racing as Remi scrambled toward them. Dave was panicking, yelling back at him to hurry up.

"Come on, Remi. Get out of there!"

Jessica backed away from the opening in a panic. Was Kyle in there? She caught a flash of something on the porch and looked up. It was her mom. El had come out in her robe and was leaning down over the rail.

"Mom! You scared us half to death," Jessica said. "What are you doing?"

"I thought I heard yelling under the floor," she said. "What's going on?"

"It's okay, Remi," Dave called in. "Sorry. It's just her mom coming out."

"Dustin's guys found some stuff under the porch," Jessica said. "Someone's been in there."

"What? Who?" El's eyes were wide.

"We don't know yet," said Jessica. "Why don't you go back inside until we handle it, okay?"

El threw her hands up and turned to go back inside as Remi climbed out, breathing hard. His clothes were streaked with dirt, and he brushed at the leaves stuck to his pants.

"Somebody is doin' stuff in there," Remi said, straightening. "They drill 'ere and dig there. They have a new sleepin' bag and cameras in 'ere. And 'ere, this is the smoke you smell."

He pulled something from the pocket of his jeans and opened his hand. He held out five crushed cigarette butts, smoked to the filter. Even burned down, Jessica could make out the brand name clear as day. Marlboro. Kyle's brand.

"They make traps in 'ere, too," he said, rubbing at his arm. "Cans, a trap. Smell, a trap. Somet'ing poke me, a trap. We gotta call the cops."

"No signal," Dave said, looking down at his phone.

"We live in a dead spot," Jessica said. "We have a landline inside."

Jessica stood by when Dave made the call, telling the dispatcher how they had found surveillance equipment and a sleeping bag under the porch, mentioning that it looked like a North Pond Hermit setup. "No one's hurt. Owner's here. Send someone fast."

"You said North Pond Hermit setup," she said as soon as he hung up. "What's that?"

"You never heard of Christopher Knight?" Dave looked at her. "He was this guy who lived in the forest near North Pond, stealing from camps and breaking into cabins. Knight may be responsible for a thousand burglaries or so. I mean, he didn't settle in like this because he was a survivalist who just wanted to be left alone. But these traps and all that reminded me of him because he'd rig little warning systems, too. You know, he would tie up cans and sticks just like you got."

"*The Stranger in the Woods*," Jessica said with some recollection. "I think I remember it."

"Yeah, that's him," said Dave. "Maybe you got a copycat."

I've got worse than that, Jessica thought. She could picture Kyle's face under the porch, smiling as he watched her and her mother go about their lives. It made her dizzy to think about it, and she had to sit down, her stomach tied in knots.

When she sank deep into the couch, Dave took the cue and told her he would wait outside with Remi until the cops came. She thanked him and said she just needed a minute.

As soon as the front door snapped shut, her mom came back into the living room. She had dressed to make herself more presentable, even if she still looked tired and worn out. Jessica did her best to balance the story, sharing details about what was found but underscoring that it wasn't something to be overly worried about.

El wasn't convinced because Jessica wasn't convincing. She wanted to tell her mom about Kyle but knew that would somehow make it worse. Isn't that what happened to Valerie Knowles? She tried to fight back, but he kept coming at her even harder. If Jessica told someone about him, who knew what he might do?

She decided to try Dustin on the landline. If anybody could make her feel better, it would be him. He might have some advice to put her and her mom at ease. He answered on the third ring as it was cutting to voice mail.

"Jess?" Dustin answered, sounding a million miles away, drowned out by the clatter of glasses and platters in the background, a busy river bar turning out lunch.

"Yes, it's me," Jessica said.

"We're in Nashua. You okay?"

"Yes, no. I mean no, Dustin," she said, voice breaking. "Your guys found some stuff under the porch."

"What?"

"You were right. Somebody has been camped out under there. They found a sleeping bag. Remi said it looked like they were wiring up cameras and wanted to get into the basement."

"They did? That's crazy. Who would want to do that to you?"

Jessica bit her lip. She knew she should tell him, but her mother wandered back into the room.

"I can't talk about it right now," she said. "When are you going to be back?"

"Late tonight or tomorrow," he said. "I'm so sorry I can't be there for you. Can we talk about it at the Red Barn tomorrow?"

"Yes, sure. I just think I needed to hear your voice."

"You'll be okay," he said, reassuring her. "If you need anything, talk to Remi or Dave. They're good guys."

"Yes, they called the cops a few minutes ago," Jessica said.

"They did what?" His voice was louder, sharper, and she was sure it was because it was hard to hear on his end of the call.

"APD," she said, louder to match him. "They called it in just a few minutes ago."

"They shouldn't have done that," he said, barely audible before raising his voice again. "Great. Just don't talk to them about the accident. You hear me?"

She frowned. Dustin wasn't making any sense.

"What about the accident?" she asked.

"How's your mom doing with all this?"

"She's spooked. We're both spooked," said Jessica. "We're just taking this one minute at a time."

"Makes sense," he said. "Hey, I have to go. We're meeting some, um, investors about my business in Texas, and it's very important. Remember what I said about the police. I'll see you tomorrow."

"Wait. What's important? The business or what you said about the police?"

It was too late. He was already gone, and she felt more alone than ever. What did his accident have to do with anything?

"You're not in any trouble, are you, darling?" her mom asked, startling her. "Your face is as white as a sheet."

"No, Mom," she said, lying again. "Of course not. The whole situation is, you know, disturbing."

"Did Dustin say anything?"

"No, not really. He was tied up with work. He asked about you, though."

"Thoughtful, I guess," she said. "Maybe I was wrong about him."

"Yeah, maybe," Jessica said, her mind drifting.

"Your dad," El said, placing a hand on Jessica's shoulder. "He was always better at this kind of thing than I was. He didn't like to talk about the war, not because of what he saw but because he said the mind is the real battleground. Let's let what we can't control go, he liked to say. He was always better at it than I was. You probably know that, given how much I glommed onto you after he was gone."

"Mom, you don't have to say that," Jessica said, placing a hand on her mom's hand and interlacing their fingers.

"I just don't like seeing you like this. You're more worried about this boogeyman than I am, I think. Let the police handle it."

Jessica squeezed her eyes shut. She desperately wanted to tell her mom, but Kyle's name burned her lips every time she tried to say it. How could she tell her mom about all that? Her daughter went to New York and got caught up in some crazy, twisted stuff that El had probably never heard of before. How could she tell her? There was this man out there, a big man, a corrections officer, who had promised he would ruin her if she ever told anyone about the games they played. And now, even after she escaped him, he had followed her more than three hundred and fifty miles to get her back.

She thought about the nursery rhyme he was fond of again. What came after being ill on Thursday? Worse on Friday? This was worse. Jessica stood up.

"Mom, there is something I have to tell you," Jessica said.

"What is it?"

"When I was in New York," she said before her voice trailed off as she looked outside. "Never mind. The police are here."

There were two APD officers outside, already talking with Remi and Dave by the time Jessica could join them. Remi was especially animated in his description of events, prompting one officer to ask Remi to show him where they found the gear under the house.

Remi was reluctant to go in again for fear of more traps, but Officer Cote coaxed him to lead the way. Dave uttered another warning as the two men entered the crawlspace. He was engrossed, but Officer Purtill seemed more interested in fishing for answers.

"Do you have any idea who might have done this?" he pressed.

"No," Jessica said, exasperated. "Dave said it seemed like a North Pond Hermit kind of thing."

"Yeah, Christopher Knight," Dave said to the officer, looking up from the darkness under the porch. "Someone trying to catch a few nights for free."

"Uh-huh," Purtill said, unconvinced. "Except for the surveillance equipment. That sounds a little more personal to me."

"It was just the first thing that came to mind," Dave said. "You know?"

"Ah, sure," Purtill said before turning back to Jessica. "Are you sure you're not leaving anything out?"

"No, why would I?"

"Now that's a good question." He put his hands on his hips. "Why would you withhold information?"

She looked at him closer, imposing in his dark blues with gold embroidery and accents. The uniform was darker than those worn by New York police and eerily similar to what Kyle wore to work, except his patches were framed in red instead of gold. His badge was silver when he wore one.

"You're Jessica Michaud, right?" Purtill asked when she didn't respond.

"I am. That's right."

"Yeah, I was talking to my partner on the way here. You're wrapped up in another case, aren't you?"

"I don't know what you mean," she said before remembering Dustin's warning.

"You're the one who called in Dustin Fields's accident a few nights ago. It's not my case, but you know, it's a small town. We talk to each other."

"This has nothing to do with him," she said.

"No?" Purtill squinted at her. "From what I understand, you weren't all that forthcoming that night. I don't think you mentioned a relationship with Dustin Fields, either. I assume you have one, given these are his guys and all."

"Hey, I don't want any trouble," Dave said. "I just came out because Mr. Fields told us to come out."

"Nah, you're good," said Purtill, not hiding his annoyance. "I'm just wondering the same thing that Ms. Michaud is wondering. Why would she withhold any information? That's what she asked, right? Most citizens want to cooperate with the police, especially those who need help. Lies around here just make things a little harder on everybody."

"We hardly have a relationship. I ran into him at the hospital the day after the accident," Jessica said. "I hadn't seen him since high school. Dustin isn't even around today. He drove down to Nashua with his dad."

If she didn't know better, there was a trace of a smile behind the officer's poker face. She caught herself. She was overexplaining, already nerved up over Kyle.

Dave took a step closer to her, apparently unhappy with the turn and tone of the conversation. He tried to diffuse whatever Purtill was trying to imply.

"Her mom has cancer, Officer," Dave said, offering it up as an excuse for him to cut her some slack before looking shyly at Jessica. "Yeah, Dustin told us. Sorry."

"Cancer, huh," he said. "I'm sorry to hear it. You give your mom my regards. Plenty of us owe her some gratitude. She made reading fun."

"I'll be sure to tell her," Jessica said, but the sudden familiarity with her mother didn't make her feel any better. He was accusing her of what he was doing.

When Remi and Cote emerged from the crawl space, they had pulled out the sleeping bag, cameras, and wiring. All of it had been tucked into plastic evidence bags, which Cote handed off to Purtill to stow in the car.

"The setup down there was real. Two cameras were wired up with these small lenses pointed up through the floor. One was by the living room window, and another was where Remi said you and Dustin had found the hole. Can I see them from inside?"

"Yes, of course," she said. "Follow me."

Before she could lead the second officer inside, Remi muttered something to Dave. Whatever Remi had told him made him feel uncomfortable. He nodded the way someone might when given bad news.

"Hey, Ms. Michaud," Dave finally said. "Remi and I have to get back to the jobsite if it's all right with you."

"Yes," she said, feeling abandoned for the second time today. "Thank you both for everything."

"If you need anything, just call the office, and they'll dispatch someone out here again."

"I appreciate it. I truly do."

On their way back to the truck, the two men stopped to talk to Purtill again. She tried to read their body language, but there wasn't enough time. Officer Cote urged her into the house.

She showed him the hole Dustin had discovered the night before and the one Remi had found near the window. Like the first one, it looked like a small split in the wood, not much bigger than a pencil lead.

"My partner said you don't have any idea who would have done this?"

"No, sir. I have no idea," she said, despite Kyle's name lighting up like a billboard behind her eyes. She felt like the cop could see it if she got too close.

"Do you mind if I ask your mom a few questions?"

"No, not at all," said Jessica. "She's in the kitchen. Right this way."

He stopped her after they took a couple of steps toward the kitchen. She tensed, looking for a signal that something was wrong.

"I'd like to talk to her alone," he said, tilting his head with a smile. "You don't mind, do you?"

"No, be my guest," she said, waving toward the kitchen. The gesture was calm, but inside, her heart was racing. There was something they weren't telling her.

He nodded his thanks and headed toward the kitchen, allowing her to return to the window. She inspected the tiny hole, knowing she would have to fill it like the other one. She felt a chill creep up her spine. Kyle had been watching them. She knew it.

She stood up and looked out the window. The two workmen were still speaking with the officer. About what? Clearly, someone had crawled under the porch and used the half-basement architecture to his advantage. End of story.

"Ms. Michaud?" Officer Cote said from behind, her mother trailing after him.

"Jessica, I told him it was mine," she said, agitated. "I told him I didn't tell you about this, and I'll take full responsibility."

"What? What are you talking about?"

"Just tell him you didn't know anything about it," El said, nodding.

"Didn't know anything about what?"

"Miss, I was asking your mom some pretty standard questions when I noticed this sticking out of a purse. Your purse," he said, holding up a bag. "It was right there on the kitchen table next to a cup of coffee."

"What is it?"

"It's marijuana," said Cote. "I wouldn't have thought twice about it, but it was too obvious. The legal limit in Maine is two point five ounces, and this is three ounces or more."

"Officer Cote," Jessica said, her voice cracking under a forced laugh. "I've never seen that before in my life. I don't even smoke."

"It's mine, Jessica," said her mom, starting to cry. "Tell him it's mine."

"What, Mom?" Jessica said, her head spinning.

"I'm sorry, Ms. Michaud. Your mom keeps saying it's hers, but it was in your purse. I might have some leeway if your mom has a medical marijuana card, but otherwise, this is over the legal limit."

"This is ridiculous," Jessica said. "We called you to investigate a prowler under the porch."

"Yes, which is why I'm sorry about this," said the officer. "Maine Revised Statutes Title 17-A, Section 1107-A is a straightforward violation. I'm going to have to confiscate it to be tested and weighed. Given the circumstances, I won't arrest you today, but I do have to issue you a citation."

"Arrest me?"

"No, we're not going to arrest you. A citation is a ticket to court. It's a summons for you to appear before a judge, where he will likely fine you for possession."

"But it isn't mine."

"Jessica. Just tell him it's mine for the cancer."

"Mom, you don't have a medical marijuana card. You have lung cancer, for heaven's sake," Jessica said, snapping at her mom. She didn't mean to, but the totality of the day was catching up to her.

"Damn it, Jessica!" El stomped her foot. "Why can't you just do as you've been told to do for once in your life?"

"The maximum penalty is a thousand dollars, but the courts often set it lower, say two hundred to five hundred dollars," he said. "Of course, they might not be as lenient if it's coupled with something else, like lying about someone smelling like alcohol after a DUI charge. That would be a false report, which, Section 509, is a class D misdemeanor with up to one year."

"Are you serious?" Jessica stumbled. "I didn't ..."

"Miss, I'm going to do you a favor and stop you right there," he said. "Whatever you say to me right now could be used against you in a court of law. So, I just need you to sign the citation. The court date is on there, Kennebec County. After that, if you suddenly have an epiphany about the accident or who might be doing this to your poor mother, you can give us a call."

Jessica tried to swallow the lump forming in her throat but couldn't. This had to be some terrible misunderstanding. Sure, she suspected Kyle, but there wasn't any proof beyond the cigarette butts. And she did lie to Danny Ouellette at the scene, but it was a white lie because nobody else was involved. But the marijuana? Where did it come from? Why was her mom trying to claim it? Did Dustin leave it behind?

Dustin's warning flashed in her mind again. *Just don't talk to them about the accident.* Then a similar, older warning from Kyle came back to her. *"Don't tell anybody about me."* She was starting to lose it.

She took the citation book and the pen from the officer and signed it. The signature didn't even look familiar, a shaky scrawl across the paper.

"As for the porch, without any other leads, we're going to start by trying to get prints off the gear we took," he said. "I suggest you think real hard about any exes or anything else you can think up. This isn't New York City, Ms. Michaud. We don't have a lot of manpower to be chasing ghosts."

"I understand," Jessica said, choking on her dry throat.

"Now, if you hear or see anything or if the perp happens to return, don't hesitate to call," he said. "Do you own a gun?"

"No,"Jessica said. "Why?"

"Just asking," he said, turning toward the door.

"Well, yes," El said quietly. "We have your father's old service pistol."

"Good to know," Cote said. "Make sure you lock the windows and the doors. I'll probably have a car pass by later tonight. As for the rest? We'll handle it."

She watched him close the front door behind him, pulling it shut hard. El slowly stood up, walked over to lock it, and put the chain on. She looked at Jessica and wrung her hands.

"You should have just told him it was mine," she said. "What difference would it have made if it was mine? I was trying to protect you."

"I'm sorry," she said, choking back tears. "I couldn't think straight. But you have to know. I don't know where it came from, Mom. It isn't mine."

"I know," she said, pulling a piece of paper from her pocket. "What does this mean?"

"Worse on Friday" was scrawled on the paper in a black Sharpie. She knew it like she knew the next line that wasn't there. Died on Saturday.

"I can't tell you, Mom," Jessica said. "I'm sorry. I just can't tell you."

CHAPTER 17

MENDING FENCES

Billy sat at the granite picnic table, watching some late-season mallards bobbing along the river at Granite City Park and taking advantage of an unusually warm October. The trees were starting to lose their fiery display of reds, oranges, and yellows in favor of browns and bare branches, but the view was still striking.

Granite City Park was one of his favorite parks growing up in Augusta. His dad used to take him to marvel at the wooden quarry crane that some folks called the "last crane standing." Billy felt a kinship with the men who worked during the heyday of the Maine granite industry in the late 1800s and early 1900s, even if his company's operation at Hallowell was informal.

Today, he was meeting Andrea here for lunch. She had picked the location because of her fondness for the Kennebec River and the park's proximity to his jobsite. She said lunch would be her treat from Hannaford's deli counter, roast beef and cheddar on sourdough. Add some horseradish, and Billy said he wouldn't argue, especially today. He was on cloud nine after his reunion with Autumn.

"It never gets old, does it?" Andrea asked as she slid in beside him.

"Hey," he said, breathing in the crisp, earthy dampness. "No. It's one of the reasons I didn't mind staying behind while everyone else chased after college dreams."

"Well, almost everyone," she said, sliding him a paper-wrapped sandwich.

"Oh, come on, now. You were never going to leave Augusta."

"I wasn't talking about me," she said. "I was talking about you."

"Yeah, well, sometimes life happens, and we adjust." He unrolled his sandwich and started to navigate one half.

"I was also talking about Stacy Brenner."

The name hit him like a fist, and he dropped his sandwich, one bite in. This was the last conversation he expected when they had so much more to talk about. He turned to face her.

"So, you're going to lead with this and ruin lunch?" His voice was tight, edged like the quarry grit that dusted his clothes.

"Billy, I know about the deal your parents cut with William Fields," she said. "We're friends. I think it's time you came clean with me. Otherwise, all the other stuff we have to discuss doesn't matter."

"You know about the Fields deal, huh?" Billy squinted at her and spoke through his teeth. "You don't know anything."

"I know William Fields bought the garage for twice its value and then somehow helped pay off your family's house without any hint of a paper trail. What did he do? Pay your family in cash?"

"You know, sometimes when people call you a pit bull, I defend you," he said. "Sure, you like being called that sometimes. But you might not if you knew what they meant. They're talking about you locking onto a story and ignoring all boundaries or fairness."

"That's the job."

"You can be a real brute sometimes, and I think that's why you like the job," he said. "But being a pit bull isn't always a strength."

"You sure seem to like it when it helps you, though," she said flatly. "Kyle Brondi from New York ring any bells? That was the cop's name who probably drugged you the other night. I haven't looked him up yet, but I sure as hell expect him to be dirty."

"How did you get that?"

"Locking onto Charlie until he pulled the tab record from that night."

"Doesn't help me," Billy said. "I don't know the guy."

"Want to know my theory?" She didn't wait for him to answer. "Dustin is back in town, and his daddy is sending you a message to keep quiet about whatever reason he had to pay your family hush money."

"It wasn't hush money, not how you think anyway."

"Then what was it, Billy?"

"It was an ultimatum," he said. "He was going to bury my family."

For the next twenty minutes, Billy did what he never thought he would ever do. He told Andrea everything. He told her about the party that set it in motion. He told her how Dustin scored some Rohypnol and convinced Billy they should slip it in their girlfriends' drinks, likening the drug to Spanish Fly or Ecstasy.

Even after he was drunk, Billy thought better of it and tossed the dose meant for Jessica in the trash. He tried to convince Dustin to do the same, but it was too late. Dustin had already drugged Stacy and was dragging her upstairs.

"I tried to stop him, you know, but I was too drunk to do much." His gaze returned to the river, looking out across the rippling water. "He raped her, and there was nothing I could do."

"Nothing?"

"I tried to stop him when they were stumbling up there, and he nearly pushed me down the stairs, calling me a coward and telling me to screw off. Even with Stacy helping him along, I didn't give up. But by the time I made it back up to the door, he had locked it. I banged on it until a couple of other guys eventually called me off, telling me to leave them alone, not knowing Dustin drugged her."

Billy looked at Andrea, her face an unrecognizable expression of pity and disgust. He couldn't tell how much of it was directed at him or Dustin, but it didn't matter anymore. He had never told anyone.

"The worst of it was that I could hear her in there. She didn't know what was happening," said Billy. "I saw her in the hallway at school a few days later, and she couldn't look at me or anybody else, really. I confronted Dustin and told him to make it right. You already know how that turned out."

He could see she understood as the pieces finally fell in place. Coach Dawson may have flipped the field that day, but Dustin took advantage of it. Dustin hit Billy as hard as he could and shattered his tibia. It sent Billy into a drug-induced haze, destroying his football career. He would never play again. His scholarships were gone. His future was trashed.

"Is that why your family took the money?"

"No, Andrea," he said. "I told you it wasn't like that. William Fields had an attorney come to the house. Unless I shut my mouth, he said they would bury us."

Billy could still see the smug suit at their dining room table, laying it out. His family could accept the "hardship donation" and sell the garage, or Fields would help the school fight their wrongful injury suit and build a brand-new garage right across the street from his dad's business.

His parents took the money but couldn't face their friends and neighbors afterward. So they told Billy to keep the house as long as he wanted and fled to the Sunshine State.

"You said he would bury you. What did he mean?"

"He'd discredit me and put my dad out of business," Billy said. "What could we do? Stacy wasn't coming forward, so anything I said would look like retaliation for the accident. You know, she didn't even visit me at the hospital. I never knew why until a couple of days ago. Dustin's dad paid her off to stay away from me. What do they call it? Divide and conquer."

"Stacy? You talked to her?"

"I saw her a couple of days ago. I had this need to see if she was okay and apologize. I don't know why. She didn't want it. She accused me of abandoning her, saying I should have come forward even if she didn't. Maybe I should have. I don't know. I wasn't in the best of places at the time, and then it was too late."

"Do you think she would come forward today?"

"No, I don't think so. She's a wreck, drugged out and hollow, living in a trailer park. She doesn't even go by Stacy anymore."

Billy watched as Andrea took a bite of her sandwich and chewed. It wasn't just the sandwich. She was digesting everything he told her, and she was weighing whether this changed their friendship. Billy braced himself for the worst outcome.

"This Kyle guy?" Andrea finally asked him. "If he roofied you, maybe there is a connection. Maybe Dustin's dad sent you a warning now that Dustin is back in town."

"A dirty cop? I don't know." Billy frowned and tried to pick up his sandwich. The theory hung heavy in the air, and he wasn't hungry anymore.

"It fits with the Fields' Boston Mob connection," she said, working the puzzle before her.

"Boston Mob? What are you talking about?"

Billy wasn't sure where Andrea got this crazy idea. William Fields was grit, not grift. He leveraged his success in trucking to start a construction company and then invested in other businesses. Dustin's dad had chalked it up to persistence. He used to tell Billy that he didn't waste time on things like fear, worry, and doubt. William said to take all that out of the equation, and everything, football included, would become easier.

Even then, Billy knew it for what it was. There was never any shortage of dads with their pulse on coaching tips and life lessons. They were quick to share recipes for success because they thought it might give the team an edge and, indirectly, their kid. Mostly, they were delusional in thinking anybody on the field was listening.

But he couldn't recall anything that would suggest Mob ties. Dustin was the only one in their friend group with real money, but that was about it.

Sometimes it was easy to forget where one came from while hanging out with Dustin. Being friends meant a sunset ride on a wind jammer in the summer, wild parties at their lake house in the spring, trips to bigger cities for concerts and football games in the fall, and skiing and snowmobiling trips in the winter.

Being friends with Dustin came with a lot of perks for kids with blue-collar backgrounds, especially Stacy. Her dad worked as a handyman, and her mom would iron people's clothes to make ends meet.

They weren't friends with Dustin because of it, but he couldn't deny that he, Jessica, Stacy, and a revolving door of other minor posse members were afforded something that might have otherwise been out of reach. It was money, but not black jackets and fedoras.

"You never heard anything about that when you two were friends?" She pressed.

"Dustin and I pretty much became best of friends during our freshman year of football," Billy said. "We were the only two freshmen to make varsity and felt we had to stick together. Jessica and I were already seeing each other, and Stacy joined the group sometime around Christmas after Dustin asked her out. You know some of them, like Izzy and Justice. Half the time, we were too busy trying not to get caught doing things to think about what our parents were doing, but I think I would have remembered if my best friend's dad was a Mob boss. I don't know, Andrea. I think you're trying to force together puzzle pieces that don't fit together."

"Maybe not a boss, but a friend," Andrea said. "Maybe he has a connection capable of very bad things. You said it yourself without saying it. Fields knows all the tricks, like he took a master class in Mob tactics."

Billy shrugged. It was so far out of left field that he wasn't convinced. The sandwich sat abandoned, horseradish prickling the air.

"Tell you the truth, I'm more concerned with Jessica getting wrapped up with him," he said, pulling the card with the dragonfly stamp from his pocket. "Jessica came by the quarry and accused me of stalking her. She said I was sending her flowers and threw this at me as part of her evidence."

"Augusta Florist? I know them," she said. "What makes her think it was you?"

"Jessica's always liked dragonflies, so I carved her a granite charm years ago," Billy said. "I wore it ever since we broke up, hoping I could give it to her someday. That day was the other night at the bar."

"So, she's pinned the flowers to you because of the stamp?"

"Like I'm the only one on the planet who knows she likes dragonflies." He snorted a laugh. "I bet Dustin sent them to make me look like a creep."

Her eyes narrowed. The gears inside her head turned again as she scooped up the card.

"Jessica's lying for Dustin about the accident," she said. "She was on the scene, and she's the only one saying he didn't smell like alcohol."

Billy bit at a hangnail on the side of his thumb. The sting of it grounded him. "You didn't tell me she was there."

"You were pretty shaken up after seeing her," Andrea said. "I was trying to protect you."

Billy rolled his eyes but let it slide. It seemed neither had been forthcoming, but his secret had dwarfed hers.

"I'm sorry," she said. "I just never thought Jessica was good enough for you."

"Yeah, well, you're not wrong," he said. "And I'm sorry, too. I would have told you about Stacy, but I knew you wouldn't let it go. I had to think of my family."

"All right," she said. "I don't like what you did, Billy. But I understand it. When this story breaks, I promise I'll be sympathetic. You were a scared kid at the time. What he did to you wasn't much different than what he did to Stacy."

"I just hope Autumn doesn't see me differently." Billy shook his head. "That's what I thought we would talk about today."

"Until yesterday, me too," Andrea said. "How did it go, by the way?"

"Better than I could have hoped and better than I deserve," he said. "I did just as you said. I was the lobster."

"You were not!" She laughed. It was the first time she even broke a smile since sitting down.

"She's moving back in on Thursday." Billy shrugged. "I'm just anxious to turn the page, if you know what I mean."

"I do," Andrea said. "I get it."

"So where does that leave us?"

"We're best friends, Billy. We have been for years," she said. "I'm not going to throw that away over this."

"I appreciate that, Andrea," he said.

"Try to eat some of it before you head back," she said. "As for me, I have a couple of stops this afternoon. I want to hear Jessica's call to dispatch, and I still have to talk to the lab technician who botched the blood draw. Then I'm going to hang Dustin on this DUI."

"If you need help, you know where I'll be."

"Sawing stone?"

"That and watering those plants before Autumn comes home."

"All right, buddy," she said.

He could see she was still processing. It wouldn't be easy, but they would have to find a way to trust each other again.

CHAPTER 18

STONE WALLS

Andrea's head was humming after lunch with Billy as she walked into the MaineGeneral Medical Center. The story was taking on a life of its own, and she was having a difficult time keeping up. She had to remind herself to keep it simple a dozen times.

There was a temptation to blow the lid off everything, but experience told her that confining the first article to the DUI was the way to go. She stopped inside the main lobby long enough to pull out her cell phone and multitask by calling APD. Strike when the story is hot.

"Augusta Police Department, Communications Center," chirped a familiar voice on the other end.

"Hey, Lydia, it's Andrea Kearney. I'm hoping you can save me some time. I'll be filing a Freedom of Access Act request on the 911 call related to Dustin Fields' case, opened last Friday. Sorry, but I don't have the case number handy. Can you have someone prep it for me?"

There was no answer on the other end of the line. Andrea looked down at her phone to make sure she was connected. It wasn't like Lydia to keep her waiting. She was neat, professional, and idealistic about law enforcement. The two had formed an unlikely connection over the television show *Blue Bloods*.

"Lydia, did you hear me?"

"Sorry, Andrea," she huffed. "I can hear you. I'm sorry to say it, but I'm supposed to deny your request by phone or in person and refer you to The Maine Emergency Services Communication Bureau. That's the statewide hub for 911 recordings."

"I know what it is, Lydia," Andrea said, pursing her lips. "What I'd like to know is why."

"I'm supposed to tell you that there is an ongoing investigation," Lydia said.

"Oh, come on. I was in there interviewing Danny Ouellette just yesterday."

"You're welcome to file a written FOAA with us and demonstrate good cause, but it will be denied. The Emergency Services Communication Bureau is your best bet if you can prove good cause."

"Good cause," Andrea said, exasperated. She took a breath and tried to soften her tone. "Can you at least tell me who's stonewalling me? It's important."

"Um. I'm sorry, Andrea. I wish I could help you out. You know that."

"District Attorney Mahoney?" Andrea pressed, knowing Lydia would have to end the call. Her question was met by silence for a few seconds before Lydia responded.

"That's where I would start if I were you," Lydia said. "Can I help you with anything else?"

"No, you've been a dear. Thanks, Lydia."

Her sneakers squeaked on the hospital floor as she headed toward the Alford Center for Health, where they did most of the lab work inside the hospital. She was gliding toward the lab, but she wanted to stomp her feet. What right did Mahoney have to bust her chops when she was so close to getting what she wanted?

As the hospital pulsed around her with monitor beeps and rattling gurneys, she dialed the district attorney's office. Two rings. Three. The greeting was crisp and indifferent.

"Kennebec County District Attorney's Office," said a woman Andrea couldn't place.

"This is Andrea Kearney. I need to talk to District Attorney Mahoney about the Fields case," she said. "He'll know what it's about."

"I'm sorry, he's unavailable at the moment. Can I take a message?"

"Unavailable or unavailable for me?" Andrea growled into the phone. "Okay, fine. Tell him I'm at MaineGeneral following up on new information about the case, and in a minute, I'm going to talk to the lab tech who can blow this whole thing wide open."

There was more silence before the concession. "Hold, please."

Andrea smirked. She knew what happened next. The receptionist would scramble, and Mahoney would bend. There was no way he could brush her off after their last conversation, dangling that ridiculous wet reckless plea. She would lay it out to him cold. With everyone corroborating that Dustin was drunk, Jessica would retract her statement at the scene.

She rounded the corner and saw the lab in sight. A white coat emerged from behind the doors, a wisp of a man with a clipboard and glasses. Andrea stepped toward him.

"Hey, excuse me?"

He glanced up at her with uncertainty. He wasn't sure if she was talking to him when Mahoney's voice cut over the phone, low and sharp.

"Kearney? This better be good."

As soon as Andrea looked down, the tech started shuffling down the hall. She held up a hand and chased after him.

"I have it all, David," said Andrea. "The witness is lying, and I'm about to talk to the tech who ran the blood. Care to comment?"

"You're out of line with all this, Andrea." His voice was loud and gruff. "Stay where you are. I'm coming over."

"Hey, fine with me, David," she said. "No time to talk."

He started to say something else, but she hung up, more intent on catching the lab tech. She dodged a nurse coming out of a room with a monitor and caught up to him.

"Hey, I have some questions for you," she said, waving after him. "You're the tech who ran the Fields sample, right?"

The guy stopped and turned toward her, brows furrowed. "Who are you?"

"Andrea Kearney, *Kennebec Journal*. I need a minute to ask you about Dustin Fields' blood draw. How was it compromised? Why was it messed up? Bad equipment? What?"

"I can't talk to you about that," he said. "Patient information is confidential."

"This isn't about the patient; it's about the procedure. Your procedure."

"I don't know what you're after. Somebody botched it. It happens."

He pushed past her, catching Andrea by surprise, and headed toward the nearest door. He glanced at her over his shoulder and ducked inside, with the lock clicking shut behind him.

"Damn it," she said, smacking the wall with an open palm.

She looked up and down the hall, trying to decide how she might cut him off somewhere. MaineGeneral wasn't huge. There had to be an access point where she could catch up to him. She wanted to talk to him more than ever now because it was clear he didn't want to talk to her. There was no doubt in her mind he had something to hide.

She wandered the halls for a few more minutes, trying to chat up some medical staff. The doctors in blue scrubs weren't any help, hunched over their laptops, but an older volunteer turned out to be a gold mine. She knew the name of the lab technician who ditched her. Devon Carver.

She wandered for a few more minutes before heading down to the cafeteria on the lower building level. Devon had to eat sometime, didn't he? She grabbed a window seat and looked at the surrounding landscape until Mahoney eventually found her.

"What took you so long?"

"Very funny, Andrea," he said, not bothering to sit down. "I think it's time you stand down. You're harassing the hospital staff. And for what? A wet reckless case?"

"He was drunk, David. And you know it," Andrea said. "The nurse confirmed it. The medics confirmed it. The officer on the scene confirmed it. Your lying witness is dating the perp. And the lab technician who botched the blood draw? He ducked me like a deer dodging headlights on Route 3."

"How do you not see it, Andrea? I can't blame the guy for running."

"Tell me why you're making me jump through hoops, and we'll go from there."

"So that's what this is about," he said. "All right, I'll be honest. You're getting too comfortable with not doing things by the books. After our last meeting, I decided it was time somebody reined you in for a change."

"I'm a reporter working a story," said Andrea. "I'm not yours to rein in. *Kennebec Journal*. Heard of it?"

"Obstruction of justice. Heard of that?" Mahoney set his jaw and used his size to his full advantage. "Don't look so surprised that I know the law. As long as I keep it open as an ongoing investigation, your actions could interfere with it."

"Bullshit," said Andrea. "It would never hold up."

"I don't need it to stick. I'll just tie you up," he said. "We'll detain you, drag you through depositions, and see how your employer likes legal fees. And then? I'll make sure it gets so much attention that your sources will dry up, and your deadlines will slip."

Andrea pulled a notebook out of her pocket and flipped it open. She poised her hand over the paper for dramatic effect.

"Can I quote you on that?"

"You really don't get it, do you?" He loomed over her, breath still sharp despite an after-lunch mint. "This isn't Denver for me. I'm not a crusader with a vendetta. I've got to balance justice in this town. I know you're only rattling Dustin to get to William Fields, but that won't end well for anyone. It's like taking a match to a tinderbox. More people than Fields will get burned, and all of them will be the wrong people."

"So what?" She stood up, signaling she wasn't afraid. "He's why Augusta is a shell of what it could be. He built the strip malls, killed downtown, and is now buying it up again to be a hero. And you should know, Mahoney, I've got more than that."

"What is it you think you have, exactly?" He leaned in. "You uncovered some secrets? Big deal. Small towns are built on secrets."

"Sorry. It's an ongoing investigation," she said, shooting from the hip. "But let's just say I know how he made his money and from what I can tell, old habits die hard."

"Now I know you're chasing ghosts," said Mahoney, stepping back and rubbing his temples. "I don't care what Fields did thirty or forty years ago. I live in the present. You should try it."

She searched his face. For a fleeting second, she saw the Mahoney she knew from the river. He was weary but casual, skipping rocks across the water and giving her history lessons. But then their friendship seemed to evaporate, replaced by the tough-as-nails prosecutor who carved his name into the underbelly of Denver.

"I'll get the 911 recording from the state. It will take a few more days, but I'll get it," Andrea said. "And if I flip Jessica Michaud's statement, you can bet I'll be running a story by Saturday."

Mahoney flinched when he heard the name. She could see it in his eyes. Something had changed.

"What about Jessica Michaud?"

"You really are a shark. I'll give you that," he said. "This town and half of Maine is messed up on fentanyl and heroin. Overdoses are up forty percent from last year. So you need to remember that whatever revenge trip this is for you, it isn't the only case that matters. Trust me. I'm doing my job."

"You need to do it better," she said through her teeth, harsher than she intended, but she couldn't help it. Her hands were shaking as the adrenaline coursed through her.

"All right, I'm done here," Mahoney said, throwing his hands up in surrender. "I hope whatever friendship we used to have was worth it. I expect you to drop this by the time I walk out the door. After that, whatever happens is on you."

"See you in print," she said, unblinking.

Mahoney turned around and walked out of the cafeteria with big, easy strides. Andrea turned back to the window and looked out over the hospital's manicured greens and surrounding trees. The quiet calm of it stood before her in contrast to her altercation with Mahoney.

Then, her eyes drifted to the architecture. MaineGeneral was a beautiful building with a clean, modern look. She remembered when the renovations were made a few years ago. It was built with galvanized steel studs and heavy wooden framing, so Mahoney's tinderbox comment carried weight. This was one of the front lines of a bigger war than the one she was chasing now.

Did she win that round, or did she lose it? She didn't know anymore. But what she did know was that she wouldn't back down. If she had learned anything since she started writing stories for her high school newspaper, it was that good reporters never gave up, even when they were dead wrong.

Tired and frustrated from her lunch with Billy and whatever had happened between her and Mahoney, she retreated to her car in the parking lot of MaineGeneral. She sat there for forty minutes, watching the clouds roll in from the south. *We could use some rain*, she thought. It had been unseasonably warm and dry for weeks.

Taking a few minutes to breathe took some of the edge off, and she considered what was left on her mental checklist. Without the lab technician or the recording, all she had left today was running by the florist as a favor to Billy. It seemed like a ridiculously trivial task unless Dustin's name did pop up on the sales receipt.

She looked down to turn the ignition key and then looked up toward the hospital. Andrea couldn't believe it. Devon, the little dirtbag, was exiting the hospital. She quickly turned off her car, jumped out, and made a beeline toward him. There wouldn't be any warning this time. She waited until she was beside him as he worked a key into the door of his car.

"Devon Carver," Andrea said, scolding him like an angry mom. "You're going to be in a ton of trouble."

Startled, Devon jumped and dropped his keys. Without even looking down, he quickly turned and put his back to the car. He brought his hands up as if she were going to punch him.

"What? What is this about?" he stammered.

"You know what it's about." It was a bluff, but she didn't think it would take much to break him.

"No, I don't. I think there is a mistake."

His head rolled back like a turtle looking for a shell. He looked away from her, eyes straining to see where his keys fell.

"Devon. What you did is going to hurt a lot of people. That's no mistake."

"I'm sorry." It came out like a low whine. "I didn't mean for it to hurt anybody."

"What didn't hurt anybody?"

"I dabbed it with an alcohol swab," he said. "It wasn't much, just enough to be sloppy. It was supposed to look like my accident."

"What?" Andrea couldn't believe her luck.

"I didn't mean to make it look like Nurse Brown made a mistake," he said. "They said it wouldn't matter because nobody was hurt, but then Nurse Brown was written up. She didn't deserve it. I did."

"She was written up? Oh, Devon. You know she's a single mom."

"I know, I know," he said. "She's such a wonderful person."

"Then why did you do it?" Andrea eased off as the man's eyes teared up.

"I don't know. It was Dustin Fields. He used to mean something to this town," Devon continued, trying to control his breathing. "Everybody has the right to make a mistake, don't they? I wanted to help."

"You said 'they' said nobody was hurt," Andrea said, circling back. "Who's they?"

"I didn't know them," he said, bringing his hands to his face to wipe his eyes under his glasses. "Two guys came in while I was working the late shift. We've been backed up. They asked if I remembered Dustin Fields, the Windsor football hero who went to Baylor. Who doesn't?"

"That's it?" She could tell there was something more.

He looked away, unable to face the truth of it. "They put five hundred dollars on the table in front of me."

"These men. Did they work for William Fields?"

"I don't know," he said, looking around the parking lot as if someone might save him. "They didn't say."

"Would you recognize them if you saw them again?"

"Maybe," he said with a shrug. "It was late, like I said. It all happened pretty fast."

"All right, Devon. Here's my card," she said. "Don't tell anybody just yet, but I'll need you to come forward eventually."

"Do you think that will help Nurse Brown? She was nice enough to buy me a cup of coffee that night, and I screwed her over. I didn't mean to hurt anybody."

"I'm sure it will all work out," Andrea said, trying to soothe the guy. "You did the right thing telling me the truth."

Andrea smiled. It didn't matter how long it took to get the recording anymore. This was the smoking gun that would flip Jessica. With all the testimony and an admission that somebody paid to tamper with the sample, Andrea had her story this weekend.

She almost felt bad for Mahoney. Unless they could connect the two men to William Fields, it seemed unlikely the district attorney would get a DUI conviction. But that was no longer her problem. She had her story, and it would blow in like a storm.

CHAPTER 19

BROKEN MOON

Autumn Larkstrom was working late, entering sales orders, reconciling invoices, and preparing end-of-the-month reports for October. It was part of a hundred tasks she juggled at Lapointe Lumber, trying to stay ahead of the looming winter slowdown.

She had also asked her supervisor, Eric, if she could cut out early tomorrow so that she could move back in with Billy. He didn't hesitate to approve it, knowing a few extra hours of light would make it easier on her if it took more than one trip. Autumn estimated only two but wanted to cook a special dinner for herself and Billy on her first night home.

Eric would have supported her either way. Lapointe was a family-owned business and known for putting people first. He also knew Autumn would likely trade the daylight of one day for the daylight of another, which is what she was doing. The sun had dropped below the horizon, giving the sky a bruised purple hue.

The building was eerily quiet. The saws were silent, forklifts were parked, and occasional bangs of lumber being loaded had faded into the background. Even Reggie, who was responsible for securing the yard after closing, had left a half hour earlier. He had to take his kids to get costumes for Halloween.

Autumn looked over the papers in front of her and started to arrange them in organized stacks so that she knew which ones deserved attention in the morning. She felt good about it. The extra hours had paid off, making her feel confident that a fresh start tomorrow would keep her on track to leave after lunch without sacrificing what needed to be done. She picked up her phone and texted Billy.

Finishing up for the night. Can't wait to see you tomorrow.

His response was immediate. Are you sure you don't want to make it tonight?

I still have to pack. One more night won't hurt.

Billy texted a smiling face with a sweat drop, illustrating his unease. She tossed her head back and laughed.

You're funny, she typed.

And you're beautiful.

Hey, I'll never get out of here if we keep this up!

All right. I'll let you go, but it's not easy.

I'll make up for it, promise.

Sweet dreams, Autumn.

She texted a heart and slipped the phone into her purse.

She couldn't remember being so happy, knowing this was going to work. Billy was starting to pack up his past and put it away where it belonged. It made her want to squeal like when she was a high school girl on the other end of the phone when the guy she was crushing on finally worked up the nerve to ask her on a date. She knew it was ridiculous, even a little childish, but she didn't care. She was in love and wanted the whole world to know it.

So she did. She stood at her desk, did a little shake dance, and managed a faint but heartfelt squeal of delight for the benefit of the empty desks cluttered with forms and coffee mugs, remnants of a busy day serving contractors. Then she laughed at herself for doing it, a sound that carried in the office and joined the hum of the heater.

Satisfied with the way she had set up everything for tomorrow, Autumn grabbed her purse and headed toward the door. She strolled past all the trappings of her second home, filing cabinets and shelves with a mismatched collection of product catalogs. Like the rest of the building, the coatrack was empty except for someone's forgotten flannel. The bowl of candy her friend Kelly brought in had also been picked over. All that was left at a glance was black licorice and Necco wafers, so Autumn made a note to contribute to the bowl when she came in tomorrow morning.

Then she caught her reflection at the front door. She looked better than she had in weeks, and the weight of her separation from Billy had finally lifted. Moving back in with him felt like stepping into a new chapter, and it might even be the one that set the tone for the rest of their lives.

She pictured them remodeling his parents' house, making it their own with an art studio for Billy to explore his true passion as a sculptor. There was no way she would let him wallow away his years working at a quarry. All he needed was a gentle push, somebody to lift him up and let him know he deserved to be successful. The image of him working stone or old car parts into something magical warmed her.

Looking out the front door, glass-paneled and heavy, she could easily see her car parked alone in the center of the lot. She flipped the switch of the last fluorescent light, plunging the open space behind her into near darkness. The only remaining illumination was security lights to the back of the building and the glow of the exit sign.

She pushed out through the door, leaving the lingering smell of wood, coffee, and damp earth behind her. It felt good to be out of the building and in the cool, crisp air. Out of habit, she glanced around the lot and yard as she headed toward her car.

She always found it peaceful, looking over the stacks of eastern white pine and other lumber that rose like silent sentinels. Next to the wood, she counted the three forklifts parked outside, ready for an early morning tomorrow. Unless there was weather, it was common to leave them out.

Less common was a truck parked beside them. Its outline was stark against the dim security lights, a hulking shape that didn't belong there. She wasn't alarmed, thinking that maybe someone left with a friend for dinner as they sometimes do. But then that didn't fit the more she looked. It was a dark-blue, almost black, Ford F-150 with New York plates.

She couldn't recall anybody driving something with out-of-state plates, so she decided to investigate, her eyes scanning the truck bed for clues. The hard bed cover wasn't giving anything up. She had to get closer.

Her walk to the truck was steady, boots crunching on the gravel as she neared the lumber stacks and forklifts. There was a newfound bounce in her step as the goofy smile emoji from Billy danced in her mind.

She closed in on the truck and reflexively slipped her keys between her fingers. *"Always be ready,"* her brothers used to tell her.

In the darkening shadows of two lumber stacks, a large man stood with his back toward her. His broad frame hunched over as if inspecting something precious in his hands, rolling whatever it was over and over.

"Excuse me?" Autumn said, her voice bright but breaking. "Can I help you?"

He froze but didn't answer as she took in his size. He was a big man with his hood down, revealing a close-cut military haircut. The way he stood there after she called out to him, motionless, as if he could turn invisible and disappear from being seen, sent a shiver up her spine.

"Hey, I don't think you're supposed to be here."

The brightness faded from her voice as she assessed her options. She could run. She could try to fish her phone out of her purse. She could tighten the grip on her keys, something her brothers taught her to do when she didn't feel safe. Nobody wants a fist full of keys, they had told her.

"No, I'm supposed to be here," he said in a low grumble.

He lifted his head, tilting enough for her to catch the curve of a strong jaw and goatee. Then he spun the rest of the way to face her, so fast it startled her. She gasped and took a step backward.

"It's okay, I'm a police officer," he said, disarming her with a smile.

"Oh, you scared me for a second," Autumn said, recovering with a nervous laugh, the New York plates slipping from her mind. "What are you doing here?"

"I'm conducting an investigation," he said. "I've been doing some intel on this guy, you see, and it led me to this lumberyard."

"Who? Maybe I know them."

"Yeah, maybe," he said. "Billy Stevens."

"Billy? Why are you investigating Billy?" She blinked, disbelieving.

He took a step toward her, still smiling. He still held something in his hands, but it was pressed into his fists.

"He gave me something the other night. Do you think you can identify it?"

She took a step back, matching him. She didn't like his smile anymore. It was less disarming and more eager, hungry for something, like a leering jerk at a bar.

"Maybe you should show me some identification?"

"Look, Autumn. Look what I have."

He held up his hands, fists unclenched to reveal a small article of clothing. She couldn't be sure, but they looked like panties. She looked closer. They were small, delicate, and pink, with a little red heart on the waistline. She remembered buying them during a weekend road trip with Billy. It was a silly impulse purchase that made them both laugh. Now, they were in a stranger's hands and he knew her name.

She could hear her heart pounding in her ears, recognizing that she was in real danger for the first time. For a moment, she was transfixed by his gaze as he stood straighter and revealed his height, several inches over six feet. She wanted to turn and run right then but found herself digging her heels into the gravel, bracing for him to make a move at her.

"Worse on Friday," he said and lunged toward her.

Autumn snapped out of her paralysis and threw a circular punch with her key hand. It wasn't fast or hard, but the man didn't expect it. The keys dragged across his face, and he fell backward. They weren't sharp enough to break the skin, but she knew she hurt him. She felt it in her stinging hand, too, nearly dropping them and losing her best chance to escape.

"You bitch!" he howled, face twisted in anger and set on her.

She turned to run for the car, trying to calculate if she could make it to the main street. There weren't many cars on the road near the lumberyard at this time of night, but maybe she would get lucky and somebody would see her.

Autumn wasn't much of a morning jogger, but she was fit. She sprinted toward the car, pumping her arms for momentum. Maybe she could make it, angling the car between him and her like a barrier.

She could feel him gaining ground on her and then felt the shock of her shirt collar cutting into her throat. He grabbed it, slowing her momentum, before ramming one of his massive shoulders into her spine. Her lungs emptied as he put his full weight on top of her, pushing her face into small stones as her keys skipped across the gravel in front of her.

She gasped for air but couldn't catch her breath to scream. She was kicking wildly, trying to wrestle herself free like she used to with her brothers. But he was too big, too strong, and he knew what he was doing, twisting one of her arms behind her back and breaking the bracelet she had worn since Billy had given it to her.

She managed to look up, seeing headlights off in the distance, a few cars passing that had no idea what was happening a few hundred feet away from the road. Their taillights faded into the night, even as she prayed someone would turn around and see her or that Billy, unwilling to take no for an answer, might pull in and save her.

He pulled her up and flipped her over, one hand on her throat as the other pummeled her cheek. It gave before he landed a second blow and broke her nose.

"A pinch and twist for being a bad girl, Autumn," he said, grabbing her breast and twisting it. "Don't fight. This only ends one way."

But Autumn did fight it. She fought him every inch as he dragged her back toward the truck and into the shadows of the lumber stacks.

"No, no, no," she cried out between bouts of spitting blood. "Please, please, please."

He hit her again. And everything for Autumn went dark, the memory of Billy's emoji fading into blackness.

CHAPTER 20

HOUSE CALL

Billy kept his promise, watering the plants on the windowsill first thing in the morning. He felt good, having cleaned the rest of the house from top to bottom the night before. He wanted it to be perfect when Autumn came home, and it had also served as a distraction so that he didn't text her every five minutes.

After watering, Billy looked at his mom's old grandfather clock, a family heirloom handed down from her grandfather. It was one of the many treasures they left behind when they moved to Florida.

He still had a half hour before work, enough time for a second cup of coffee. He headed toward the kitchen, mug in hand, stopping short as a vehicle parked in front of his house.

Pulling back the curtain from the window, Billy saw a Silver Ford Explorer parked in front. A second vehicle, a black and white Ford Police Interceptor Utility with *POLICE* written in all caps across the doors, was parked across the street.

Billy wondered what might be happening in the neighborhood that would warrant a couple of officers from the Augusta Police Department. He headed into the kitchen to retrieve a second cup. There was time to poke his head out and see which neighbor might have attracted the APD before sunrise. By the time he returned, there was a loud, sharp knock at his door.

Two men hovered on his porch. One was in a navy windbreaker, and the other was in uniform. He knew it couldn't be good. Cops didn't show up this early for a friendly chat.

He set the mug on the coffee table and opened the door. The one who knocked was a tall man in his midforties, wearing a collared shirt under the windbreaker. Billy didn't know the older one but knew the one in uniform.

Derrik Mills had gone to Cony High School, his high school's biggest football rival. Billy had tackled this flashy running back a few times before Derrik had earned the nickname "Diesel." After graduation, Derrik was drafted by the University of Maine at Farmington and then dragged back for a family emergency. He never went back to college, enrolling in the Maine Criminal Justice Academy instead and being hired by the APD last year.

"Billy Stevens?" asked the older man.

"Yeah, good morning," Billy said, before turning to Derrik. "Hey, Derrik. What's this about?"

"Heya, Billy. This is Detective Benjamin Metcliff," he said. "Do you mind inviting us inside? I think that might be for the best."

"Sure," he said, a frown creeping across his face. "This won't take too long, I hope. I have to leave for work in a few minutes."

"It won't take long, Mr. Stevens," said Metcliff. "You might want to sit down."

"If it's about those overdue library books, I promise to return them," Billy said, trying to mask his unease. "Sorry, morning humor. Have a seat."

"I'll let the librarian know you're good for it," Metcliff said, shooting a look at Derrik. The officer returned a pained expression. Billy sensed it wouldn't be good. Did something happen at the quarry?

"We're here about Autumn Larkstrom," Metcliff said, so quiet that Billy almost didn't hear him. But he did hear her name, and every synapse in his head fired at once.

"What about Autumn?" he asked, standing up. "Has there been an accident?"

The words of their last few texts burned in his head. Finishing up for the night. Can't wait to see you tomorrow. This had to be a mistake.

"We'd rather be anywhere but here, Billy," said Metcliff, but it sounded like gibberish to Billy. "Ms. Larkstrom was found dead this morning at the lumber yard."

The room tilted, and Billy's knees buckled. Derrik rushed to his side, guiding him to the armchair that his dad once claimed as his spot. Billy looked up, trying to speak, but no words came out. He put a shaking hand to his head and tried to find them. He didn't have to. Metcliff trudged forward.

"It appears she was killed last night. Her body was found between the lumber stacks out in the yard." His voice was low and firm. "Whatever happened was out of sight from the yard's security camera."

Derrik squeezed Billy's shoulder, an empathic gesture letting him know he wasn't alone. The two weren't friends, but they shared a mutual respect.

"Who did it?" Billy asked in a growl, the initial shock turning to anger.

"We don't know. That's why we're here. We need your help."

"My help?" Billy narrowed his eyes. "The guy who did it is out there."

"We know, we know," said Metcliff. "But I do need to ask. Where were you last night?"

Billy's mind spun. Was he really asking him that question?

"I was here all night, cleaning," Billy said, starting to explain and then trailing off. "She was moving back in today, and I wanted to make the place, you know, perfect."

"Can anyone verify that?" Metcliff asked.

"No, I was alone," he said. "What are you getting on about?"

"You're the boyfriend, right?"

"Yeah, we were split for a few weeks, but we worked it out on Tuesday. She was moving back in tonight."

"As the boyfriend, we have to ask you these questions. It's all pretty standard."

"You know how it is, Billy," Derrik said. "We have to clear you, given your record."

"That was all different. Those were all drunk nights and bar fights," Billy said, incensed at the comment. "I've never hurt Autumn. I could never."

It was starting to sink in deep. She was gone. He would never see her again.

"Is that why you came along, Mills? To soothe the savage beast?" Billy said, snarking at him.

"Hey, man. I requested to be here for your benefit," said Mills. "I knew this wouldn't be easy."

"You got that right," Billy said. "Guess what? I'm not that guy anymore. I haven't been in a fight this year."

He had met her on New Year's Eve, and she had changed him. He had never connected the dots before, but that was it. Sure, there were a couple of nights he got out of hand, including the one that caused her to move out, but no more violence. She had grounded him. She was the one. What was he going to do now?

"This isn't an interrogation," said Metcliff, trying to guide the crashing waves of emotion Billy was going through. "We just need the facts. Did Autumn mention any problems at work? A disagreement? Maybe one of her coworkers making advances?"

"No," Billy said, realizing he said it too fast. He really didn't know. They'd been apart for weeks.

"Mr. Stevens, I need you to think long and hard about this."

"We mostly talked about moving back in, my parents, and her cousin getting a new job in Kennebunk," Billy said, rehashing some things about their reunion at Two Guys. "Hell, we texted each other last night."

"And? Did she seem distressed or frightened, like somebody was with her?"

"No. She had stayed late so she could get off early today," he said, voice wavering between anger and anguish as he relived those last tender moments with her. "She just said she was going home to pack. I'm sorry. This can't be happening."

She had signed off with a heart emoji. It was the last thing she would ever text him after he had joked and told her to move in sooner. Why hadn't she? If she had come home last night, she would be here right now, waking up with him this morning.

"Billy, stay with me, okay," Metcliff said. "Did she try to reach out again after the texts? Or maybe you tried to call her later that night to say good night."

"No, I told you. It was a couple of texts," he said. "She said if we kept on, she would never get her work done."

Billy didn't know what to do, his head aching from the questions and his heart breaking from the loss. He wanted to hide under some covers like a kid. He wanted to punch the walls until his knuckles bled. He wanted to kick these intruders out of his house.

An insistent knock at the door jarred him back into focus. It was hard and hurried. Derrik opened it and immediately recognized Andrea Kearney.

"Expecting someone?" Metcliff asked without turning around.

Andrea pushed her way past him and ran over to Billy. She threw her arms around him and squeezed harder than she ever had before.

"Oh, Billy, I am so sorry," she said. "When it came over the scanner, the newspaper called me, and I came right here. Is it true? What happened?"

"I don't know," Billy said. "Oh my God, Andrea. This can't be happening."

"I take it you two know each other," Metcliff said. "You heard a dispatch, and what? You decided it was a good time for a high school reunion."

"Back off, Ben," said Andrea, turning to Metcliff with a set jaw. Her eyes were red from crying on her way over. "This is my job. As soon as I heard Autumn's name, I knew this was the place I had to be. Billy's my friend, and she was mine, too."

"They say she was killed at the lumber yard," Billy said. "And they're here asking me all sorts of questions."

"Asking you questions? They need to be answering them," she said, turning back to the detective. "What happened to her, Ben? You must have something? Leads?"

"There are no details to share, Ms. Kearney," Metcliff said, unaffected. "This is an active investigation, and I'd appreciate it if you let us finish asking Mr. Stevens some questions."

Andrea waved her hand at him to continue, but her eyes darted to Billy in a search for permission. He gave a slight nod. She sat in the armchair opposite him, offering to be his anchor in the storm.

"I'm not sure this is appropriate, asking you questions in front of a reporter," Metcliff said.

"She can stay," he muttered.

"Fine," Metcliff said, annoyed enough to change his tune. "You said you were here all night. No one saw you. No one called you. There is nothing to confirm you were here."

"No, I told you, I was alone," Billy said, his head clearing again.

"When we pull your texts, and we will pull your texts, will we find anything troublesome? Spats? Arguments?"

"No, it wasn't like that," Billy said. "We had a fight a few weeks ago over some old pictures, and she moved out. We didn't keep fighting about it. We gave each other space."

Even with Andrea sitting right there, the walls felt like they were closing in on him. If the questions were all about him, the narrative was set. Bad boy Billy Stevens didn't like getting dumped. With his history and a motive, it could be a slam dunk.

"Her car was parked in the center of the lot," he said, looking down at some notes. "But her keys were dropped a few feet from the car. Her purse and part of a bracelet, apparently broken, were found about halfway between the car and the stacks. Can you explain any of that? Why might she run away from her car or maybe walk over to the stacks and then run toward her car?"

"What about security footage?" Andrea asked, unable to help herself.

"Ms. Kearney, please. Don't make me ask you to leave," Metcliff said. "Billy, I'm sorry. I will have to ask you to come to the station to make a formal statement. You understand what that means?"

"You think I'm a suspect," Billy said, his first cup of coffee wanting to come back up.

"All it means is that we think you have information that will help us solve this crime," Metcliff said. "Maybe you don't remember everything now because this is a shock to you. Maybe you'll remember something later. Maybe we'll find something or learn something that jogs your memory. We want to find who did this, just like you do."

"I heard what you said and know what you think," Billy said. It landed flat and created an uncomfortable vacuum. Metcliff sat back on the couch, looking to Derrik for help. The officer didn't have any to give.

"Billy, did you tell them?" Andrea said, nudging Billy to speak up.

"Tell us what?" Metcliff asked, anxious for a breakthrough.

"She's talking about last Friday. I was at the Bear Paw and somebody roofied my drink. I don't remember coming home that night, but I got home. When I woke up the next day, somebody had gone through the house. It wasn't trashed, but somebody rifled through my stuff and some of the things Autumn had left here."

"What, like a break-in?" Metcliff asked, writing something in his notebook. "Did they take anything?"

"No. I don't know," he said. "It didn't look like anything was missing. It was more like snooping. More like a prank or kids' stuff."

"Why didn't you report it?"

"I don't have the best of luck with you guys," Billy said, remembering that Delores, the nurse who saw him the day after, had urged him to report it. "There's a record of my visit to the Quick Care the next day."

"Interesting. You had nothing, and now there's a break-in with a mystery intruder," said Metcliff. "You know we'll have to check into all this now, right? The Bear Paw. The Quick Care. All of it?"

Andrea started to speak again, but Billy waved her off. He wasn't sure if Derrik or the detective saw him do it, but he didn't want them to know they suspected a New York cop had roofied him or that the guy might have been working for Fields. Billy was too vulnerable to toss it on the table and let them pick it apart.

Detective Metcliff stood up. "People never want the cops involved until they do. Isn't that right, Ms. Kearney?"

"They never want a reporter around, either, Ben," she said. "Until they do."

"Anything else you can remember, Mr. Stevens? Maybe with Ms. Kearney's help?"

"No," Billy said, exhausted. "I can't give you any more right now."

"All right. Take a day to decompress and come see me or Officer Mills at the station tomorrow. It would be best if you didn't leave town," he said before turning to Andrea. "I don't think I have to tell you to keep this out of the paper for now."

"I know what's fair game and what's not," Andrea said. "I haven't looked, but I'm sure some stations already have it up on socials."

"Have you told her parents?" Billy suddenly asked. They were going to be crushed.

"Not yet, but we're working on it," he said.

"Do you think I should call them? They might take it better coming from me," Billy said, searching the man's face.

"I know this is an incredibly impossible position for you to be in, but I think you should let us take care of that," Metcliff said. "I don't want anything to make this unintentionally harder on the family or you."

Billy nodded, lips pressed tight. They might as well book him now.

"You two, take care," Metcliff said at the door. "And Kearney? I wouldn't mind talking to you a bit, too."

Derrik followed close behind the detective but stopped at the door. He turned back to look at Billy.

"I can't imagine, Billy. Sorry."

Billy raised a weak hand in appreciation before the storm door slammed behind the two men. As soon as they were out the door, Andrea rushed over to Billy and put her arms around him again. He was crying, so she pulled him into her, gently rocking him back and forth.

"We'll find out who did this, Billy," she said. "I promise. For you. And for Autumn."

Billy's thoughts drifted back to when this all started. He ran into his high school girlfriend, Jessica Michaud, almost a week ago, the same night he was roofied. She was back in town to help her dying mother. It wasn't clear then, but Dustin Fields was back in town, too.

Maybe Andrea's speculation yesterday wasn't so far-fetched after all. Somehow, Fields was no longer satisfied with how they left things when his parents took a payout to silence him about Stacy and the football injury.

Maybe they wanted something more now that Dustin had returned home. Maybe the roofie had been a warning, and he didn't get the message, so they had Autumn killed. If that was true, he was going to make them pay.

"Do you think the Fields family did this?" Billy asked.

"I don't know, Billy. I just need to keep digging," she said. "I know they paid off the lab technician to cover up Dustin's DUI, and we still have the name of that cop who roofied you. The pieces are falling in place."

"Yeah, Kyle Brondi," he said. "I know you wanted me to give up his name to the cops, but if Fields has one cop on the payroll, who's to say he doesn't have more?"

"We'll get this," Andrea said. "I'll focus on Fields, and you focus on you. After my run-in with the DA yesterday, I think we need to be honest but careful."

They didn't say anything for a long time, preferring to comfort each other over the loss. Autumn was Billy's girlfriend, but Andrea had always known what he refused to see. He was never destined to be with Jessica. Her memory was holding him back.

Eventually, Billy broke away and walked over to the plants. He brushed a light hand across their leaves.

"I watered them this morning," he said. "I loved her. All this time."

"I know," Andrea said. "We'll find out who did this."

"I can't believe it," he said with a snort. "I haven't even called in to work."

Andrea took it as a cue and picked up her notebook. She held it up before putting it in her purse like an unspoken promise between them.

Billy picked up his coffee mug. It was cold. And now, he felt cold, too.

CHAPTER 21

BAD ACTOR

Andrea burst through the doors of the *Kennebec Journal*. She hadn't been in the office for a week, preferring to work on her feet rather than sticking to one of the desks arranged in clusters of four to facilitate communication among coworkers. Even with a small staff shared between two newspapers, the other being the *Morning Sentinel*, covering Waterville to the north, it was often too noisy.

It was loud now, her colleagues bantering over state legislators, who were reconvening for a second special session to address marijuana legalization. Voters favored recreational use the year before, a bitter pill for the community given the opioid crisis. Andrea ignored them all and focused on the receptionist.

"Who's working the Larkstrom murder?" Andrea asked as she passed the desk.

"Um, Steve has it," Julia said.

"Steve? Why not Betty?" Steve was a good reporter, a couple of years older than Andrea but without the same fire. Betty was hands down the best crime reporter in the building.

"She's digging deep into the backlog at the county court," said Julia. "The slowdown has been brutal on victims of violent crimes."

"All right, tell Steve to meet me in Edith's office in about five minutes," Andrea said as she reached the editor's door and walked through without knocking.

"The prodigal daughter returns," Edith said without looking up as Andrea plopped into one of the chairs facing the editor's desk.

"I want in on the Larkstrom case," said Andrea.

"It's too personal to you on every level, and Steve is already on it," she said. "Next question?"

"Fine. He can be the lead reporter, but I want to assist," Andrea said. "I have information that may help break it wide open."

Edith stopped reading whatever was on her computer screen and pulled down her readers. She looked good for her age, gray overtaking her brown hair, cut short above her shoulders so that she never had to tie it back. If she dyed it, most people would guess she was in her late forties or early fifties instead of her sixties because she had wrinkles, a combination of good genes and a few extra pounds.

"What do you have?"

"We have a bad actor in Augusta," Andrea said. She knew it was a leap of faith, but nothing else would convince her boss to reevaluate the decision. "A New York cop named Kyle Brondi."

Edith didn't react at first but gave it away with her only tell. She bit one of the temple tips on her readers and considered, knowing this was something new. The police didn't have it.

"I'm listening, but I still don't like it," Edith said. "Everybody knows you're friends with Billy Stevens. I heard you headed to his place as soon as someone told you that it came over the scanner."

"The police were already there," Andrea said. "They're leaning into Billy. Not hard, but they haven't cleared him."

Edith shook her head. "Reporting on your friend's murder is like being a surgeon and operating on a loved one. You're putting on a good show, but I know you. You're a mess of grief, loyalty, and self-doubt on the inside."

Edith did know her, but the control she was showing wasn't merely an act. Andrea had deeply buried her feelings about Autumn's death and Billy's tragedy. Working on the case might be the only thing that helped her keep it together.

"We already agreed this is Steve's story," Andrea said, pressing. "I just want to explore a couple of angles. This might even bump up against something else I'm pursuing."

"Yes, I've heard about that," Edith said. "District Attorney Mahoney called me."

"He called you?" Andrea asked. She couldn't help feeling shocked and betrayed.

"He said you have a 'hard-on,' his words, for the Fields family," she said. "You've been chasing the same story since college. The decline of small-town America at the hands of big business. You're a great reporter, one of the best, but this isn't a college newspaper."

"Damn it, Edith," she said. "It isn't like that."

"Let me jump in here," Edith said. "When I was in school, just a little younger than you are now, I had a journalism professor ask the class to raise their hands if they would withhold the name of a thirteen-year-old rape victim. Almost everybody raised their hands. Then he asked if they would if the rapist was her uncle. About half the hands went down. Then he asked if they would if her uncle was the mayor. There might have been only two or three hands up after that, and they weren't going to be reporters. My point is that this job is like walking a tightrope over an alligator pit. We must always balance protecting the vulnerable and the public's right to know."

Andrea didn't have to respond. Steve was knocking lightly on the door.

"Come on in, Steve," Edith said. "It's so good to know somebody around here has the courtesy to knock."

"Good morning, Edith," said Steve before looking at Andrea. "Andrea, I'm sorry for your loss. I know Autumn was a friend of yours."

"Thanks, Steve," Andrea said, still mulling over Edith's cryptic lesson.

"Steve, what do you have on the Larkstrom case?" Edith asked. "I know some of it, but go ahead and don't hold back."

Steve looked at Andrea. He was clearly uncomfortable, eyes wide.

"I said don't hold back," Edith said.

"The scene, as you know, was gruesome, to put it mildly," Steve said, swallowing. "The police think it implies intense emotion or rage, which is common in crimes where the victim knew the killer."

Andrea slouched in the chair. She wanted to hear it but didn't want to hear it.

"The body was found, badly beaten, between the lumber stacks toward the back of the yard, an area where the one working camera on the property couldn't see what happened," he said, continuing. "Police suspect she knew the killer. That he was familiar enough with the yard that he would know this area of the lot wasn't on camera. That he stood over there and beckoned Larkstrom over to him. She obliged, not thinking anything was wrong until she realized something was wrong. She tried to flee but couldn't make it back to her car, let alone the safety of the building. Evidence suggests she fought back hard."

"Hold on a sec, Steve," Edith said. "I think Andrea is starting to get my point. Can we focus on what the police were doing?"

"One of the employees, Reggie Coleman, found the body when he arrived early this morning. He was the last person, aside from the killer, to see her last night, but the police were questioning everybody there. They've roped everything off, collecting initial evidence. The body is with the coroner so they can scrape the nails and estimate the time of death. I know they've already interviewed the boyfriend. Sorry, Andrea. They should release forensic evidence in a few days, canvass the area for witnesses — but I don't expect much — map her whereabouts over the last few days, and narrow a suspect list. Oh, we have her name but aren't releasing it yet. The Larkstrom family is still being notified."

Andrea's head rolled as Steve droned on, feeling like she was lost at sea and the waves were growing larger around her. Autumn was a special person, grounded in a way Andrea could never be because she was too busy picking fights with the world.

"I'm just asking permission to dig into this Kyle Brondi guy," she said. "I have reason to believe he might not be operating alone. He might have even been hired."

"Who's Kyle Brondi?" Steve asked, writing the name in his notebook.

"He's a New York City cop. I think he roofied Billy a few nights ago and then used it to his advantage to search Billy's house. For what? I don't know. APD knows this but not the name. If they keep their investigation close to home, Brondi won't even factor into the equation."

"You were at Billy's house with the police this morning and withheld this information?" Edith said, narrowing her eyes.

"He's a cop," Andrea said, matter-of-fact. "Trust me. They didn't want to hear it."

"Let me guess," Edith said, waving her hand like it held a magic wand. "You think he was working for the Fields family."

"I didn't say that," Andrea said defensively and then reconsidered. "Okay, fine. I'm sure the Fields family is working to cover up what should be their son Dustin's DUI last Friday, and they are doing it because they're afraid his vulnerability will prompt several young women to come forward and press charges for sexual assault or rape."

Edith threw her hands up and leaned back in her chair. Steve's shoulders tensed, an early warning signal that he knew what might be coming next.

"This is what you've been working on all week?" Edith asked, but not as a question. "Investigative reporters are being dropped from newspapers all over the country, and you're on a crusade to save small-town America?"

"Some of it lines up," Andrea said, shooting back. "The lab tech at MaineGeneral admitted to me he was paid to make Dustin's BAC sample inadmissible. The police officer on the scene, medics, nurse, and doctors all say Dustin was drunk. In fact, the only person saying otherwise is Jessica Michaud, and I'll be visiting her tomorrow."

"Jessica Michaud?" Steve asked, surprised to hear the name.

"Yes, why?"

"Daniella is looking into a weird report at Muriel Michaud's place," Steve said. "Seems they might have had a North Pond Hermit kind of thing under their porch. Weird stuff. Oh, and get this, the cops were interviewing Muriel when one of them spotted three ounces of marijuana sticking out of Jessica's purse. Bad luck for her. They issued a citation. Any credibility she had as a witness isn't going to help Dustin Fields now."

"Welcome to the land of legalized recreational marijuana," Edith said, shaking her head. "Steve, do you mind giving Andrea a minute alone with me?"

"Oh, sure," Steve said. "See me when you're done, Andrea. I'd like to know more about this Brondi character."

"Yeah, sure," Andrea said, casting her eyes down like a high school student in the principal's office.

Steve shut the door on his way out, and Edith wasted no time. She stood up and paced behind her desk, searching for the right words.

"I had to send him out because you can't even hear yourself right now," said Edith. "You're spinning like a toy top, around and around and around."

"Edith, I'm so close," Andrea said. "I have all the pieces. I just need to put them in the right places."

"I'll tell you what I'm going to do," Edith said. "I don't want Steve wasting his time with this left-field Kyle Brondi business. You can do it. But that doesn't mean you are working on the murder case. Are we clear?"

"Yes, I get it," Andrea said, disappointed but willing to accept any small victory.

"Do you know where to start?" Edith asked.

"I'm going to start with public records and online databases, maybe a stateside criminal history search with the New York State Office of Court Administration. I'll check the NYPD personnel records unless they stonewall me, of course. I don't know. Maybe one of my friends at the sheriff's office can ask around for us."

Edith considered and then peered at Andrea. Whether she was judging the work or the reporter, Andrea didn't know.

"Don't waste your time with the criminal history search if you don't have his date of birth," she finally said. "There's too big of a chance for incomplete or inaccurate records."

"Right, thank you," Andrea said, a sigh of relief in her voice.

"Don't get too excited, Andrea," Edith said. "This isn't a reward. It's a punishment because I will also ask you to tread lightly on this weird Fields fixation. Go ahead and talk to Michaud if you want, but there's no DUI story unless I can see the high caliber of work I've grown to expect from you. We have bigger fish to fry than a spoiled rich kid home from college, or whatever, who gets a break."

"But," Andrea started and then rethought her position. "I understand. Thank you."

"But?" Edith says. "I've been doing this job all my life. But nothing. I heard you. This all links together in your mind. Without something concrete, it doesn't. They are separate stories until you can bring me something as solid as the granite mined out of the Hallowell Quarry. Am I clear?"

"Yes, ma'am," Andrea said. "I think we understand each other."

"Get out of my office," Edith said and sat back down in front of her computer.

Andrea didn't waste any time. She had never been on thinner ice but got part of what she wanted. Edith gave her permission to pull together a backgrounder on Kyle Brondi, which would likely take the rest of the day or longer. If it turned out to be a dead end, at least they would figure out why Brondi targeted Billy.

Walking back to her desk with a chair two weeks cold, Andrea remembered another breadcrumb she had been carrying around with her. She still had the card with the name of the florist that Billy had given her. She stopped by Daniella's desk on her way.

"Here," Andrea said. "I heard you're looking into the North Pond Hermit thing at the Michaud place. This might be nothing, but Jessica had been getting flowers from a secret admirer. Maybe the two things are connected."

"Hey, thanks, Andrea," Daniella said. "I'll let you know what I find out. And, oh, I'm really sorry about your loss. We're all hoping they catch the guy."

Catching the guy wasn't what was troubling Andrea. She wanted them to catch the right guy. Her money was on mystery man Kyle Brondi. But only if she could catch a break for Billy.

CHAPTER 22

COMES AROUND

After discovering someone had camped under their porch the day before, Jessica was reluctant to leave her mom alone. But El finally convinced Jessica to go out by telling her daughter the ugly truth. She needed a break from Jessica.

It stung Jessica to hear it, but she knew it was true. Ever since the chilling discovery, followed by the citation for marijuana that wasn't hers, Jessica had spiraled into a quiet panic. She couldn't shake the feeling. Kyle was out there somewhere, watching the house from a new location.

When Jessica wasn't patrolling the house every two hours, looking for new signs of intrusion, she shadowed her mom's every step. El continually reassured her daughter that everything was fine. She didn't need another pillow or a back rub or Bible verse. What El needed was whatever truth Jessica wouldn't relinquish. Every time that came up, Jessica would retreat into a shell of shame and stigma.

When Dustin called and asked if Jessica was still up for their reunion, Jessica had decided to say no. But now they were pulling into the familiar parking lot, an old high school haunt that proudly claimed to be one of the area's busiest family-owned restaurants.

The drive over wasn't easy. She rattled on about everything that transpired the day before while he was in Nashua with his dad, except for one crucial detail. She didn't dare tell him about the man who introduced her to an exhilarating and twisted world of submission and abuse or how Kyle was now poised to keep his promise to make everybody she ever cared about suffer and get her back. And if he did get her back?

"Hey, I've got to tell you," Dustin said, trying to ground her. "I know everything that happened was terrifying, Jess. I'm here for you now. I think your mom is right. You need to give your mind a rest, even if it's only a few hours."

"I know you're right, and she's right," Jessica said. "But that doesn't make it easier, Dustin. Somebody was spying on us. Do you have any idea how that feels? We were up late some nights on the couch, her in a nightgown and me in a T-shirt, talking about her condition and my childhood memories or my dad, with some guy down in the dark, watching, listening, planning, and plotting."

"No, I can't imagine," he admitted. "Nobody can blame you for being on edge, especially after the cops pinned the drugs this creep planted on you. That's messed up. All I can say is that there are some real weirdos out there. So the best thing you can do is give yourself time to breathe, and then if you still need to vent, I'm here for you. No judgment."

Jessica looked out the window of the truck Dustin had borrowed from his dad's construction yard, his dark-blue Challenger totaled less than a week ago. Even through the smear on the passenger-side window, the busy lot was a sight for sore eyes. The crazy sign that sported little bits of wisdom in big block letters gave her a lift: DIFFICULTIES ARE MEANT TO ROUSE. NOT DISCOURAGE.

Dustin turned off the engine and smiled at her. She could tell it wasn't as genuine as the one he gave her two days ago. He was studying her, and it made her self-conscious.

"I know, I look like a wreck," she said. "I didn't sleep much last night."

"Don't worry about that," he said, brushing her hair back with a gentle hand. "Worry about chicken or fish or shrimp or scallops."

She smiled, one of her first since yesterday. Then she took in a deep breath.

"Okay, I'm ready. Let's do it."

As planned, Dustin claimed the picnic table that was the farthest away from the original barn and expansion buildings. The choice made her feel slightly awkward, which surprised her because it had sounded so perfect last Saturday. But today, all it made her think about was that this was the same table Billy favored when they dated in high school, back when Dustin was going out with Stacy. Whatever happened to her?

"We might as well enjoy the warm weather while it lasts," he said. "Can you believe it? It's even Thursday, just like old times."

"All we need is Pete in a chicken suit chanting, 'Where's the beef,'" she said, trying to revive happier conversations from a week ago.

He laughed, throwing his head back like he didn't have a care in the world before leaving her to place their order at the counter. She wanted to taste the nostalgia that the Red Barn made her feel and had zeroed in on a lobster roll and Laura's famous seafood stew. She would never finish all of it, but it wasn't about that.

She had offered to join him at the counter, but Dustin insisted she stay. He didn't want to lose the table. She agreed but regretted the decision soon after. It was only 4 p.m., but every long shadow caught her attention. Every shed and tree could hide someone. Every man the same size as Dustin or bigger was a potential threat.

Suddenly, the opening to the song "Slide" by Calvin Harris sounded from her purse, an incoming call from Kennedy Sloane, the agency she worked for in New York. She reached in, moving the note Kyle had left with the marijuana out of the way.

"Jessica Michaud," she said, forcing a smile so that whoever was calling on the other end could hear it.

"Hey Jessica, it's Keiko."

"Oh, Keiko!" Jessica was happy to hear her voice.

"How are things? I mean with your mom?"

"Good. Well, not good, as you know, but as good as we can expect."

"I get it," Keiko said. "Hey, I'm calling for two reasons. It's sort of a good news, bad news thing."

"I could use some good news." Jessica braced herself.

"Kennedy Sloane is going to stand by you."

"Oh my goodness, thank you!" Jessica had been waiting to hear back from them since her mom's prognosis was official. "It hasn't been easy here, but this is like a light in a very dark tunnel, Keiko."

"Don't thank me yet," Keiko said. "You're eligible for twelve weeks of FMLA, but it won't cover everything. Even with the vacation time, you're coming up short."

"What about sick days?" Jessica asked.

"Paid sick leave counts against your FMLA, but on a brighter note, New York just passed its own family leave act, which could give you an additional eight weeks at fifty percent of your salary," she said. "It's a bit of gray area because it isn't effective until next year. So, how we plan this makes a big difference."

Trying to focus on everything Keiko was throwing at her was like drinking water from a firehose. She couldn't even think it through right now.

"I need to stay with her the entire time," Jessica said. "I don't know how long."

"I'm sorry, sweetie," Keiko said. "That's not in the cards. Maybe we can refer you to the American Cancer Society for hospice information?"

Jessica swallowed. She wasn't ready to think about that. She always imagined her mom dying peacefully at home.

"I can't, um, can I have a few days to think about it?"

"Yes, sure," Keiko said. "Just don't think too long because there's the second reason I had to call."

Her heart dropped. "He's not still calling the office, is he?"

"No, but someone else called," Keiko said. "Is it true you received a citation for possession of marijuana over the legal limit in Maine?"

Jessica nearly dropped the phone. She couldn't believe it.

"Yes, but it wasn't mine," Jessica said, blurting it out and quickly following up. "Who called? The police?"

"No, it wasn't the police," said Keiko. "Look, don't lose it. We're an agency. Most of the creative team partakes. Whatever gets them through the night and coming up with crazy stuff, right?"

"Oh, yeah, right," Jessica said.

"It's the optics," Keiko said. "They aren't good. We're fighting for your FMLA request, and you're up there in Maine smoking dope with lobsters or whatever."

"No, I understand,"Jessica said. "I get it."

"No more mess-ups," Keiko said, flatly this time. "No more ex-boyfriend calls. No more citations. No more whatever else is going on up there. None."

"Okay," said Jessica.

"All right, let's talk again soon, and try to have a nice night," Keiko said. "Where are you anyway? I called the house first, and your mom said you had a date?"

"No, nothing like that. It's an old high school friend."

"All right, whatever," she said. "Bye-bye, Jessica."

"Bye," Jessica said and hung up as Dustin returned to the table with drinks.

"What was that about?" he asked. "You looked intense."

"Oh, nothing, just work," she said, looking down at her phone. "Oh, shoot. The garage called earlier, and I missed it. The calls pile up without service at the house."

"Hey, no worries," he said. "Give them a call."

Jessica smiled weakly and tapped the recent number button. It rang, and a young man answered. "Pine Hollow Garage."

"Hi, this is Jessica Michaud," she said. "I think I missed your call?"

"Oh, right," he said, snapping gum. "Eddie wants to know if you want two new tires or all four plus the spare."

"Two or all five? No, there must be a mistake," Jessica said. "I just need one new tire. The other just needs air."

"Ah, no," he said. "You have two tires with punctures that can't be fixed. So you can replace just the two or go with all four plus the full-sized spare. With the wear I'm seeing, leave it over the weekend for all five. Go for two, and pick it up tomorrow."

Dustin tried to get her attention. He wanted to know what the mechanic was saying. She held up a hand to stave him off.

"Two is fine. What time tomorrow?"

"Around ten, maybe?"

She looked at Dustin.

"Can you give me a ride to the garage tomorrow around ten?"

He didn't hesitate, giving her a nod, then, a thumbs-up.

"Ten is fine," she said into the phone.

"Thanks for calling Pine Hollow Garage."

Dustin slid two drinks to her, a Coke and water, as requested. He had iced tea.

"You're popular tonight," he said. "What's going on?"

"This is weird," Jessica said, trying to ignore the painful and obvious truth that this was all Kyle again. "I thought the spare needed air, but it was punctured just like the one I changed."

"That is weird," Dustin said, his brain working over the odds.

"You know, you were right," she said. "Let's talk about something else. I didn't even ask you about Nashua. How did the trip with your dad go?"

"Oh," he said, as if he was hesitant to talk about it. "Good, you know. Road trip with my dad. He's not the easiest guy to get along with at times. But hey, he's helping me out."

"You said something about investors?" Jessica said. "What's going on?"

"Not investors exactly. More like business partners," he said. "I opened a construction company in Waco after I left school. Thought I told you that."

"You mentioned something, I think," Jessica said, searching her memory. So much had happened since then.

"Anyway, I hit a snag and thought Dad could help me," he said. "I have a cash infusion but need a way to funnel it back into the company. Ah, it's boring business stuff. I just like to build things."

"Oh, so you're not staying in Augusta long?" Jessica said, disappointed. "I didn't realize."

She could tell Dustin understood her immediately. He took her hands in his, giving them a gentle squeeze.

"Hey, don't worry about it, silly," Dustin said. "I'll be here for weeks, maybe longer if I'm needed. I won't run out on a friend, Jess."

"I appreciate that, Dustin," she said. "I don't know what it is. I'm usually stronger than all this. You know, tough-as-nails account executive at a big-time New York ad agency."

"No, yeah, I get that from you," he said. "Funny. We escaped Augusta, and family ties brought us both back for a little while. Kismet, like I said."

"It wasn't all bad," Jessica said, looking for a way to salvage the night. "Remember walking the mall and trying on tees at Hot Topic? You'd always go for a tee that was two sizes too small to show off your muscles."

"They used to get so mad at me for stretching them out," Dustin said, laughing and then imitating the store manager's nasal monotone. "'Mr. Fields? If you stretch them out, you have to buy them.'"

"Or remember when my mom told everybody about the phantom of the Maine State Library?" Jessica said. "So we started a rumor that there was a ghost at the Lithgow Library, too?"

"You kept sneaking in there to flip the books on the shelves so that nobody could read the spines." Dustin was animated again, making big gestures. "'Not me, not me, there's a spirit in the stacks,' you'd say."

"So many memories," Jessica said, trying to remember the next.

Before she knew it, she had proven Dustin and her mother right. She needed some time to reclaim normalcy. It was working, each of them taking turns remembering something about the other over their food. All her troubles drifted away, right up until her phone pinged with a text message. She flipped it over to see a message from Kyle and a video attachment. She pressed play.

"See, you are popular." Dustin smiled, but it faded as her face lost color and her hand started to shake. "You good?"

"Wrong number," she said, dropping the phone as her stomach churned. "Excuse me."

Jessica couldn't sit still as the wave of nausea came over her. She needed to throw up.

She flipped her legs over the bench and headed to the bathroom. She remembered the night explicitly but didn't know there was a video. She stumbled toward the outdoor porta-potties, rubbing her wrists where ropes once burned them.

In the porta-potty, she gagged from the memory as much as the smell. She had been blindfolded in the video, a game they'd played before. Except that time, there was another presence in the room besides Kyle. It didn't feel like Kyle between her legs, and it wasn't. Kyle's hot breath was on her neck, telling her to relax through his mask. It all came up, acidic and sour.

Her head spun, and she put her hand on the plastic wall. It wasn't just the video but the message that came with it. She gagged again, wishing there was something she could use to clean up. She needed to get out and get some air. She wanted to go home.

She struggled with the latch but managed to wrestle the door open. She took two huge gulps of air and looked back at the table where they had been sitting. She half expected Dustin to be looking her way, concerned and worried. He wasn't. Even in the shadows, she could see his head down, looking at something else. Her phone?

Heart pounding, she ran back to the table. She was calling to him, trying to get his attention as she tripped her way to him, ready to smack her phone out of his hands.

"Is that my phone?" she asked, sharp and desperate.

"What?" Dustin said, looking at her perplexed and turning to show her something. "No, this is my phone. Jess, are you okay?"

She scanned the table, searching for her phone. Then she saw it, facing up and dark in the middle of the table. Was that how she dropped it?

"Did you touch it?" She knew something was wrong.

"You dropped it. It almost fell off the table," he said, eyes glancing at her phone.

He looked back at her, and she closed her eyes, unable to look at him or the table with the half-eaten lobster roll and cold stew. She took another breath.

"I'm sorry, Dustin. I'm done," she said. "Take me home."

He didn't argue. Instead, he muttered that he was sorry the dinner didn't sit well with her. His words were lost on her. She couldn't hear a thing, not even the rumble of conversations around them.

In the truck, he rambled on about making it up to her tomorrow. He'd pick her up so that they could get her Jeep. She nodded, agreeing with him. But she wasn't listening. She was thinking about what would happen tomorrow with Kyle's text burning behind her eyes.

Sending to Kennedy Sloane tomorrow. Died on Saturday.

Kyle was going to do to her what he did to his last girlfriend. Her job. Her life. It was all over.

CHAPTER 23

BAR FIGHTS

Billy felt like he was going insane. He had called off work because he knew he couldn't operate the granite cutter. But staying home was taking its toll. Everywhere he looked, he saw Autumn.

The plants on the windowsill were freshly watered in the morning. Her clothes in the dresser were refolded after someone had searched through them. The scrunchie she had left in the bathroom was untouched. The photo of them mimicking the pose of a statue at the Morris Museum of Art was unmoved. The cutting board in the kitchen was unused.

Nobody ever thinks about the stuff accumulated while living together until one person is gone. While they're alive, it bleeds into the background of life. When they're gone, it pops with intensity. The most trivial things become tethered to sentimental value, like a stupid blue hand towel. These were the kind of thoughts that convinced him. He was going insane, wandering the house and finding something new to drive another nail into the coffin of his depression.

Then Conner McGrath called because he had heard about what happened. Billy figured everyone had by then, but he didn't know for certain. He had been too afraid to turn on the television. Conner wanted to know how he was holding up.

"I'm dying here, Conner," Billy said, rasping into the phone.

"Want me to come over?"

"No, I can't stay here anymore," he said. "Autumn is everywhere."

"Want to go for a drink?"

"I don't know if I could take the attention," Billy said. "Everybody would be looking at me, consoling me, or damning me."

"I've got a place," he said. "Why don't you meet me at the Woodshed in Manchester? Nobody's going to know you there."

Billy frowned into the phone. Metcliff had told him to stay in town, but Manchester was seven miles northwest of Augusta. Did that count? Did he care?

"Yeah," Billy said. "I'll see you there in twenty minutes. Oh, you're not bringing Hope, are you?"

He liked Hope. But it might break him to see her right now.

"No, buddy," he said. "It's just you and me."

The Woodshed was perfect. Nobody from the Augusta or Hallowell scenes would likely be there, even on a Friday night. It was a working-class crowd, and the vibe was casual. It was the kind of place you could blend in and not be noticed over beer, darts, and the jukebox.

When Billy arrived, Conner had already staked out a spot at the far end of the bar. He waved at his friend as someone pushed inside behind him. He turned to look, but nobody was there. So he brushed it off and headed back. Conner shook his hand and pulled him in for an embrace. Billy returned it, strong and hard.

"Four shots, Old Route 8," Conner said to the bartender as Billy took the stool against the wall. "Beer backs, whatever's good on tap."

As soon as the whiskeys arrived, they toasted Autumn and threw back the first shots. Conner positioned himself like a wall in front of Billy, a barricade between him and the growing crowd. It was loud, a thousand conversations rumbling in the background, food coming out of the kitchen, and Guns N' Roses covering Bob Dylan's song "Knocking on Heaven's Door." Billy leaned in to be heard.

"Are you sure we can blend in here?" Billy said. "I feel like everybody is looking at me."

"Nobody can see you back here," Conner said. "It's all over the news, but you haven't been mentioned yet. Have you seen it? It isn't good, Billy."

"I don't want to know right now," Billy said. "I want the guy who did it."

"If they ever find him, I'll be right there with you," Conner said. "Do they have any leads?"

Russell must have told Conner the cops had come out to his place in the morning, which is why Billy didn't make it in to work. Billy didn't care. He just shook his head and looked at Conner dead in the eyes.

"They think it's me," said Billy and slammed the second shot down.

"What? That makes no sense," Conner said. "You loved Autumn. Any fool could see that, even when you couldn't see that."

Billy knew what Conner was getting at. Everybody who knew him did. Part of him could never let Jessica go enough to make room for anybody. It took months for him to believe his feelings for Autumn were real. He just needed to see Jessica again for closure. He was an idiot, so he held up two fingers to the bartender and pointed to his spot and Conner.

"This ain't a funeral, my friend," Billy said. "It's a wake."

They sat there for the next two hours, letting the conversation drift from Autumn to growing up in Augusta. They had lived in different neighborhoods but were often in the same orbit, eventually playing football together.

Conner never got the attention that Billy did, and with his grades hovering around a C, college wasn't an option. He drifted into the workforce after graduation, bouncing around jobs before landing a spot at the quarry.

As the drinks poured on, the two lamented that they weren't close friends in high school. Their friendship had come later at the quarry.

Conner loved the physicality of the work and was content with saving up for his next hunting trip. Billy shared a new revelation that maybe it was time he looked for something better, like Autumn always wanted him to do. Augusta wasn't the right place to challenge him as an artist. Head west, she had told him.

"I've got to take a leak," Conner said, sliding off the stool. He was drunk but working toward sobering up. "Save my seat and no more whiskey."

"Lightweight," Billy said, calling after Conner and then adding to no one, "Good friend, but a lightweight."

With Conner gone, Billy tucked himself deeper into the corner of the bar against the wall and closed his eyes. The haze made it almost feel normal, listening to a crowded bar over Lynyrd Skynyrd chords. He found peace until the sudden sting of stale cigarette smoke, an acrid stench from a few days ago.

Billy's muscles tightened as he looked up. A bear of a man was sitting on Conner's stool, back toward him. Some weirdo with a black hoodie pulled up around his head.

"Hey, buddy," Billy said. "Seat's taken."

The man ignored him, so Billy reached out to grab the man's shoulder. As his fingers brushed the fabric, the man shifted, backing off the barstool and into Billy.

"What the hell?" Billy said, losing his balance.

The man was on him, turning around to catch his balance while pawing at Billy's flannel jacket. Billy pushed back, feeling taut muscles under the hoodie. Billy was formidable, but this guy was stronger, lifting his head so that Billy could see his face.

Billy's stomach twisted. He knew those eyes. It was Kyle, right there in front of him. He reached out to grab him, fingers looking to lock onto something. But Kyle jammed his shoulder into him, and Billy fell, landing hard on the wooden floor.

He hit his head but ignored the pain, struggling to get up and confront the man he knew killed Autumn. But Kyle was drifting into the crowd as a couple of people nearby helped Billy up.

They asked if he was okay as Billy adjusted his jacket, hand brushing against something metal in the outside pocket. He never kept anything in his coat pockets. He pulled it out. It was part of a broken bangle with a tiny crescent moon and a single star, shining in the light of the backlit bar wall. Autumn's bracelet.

Billy's mind reeled. There was no question now. Kyle killed Autumn brutally and savagely in the lumberyard where she worked. Desperate to find him, Billy started pushing through the crowd, scanning for the big man with a black hoodie.

He could see it in the distance near the front door. His pulse quickened as he moved toward the door, pushing past agitated patrons, strangers, and familiar faces like Conner and then Derrik, even though that couldn't be. He was seeing things. His heart thumped as he closed in on the monster.

He grabbed Kyle's shoulder, dizzy with rage, and threw a wild, glancing punch. Kyle turned, scowling at him. Except it wasn't Kyle. It was a large bearded stranger in a black shawl-collared sweater and jeans. He was shouting at Billy. His curses were joined by the chorus of an angry mob and the smell of spilled beer. He made a mistake.

The stranger growled, stepped on Billy's foot, and threw a punch of his own. It wasn't wild, a jab hitting Billy like a sledgehammer. A flash of white light replaced the dark bar, his vision failing and his feet slipping, hands from the crowd grabbing him and yanking hard.

"Get him out of here," someone said as the strong hands on either arm guided him toward the door and out into the cool air.

"Easy, Billy, I got you," Conner said on his left.

"It was him," Billy said. "I had him."

"Yeah, buddy," Conner said. "Calm down. It's okay."

"Can you get him home?" asked a voice, controlled and familiar.

Billy turned to see who was to his right. It was Derrik. As soon as he recognized him, Billy instantly wrested the officer's hands off him, confused by seeing the man in plain clothes and not a uniform.

"What are you doing here?" Billy asked, taking a step back toward Conner and away from Derrik. "You shouldn't be here."

"Easy, Billy," Derrik said. "I followed you over for your own safety."

"Are you with them?" Billy said. "Fields?"

"I'm doing this for you," Derrik said. "If that fight escalated, nobody would have been able to save you."

"Why would you do that?" Billy said, anger rising in his slurred speech.

"Not everybody is against you, Billy," he said. "You're a drunk, a hothead, an idiot sometimes, and a pain in the neck, but I saw you this morning. There's no way you killed that girl."

"She wasn't just some girl," Billy said, spitting over his busted lip. "He was right here. Did you see him?"

"I didn't see anybody, no," Derrik said. "I just saw you hit the guy at the door."

"I saw some big guy bolt out of here," Conner said. "Hard to tell why with everything going on."

"Can you get him home?" Derrik again asked Conner.

"Yeah, sure," Conner said. "What about his truck?"

"Give me the keys, and I'll take care of it," Derrik said. "Damn it, Billy. You're lucky I was here."

"Yeah, I'm lucky," Billy said, trying to keep his balance as Conner fished the keys out and tossed them to Derrik. "Real lucky."

Billy made a pistol out of one hand and put it to his temple. He dropped his thumb like a hammer. Conner pushed it down and guided his friend toward his pickup.

"He was here," Billy said to Conner.

"I know, Billy," Conner said. "I believe you."

Billy heard the words but couldn't tell if Conner believed him. Billy's thumb traced the crescent moon in his pocket. He needed to get home. He needed to sober up. He needed to find Kyle.

CHAPTER 24

STORM WARNING

The possibility of a storm rolling in over the weekend dominated the morning news. It foreshadowed a dramatic change in the weather, as the last two months had been unusually warm. Now, meteorologists were urging Mainers to keep an eye on updates about a powerful low-pressure system, fueled partly by moisture from the remnants of Tropical Storm Philippe merging with a cold front from the Midwest.

El had been glued to the television all morning, flipping from one station to the next to "get ahead of the storm." El's behavior was a complete about-face from the day before. She had turned off the news because she didn't want to hear anything more about the poor girl found dead in a lumberyard.

El's focus on the potential nor'easter foreshadowed her conversation with Jessica when Dustin came to get her to retrieve the Jeep. She told Jessica to stop by Shaw's and pick up a long list of provisions. Jessica knew the list by heart: canned goods, batteries, toilet paper, wine, water, and the usual paranoia.

Jessica promised her mom that she would stop by the store, but wasn't going to stop by Shaw's. The Hannaford Supermarket was cheaper and closer to the garage that had replaced a flat tire on her Jeep and the spare. She didn't want to leave her mom alone in the house any longer than she had to, with Kyle lurking around out there somewhere and now some killer on the streets.

The ride over to the garage was mostly quiet; it had been awkward since Jessica had accused Dustin of looking at her phone while she was throwing up in the porta-potty. She had told him it was the wrong number, but it was a text from Kyle with a video attachment. The video was a sex tape she never knew he recorded. It was from the night Kyle had deceived her and invited a stranger into their bedroom.

This was the kind of tape that Jessica knew would get her fired if Kyle followed through on his threat to send it to Kennedy Sloane, especially after being warned by Keiko. So while her mom was busy monitoring the weather, Jessica had spent most of the day waiting for the boot to drop. There was a good chance it would. He had done the same thing to his former girlfriend.

"You're not very talkative today," Dustin said early into the ride.

"Just tired," she said, staring out past the smear on the window.

By the time they reached the garage, the tension between Jessica and Dustin had dissipated. She decided there was no way he could look her in the face had he seen that video. But other than walking on eggshells around her, it was the same old Dustin she had gotten reacquainted with this week. He was strong, safe, handsome, and charming.

"El's list sounds like my dad's list," Dustin said, trying again. "Do you mind if I tag along to the store?"

"I'm only going to be in and out," she said before the urgency in his expression convinced her to reconsider. "All right, I wouldn't mind the company."

"Love the quality. Trust the save," Dustin said, reciting the grocery's tagline to lighten the mood.

"Very funny," Jessica said. "You're a junior advertising executive's dream come true."

The banter helped ease her mind, but Jessica was still on guard, especially after inspecting the damage done to the old tires. The punctures were in different locations but too similar to be an accident. The young mechanic said it looked like somebody took a plasterboard punch to them.

"I'm not saying that's what it was," the kid said, snapping gum and pulling one earbud out of his ear. "Somebody would have to be pretty strong to manage it, like bench pressing two hundred and fifty pounds or stronger."

Jessica didn't say it, but Kyle was easily that strong. He spent much of his free time at the gym, maxing out above three hundred. Not that it mattered. Jessica already knew who did it. Kyle was behind all her problems, and they were only getting worse.

She had read the police reports of the last woman he terrorized, driving his truck through her neighborhood, lingering at a neighbor's house three doors down, spamming her email with burial insurance, and lighting up her social media accounts to brand her a cheater. Valerie's plight lived like a phantom in Jessica's head because it was happening all over again, except it was happening to her this time. And the more she thought about it, the more having Dustin at the store made sense.

When they arrived, Hannaford's was packed. As much as she and Dustin made fun of their parents, they knew that a nor'easter was serious business. Their winds could reach hurricane-force speeds and tear up trees, houses, and power lines. Worse, they didn't pass by over an area in a few hours. They could last days.

Make fun of an old-timer's insistence on preparedness, and they'd likely tell you about the Halloween storm of 1991 that killed thirteen people and resulted in more than $200 million in destruction along the Massachusetts and Maine coastline. It was etched into their cultural memories, even those of locals like Jessica and Dustin, who were born after it happened.

Inside the store, they faced a different kind of storm. The aisles were packed with Mainers, many of them older, swirling about the store and crashing up against the shelves that mattered most. Those with lists were cleaning out the canned soups first. Experience told Jessica the tuna would be next. Single moms with their children were bunching up in the cereal aisle, checking the boxes against their coupons.

"This is nuts," Dustin said. "I can't remember it being this bad."

"It's all this warm, dry weather," said an old man in a flannel coat and cap, carrying an odd combo of batteries and kerosene. "It's going to snap those trees up like nothing. Mark my words."

Jessica would have marked them, but something caught her attention out of the corner of her eye. When she turned around, she saw the flash of a large man in a black hoodie with a back and shoulders as broad as Kyle's. At first, she doubted herself, thinking her mind was playing tricks on her. But then again, this was precisely the kind of trick he did, making his presence felt.

"Hey, watch the carts," she told Dustin behind her. "I just need to check something out."

"Are you sure?" he asked. "I can go with you or get what you need."

"No, it's okay," she said. "It could be nothing."

She walked briskly to the aisle where she saw him and turned down it. As she did, it looked like the same large man was turning the corner again. Seeing him duck around made her furious, and the sudden rush of anger surprised her. Maybe it was the amount of people in the store, but she wasn't afraid as much as she was angry. She picked up her pace to catch him. If she did, she would give him a piece of her mind.

By the time she reached the end of the aisle, Jessica was nearly jogging. Her heart pounded, sure that Kyle was taunting her again. She clenched her fists and gulped air as she prepared for a confrontation.

She rounded the end deck, braced for a fight, and plowed into a thin woman with a handheld basket, sending some processed meats, cheese, chips, and a loaf of bread flying.

The woman screamed at her. "Watch where you're going, you dumb bitch!"

"Oh, I'm so sorry," Jessica said, stopping her pursuit and bending down to pick up some of the items that spilled out.

She came up with a summer sausage and two candy bars, and the woman in torn jeans stood up with a can of lima beans. Her skin had a gray tinge, and there were dark circles under her eyes, but Jessica knew her.

"Stacy?" Jessica asked. "It's me, Jessica. What are you doing here?"

"I should ask you that question," Stacy said. "You strike me as a Shaw's shopper."

"I just picked up my Jeep from a garage near here," she said, as if that explained everything. "Wow, I haven't seen you in years."

"Get a good look, then," Stacy said, disinterested. "Maybe you can gloat."

"How are you? How's your family? Your sister?"

"Look, Jessica," Stacy said. "I'm fine. They're fine. You're fine. We got nothing else to talk about, so let's just move on. Okay?"

"No, wait, I'm here with Dustin," she said. "Let me get him."

"Dustin Fields?" Stacy asked, her words laced with disgust. "Why on earth would you be with him?"

"We ran into each other earlier this week," Jessica said, motioning to the aisle's end. "Look, he's right over there."

"Over there?" Stacy said, squinting. "What are you smoking?"

Jessica looked back. She thought he was right there, navigating their carts.

"Sorry," Jessica said. "He was just there."

"Good thing he isn't," Stacy said. "I'd scratch his eyes right out of his head."

Jessica looked at her, eyebrows knitted in confusion. Stacy's face hardened.

"Oh, you don't know? Billy never told you? Dustin Fields raped me."

"What are you talking about?" Jessica took a step back.

"That night at the party? You know, the last one we ever went to together? Dustin roofied me and then raped me. I'm surprised Billy never told you."

Jessica looked back toward the carts to see if she could spot Dustin. He wasn't anywhere in sight.

"Maybe I shouldn't be surprised Billy never told you," Stacy said, becoming more agitated as she continued. "He came to see me the other day, you know. He came to apologize. But I set him straight. I didn't need his apology any more than he needed my forgiveness. We all get what we get."

"I don't understand. Why would Billy apologize?"

"Because he was there," said Stacy. "He tried to stop it but failed. Oh, wow. You really don't know any of this. Little Miss Perfect. You are so stupid, Jessica. Why do you think Dustin jacked up Billy's leg?"

"Coach Dawson was teaching head-down tactics, and he flipped the field," she said. "Everybody knows that. That's why they eventually let him go."

"Yeah, and I've got a bridge in Brooklyn to sell you. You live in New York now. Maybe you've seen it," Stacy said. "You do live there now, don't you?"

Jessica's mind whirled around what she was saying. It couldn't be true. All she had to do was ask Dustin, and he'd set everything straight.

"Earth to Jessica?"

"Sorry," Jessica said. "You caught me by surprise."

"Well, you caught me by surprise seven years ago," she said. "I know we were friends because Billy and Dustin were friends, but I kind of looked up to you as my best friend until you never even bothered to reach out to me. Not once, Jessica. Not a call. Not a text. Not a snap. Not a fine how-de-doo at school in the hall."

Jessica tried to think back to high school. She heard what Stacy was saying but didn't remember it that way. She remembered Stacy ghosting everyone after breaking up with Dustin. A few days after that, nobody had time to think about it as everyone rallied around Billy before the pain meds and coaching accusations started to take their toll. It was all muddled.

"Oh, and by the way, I don't go by Stacy no more," she said. "My name is Sarah. Now, kindly get out of my way and be more careful. Even us EBT folks got to eat."

Stacy pushed past Jessica, leaving her there, stunned, in the aisle. She was still holding a bag of Stacy's chips, forgotten during the clipped conversation.

Jessica turned back toward the shopping carts, now abandoned. She tugged her cell phone out of her back pocket and texted Dustin.

Hey, where did you go?

She stood by the carts, wondering what to do. Where did he go? Was he coming back? An ellipsis blinked on her phone.

Sorry. My dad called and I had to run out.

What about your stuff?

All good. Just leave it.

Jessica looked at his cart. It was unbelievable to think he wasn't coming back, especially now. She needed him to be here, explaining away all the crazy talk. She closed her eyes, thinking, and decided to ask him.

What happened between you and Stacy?

He started to type. Then he stopped and started again.

Don't believe anything that crazy bitch says. She's a meth head.

Jessica read the message twice. He had seen Stacy and bailed. Why?

I'll call you later and explain. Got to go.

She texted him a heart, and he gave it a thumbs-up. Then she put the phone away and stood there trying to wrap her head around everything. If any of it was even close to true, she would have to rewrite her entire high school memories as she knew them. And if all of it was true, it would change everything.

Jessica looked at the carts again and slowly pulled hers away from the one Dustin left behind. She didn't have time to think about it anymore. She had to get home.

CHAPTER 25

PRIME SUSPECT

Billy sat in interview room two of the Augusta Police Station, sipping the sour coffee Detective Metcliff had brought in from some out-of-the-way break room. Metcliff warned Billy about the coffee when he offered it, joking that he had a predilection for finding the worst coffee in Augusta because it helped keep him grounded. APD coffee, he claimed, was the worst.

Under normal circumstances, Billy wouldn't drink coffee in the late afternoon, but he had slept in late to clear the hangover from his head before coming into the station. So he gulped down the first drink before realizing that was a mistake. What it lacked in taste it made up for in grounding him as Metcliff suggested.

Sitting at a gray table in a gray room was the last place he wanted to be. As shaken as he was over Autumn, he would have rather left for the quarry with Conner than sleep a few more hours. The jobsite needed him to be there. The high-level clouds he saw while driving over reinforced what the rest of Augusta knew. The warm air and mild weather were a false calm.

"Before we start, I need you to sign this," Metcliff said, sliding a piece of paper and pen toward Billy.

"And what's this?" Billy said, pulling the paper toward him.

"They're your Miranda rights," Metcliff said. "I need you to acknowledge that you understand your rights."

"I thought you just wanted to ask some questions. Give a statement."

"You're not under arrest," he said. "But it's important you understand your rights because I'm going to ask you questions about your relationship with the victim."

"Her name is Autumn," Billy said, correcting him.

"I apologize," Metcliff said. "You're free to ask for a lawyer or leave anytime."

Billy spun the paper around and squinted at it in the dim light. He picked up the pen and signed.

"But that wouldn't look good. I got it," Billy said. "Where's Derrik?"

"Technically, Officer Mills isn't assigned to this case," said Metcliff. "But with the department stretched thin, doubly so in preparation for a storm, he is assisting me. I suspect he'll show up sometime after seeing to his normal duties."

"You're taping this?" Billy said, motioning to the mirror behind the detective.

"Yes, Billy. You ready?" Metcliff's question was met with a nod. "I know we've asked you some of this before, but I need it as part of a formal statement. Can you tell me about your relationship with Miss Larkstrom?"

"Autumn," Billy said, emphasizing her name again. "We started dating this year. We met on New Year's Eve, and she moved in with me around April."

"But she wasn't living with you now, correct?"

"Yes and no. She hasn't been living with me for a few weeks, but Autumn never completely moved out," Billy said. "She was supposed to move back in yesterday."

"You said she hasn't lived with you for a few weeks," Metcliff said, more methodic in his approach than the questions he asked Billy at the house. "Why did she move out? You had a fight?"

"Something like that," Billy said, impatience undercutting his response. "It was a misunderstanding more than anything. Look, are all your questions going to be like this? Because I have something to tell you."

Metcliff winced. Billy caught him off guard. He gestured for Billy to go ahead.

Billy reached into an inside pocket of his flannel jacket and pulled out the broken bangle. He put it on the table and drew his hand back across the cold surface.

"A guy named Kyle Brondi gave this to me last night. He's a New York cop. I met him at the Bear Paw last Friday," Billy said. "You know what it is, right? It's part of the broken bangle you found at the scene. I gave it to Autumn the night before."

Metcliff stiffened and stood up, looking at the bracelet as if it were a time bomb. He walked over to a small wall-mounted cabinet and unlocked it, producing gloves and a small evidence bag.

"You said you got this last night in Manchester?" Metcliff said, studying the bangle for its secrets before bagging it.

"I never said I was in Manchester," Billy said. His head started throbbing again. He was taking a big chance here, not knowing who was pulling the strings.

"No, Officer Mills told me you were in Manchester," Metcliff said. "He said you thought you saw somebody at the Woodshed, where you shouldn't have been."

"Give me a break. It's seven miles out," Billy said, irritation cutting his voice.

Metcliff's scolding irritated him, but Derrik's betrayal made it worse. He thought Derrik said he was off duty last night.

"Let's get back to what's important. You're saying a New York cop gave you evidence from a crime scene in Augusta while you were in Manchester?" Metcliff said, slipping on the latex gloves and carefully placing the bracelet in the bag with practiced care. "This is that mystery intruder you mentioned yesterday morning?"

"Yes," Billy said. "If you get Brondi, you get Autumn's killer."

"Wait right here," Metcliff said, snapping the evidence bag shut. "You'll have to be patient. This may take longer than a bad cup of coffee."

As Metcliff left the room, Billy stared at the empty table. The bangle was gone. It was the last gift he ever bought her. Before the pain of his loss could seize him again, he took another gulp of coffee. It was hot and black and tasted like cardboard. He didn't want to lose it with a camera humming hot behind the glass.

To distract himself, he pulled out his phone. Andrea had called again. He never called her back last night. She might have another hint about the involvement of the Fields family, or maybe she wanted to check up on him.

"You can't drink the pain away," she would quip.

"I can try," he would have told her, warm and dry like the weather.

He looked at the mirror and decided to put the phone back in his pocket. He didn't know the protocol anyway. Metcliff didn't mention phones, but Billy was pretty sure he shouldn't place a call.

The door opened, and Derrik stepped inside. He was in uniform again and paced the room. Billy still didn't know why he'd been at the Woodshed last night.

"What is this? You're not a running back anymore, Diesel?" Billy said sarcastically. "You here to tackle me again?"

"You're not funny, Billy," Derrik said. "This is serious."

Billy shrugged. "You said you were off duty like it was a favor to me."

"I said I followed you for your safety," Derrik said. "A police officer is never off duty. I had to report your altercation last night. Besides, it would have gone sideways if I didn't report it and someone else did."

"I didn't get the memo," said Billy. "If I had, I would have told him."

"You can sit there and try to be cute all you want, but you just walked into a police station with evidence from a crime scene."

"Yeah, and I told Metcliff who gave it to me," Billy said. "What's the problem?"

"I would call that a fumble," said Derrik. "You just put yourself at the crime scene. Odds are, you just made yourself a suspect."

Billy never considered it as a possibility. He was normally steadfast when he was sober, but now it was apparent he was slipping. The traumas of the past week were piling up.

"What was I supposed to do? Keep it and have it incriminate me later?"

The door opened and Metcliff walked into the room, hands on hips. He looked down at Billy, pushing his chest and stomach out, making the skin bunch up around his neck. He was frowning. Billy couldn't tell if Metcliff was unhappy with him or the added workload.

"I've got someone checking with NYPD," he said. "Why don't you describe Brondi and his connection to you and Autumn. And Billy, don't leave anything out this time."

"I don't remember as many details as I would like," said Billy. "It's the cigarette smell that stuck with me. Other than that, I'd say he was a big guy, maybe an inch taller than me, so six foot two, built like a bear, all arms and broad shoulders. Close-cropped hair, like a military haircut. He had the start of a goatee. You know, tight and neat?"

"Any tattoos or scars, something that made him stand out?" Derrik asked.

Looking over Metcliff's shoulder, he could almost see Kyle's reflection in the mirror, an apparition coming at him out of the haze and shadows. Kyle was grinning at him from the crowd in the Woodshed. He was pinching the butt of a cigarette outside the Paw. He was watching Billy drugged on the couch and laughing at him for being a sap and a sucker.

"I can tell you I didn't like the guy," Billy said. "Andrea showed me the texts I sent her that night when I was stuck at the bar with him. It's pretty clear I didn't want him to take me home."

"Why you?" Metcliff said. "You're a good-sized scrapper."

"I was an easy mark that night, I guess," Billy said. "I had just run into my girlfriend from high school, and it hit me funny. Charlie could tell. He tried to cut me off, and this cop came in like a knight in shining armor. 'Oh, it's okay. I got him,' he says."

Metcliff and Derrik exchanged a look. Metcliff was taking notes, clicking his pen.

"I don't remember anything after that," said Billy. "It hit me so hard that Andrea told me to go into Quick Care the next day. The nurse told me I was roofied and should check my house to see if something was missing."

"Was there?" Metcliff.

"Not that I could tell," Billy said. "Anyway, Andrea's the one who got the name from Charlie. I thought it was Dale, but the tab was under Kyle Brondi."

"So, what's your theory?" Metcliff asked, punctuating it with another click. "You think he's some psycho who targeted you and then went after Autumn?"

Billy thought about Andrea's theory about the Fields family and decided against sharing it. If he went down that road, everything sounded even crazier. This idea that Brondi was a dirty cop hired to cover up a rape that happened seven years ago wouldn't do him any good. It might land him behind bars.

"I wasn't sure before," Billy said. "Last night suggests something like that."

"Or maybe it's clear," Metcliff said. "A quarry grunt couldn't take it when his girl left him."

Billy clenched his jaw, but he knew the jab was to see how he would react. Billy wasn't going to give him the satisfaction. This wasn't a bar, and he wasn't drunk.

"Hey, Ben," Derrik said gently. "We don't believe that, do we? Plenty of plays need to be called before that's our angle. If there is a credit card receipt at the Bear Paw, this mystery intruder obviously exists."

"You're right. We have to pull any surveillance footage from the Woodshed, too. Maybe we'll get lucky," he said to Derrik. "You didn't see anyone?"

"I only saw the guy Billy punched by mistake," Derrik said. "The place was packed. His friend saw a big guy leave in a hurry, but everybody blends in there."

"So, what?" Billy said. "You guys believe me?"

"The bracelet is a big deal. The lab will get it on Monday," said Metcliff. "I don't know if this Brondi guy left any DNA on it, but I know yours is all over it."

"There's plenty to check into, but I'm afraid if this storm comes in like they say, then it's going to slow things down," Derrik said. "Maybe it will give you time to regroup, Billy."

There was a knock at the door, and Metcliff told them to enter. With the door open, Billy could hear radio chatter as the department prepared to shift gears from crime fighters to first responders. An officer came in and whispered something in Metcliff's ear.

"NYPD doesn't have a police officer named Brondi," Metcliff said, clicking his pen closed and tossing it on the table. "So, Billy, I suggest you prep for the storm, go home, don't leave town for real this time, and get a lawyer."

"If anything comes to mind before then, give me a call," Derrik said and flipped Billy a card. "My direct number is on it. The storm will keep us busy, but we're still going to bring this killer to justice."

Billy picked up the card, but all he could think about were the last three words that Metcliff said. *Get a lawyer.*

CHAPTER 26

WHITE LIES

Andrea stood on the porch of the Michaud residence and gently knocked on the door. It was her last task in a long day of dead ends. Every proverbial door she had knocked on to identify Kyle Brondi as an NYPD police officer came up empty, so she'd decided to knock on this one.

If she couldn't break Autumn's murder wide open, at least she would be able to put Dustin's DUI story to bed. Even without the 911 recording, a change in Jessica's story could be the linchpin, enough to call Dustin or William Fields for comment.

She could easily write the story tomorrow and send District Attorney Mahoney an advance copy, forcing him to backpedal on offering Dustin a wet reckless plea. If he didn't, it would look like he was unjustly protecting one of the most influential families in Augusta. A story like that would easily be used by whomever ran against him in the next election cycle.

Newspapers might have been struggling in the age of new media, but they still had teeth. After trying to stonewall her at the hospital and then calling her editor, Mahoney deserved a refresher no matter how much she liked him. She almost felt guilty.

She knocked on the door again and took a step back like a solicitor after sunset. This time, someone inside turned on the porch light. As the front door opened and then the storm door cracked, Andrea felt a sudden chill in the air as a prelude to the storm everybody expected to arrive tomorrow. *Keep an eye on updates*, Andrea reminded herself.

"Can I help you?" Jessica said, tilting her head as if to hear better between the narrow opening. Andrea noted that Jessica was still beautiful, even if she looked tired.

"Jessica, it's me. Andrea," she said. "Andrea Kearney from high school."

"Andrea?" Jessica said, trying to place the name. "Billy's friend after the football accident? The school reporter?"

Andrea didn't know what she expected coming here, but she was glad it wasn't flattery. Jessica had always been distant from her, and it wasn't easy to reconcile that this woman played a much larger role in Andrea's life because of Billy and not any tangible connection. Yet in Jessica's life, Andrea was part of the background.

"The *Kennebec Journal* now," said Andrea. "That's why I'm here. Mind if I come in and ask you a few questions?"

"Yes, sorry, I do," Jessica said as she came out on the porch. "My mom's sleeping on the couch. I don't want to wake her up."

"Oh, right. How is she doing?"

"Honestly, some days better than I am, I think," Jessica said with a little laugh. "You said you had some questions for me? I already talked to one reporter from your paper yesterday. About the prowler under the porch? There's nothing new to report."

"Oh, right. That's so terrifying. How are you holding up?"

"We're doing better now," Jessica said. "The police have been so supportive through all this. They send a car around every now and again."

Andrea let the partial lie slide, not wanting to bring up the marijuana citation until later in the conversation. She still made a mental note. Jessica was a practiced liar.

"So good to hear," Andrea said. "There are a lot of great officers with the APD these days. In fact, I wanted to talk to you about one of them."

"Oh?" Jessica said. "I don't know if I can help you. Several have stopped by, and I can't seem to keep them all straight."

"This one you'll remember," Andrea said, setting the hook. "Officer Danny Ouellette? He's the one who arrived first on the scene at the crash you called in last Friday, remember?"

"Yes, I remember. He had a boyish charm about him," Jessica said, trying to find something that might help her retain her cautious, pleasant smile. "Funny thing. He remembered me from a biology class at Windsor High School. What about him?"

"Well, he seems to think you might have misspoke about whether or not the person driving smelled like alcohol," Andrea said, letting it fall from her lips as smoothly as she might mention the weather. "Any thoughts about that?"

Jessica's smile faded, waving a hand at two autumnal moths attracted to the light. They ignored her and continued to thud against its casing.

"What now?"

"He's not the only one wondering," Andrea said, pen poised over her notepad. "I can't seem to find anyone who remembers it the way you do. Not the medics or nurses or doctors. Certainly not the lab tech paid five hundred dollars to make the BAC test inadmissible."

Jessica blinked, and her lips rolled back. Andrea could see it. Mentioning the bribe had hooked Jessica, and it was time to reel her in for the prize.

"Before you answer me, I might mention that your statement at the scene, if proven false, could land you in jail," said Andrea.

"That's hefty, especially with a citation for possession. I've seen this before. The judge will say it's a pattern."

"How do you know about that?" Jessica asked, retreating to the door and placing her hand on the handle.

Andrea could have kicked herself. She had her and pulled the line too hard. She would only have one chance to salvage it.

"Think carefully before you go back inside," Andrea said, hoping to yank her back. "If I write the story I have, the police will have no choice but to investigate you. What else might they find out?"

Jessica paused at the door, weighing her options. Her rigid shoulders relaxed as she seemed to make a decision.

"It was almost a week ago," Jessica said. "It was late and I was just driving home from the Bear Paw. I saw Billy there, you know. Are you two still friends?"

Andrea decided to follow the deflection, anticipating Jessica would bolt inside if she were needled any more. Andrea had her story, but a confession was stronger than an evasion.

"We've become close since high school, sure," Andrea said. "Why do you ask?"

"I'll answer your question, but I want you to answer mine first," Jessica said. "Did Billy ever mention something about Stacy Brenner to you?"

The conversation Andrea had with Billy was still fresh in her mind, like a newly scabbed injury. She gathered her thoughts and carefully crafted a response.

"Yeah, he mentioned Stacy. He mentioned all of you back then, how close you all were," Andrea said. "Why do you ask?"

"I ran into her at the grocery store earlier today, literally. I knocked her stuff everywhere." Jessica closed her eyes, remembering. "We chatted for a minute. Can't say she was happy to see me. Did you know she goes by Sarah now?"

"No, I didn't know that," Andrea peered into Jessica's eyes and could tell it was brought up for a reason. "Did she mention anything from high school?"

Jessica hesitated, her hand tightening on the door handle again, the moths dancing around the dim porch light, a tiny but persistent beat as they bounced off the bulb. Jessica shrugged and then settled back into a casual demeanor like this was a friendly high school reunion.

"She brought up some old drama, you know, how we all supposedly ghosted her after she broke up with Dustin when she was the one who ghosted everybody else," Jessica said. "I didn't get in too deep with her, but I thought maybe Billy might have said something."

Andrea smiled despite screaming on the inside. Jessica was dancing around something she wanted to know but wouldn't ask it. Andrea guessed it was about the rape.

"He mentioned a few things," she finally said, hoping to probe more without betraying Billy's confidence. "Did she tell you why she broke up with Dustin?"

Jessica glanced toward the front door as if her mom had woken up and was calling to her from inside. A cool breeze kicked up, and the darkness around the porch seemed to close in as the cloud cover blotted out the moon.

"I don't know. It's probably nothing," Jessica said, retreating. "She looked like she had a rough go. I think it made her bitter. She said if she saw Dustin again, she might even scratch out his eyes."

Andrea was certain Jessica was lying to her. If Stacy had said she wanted to scratch Dustin's eyes out, then Stacy must have confessed. All of her questions made sense now. Jessica wanted someone to verify or refute the claim.

It also meant Jessica hadn't asked Dustin. Was she afraid? Andrea wasn't scared. If she could get Dustin Fields on the phone, she knew exactly what to ask him.

A chill swept across the porch, scattering the moths into the darkness on their sluggish wings, silencing the night's gentle percussion. Andrea decided to cut her losses and pivot to the DUI before she lost out on the reason she was here.

"Sounds like she is carrying a lot from back then," Andrea said, closing her notebook. "I'll have to ask Billy if he's seen her lately. But about that crash again. The report is pretty clear. You said there was no hint of alcohol. Everybody else disagrees. If there is more to the story, now's the time to tell me."

"I already told you it was late, and I was driving home," Jessica said with a sudden surge of confidence. "I hate to admit it, but I had a few drinks at the bar with Billy that night. If I smelled anything, and I'm not saying I did, who's to say it wasn't me?"

"Now there's a great question, Jessica." Andrea smiled. "I might even ask Dustin that myself. He's my next call."

"Good night, Andrea," Jessica said, her face hardening as she slipped inside. The storm door clicked shut, and Andrea could hear the safety chain slip into place.

Her departure left Andrea frustrated but energized. She didn't get the confession, but the evasiveness about the crash was good enough to print, especially her attempt at being clever. As a standalone quote, it was practically the headline.

Once the DUI story ran, Andrea resolved to follow up with Billy about Stacy. Maybe Stacy was ready to come forward and confirm that she was assaulted. Or maybe when Andrea called Dustin, she could tag that question at the end.

Andrea hopped off the last step of the porch and turned back to look at it. Suddenly, part of her wished she was here working on the prowler story. Coupled with Autumn's murder, there wouldn't be a newspaper on any news rack left anywhere.

The porch light turned off, plunging Andrea into darkness. She pulled her phone out of her pocket to light the way back to her car. As she headed toward it, her mind raced ahead. One call to Dustin Fields would do the trick. She could lead by asking him why Jessica was willing to go to jail for him and end with why Stacy Brenner wanted to claw his eyes out.

At this rate, she might break her story before the storm. All thanks to Jessica Michaud's attempt to be clever.

CHAPTER 27

LIVE WIRE

The phone's incessant ringing woke Jessica up from a restless sleep. She had fallen asleep on the couch after the reporter had left and she'd helped her mom upstairs to bed. Nightmarish dreams from high school had plagued her all night.

The worst of them placed her on the sidelines of the Windsor High School football field. She had forgotten her Spanx, and for some reason, the team managers couldn't find any backups in her size.

She tried to persevere and perform anyway, sticking to the safest cheers until the coach forced her to be the flyer. She executed the stunt perfectly, but not without drawing unwanted attention. Everyone in the stands and on the field stopped what they were doing and looked at her.

Jessica tumbled off the couch and stumbled toward the phone. It was still dark. The sun hadn't even started its ascent. Her mom, thankfully, was still asleep upstairs.

"Hello?" Her voice was dry and raspy, the sleep shaking off her vocal cords.

"Jessica?" It was Dustin.

"Dustin? Why are you calling so early?" Jessica asked, peering at her mom's digital clock on the bookshelf. "It's barely five."

"I'm calling because I want to know why you did it."

"Did what?" Jessica asked.

"Why did you talk to that, that snoop?" His voice hot and harsh.

"What?"

"The reporter, Andrea Kearney," he said. "She called and asked me why you were willing to go to jail for me. Go to jail for me? What is she even talking about?"

"Slow down and give me a minute," Jessica said, trying to clear her head. "Yes, she was here last night. She tried to intimidate me, Dustin. She said everyone says you smelled like alcohol except me."

"So, what?" he asked, cutting her off. "Why did you change your statement?"

"No, I didn't change it. You've got to believe me."

"You have no idea what you've done," Dustin said, every word strained. "I can't afford this kind of attention right now, and you go ahead and do the one thing I asked you not to do. I said don't talk about the crash. Why? Is it because of what the meth head said? I told you not to believe her."

He was yelling now, and Jessica held the phone away from her ear. The escalating anger in his voice reminded her of Kyle coming home to their apartment after a bad day. She was home, reading a romantasy on the couch with her feet kicked over one arm.

A thunderclap suddenly broke the quiet. Kyle burst into their apartment and yelled something about needing a drink. She ignored it until he stormed out of the kitchen, asking why she didn't take out the trash before he got home. He knocked her feet off their perch, startling her when he grabbed one ankle and dragged her into the kitchen to get the job done.

"That night Stacy is talking about? You need to know what happened so bad, I'll tell you. She got smashed, came onto me, and we went upstairs like we had done dozens of times before." He was screaming it. "Except the next day, she hits me with this victim bullshit. She tells me she was not herself, like somebody must have drugged her or something. That it was my fault, not her fault for playing along."

The words burned her ears. His accusations were a mirror image of those used by Kyle to explain his actions. The stranger in the bedroom was her fault for playing along. The cigarette burns on the tender part of her skin, her doing. The bruise on her breast because she wouldn't fetch him a beer on command, justified.

"This is how you repay me after everything I've done for you over the last few days," he said, hissing. "Every time something goes wrong, I've been there for you."

"I don't know what she told you, but she's lying, Dustin," Jessica said, trying to make her case, but there was no use. He wasn't hearing her.

"She's running the story tomorrow in the Sunday paper," he said. "Guess whose quote is in the headline? 'If I smelled anything, who's to say it wasn't me?' Sound familiar?"

"I didn't say it like that," Jessica said, as if trying to fend off the punches.

"You need to get something straight right now. If you are called to testify, you better stick to what you said that night and not whatever this crackpot reporter put in that pea-brain head of yours," Dustin roared. "And if I lose my connection in Nashua over this, you can mark my words, Jess. I will bury you."

His choice of words struck a chord. Buried on Sunday was the next line in Kyle's favorite narrative. It was always the end of everything.

"Dustin," Jessica said in a broken whisper, "I didn't tell her anything. I was trying to protect you. You have to believe me. You have to."

He didn't respond. She thought he might have hung up at first but then heard his heavy, rasping breath on the other end of the phone. Maybe he had heard her.

"Look, Jess, I'm sorry," he said, quieter and controlled but cold. "Imagine having your deepest, darkest secrets suddenly exposed to the world. Do you have any idea how that might make you feel?"

She did. And every hour Kyle held off from making good on his threat to release the video he had secretly taped was a reprieve.

"Well, maybe you should," he said. "Maybe then you wouldn't be so selfish to think of yourself first all the time, just like you did in high school. I always told Billy you weren't worth a cup of spit. I bet he believes me now."

She let the phone fall from her hand when he hung up. Her head felt heavy and swollen, pummeled by a man who didn't sound anything like one who had made her feel safe for the first time in months. Did she look so vulnerable that she attracted abusive men? Was she such a bad person that she deserved them?

Jessica had read plenty of articles about it. So many of them claimed that her mind wanted to find a safe and familiar place. But that never made any sense to her. Her dad was such a strong, positive presence in her life before he died. He was the one who encouraged her, challenged her to try out for cheerleading when she was too scared, and introduced her to new experiences that made her feel strong.

She thought she had found those kinds of men but never made them happy or showed them who she really was. The only man who ever came close to anything like that was Billy, and she pushed him away because he crumbled after the accident. Dustin had said it was kismet that they met again. Maybe it was karma, but not in the way he thought. Maybe she was being punished for abandoning Billy.

Jessica sat on the floor, crying. The phone still dangled from its old wire cord, the fast busy signal sounding far away. One of the living room lights flickered to life.

"Jess? Jess, honey," El said, voice rising in the background. "Are you okay?"

"No, Mom, I'm not," she said.

Her mom placed one hand on her shoulder and hung up the phone with the other. Then she gave Jessica's T-shirt a gentle tug.

"Come on, get up," El said. "I can't get down there with you, so you'll have to get up and come over to the couch. Then you can tell me everything. I think it's time."

El led Jessica to the couch, guiding her to sit together like they used to when she was eight. Jessica didn't know where to begin, so she started with Dustin, telling her mom that a reporter had come by last night and threatened her. And then, this morning, the reporter must have lied to Dustin.

El told her not to worry. If it was meant to be, it would all work out. Dustin would come around when he learned the truth. But that wasn't what was eating at Jessica. It was the opposite. His temper reminded her of cracks on the Kennebec when it froze over. Everyone knew there were dangerous currents underneath, but she always felt compelled to walk out on the ice anyway.

Except, she wasn't talking about Dustin anymore. She was talking about a man she met in New York named Kyle. He was the reason she wanted to come home to Augusta even before El had told her about the cancer.

"The first thing you need to know is that this isn't your fault," said El, running her fingers through Jessica's hair as if it were still as long as it was in high school. "You didn't choose an abusive partner in New York. He chose you. The choice you made is when you chose to leave him."

"I'm just afraid, Mom," she said. "I didn't mean to bring these problems home. I should have known he would follow me, but I didn't want to believe it."

"It took a lot of courage to leave and a lot of courage to tell me about it," El said. "Now I need you to stay strong. I think it's time you told the police."

"Maybe," Jessica said. "I'm just afraid if I report him, it will make everything worse. Oh my God, what if he tried to hurt you?"

"He's not coming after me," El said. "Even if he did, so what? It won't change anything. Don't let him use me to keep you quiet."

"It's not just that," Jessica said. "The cops won't listen. Kyle works in law enforcement. He knows how to manipulate the system. That's why he planted the drugs on me. We caught onto his hiding place under the porch, and planting the drugs was the punishment for calling the police."

"When your father was alive, there was a neighbor who came to him about being abused by her husband. You might remember her, Mrs. Blondeau," El said, squeezing her daughter's shoulder. "She didn't want to go to the police either. So he suggested that they start out by writing everything down. Maybe you and I could do that. We'll start by writing everything down before we decide on the next step."

"Yes, I think I can do that," Jessica said, squeezing her mom's hand in return. "Let me get a notepad from the kitchen."

Jessica started toward the kitchen when the phone rang again. Her first reaction was to stare at it, unsure if she should answer it. What if it was Dustin again? She didn't know if she could take another round of his fury. It rang again.

"Jess, do you want me to get it?" Her mom called from the living room.

"No, I got it," she said, hesitating and picking up the receiver. "Michaud residence."

"Jessica, it's Keiko," Keiko said, clipped and nearly out of breath.

"Keiko?" Jessica said. "It's so early. Is everything okay?"

"No, Jessica. It's not," Keiko said. "I was called in this morning because we have an emergency. It seems somebody sent a rather repulsive video to everyone in the office."

"Everyone?" Jessica said, feeling like the world was shifting under her feet.

"Everyone and all our clients," Keiko said. "We're doing the best we can to contain the damage, but it's bad, Jessica. Real bad."

"What does that mean?"

"You might want to check your socials," said Keiko. "I think somebody loaded it up and tagged your accounts."

Jessica's stomach dropped. She wouldn't be able to check her socials at the house. She would have to find another location.

"Jessica, I don't have time to talk to you about this," said Keiko, exhaling sharply. "But there's nothing I can do. We have to let you go. Your last check will be directly deposited into your account."

Keiko didn't wait for Jessica to respond. She hung up, leaving Jessica holding the phone with her head on the wall to steady herself. Her mom was calling from the other room, asking if everything was all right. It wasn't. Jessica felt like her world was ending.

Outside, the world was not ending. It was only beginning as clouds continued to roll in, an eerie gray gauze that muted the sunrise. Remnants from Tropical Storm Philippe and the cold front from the Midwest were making their presence known. Weather reports said to brace for a major storm, with rain starting around noon.

CHAPTER 28

EVEN TRADE

When Andrea arrived, District Attorney David Mahoney was sitting at a small table against the far wall of the yellow wainscoted wall of Slates Bakery. She had been reluctant to meet him because it could only mean one thing. He didn't like the advanced copy of the story the *Kennebec Journal* would publish tomorrow.

Andrea saw him as soon as she opened the front door. He was hunched over a large roast beef sandwich with a side of chips, looking out of place under the eclectic collection of local art that filled almost every inch of wall space above the high chair rail. She armed herself with the first question. Why were they meeting at such an off-the-radar spot?

"Afternoon, Ms. Kearney," Mahoney said, not looking up. "Have a seat."

"If we would have met in your office, I would have told you I'd rather stand," Andrea said, grabbing the chair opposite him. "Why Hallowell and not State Lunch?"

"Maybe I wanted someplace where we could talk without being overheard," he said with a shrug. "Or maybe I'm just fond of the roast beef. Want something? I'm buying."

"No, I'm not expecting to stay long enough to eat because I have a story to finish," she said. "But you go ahead. It looks good, if not on the heavy side for lunch."

"Look outside," Mahoney said with a smirk of approval as if they were friends again. "Those clouds are about to open up out there, and when they do, there is no telling when I'm going to have a chance to sit down and eat again."

"Don't tell me you're on a call with Kennebec County's EMA," Andrea said, chuckling. "You trying to earn a Boy Scout merit badge or just earn some karma points for running interference for William Fields?"

Andrea thought she was on a roll, but Mahoney didn't find that funny. He scowled at her, giving her a flash of the enemy she'd made at the hospital. She recognized it for what it was. This meeting could go either way.

"This is the second Saturday you interrupted me from time with the family," Mahoney said. "I'm going to forgive you for it, but I expect a little less sarcasm and a little more grace."

The front door banged, glass rattling as an older couple came in. The man was holding a bush hat to his head of thinning hair. The woman had a scarf tied tightly to her head. They laughed, embarrassed that a gust of wind had caught them off guard.

"How bad do you think it's going to be?" Andrea said, momentarily distracted.

"Two to three inches of rain, maybe," Mahoney said. "It's the wind that has everybody worked up. Some folks at the EMA are saying gusts of sixty or seventy miles per hour. It should keep people distracted for a few days. So, I don't expect anybody will see your exposé tomorrow. Maybe you should wait until, I don't know, Tuesday?"

Andrea chortled at his nerve. Was Mahoney asking for a rain delay?

"I don't think so," said Andrea. "Besides, the next story is even better. What Dustin Fields lacks in character, he makes up for by saying all sorts of stupid things."

"Jessica Michaud broke this wide open for you, huh?"

"Yeah, she's a real peach," Andrea said.

"I'm surprised you didn't make her look better in the piece," Mahoney said. "You made her look almost as bad as me."

"You should meet her sometime," Andrea said. "I bet you two would hit it off."

"All right. Look, I'm just going to come right out and say it," Mahoney said, pausing to take a bite of his sandwich. "I'm asking you for a favor."

"I'm sorry." Andrea smiled. "Did the district attorney just ask me for a favor? I don't even know if I ever added that one to my bucket list to cross off. Why would I do that?"

Mahoney chewed slowly and wiped his face with one hand, which he then wiped on the napkin on his lap. He swallowed and took a drink of soda. Andrea guessed Sprite or 7UP.

"I'm going to do you a favor," Mahoney said.

"You're going to do me a favor?" Andrea said, laughing. "What favor could you possibly do for me? Not call my boss again? How did that work out for you anyway?"

"No, Andrea," Mahoney said, narrowing his eyes. "I'm going to let Billy Stevens enjoy one more weekend of freedom before we arrest him for the suspected murder of Autumn Larkstrom."

"This is a joke, right?" Andrea said. "He didn't kill Autumn. Not a chance."

"Maybe so," Mahoney said. "But we're still going to book him."

"Why?" Andrea said. "To stop me from publishing this story? Come on. This is a puff piece for the likes of the Fields family."

"No, we're bringing Billy in because we can't reconcile how he managed to end up with a piece of evidence from the crime scene," Mahoney said, searching Andrea's face for a reaction. "You didn't know that, did you? Yeah, he came in to give his statement yesterday and tossed a piece of the victim's broken bangle onto the interview table."

Andrea reeled. She hadn't been able to get ahold of Billy since Thursday. She didn't even know what to say. There had to be an explanation, and it was difficult not to reach into her pocket and call Billy to find out what it was and to warn him about the impending arrest.

"You haven't talked to him, I take it," Mahoney said. "The broken bracelet he surrendered, his record of violence, and a clear motive. The department would be negligent not to bring him in while we wait for lab results on the bracelet."

"It's not Billy," Andrea said under her breath. "It's a New York cop named Kyle Brondi."

"Oh, he told us that one, too," said Mahoney. "NYPD doesn't have a Brondi on the payroll."

"You know that?"

"He said that's who gave it to him. Kyle Brondi."

No wonder she kept hitting a wall. Billy and Charlie had been wrong. Brondi wasn't a cop. It was a surprise, but not a shock. Brondi had introduced himself as Dale, but the first name on his credit card was Kyle. Andrea decided to push back.

"No deal," Andrea said. "Not unless you tell me what the hell is going on, and I mean, no holds barred. On the record."

Mahoney leaned back, clearly not expecting her to kick away the offer. He stopped eating and folded his hands on his lap. He ran his tongue over his teeth and dabbed his lip with a napkin, an early warning sign he would try to dazzle her with some legal buffoonery.

"Did you know the sandwich was invented by the fourth Earl of Sandwich in 1762? He was just a guy who wanted a convenient way to eat while playing cards," Mahoney said. "He requested roast beef between two slices of bread, just like the one in front of me. No horseradish, though. That came later. You know what I like best about horseradish?"

"I'm all ears," Andrea said, already impatient.

"Horseradish doesn't have any connection to horses. In fact, if you can believe it, horseradish is poisonous to them. The name horseradish, as best as any can figure, was an English mispronunciation of the German word *meerrettich,* or sea radish."

"And your point?"

"Not everything is always as it seems, Andrea," said Mahoney. "You're sitting across from me thinking you have all the cards, and I admit you do for the game you are playing. But we're not playing the same game. You're playing go fish, and I'm playing contract bridge."

"Mahoney," Andrea said. "I'm going to walk out of that door in thirty seconds."

"This is off the record."

"Fine."

"William Fields called me about a week and a half ago. It seems Dustin ran into some trouble in Texas with the construction company he started in Waco," Mahoney said, his voice dropping to a whisper. "To get out of it, he ordered materials at inflated prices, and his supplier delivered substandard materials."

"Why would he do that?" Andrea leaned in to hear him over the clatter of the window panes as the wind picked up.

"The supplier was giving him a kickback on the overpayment in cash to the construction company. The only problem? He needed a way to clean the money."

"Unbelievable. That's not far off from how his dad made early money," Andrea said, trying to control herself from pulling out a notepad. "So what's the angle? Why did Daddy Fields call you?"

"He offered to set up a meeting with a money-laundering operation in Nashua, some bar called Crabby's," said Mahoney. "In exchange, his kid gets to walk."

"And you guys took it?" Andrea asked, disgust rising in her voice. "Pathetic."

"If you run the DUI story now, this is going to fall apart," Mahoney said, ignoring her. "It took a lot of work to get everyone on board. Multiple local, state, and federal agencies."

"So you are protecting Fields," Andrea said. "He's a Mob informant."

"No, not really," Mahoney said. "Fields has been out of the game for a long time. He's no more connected to the Mob than the Super 8 or the Liberal Cup, where some of them used to hole up. That's why he came to us. Heck, he didn't even tell Dustin about it. He just wants to protect his kid."

"His kid is a menace. He needs to be locked up like an animal. And Daddy Fields hasn't given up all his old habits, like bribing a lab tech."

"Dustin is the oldest," Mahoney said, as if that explained anything.

"Tell that to the women he raped here and in Augusta," Andrea said. "The DUI story was only a warmup."

"You're back to that now, too?"

Andrea held up a thumb and index finger. The space between them was less than an inch.

"The *Kennebec Journal* doesn't pay you enough."

"That's not why I do it, and you know it," Andrea said.

"Andrea," Mahoney said with a sigh. "I'm not asking you to let him go on whatever you want to dig up. I'm asking you to wait a few days, maybe a week. You do that, and I'll give Billy the same courtesy. It's an even trade."

"Not good enough," she said, shaking her head. "I want you to expand your search on Kyle Brondi. I'm getting nowhere, but you shouldn't have that problem with an open murder investigation."

"Anything else?"

"It wouldn't hurt to put two detectives on a murder case," she said.

"I'll see what I can do," Mahoney said.

"And I want an exclusive on Crabby's when it all goes down," Andrea said as an afterthought. "I want it all. It might even get picked up by the national circuit."

"Sure," he said, but he wasn't happy about it. "And maybe you can revisit the DUI story so I don't sound like a total idiot."

"All right, deal," Andrea said. "Does this mean we're friends again?"

"No, Andrea," he said. "I don't make friends with sharks."

"You say that like you mean it, but I think you like me." Andrea smiled as she stood up. "Heck, I'm even a cheap date."

"One more thing, Andrea." His jaw was set. "If it turns out Billy did do it, then we won't have a relationship anymore. Not even a tenuous one."

"He didn't do it," she said and flipped him off.

Andrea turned and marched out the door. The wind was picking up, and it had started to rain. She could only imagine what the weather reports were like now. Reporters were likely buzzing Central Maine Power for interviews, shifting the tone from "stay tuned" to "stock up now."

She turned on her radio to catch an update. Mahoney was right. The National Weather Service had issued a high wind warning and flash flood watch. Central Maine Power was already preparing for a multiple-day restoration effort. The worst of it was expected to hit sometime tomorrow night.

She shook her head and started her car when her phone rang. It was her coworker Daniella. She had the name of the guy who bought the flowers for Jessica. Andrea couldn't believe it. She had to find Billy before the storm broke.

CHAPTER 29

SHATTERED HEARTS

Jessica could barely make out the sun when she looked outside as part of her hourly patrol. It had been diminished to a muted glow on the western horizon, hidden by the dark clouds and hazy grayness that had appeared yesterday afternoon.

Between the storm, fallout with Dustin, and damaging video, Jessica and El had decided to skip church and hunker down for the day. They unplugged the phone to stop the frantic calls from friends and neighbors, turned on the television as another window on the weather, and huddled on the couch with a bowl of pizza rolls.

They were going to weather the storms together. The real one was a cold front pulling moisture from what was left of Tropical Storm Philippe. The other one cost Jessica her job.

Kyle had done her even dirtier than his threat. He had uploaded it everywhere, making it a spectacle that Jessica could never live down, even after driving over to the nearest restaurant parking lot and deleting every social network account she'd ever opened. Everything was gone now, a lifetime of memories shared across the net.

"Maybe we can make some popcorn and watch a movie later?" Jessica asked her mom as she headed to the bathroom. "How about *The Sandlot*? We haven't watched that one in a while."

"Is that the one with the baseball game under the fireworks?" El asked.

"Yes, that's the one," Jessica said as she headed down the hall.

"Good pick," El said, calling after her. "I could use some summer cheer. You too, I think."

As she closed the door, Jessica reflected on her mom's resilience again. They had made each other a pinkie promise to try their best not to talk about Jessica's troubles or El's cancer for the day, and so far, it had been working. Jessica still made her habitual security rounds with increased frequency, but her mood improved with her mom's theory of familiar insulation.

Jessica noted there wasn't much toilet paper left as she tore a few sheets from the roll. She would have to go to the basement, where her mom kept extra supplies. She was still sitting there, trying to decide whether to wait on the chore or get it over with, when she heard a heavy knock at the front door.

"Mom, don't answer that," Jessica called from the bathroom. "Let me get it."

"What?" her mom called back.

"I said I'll get it!" Jessica said while flushing the toilet.

It was too late. El had opened the front door, and there was the silhouette of a man standing in the entryway. Jessica's heart stopped, eyes frantically searching for anything she had stashed around the house to defend herself and her mom.

"Hey, Jessica," El said with inexplicable brightness. "It's Billy Stevens!"

"Billy?" Jessica felt the tension in her body ease.

"Hello, Jessica," Billy said. "I would have called, but your phone is out."

"We took it off the hook," El said. "Everybody's been calling Jessica because of that video. I just wish they would all go away for a while."

"Video?" Billy said, standing just inside the door, water dripping off him and onto the floor.

"You haven't seen it?" El said. "That's a small miracle. Why don't you come in?"

"No," Billy said. "I can't stay if I'm going to make it home before it gets worse. Besides, I'm all wet, and I'll just make a mess all over your place."

"You always were a gentleman," El said, returning to the couch. "Well, don't mind me. I'll get out of the way so you two can talk."

"Why are you here?" Jessica asked him.

"I need to know," Billy said, pursing his lips as if what he had to say was one of the most difficult questions he ever asked. "I need to know who Kyle Brondi is, and I think you know him."

"Where did you hear that name?" Jessica said, her eyes growing wide.

"He's the one who sent those flowers to you, not me," Billy said. "Andrea Kearney got a hold of me about an hour ago. She had been trying for days, I guess. One of her coworkers tracked down the sales receipts from the florist."

"That doesn't make any sense," Jessica said. "He doesn't know anything about me liking dragonflies in high school."

"He does," Billy said. "He was there last Friday at the Bear Paw. He saw us together and has been making my life a living hell ever since."

"What did he do?" Jessica asked.

"I can't even get into all that right now," Billy said. "I just want to know how you know this cop and where I can find him."

"Cop?" Jessica said. "Kyle's not a cop. He's a corrections officer."

"Corrections officer?" Billy narrowed his eyes.

"Yes, he's a New York corrections officer," she said. "He's also ex-military. Well, discharged for insubordination and fighting. My point is that he's dangerous. Stay away from him."

"It's too late for that," Billy said, a cloud of anguish coming over his face. "Who is he to you?"

"He's my ex-boyfriend," Jessica said. "I left him, and he came up here to destroy my life."

"Well, he's doing a pretty good job destroying mine," he said. "Do you know where I can find him?"

"What's wrong? What happened?"

"Everything's wrong," Billy said. "He killed my girlfriend."

"Your girlfriend?" Jessica said, bringing her hand up to her chest as the realization hit. "Your girlfriend was the one at the lumberyard?"

"Her name is Autumn," Billy said, choking back tears and looking away.

"I didn't even know you had a girlfriend. I'm so sorry," she said, taking a step toward him. "I can't tell you how sorry I am. It's Kyle. He's crazy, Billy. He said he would hurt everyone I care about and cared about. This is awful. I'm so sorry."

"Sorry? Sorry?" Billy said as the tone in his voice shifted from sorrow to disgust. "You brought this psychopath into my life and say you're sorry? No. That's not going to cut it. I want to know where he is, and then I never want to see you again."

"I don't know where he is," Jessica said. "He could be right outside for all I know."

"Right outside?" Billy glanced over his shoulder.

"You have to understand. He's relentless. He was camped out right under our porch for a few nights, trying to spy on me and my mom. I haven't seen any signs of him since the cops cleared out his setup, but I know he's still around, trolling the neighborhood."

"Can you get ahold of him?" Billy asked. "Flush him out?"

"I can text him," she said. "I can't do it from here, as you know. But I will. I'll help you find him. I will. Come back after the storm passes, and we'll find him together."

"What about right now?" Billy said, biting the inside of his cheek.

"I can't leave my mom right now. Not in this storm."

Billy clenched his fists and looked like he was about to punch the wall. He turned around as if wrestling to control himself and show restraint.

"Fine," he said. "That's just fine, Jess. I'll tell you what. I'll come back. But if he shows up around here or drives by or anything, you call me."

Billy pulled a card from his pants pocket and placed it on the entryway table. He tapped it.

"You call me," he said. "I mean it."

"I will, Billy, I promise," she said, adding an afterthought. "He drives a dark-blue, almost black Ford F-150 with New York plates. If I know him, he's probably staying somewhere along Route 3 or maybe even at a state park. But if you see him, call the cops. I could never forgive myself if something happened to you."

"That would make two of us who will never forgive you," Billy said. "Tell your mom I said good night."

Jessica watched him turn, not even looking at her again, and open the front door. The weather was getting worse by the hour. He pulled up a hood from under his jacket and stepped outside into the blackness, the last remnants of the sun long gone.

Jessica walked over to the entry table and picked up the card. It was white with his name and phone number in black ink. On the other side, it read *Sculptor*. Jessica carried it into the living room, his words still stinging her. She had been the one to end it in high school and had been unkind to him at the bar and quarry, but she never meant to lose him completely.

Her mom was still watching the weather report. While it was impossible to tell looking out the window, newscasters were raising the alarm that this wasn't a typical storm. There would be power outages, structural damage, and flooding, with road closures along I-95 and Augusta's bridges.

"What did Billy want?" El asked. "It's awful reckless driving around out there in this weather."

Jessica couldn't bear to tell her mom the truth. El had already been worked up over the murder of the girl in the lumberyard before the storm eclipsed it as a news story.

"He's looking out for us," Jessica said, setting his card on the coffee table. "Just as you might expect. Hey, how about that movie? I'll make the popcorn first."

"All right, hon," El said. "You should have asked Billy to stick around. He was the one you let get away."

Jessica rolled her eyes despite knowing her mom might have been right. She took a deep breath and walked into the kitchen. The light flickered when she turned it on, and she said a little prayer. The last thing they needed was to lose power.

"Hey, Mom?" Jessica called as she rifled through the cupboards. "What do you want? Microwave or stovetop?"

"Stovetop is better," El called. "I don't want anything microwaved. Radiation freaks me out now."

Her mom was being funny, but Jessica still didn't have it in her to laugh. Billy's accusation that Kyle had killed his girlfriend was weighing heavily on her. If Kyle were willing to risk everything to punish her, it would only end one way. Somebody else was going to die.

Jessica pulled the jar of popcorn from the shelf and set it on the counter. As she washed her hands, she noticed her reflection in the kitchen window above the sink. She looked as tired as she felt, puffy under the eyes and without makeup. She grimaced at her reflection to express the anger she harbored toward herself.

As she scowled again, the lights flickered and revealed another face. It was the white death mask that had become a symbol of his power and her shame. Kyle had been wearing it when he secretly recorded her, using it to stimulate fear in her and detach himself from the events he set up, one of his favorite games.

She jumped back from the sink, her heart pounding in her ears. All Jessica could see was her reflection again, twisted, with her mouth gaping open. She wanted to check the kitchen door's lock to ensure the entry was secure, but she couldn't tear her gaze away from the window.

The lights flickered again and died, plunging the house into darkness. The television, previously blaring to accommodate El's hearing loss and drown out the storm, fell silent. But now the window was empty, as if what she had seen was a hallucination.

"Jessica," El said, calling from the living room. "The lights are out. We'll need to light those candles."

"Mom! Never mind that," Jessica said in a panic, unwilling to take any chances. "Go upstairs to your room and lock the door."

"Why?"

"Just do it, please," Jessica said, rushing over to the knife block. She grabbed the eight-inch chef's knife and wrapped her fingers around the handle. She faced the back door, her feet shoulder-width apart and the knife thrust out in front of her.

She couldn't see the deadbolt in the darkness, even as her eyes adjusted. She was sure it was locked but felt compelled to check.

As she took a few shuffle steps closer to the back door, there was a sharp knock at the front door. Every muscle in her body tensed.

"Somebody's at the front door," El said. "Maybe it's Billy."

"Mom, it's not Billy. Don't you dare open that door!" Jessica said, turning from the back door toward the hall that connected the lower rooms. "Mom, did you hear me? Get upstairs!"

Jessica swiftly navigated back to the living room, worried her mom might open the door. There was another sharp knock, followed by an urgent banging.

The pounding increased until the door sounded like it would give against the force. Jessica screamed with a terrible revelation. She never put the security chain on the door after Billy left.

"Kyle, I see you out there," she yelled, hurling herself toward the door to support it. "I know it's you. Get out of here!"

With his death mask still burned into her mind, Jessica pressed her shoulder against the door. She momentarily took one hand off the knife and felt for the security chain. She couldn't seem to find it as the door buckled from the assault, and the front windows rattled with every successive blow.

"Mom, we have to call 911!" Jessica said urgently before her heart sank. She had unplugged the phone.

"We unplugged the phone!" El called back from the stairs.

"Please, Lord, please," Jessica whimpered as her hand found the slider.

She lifted it and set the lock when a massive blow against the door bounced her off. It sent her sprawling on the floor. She chased after the dropped knife, feeling around the floor, sure that Kyle would break into the house at any moment. Except he didn't. The banging suddenly stopped.

Jessica didn't know what he was doing outside but could hear the porch creak under his weight. He was out there, pacing back and forth on the rain-soaked planks. Her fingers brushed against the knife handle, and she slid toward it on her belly.

The pacing stopped, a momentary quiet except for the rain on the house and the wind whistling through old imperfections. Then, the hooked end of a crowbar broke through the front window, shattering the glass and scattering shards across the floor.

It was immediately followed by a gust of wind that sent the curtains flying as rain blew into the room. Jessica heard El scream and scramble up the stairs while she focused on regaining her grip on the knife. She stood and tried to figure out a better defensive stance in front of the broken window.

She stood a few feet from the door, knife trembling, unsure what to do. Wind and rain whipped through the shattered windows, soaking the floor. She wanted to barricade the broken window, but it was impossible now. With no sign of Kyle, she braced for his next attack.

"Say something, you shit," Jessica screamed at the window, unnerved by the absence of his usual verbal taunts. "Say something!"

Her screams were answered by breaking glass in the kitchen. Knowing he must have circled around to the weaker door, she raced back toward the kitchen, her knee smacking against a wall as she did. A picture fell as she brushed past, and it crashed on the hardwood floor.

Rain was coming in from the broken window above the sink, where she'd first seen him peering in at her. The back door rattled violently, confirming her worst fear. Kyle was testing another entry to gain access to the house. Jessica took a deep breath to calm her shaking hands.

A heavy blow punched the door near the lock, and something tore into the wood of the outside frame. Metal scraped and wood splintered as he used the crowbar to pry the door off its frame. There was nothing she could do to stop him.

"Leave us alone!" Jessica yelled at the door, but it sounded more like a plea. "I have a knife! Just leave us alone!"

Another smashing blow fractured the door further, but the deadbolt held. He hit it again, and the wood groaned from the force as a gust of wind blew more rain into the kitchen.

Jessica's breath caught as the door splintered under a final, heavy kick. It flew open, and she could see him step through the broken frame and into the kitchen. He stopped, wet with rain, and assessed her as she jutted the knife outward at him.

"Stay away from me," said Jessica as he took his first cautious step toward her.

She already knew warning him off wouldn't do any good. He had terrorized her for months, proving he could overpower her time and time again. But this time was different. She wasn't just protecting herself. She couldn't let him hurt her mom.

She thrust the knife toward him again, and he moved in quickly to counter her. Kyle lunged forward, closing the distance in three quick steps to bypass the knife. She slashed awkwardly at his left arm, and he blocked it with his wrist, something hard under his shirt blocking the blade. He didn't flinch, stepping forward on wet tile.

She screamed in terror, flailing, as he threw the crowbar aside and drove a fist into her forehead. It was a quick, brutal punch that sent her staggering back and slipping on the wet floor.

He advanced on her in the open space near the counter, punching her in her ribs and doubling her over. He followed it up with another punch that landed on her temple, sending her sprawling into the stove, her vision blurring and the world falling away. Her senses dimmed as even the sound of the storm seemed to fade into the distance.

She tried to turn over, barely hearing her mom's panicked voice. She was no longer upstairs but only a few feet away. She tried to tell her mom to run but had no breath in her lungs to speak.

"Put down the gun, Ms. M." His voice was distorted and laced with menace. His words barely registered with Jessica, lost in the haze enveloping her.

Jessica strained her neck to see her mom. She was a slight silhouette facing off against a monster. But she had her husband's service weapon, held tight in both hands with shaking arms.

Calling upon a last surge of adrenaline, Jessica tried to find one of Kyle's legs to trip or stop him from advancing. There was the roar of a gunshot as Kyle kicked Jessica away, landing one wet boot heel to her face. Everything went black.

CHAPTER 30

STORM BREAKS

Billy was standing in the rain and securing his Marlin lever-action rifle by the passenger seat of his truck when his phone rang. He knew the number from what seemed like a lifetime ago. It was the Michaud house. Jessica was calling him.

"What is it, Jessica?" He said flatly and still irritated after seeing her.

"Help," said a frail voice on the other end of the phone.

Billy looked down at the screen, thinking he misread the number. "Who is this?"

"Help, Billy," said the voice. "He took Jessica and, and I'm hurt."

"Who took Jessica?" Billy said, his voice rising in alarm. "Mrs. Michaud? Who took her?"

"He hurt me," El said, her voice fading under the static. "And he left with her."

"I'll be right there," Billy said, slamming the passenger door. "Find a safe place and call 911."

"I tried, I really tried," she whimpered. "But all the lines are busy. That's why I called you."

It made sense. As the storm continued to grow in size, more and more calls would tie up the lines. The rain had already progressed from light to moderate, with wind gusts between thirty-five and forty-five miles per hour.

He knew the roads would be slick with scattered debris, and the radio had reported that some areas had already lost power. The growing severity of the storm made him question his resolve to go hunting for Kyle Brondi, but guilt from his inaction against a misogynist in high school still haunted him. He hadn't done enough to protect Stacy from Dustin back then.

There would be no excuse this time. He hadn't had a drop to drink since his last encounter with Kyle at the Woodshed and had resolved that there was no way he was going to let this madman hurt another person. Storm be damned. He had prepared to hunt Kyle all night, only to find out he was too late.

"How bad are you hurt?" Billy asked as he climbed into the cab of his truck.

"It's bad, so bad," she said.

"Can you get somewhere safe?" Billy started the truck. "If you can, get somewhere safe. I'm on my way and calling for help."

"Hurry, Billy. Please hurry."

Billy didn't waste any time. Given the weather conditions, he plotted the fastest route to the Michaud home. The trees were swaying, bending in the wind. If it continued to get worse, branches would start snapping, and the pockets of darkness he experienced as he drove on would eventually envelop all of Augusta, if not the entire state of Maine.

As he drove, visibility diminishing to a few hundred feet before him, Billy decided to take a leap of faith. If emergency numbers were overwhelmed by calls, he might be able to get through to Officer Derrik Mills on his direct line. He had saved Derrik's number in his phone after the officer had given him a card.

He still didn't trust Derrik, but decided it might not matter, given the circumstances. If he wasn't dirty, Derrik would be an asset. And even a dirty cop working for Fields would have to reevaluate what side he was on if a killer intended to take yet another woman's life. At least, Billy hoped that would be the case.

The phone rang and went to voice mail. Billy didn't care. He anticipated it. Derrik could be answering any number of calls on a night like tonight.

"Derrik? This is Billy Stevens. There has been a break-in at the Michaud house. Muriel Michaud has been hurt. Jessica Michaud has been abducted. Send help."

He rattled off the address and continued to drive, intending to turn on the radio for weather updates after one more call. He momentarily took his eyes off the road to find Andrea's most recent call and instantly regretted it. He had to swerve to avoid a branch drifting onto the road, snapped from a red maple.

"Billy? Is that you?" Andrea called out on the other end of the line.

"Yeah, it's me," Billy said, nearly drowned out by the storm around him.

"Are you crazy?" she asked. "What the heck are you doing out in this storm?"

"Andrea, no time for that," he said. "I need your help. Can you meet me at the Michaud place?"

"I don't have the car for that kind of adventure," she said. "What's going on?"

"Kyle Brondi broke into the Michaud place, took Jessica, and hurt her mom," Billy said. "Are you sure you can't meet me there?"

"I'm already getting my coat on," she said. "Have you called 911?"

"Nothing's going through," he said. "We're all there is."

"All right, Billy," she said. "Please drive safe. You aren't going help anyone if you're sitting in a ditch."

"Yeah, I know. You too," he said. "And Andrea? Thanks a lot."

"You don't have to thank me. If we can bring Autumn's killer to justice, I'm all in with you."

"Yeah," he said and hung up.

As soon as she was gone, he turned on the radio. The signal was weak but enough to catch some bits and pieces. The Kennebec River was rising and expected to flood. The Augusta Police Department was urging people to stay indoors, away from windows, and use extreme caution. People were calling into one station, fretting that the storm might cancel Halloween.

Halloween? Billy hadn't even thought of it. It was the last thing anybody needed to worry about.

He'd heard enough about bombogenesis, too. The fancy weather terms were exhausting. There was no such thing when he was growing up. It was a nor'easter, simple as that, with heavy rain and strong winds that could tear the world apart.

"Whatever you do," the newscaster continued, "don't go outside." Wind speeds were reaching forty-seven miles per hour near Cape Elizabeth. If the winds were that bad there, it would only be a matter of time before they would be just as bad, if not worse, in Augusta. None of it would surprise him. The rain drummed on the cab's roof, and an occasional small branch pinged off the bed of his truck.

Twenty minutes later, Billy arrived at the Michaud house. As he pulled up, it looked dark and lifeless, so he pointed his brights at the porch and left the truck running. He immediately noticed the window was smashed, and soggy curtains were being sucked out and then blown back into the house by the wind.

Seeing the destruction, Billy knew he had no time to lose. He took the porch steps two at a time, nearly slipping as he reached the top. The front door was damaged, but it didn't look like Kyle had gained entrance that way. Billy thought about going around the back, but another gust of wind convinced him otherwise. He didn't have any more time.

He kicked the weakened door near the lock, and it burst inward. He rushed in and called for El. He found her quickly, sitting on the stairs in the hallway.

"El, are you okay?" He asked, tapping her gently to see if she was conscious.

"Billy," she said, wheezing. "He took Jessica. You have to save my baby. She's all I have."

"Sorry, El," he said, noticing the blood trickling down one side of her head. "I have to fix you before I go after Kyle."

"No, it's not Kyle," she whispered.

Billy didn't wait for an explanation. He went into the kitchen to retrieve a dish towel so that he could apply pressure to her head injury. When he returned, he asked her where else she was hurt, and she pointed to her arm. He found a towel and a blanket in the linen closet off the hall to make a makeshift splint and keep her warm, suddenly grateful for the safety classes he received at work.

"Hey, I've called for more help, El," he said, quietly reassuring her. "Now what were you saying about Kyle, not Kyle?"

"It wasn't Kyle," she said, her voice weakening. "He wanted her to think it was Kyle because he was wearing this weird mask, but it wasn't Kyle."

"I don't understand," Billy said. "Who was it then?"

"Jessica kept calling him Kyle, but I think she was scared and confused."

"How could you know this?"

"I never met this Kyle character before," El said. "He wouldn't call me Ms. M."

Billy's mind spun. He had surveyed some of the damage in the house. Dustin had done all this on his own? It was almost impossible to believe, but it also made perfect sense. Kyle would never have left Muriel Michaud alive if he had been here.

"All right," Billy said. "I know this is hard, but did he say where he might go? Anything like that?"

"No," she said, forcing the words through a cough. "I tried to shoot him, but the gun kicked back in my hand. I didn't expect it. Then he knocked it out of my hand and hit me on the head. I tried to stop him, Billy. I did. And now he has my baby."

"You tried to shoot him?" he asked. "Do you know where the gun went?"

"I don't know," she said. "It's probably in the kitchen somewhere."

"Okay," he said. "Stay here."

Billy went back into the kitchen. The scene was worse than the living room. Broken glass and unpopped popcorn kernels were scattered across the wet floor. The window was smashed, and the door was blown open, a giant ragged gash where the lock had been, the door frame obliterated.

He searched the floor, coming up with a crowbar first. Then he found the handgun. It was a standard-issue M1911 .45 caliber Colt. He checked it and tucked it into the back of his pants behind his jacket. From what he remembered, it likely had a seven- to twelve-round feed, minus the bullet El had put into the kitchen ceiling. He could see a car pull up next to his truck as he returned to her side.

"El, I'm pretty sure this is Andrea," Billy said. "She's a good friend of mine, and she's going to stay with you until help arrives."

"Okay," El said, her breathing labored.

"I'm going to find Jessica," he said, clasping her uninjured hand. "I'll find her and bring her home."

El squeezed her hand. "Thank you, Billy. I always think of you as family."

"I am," he said. "We're family."

He stood up and headed back to the front as Andrea cautiously climbed the steps. They met at the front door.

"Look at this place," Andrea said. "Kyle did all this?"

"No, El says it was Dustin."

"Dustin?"

"If this was all him, he is off the rails," Billy said. "I've got to find him and put an end to this. I'll worry about Kyle later."

"Are you sure this is a good idea?"

"It's a terrible idea. But if I don't do something, who will? The cops are spread out everywhere, nobody can get through to 911, and the storm is getting worse by the minute. Look, I called Officer Derrik Mills. I think he's one of the good guys. He should be here soon. Stay with Ms. Michaud until he gets here."

"Where are you going?"

"If Dustin took her, I bet he brought her to his parents' lake house near North Belgrave. Hatch Cove," he said. "I don't have an address, just a vague memory. I'll drop you a pin once I'm there. You won't get it here, though. The dead zone around here is about a half mile or so."

"And if you're wrong?"

"Then it won't really matter," Billy said. "If this keeps up, I don't think I'll make it back tonight."

"Billy, if Dustin did all this, it might be my fault," Andrea said. "I hit him with everything I had the other night. The DUI story and the date rapes. He flew off the handle."

"So?"

"I implied Jessica told me everything," she said. "And there's more. Dustin has gotten himself in deep with organized crime."

Billy shook his head. "I should have stopped him back in high school."

He started to turn out the front door and into the rain, but Andrea grabbed his arm. He looked at her, waiting for her to say something. She didn't. She pulled him in and hugged him. He hugged her back, grazing her with the crowbar.

"And what are you going to do with that?" Andrea said, pointing to the crowbar.

"Heck, Andrea," Billy said. "I have no idea what I'm doing with anything."

"Just be safe."

He looked down at her as if he was going to say something. Then he changed his mind, and came up with something else.

"Looks like you got one heck of a story," he said, walking out the door into the darkness, gripping the crowbar tight. He hoped there was enough time.

The rain was heavy now, with the wind whipping at everything it could grab. As Billy approached his truck, the radio droned on with a newscaster saying the worst was yet to come, something comparable to the 1998 ice storm when almost a million lost power for nearly a week, some for over three weeks.

CHAPTER 31

DEATH MASK

Jessica woke up with a pounding pressure in her head, sharper than any headache she could remember. Coarse rope cut into her skin, rough fibers biting into her wrists with every movement. She was on a bed, stripped to her underwear.

She twisted her body, ankles bound just as tight as her hands. Every move seemed to make them tighter, searing her flesh. *"Don't struggle,"* she remembered Kyle telling her once. *"It will only make things worse."* His words fit, especially because the ropes weren't paracord like he usually used. They burned her wrists and ankles.

She took a deep breath of damp air scented with wax. Flickering candles cast looming shadows across the wood-paneled walls. She was at a cabin, maybe a lake house, with the storm still shrieking through the walls and rain hammering the roof and windows.

The realization of what happened crashed over her like a wave. Kyle had used a crowbar to shatter the back door, break in, and knock her out. And her mom? What happened to her mom?

She thrashed, desperate to sit up and search for her mom. Then it hit her. She remembered the sound of a gunshot. It was tangled up with flashes of Kyle's white death mask, shattered glass, and the storm raging through their home. The hazy fragments made her sick, but she couldn't fully grasp what had happened.

She turned her head to the left and saw two candles on a dresser with picture frames and a collection of small wooden animals — a duck, a moose, a bear. She turned to her right, trying to let her eyes adjust after looking at the tiny flames and peering deeper into the darkness. She winced. Kyle was sitting there in the dark, one hand under the chin of his white death mask like a grotesque reimagining of the Thinker.

"Where's my mom?" she asked, her voice rising above the outside storm. "What did you do to her?"

He stood up, stepping into the dim glow. A white death mask floating in the dark, tilted to one side in mock confusion. He spread his hands with a shrug like a cruel mime.

"Quit playing games, you bastard," she said, wanting to spit at him but found no saliva left in her dry mouth. "What happened to my mom?"

Kyle answered with a slow clap. Each smack was a silent taunt. Jessica's stomach twisted, bruised where he had punched her earlier. This wasn't Kyle. He was using the mask as a dramatic prop, not to detach himself from events. He was big, but not nearly as big as Kyle. One of his hands, the left one, sported a cast.

"If you could see your face," said Dustin, slipping off the mask. "He must really terrify you. What is it? The mask? Or did he do terrible things to you like in that video?"

She studied his features in the flickering light. This wasn't the man she had spent so much time with over the past week. This was somebody else, a man who didn't need a mask because he woke up in one every day of his life, his charm and charisma hiding something else inside.

"Where's my mom, Dustin?" Jessica asked again. "What did you do to her?"

"She's back at the house. Shaken, but fine," he said, smile fading. "She almost shot me, you know. I didn't want to hurt her."

She felt some immediate relief, but doubt still gnawed at her bones. He could be lying to her.

"I needed her to see me," he said, holding up the mask. "Well, see this Kyle guy anyway."

"What is this about?" Jessica asked. "Why are you doing this?"

"I tried to ask you the same question yesterday, remember? And all you did was lie to me. You fed that tramp reporter scraps about me and about Stacy Brenner."

"I didn't tell her anything."

"I was going to let it go at first. Take you at your word that you wouldn't flip your story. I was," he said. "But then I thought about it. How would Jessica feel if her deepest, darkest secrets were suddenly exposed? That video on your phone at The Barn. That's some messed-up stuff."

The revelation caught her off guard. He had seen the video that night, after all, and then lied to her face that he hadn't been looking at her phone. She should have trusted her gut but didn't want to believe it then.

"So, I did something about it," Dustin said. "I posted it online, tagged your socials, and sent it to your work. So now you know. Andrea Kearney won't have such an easy time dragging my name through the mud. You have no credibility."

Her head swam. It wasn't Kyle making good on his threat to share the video. It was Dustin. He had betrayed her, even then.

"How did you even get it?" Jessica asked, angry and hurt.

"That night at the Barn? I airdropped it to myself," he said. "I was curious, mostly. It's some kind of crazy, kinky stuff but kind of hot, too. I never intended to do anything with it, except see what you were into."

"It wasn't like that," she said. "You don't understand. You couldn't understand."

"Whatever, Jessica," Dustin said, growing agitated. "You set everything in motion. You could have told Kearney no comment and left it at that. But instead, you go on about the accident and then dredge up Stacy, Billy's injury, all of it. You have no idea what you've done."

"I didn't tell her anything, Dustin," Jessica said. "I told her it was late and I was driving home."

"I told you before, Stacy is a meth head. Did you know she practically extorted my family seven years ago?"

"No, I didn't know," Jessica said.

"I was being looked at by multiple schools at the time, Baylor included. And Stacy Brenner hits me with this idea that I raped her. No medical exam. No pictures. No report. But she wants a payday. It broke my heart, and I told her to screw off. But you know what she did next? She convinced Billy to turn on me, too. My best friend."

"Dustin, I didn't know any of this," Jessica said. "Billy never told me."

"Billy wanted me to cop to something I didn't do," Dustin said. "And then the accident happened on the field, and bam, our friendship was over. You know his family took a payout, too? I bet you didn't know that."

"I wish I had," Jessica said. "Maybe I could have done something to help."

"Yeah, right," Dustin said. "You were always off in your own little world. You still are in some ways. When this story breaks about me, everything I've worked to set up will evaporate. My family? Embarrassed. Those business partners in Nashua? They'll cut me loose. My construction company in Waco? Gone. I'll lose everything."

"Maybe there's another way. I can deny whatever is put in print."

"But then it hit me," Dustin said, looking down at her. "What if Kearney's source was out of the picture? The headlines wouldn't be about me. They would be about your weird secret lover and this crazy mask. He drove up here from New York, and that was the end of you."

Jessica tested the ropes again, panic rising up in her chest. She had to remember he wasn't Kyle. Maybe he didn't tie the ropes right. Maybe she could loosen them and slip out.

"Go ahead, struggle," Dustin said. "The more you struggle, the better. That's the idea. Rope burns and blood."

Dustin drew a knife, its black blade glinting in the candlelight. Jessica's pulse quickened as she took in the four-inch blade.

"You don't have to do this, Dustin," she said. "There's a better way."

"You don't think I thought about that? I did, Jessica," Dustin said. "I thought about a lot of things. We might have made a cute couple, you know? I thought about that. I could have bludgeoned you to death in your house with your mom, making it look like that lumberyard killer. But with that video all over the net and your mom witnessing a man in a death mask break into your house? It's too perfect."

He brought the knife closer to her body, and she temporarily froze, afraid she might accidentally cut herself on it. He drew the tip of it up her leg and waist to her breast. He rested it there, with the tip of it under her nipple, her bra the only thing between the skin and cold steel.

"I'm wearing gloves, Jessica," Dustin said. "But do you think they would find any DNA if I wore a condom? I read once that a rapist got away with it because of that."

Jessica could see the truth as the words tumbled out of him like a confession. He had raped Stacy Brenner. He had hurt Billy to shut him up. Jessica had been wrong about him, and he was going to kill her.

"Dustin, don't," she whispered. "I'm sorry. I shouldn't have said anything."

She couldn't see what he was doing but immediately felt pressure against her skin. It was a sharp, pricking sensation as the fabric resisted. He pressed harder.

"No, you shouldn't have," said Dustin. "You screwed me over with people who don't play games, and this is my only way out. With you gone, there is no story, and everything happens the way it should."

Every tiny hair on Jessica's body felt electrified as her sense of fear heightened. The material was tearing, and she suddenly felt a throbbing and burning sensation. Her skin, cold only seconds before, registered a warm, wet trickle of blood.

He held up the knife to show her. Even in the dim light, she could see blood, her blood, glistening on the end of it.

"I'm sorry, Jessica," he said. "This only ends one way. The only question is how we get there."

"Please think this through," she said, gasping for air. "This isn't like anything you've ever done before. You'll have to live with it."

"I'm going to dump you in a lake and let the storm finish the job," he said. "Then I'm going to burn everything else to the ground. My dad can collect the insurance."

There was a sudden furious banging somewhere toward the front of the house. It was loud and rhythmic, impossible to mistake as branches or trees being battered by the storm outside.

Dustin stepped back and lowered the knife. His body tensed as fear washed over him. He looked out the bedroom room door toward the pounding, trying to assess the unexpected threat. He moved toward the door, taking a second to glance at her.

"Shut up," he said. "Don't say a word!"

Jessica didn't plan to say anything while he was in the room. She was working on one of the ropes, the loosest on her left ankle.

Dustin peered out of the bedroom into the hallway. The pounding was replaced by a tremendous thud, as if the door were being pummeled by a battering ram. Dustin held up the knife and moved stealthily out of the room.

As soon as he was gone, Jessica started pulling on the rope to create friction against the bedpost. She pulled her foot toward her body, testing how much slack she could find. She started rotating it in small circles, muscles straining against the rope as it slackened, inch by inch.

Her wrists burned, and her skin was rubbed raw as she worked the rope faster. Another loud bang hit the door, followed by a third, then a splintering crunch and the roar of wind and heavy rain coming through an open door.

A voice boomed over the wind and rain. "Police! Coming in!"

"He has a knife!" Jessica yelled out as the rope on her ankle pulled free.

Her ankle throbbed from the rope burn, but she knew there was no time to lose. Another surge of adrenaline propelled her to use her free foot to work on the other rope, the pain in her head and chest falling away and distant. She had to work fast.

Two successive gunshots ripped through the night, slicing through the storm's howl. The shots were followed by a crash. Two forces of nature slammed together, toppling over furniture and breaking ceramics.

Jessica tried to ignore it as her second ankle came free. Curling her body, she brought both feet up to work on her right wrist despite the burning in her breast as it came into contact with her waist. She pushed past the pain, urged on by the promise of freedom.

As the howls and grunts of two men fighting it out in the living room beyond the hall continued, Jessica pressed both feet against one of the knots. The bedpost creaked as she put all her weight behind it.

The maneuver worked, giving her just enough slack to wrestle her right wrist free. She quickly sat up and glanced at the door. The fighting had stopped, drowned out by the wind and rain coming into the house. She wanted to call out, but without knowing who the victor might be, she decided against it.

She sat up and started working on the last knot, the tightest of the four. She heard somebody sliding furniture around in the other room, propping a heavy chair against the front door to shut out the storm. She quickened her pace, pulling and tugging and then trying to undo the knot.

"Hey, Jess," a familiar voice sounded from the door of the bedroom.

She stopped trying to undo the remaining knot and froze. It was the last voice she wanted to hear. Terror seized her, every nerve coming to life as his presence loomed in the doorway. She could hear the familiar sound of a Zippo lighter coming to life and a deep inhale of smoke.

"Let me help you with that knot," Kyle said.

She turned her head to look at him, defeat in her eyes. She wanted to cry.

"You don't seem happy to see me, Jess," Kyle said, walking over to the last rope with the knife. "Aren't you glad I staked out your house? I just saved your life."

He cut the rope with the knife that Dustin once bandied about, and she immediately withdrew her hand, rubbing at her wrist. She kept her head down, unable to look at him, wondering if she could make a run for it.

"Nope, you can't run," he said, as if reading her mind. "There's nowhere to go, and the storm outside will tear you to shreds. Come on. Let's go see lover boy."

Without making eye contact, Jessica eased herself off the bed. She followed Kyle into a short hallway adorned with pictures of what Jessica knew would be the Fields family on various vacations. Jessica didn't have to see them to know. She had been here many times when they were in high school.

The hallway opened into the sunken great room, lit by a mag light set on an elevated kitchen counter and breakfast bar. In the recessed area of the home, furniture was askew, and shards of glass and ceramics littered the floor. In the center, Dustin was unconscious, tied to a chair brought down from the dining area.

"Don't go down there without shoes," Kyle said. "I found yours in the foyer and tossed them over there by the fireplace. You feel like a fire? I feel like a fire."

Jessica obeyed his passive direction, knowing what might happen if she didn't. She put on shoes, and he went to work on starting a fire.

"Did you find my clothes, too?" Jessica asked when she finished tying them.

"They're all wet," he said, poking at the fire. "I kind of like you that way anyway, babe."

"Okay," she said, surveying the room and looking for something to use as a weapon, like the poker he was holding. "What now, Kyle?"

"What now?" Kyle asked as if she wanted to know the meaning of life. He stood up. "I'm going to shut the flashlight off, and then I'm going to wake up lover boy."

Kyle lumbered across the room to the kitchen counter. Jessica noticed an uneven gait and wondered if Dustin had done any damage. She licked at her lips, mouth feeling even drier as Kyle filled a glass of water from the refrigerator's dispenser.

Her eyes turned toward Dustin. His head was down, but she could see swelling and bruising across one side of his face. Kyle had tied Dustin to the chair, broken his cast, ruined his wrist, and then tied his hands behind his back. Each foot was tied to a different chair leg. It wasn't the rope Dustin had used on her. It was what Kyle liked best. It was paracord, something Kyle once said he never left home without it.

"Come on," he said, waving her over to where he was standing in front of Dustin. "Let's get this over with."

"What?"

"Come on," he said, firmer to remind her that he didn't like to repeat himself. "Come on and take it."

She didn't wait to be told again. She stepped down into the depression, shoes crushing broken pottery and the fragments of a glass coffee table. He waited for her, holding out the knife. She hesitated to take it from him, but he shook it impatiently.

As soon as she did, Kyle splashed water on Dustin's face, and he immediately woke up choking. He didn't look like the same strong, handsome, and safe man she knew from a few days ago. He was broken, a spider caught in its own trap.

"Morning, lover boy," Kyle said. "I'm going to teach you a little lesson, and then we're going to play a game."

Jessica tightened her grip on the knife, wondering if she would be fast enough to stab him in the kidney or groin. And if she was, would that be enough to put him down long enough to get away? But get away where?

"Let me go," Dustin said, testing his bindings.

Kyle didn't say another word. He cocked a meaty fist and hit Dustin in the eye that wasn't ruined.

"Talk again. See what happens," Kyle said. "Now, here's the lesson. My daddy was a great man. He took no crap from anybody. Not from my mother. Not from his employer. Not from the police. Not anybody. But one day, he let himself get arrested for assaulting a coworker. He was locked up. Lost his job. It was embarrassing. It put a real strain on the family. Anybody want to guess the lesson?"

"He was a loser like you?" Dustin said.

"Wrong!" Kyle yelled and stomped on Dustin's foot. "He was a loser like you."

Dustin howled, his toes broken under the weight of the man. Jessica flinched.

"Let me spell it out," Kyle said, smiling. "Unless power is absolute, it crumbles. Like you. You had some power. Yeah, you had some. But it's crumbling, crumbling down."

"You want power?" Dustin said. "My father can give it to you. Whatever you want."

"You're not hearing me. I already have absolute power," Kyle said, turning toward Jessica and pointing to her chest. "He cut you, right? Cut him back."

Jessica wasn't sure what to do, so Kyle took action. He ripped open Dustin's shirt and pointed to his chest.

"Cut him back," he said.

Jessica's muscles tensed. She had never hurt anyone like that before. And she had never wanted to hurt anyone like that before. But now, a strange feeling started to creep over her. This was the man who lied to her, got her fired from her job, broke into her home, hurt her and her mom, and planned to kill her and maybe rape her in the most brutal, unforgiving way. And for what?

"You don't have to do this, Jess," Dustin said. "Don't you see? This is your only chance to get away from him. I'll help you."

Anger bubbled up inside her, and part of her wanted to do exactly what Kyle wanted. He had cut her, and he deserved to be cut.

She felt Kyle's hand on her wrist, ready to guide her if she resisted. She shook him away, anger growing as Dustin made his feeble pleas. He deserved to pay for what he did.

She dragged the knife down from his clavicle, across his chest, and the muscle opened up. Dustin screamed as blood streamed from the open wound. Jessica stopped and looked at him, almost disbelieving that this coward had terrorized her just a few minutes before.

"Yeah," Kyle said with a chuckle. "Cut him again."

She didn't hesitate this time, zeroing in on the other side of his chest. The knife was sharp, and she couldn't believe how simply it sliced through his flesh and how easily she could block his cries from her mind.

"That was for Stacy and Billy and my mom," Jessica said, overwhelmed with emotion and near tears. "I hope you rot in jail."

"No," Kyle said. "He's not going to rot in jail. You're going to finish him."

"What?"

"He's buried on Sunday," Kyle said. "This is the end. Of Solomon Grundy."

"What?" Dustin said, sobbing. "What is he talking about?"

Jessica looked at Dustin. He was broken in the chair before her. She wrestled with the idea Kyle had put before her. Did he deserve it? Could she do it? What would that make her if she did?

"There," Kyle said, pointing to Dustin's neck. "Cut him there, and he'll bleed out in no time."

Jessica lifted the knife and pointed it at Dustin's neck. He was wailing, trying to scoot the chair back and away from her. Seeing him like this made her feel nauseous again, and she knew she couldn't do it. She let the knife fall to her side, and she shook her head.

"No, Kyle," she said. "I won't do this."

"Suit yourself," Kyle said. "But this is the end of Solomon Grundy."

He reached under his arm and drew his .38 special. There was a deafening roar as the gun exploded and Dustin's head snapped back, blood glistening in the firelight.

Jessica looked at Dustin's ruined head and then up at Kyle. He was looking at Dustin, too, but with a grin. Then he turned his head to look at her.

"Now, what to do about you?" he asked her.

CHAPTER 32

QUARRY MAN

Billy was looking through the scope of his Marlin lever-action rifle when he saw a muzzle flash and Dustin's head snap back. Instinct had told him to shoot. But in the maelstrom surrounding him, he was just as likely to hit Jessica as the monster who shot Dustin.

Billy had no choice. He had to get closer to the back of the house and break in through the lower level, using the crowbar on the sliding glass door. He'd have to move fast to keep the element of surprise and use the Colt tucked under his jacket.

A couple of minutes earlier, he had parked his truck a few hundred yards from the Fields family's lake house driveway and scrambled through a dense wood, circling the property to the back of the house. His initial idea was to find the right vector and take a shot at Dustin from a safe distance, aiming for an arm or leg.

But by the time he found a good position, he made a startling discovery. It wasn't Dustin that he had to worry about. Kyle was there, looming over everything like an apex predator. Between not having a clean shot and the fury of the storm, the rifle was all but useless.

As the Fields family's boat slammed into the dock behind him, Billy kept low and scampered up to the back of the house, rifle in one hand and the crowbar in the other. Long grass, mud, and wind gusts as high as seventy miles per hour made the ascent from the lakefront difficult, but he eventually reached the back of the house.

The lower level was set in a depression from the excavation needed to build it ten years ago. It offered partial shelter from the storm.

Billy was grateful to be partly out of the rain, which had poured buckets on him. He was soaked and was starting to wonder if the Colt was even up to the job, likely unserviced since Ed Michaud, Jessica's dad, was alive.

He took a deep breath. There was only one way to find out. He set the rifle down and crouched by the sliding glass door, positioning the flat end of the crowbar between the side jamb and operating panel lock.

His muscles tensed as he tested the resistance, metal softly scraping against the aluminum frame. The lock held, but there was the promise of a slight give. He leaned into it until he heard the sharp crack of the lock mechanism buckling.

He froze, heart pounding, wondering if he had been heard or if the noise blended in with the storm. He didn't hear anything. With a final heave, Billy slid the panel open and quickly ducked inside before the roar of wind and rain betrayed him.

Once inside, he laid down the rifle. It would be nearly useless in such close quarters. Then he tried to remember where the stairs were to the upper level. He stumbled in the dark past the pool table and toward the back of the room, trying not to make any additional noise. At the beginning of the carpeted stairs, he listened for anything louder than the pelting rain and whistling wind.

He couldn't make out the words, but the timbre of Kyle's voice was a distinctly controlled growl that rose and fell with Jessica's tears. Her sobs triggered something deep inside him, imagining that his girlfriend must have sounded just like Jessica, pleading for her life.

He crawled up the stairs, feeling sluggish in his wet clothes, voices growing louder with each step. Her pleas tore at him, urging him to move faster. At the top, he looked down a short hallway to a doorway with the soft illumination of firelight. The smell of burning wood would have been welcoming under different circumstances.

He remembered the night at the Woodshed and how intimidating Kyle could be, even to someone his size. The memory filled him with rage. Kyle had jammed one massive shoulder into him, knocking him off the barstool and into the wall. He had been caught off guard in a crowded place when he was drunk. But Billy wasn't drunk this time.

It was now or never. Billy passed the crowbar to his left hand and drew the Colt with his right. He stood up, took a deep breath, and charged the doorway like strong safety might charge a running back breaking through the line.

He was screaming like a madman, propelled by his need to avenge Autumn's death and save Jessica from becoming another victim. The two of them came into focus as he rounded the corner. Jessica dove into a hundred sparkling shards of glass on the floor while Kyle, startled, turned to look in Billy's direction, raising his .38.

Gunshots rang through the house as Billy emptied the clip, six shots to the two Kyle squeezed off. The first bullet hit Kyle in the shoulder of his gun hand, saving Billy's life as Kyle's shots whizzed high and to the right. A second bullet grazed the monster's leg with less effect than the first, whereas the others went wide.

Billy's heart sank. There weren't enough bullets to do the job, so he dropped the empty Colt in favor of the crowbar and charged at Kyle, swinging it downward with both hands. Kyle, still recovering from being wounded, twisted away from the attack, taking a hit on the back of his other shoulder. He grunted and dropped his gun but didn't falter, throwing a punch at Billy's unprotected jaw.

The blow grazed Billy's ear, and he countered it with a sharp blow to the bear's ribs. Kyle didn't flinch, absorbing it like a tank. They crashed into the couch, sprawling away from Jessica, who had tucked herself into a ball.

As Kyle clamped Billy's shoulder, he felt the brute strength of a corrections officer who had wrestled more than one unruly prisoner to the ground. He was being collared as Kyle tried to use all his weight to pin him. Panic hit Billy square in the chest, flashes of bar fights when he was outnumbered and outmatched. He wouldn't hold up in a grapple.

He jammed the crowbar into Kyle's hip, hitting a wound that Dustin had made minutes before. Kyle roared, loosening his grip for a split second. Billy took advantage of it and broke free, tripping backward and losing the crowbar.

"Look out, Billy!" Jessica screamed, coming to life again.

Kyle was on him in an instant, blood dripping from his hip. There was no smile on his face this time. Kyle's eyes burned with fury, raging at the man who dared to challenge him. He grabbed Billy by the collar, hauling him up into his crushing arms. Billy, desperate to avoid the hold, clawed at Kyle's eyes. The big man recoiled and released the barroom scrapper as a gust of wind fanned the flames inside the fireplace.

Billy spied the crowbar and dove, fingers closing around it as Kyle charged him again. He swung upward from the ground, the crowbar catching Kyle's knee with a thud. The big man staggered, his injured leg buckling under a new wound.

Billy found his way up again, sensing his only advantages were the crowbar and speed. He feinted a high swing and then drove the crowbar into Kyle's gut, doubling him over. He swung again, a glancing blow off the side of Kyle's head. Kyle swayed as another wound opened up, blood trickling from his scalp. Billy pounced, tackling Kyle and sending him into the sharp steps of the recessed living room.

Kyle grunted again, but Billy's gamble sacrificed advantage. Kyle wrestled Billy around, flipping him onto his back. One giant hand grabbed his wet jacket while another landed on his forehead.

Dazed, Billy tried to fend off Kyle's next attack with the crowbar, but the giant's hands scrambled for a hold. Kyle pushed down, cold iron slipping under Billy's chin.

"Time to join your girlfriend, quarryman," Kyle said. "Time to die."

The pain of failing to stop Autumn's killer washed over him, exceeding the physical pain that racked his entire body. Billy tried to press the giant's weight off him, but he was choking. The crowbar had suddenly become a liability.

Billy kicked his legs and arched his back, hoping to shift the man's weight. It didn't work, and his hands strained to keep the crowbar from crushing his windpipe. Billy faced the hard truth. There wouldn't be an escape this time.

"Don't kill him, Kyle," Jessica said. "I'll go back to New York with you. Just don't kill him."

As the room began to fade into the background, Billy heard only the fury of the storm. It was a tempest, reminding humankind that their triumphs and tragedies were trivial in comparison. The world would not remember Billy Stevens.

His thoughts began to darken with his vision when Jessica screamed in wild desperation. She stood behind Kyle with a knife that Billy didn't know she had.

She brought it down into Kyle's back, then up and down again. Kyle screamed, hands loosening on the crowbar. He reeled backward as another thrust cut deep into his muscular neck. She had given Billy a second life, a surge of exhilaration and adrenaline.

Billy coughed as he rolled free with the crowbar. Still gasping for air, he got up and looked down at Kyle. The monster was holding the back of his neck where Jessica had stabbed him. Billy roared and brought the crowbar down on Kyle's head with everything he had left. The crack echoed like a gunshot as the bear collapsed, blood pooling beneath his head.

Billy, panting, stumbled back and dropped the crowbar. His throat burned, his ear throbbed, and his head ached. But he was alive. Jessica had saved him.

Almost immediately, Jessica was by his side. She brushed his hair back and looked at him, a bruise spreading across his forehead where he had been hit.

"We're still here, Billy," she said softly, gripping his hand. "You saved my life."

"No," he said, voice nearly broken. "You saved mine."

She bent down and kissed him on the lips. Billy flinched, but he was too tired to stop her. It was deep and passionate, wet like they once kissed in high school. A different time and place that felt a million miles away, much like the last time he saw Autumn. And much like the raging storm outside.

CHAPTER 33

HERO'S END

Andrea left the Michaud house shortly after the heavy rain began to taper off. Officer Derrik Mills had made her promise to wait. He had arrived almost two hours after Billy had left.

When he got there, he'd reassessed Muriel Michaud, reinforcing the splint Billy had made, and called for an emergency evacuation. Even as a priority, they waited another two hours before an ambulance arrived.

Mills left after handing off El for medical transport. He needed to respond to a flurry of new calls not far from their location.

Early risers and those who couldn't sleep were out with flashlights, inspecting the devastation. News outlets reported that the storm had caused historic damage, worse than the 1998 ice storm. Trees were uprooted, roofs collapsed, buildings were marked unsafe, and roads were closed. It was only a matter of time before Governor LePage declared a state of emergency.

While schools and businesses would remain closed, Andrea belonged to a foolhardy troupe of daredevils responsible for gathering the news, and she had a very specific story. Once she was five minutes away from the Michaud house and out of the dead zone, she knew exactly where to find it. Billy's pin drop lit up her screen.

He was at the once-infamous Fields family's lake house, where red cups and kegs flowed freely like the tributaries surrounding the property during their high school years. Andrea had never been there, but the stories they spun from all the foolish and often illegal fun her classmates reported were akin to local legend.

Andrea was supposed to call Officer Mills as soon as she got a location, but her gut told her to wait. She wanted to assess the scene before contacting him. What she didn't count on was that it would take yet another hour to get there after being rerouted a half dozen times to avoid flooded rivers and downed power lines.

When she arrived, she was surprised to pass Billy's truck, which had been abandoned on the road to the house. But then she was even more surprised when she saw not one but two more trucks in the driveway. One was a Fields Construction pickup truck. The other was a Ford F-150 with New York plates. Her pulse quickened, and she picked up her phone. She dialed, and her call went right to voice mail.

"Officer Mills, this is Andrea Kearney," said Andrea. "I'm at the Fields' lake house, and I'll pin you the address. I think they're all here — Billy, Jessica, Dustin, and Kyle Brondi. I'm going to investigate."

She immediately sent the officer a pin and opened her car door. Like many of the houses she passed on the way over, the lake house property was in disarray. A white pine, uprooted, rocked against the Fields Construction truck in the debris-strewn drive.

She got out of her car and stepped into the cold rain. The storm was dying down, but an occasional gust blew up a sheet of water that tugged at her windbreaker.

The sun was slowly rising behind thick clouds, offering a lighter shade of gray than the predawn twilight during her ride over. The effect was subdued, almost mournful, as the storm's lingering presence overshadowed any hope for renewal.

The lake house itself looked mostly intact, with loose shingles and gutters creaking in the wind. The small, twisted two-foot satellite dish hung down from the roof, its mount bent by the tree branch entangling it. The windows were dark, one sporting a jagged crack that ran diagonally down the upper right corner of the frame before branching out like a lightning strike.

As she cautiously approached the house, she could see the still-turbulent lake down the hill. Its surface rippled with waves aggressively lapping at the shore and into the grass. The Fields family's boat looked forlorn, partially capsized. Its hull was broken by the pier.

Her heart raced as she reached the front door, sitting slightly ajar. The frame was misaligned, splintered from some unknown impact, like someone had kicked it in. Andrea pushed against it, anxious to get out of the rain. As she leaned into it, the door tilted, opening a small gap before something prevented her from entering. She pushed harder, feeling whatever was blocking the door shift and grind across a tile floor. With just enough room to squeeze in, Andrea slid inside past the chair propped up against it.

While the sun had started to illuminate the storm-soaked world outside, the inside of the house remained dim, lit only by a dying fire in the fireplace. Andrea reached for her phone and turned on its flashlight. She shined the light into the living room and gasped in horror.

Dustin was tied to a toppled-over chair, his ruined head lying lifeless on a bed of shattered glass and broken art. Not far from him, a monstrous man lay unblinking, the center of his scalp matted with blood. Andrea looked away in revulsion.

She tried to ignore the gruesome scene and headed to the hallway toward the bedrooms, pulse racing as she imagined the worst for Billy and Jessica, the girl he tried to rescue.

"Billy?" she called quietly as she reached the main bedroom with a lakefront view.

The room was empty and smelt of burned wax and scorched wood, as two candles on a dresser had melted away. She noticed the ropes dangling from each post of the poster bed. The comforter was tousled, and a lifeless white death mask lay on top of it.

"Billy?" Andrea called again as she headed to the smaller rooms on the other end of the hall.

The door of the first room was partly open, and she looked inside. Billy was lying on a queen-size bed, covered by a warm winter comforter, and Jessica was wrapped up in his arms.

"Billy?" she called again, louder and sharper this time, partly disgusted by seeing them together in bed.

"Andrea?" Billy said, turning to reveal his near nakedness.

She frowned, made a guttural groan, and then turned away to leave the room.

"Wait, Andrea," Billy said. "It's not what you think."

She stood in the hallway, back turned toward the door, as Billy came out of the room in a blanket. She heard him gently shut the door.

"Autumn's body is barely cold, Billy," Andrea said.

"It wasn't like that," he said. "We were cold and wet and tired, and there's no electricity or heat."

Andrea weighed his words and turned to look at him, his bruised and bloodied face. His eyes were sad and tired. His hair dried into a matted mess. Of course he was telling the truth.

"Damn, Billy," Andrea said and embraced him. "I was so scared for you."

Billy groaned as she touched his shoulder but embraced her back. It was comforting, like two friends who hadn't seen each other in years.

"It's so good to see you," he said. "You wouldn't believe what happened last night."

"Dustin?"

"Dustin was going to kill Jessica, but Kyle followed them here," Billy said. "And then I got here. I didn't have any choice. I had to kill Kyle."

"Let's find you something to wear," Andrea said. "And then I want you to tell me everything before the police get here."

After finding a robe in a linen closet, Billy took Andrea through the chain of events, piecing together what Jessica had told him with what he had experienced. He told her how Jessica had woken up to Dustin standing beside her, wearing a white death mask like the one in the sex video used to destroy Jessica's reputation, how he intended to kill Jessica, making it look like Kyle.

Dustin's plan was to use her murder as a smokescreen for his money-laundering deal in Nashua, among other crimes. But before he could do it, Kyle had broken into the house, subdued him, and later killed him. Then he walked her through how he broke in and faced off against Kyle and was nearly killed before Jessica intervened.

Andrea didn't say anything for a long time. Then, she shook her head.

"It's no good, Billy," Andrea said. "Nobody will believe it."

"What? But that's what happened."

"There's more to this than you know," Andrea said. "Dustin's dad had set up an out for the kid. And if his dad says Dustin knew about the deal with law enforcement, nobody will believe your story. Add in that stuff you told me about Jessica and how she willingly cut into him?"

"She didn't have a choice," Billy said. "Kyle made her do it."

"Yeah, we'll see how she holds up to those questions on a witness stand," Andrea said. "If even a little part of her wanted to do it, they'll try to hang her."

"Look, I'll testify, too," he said. "Kyle was a monster. Nobody could stand up against him."

"But you did," Andrea said, looking at him in the eyes. "They're going to ask you about that. If you broke into the house, playing a self-defense card might not work here. I'm not saying they won't believe you. I'm just saying it's a crapshoot."

"What does that mean?"

"I'm saying we get Jessica and her mom to go along with a different story," Andrea said. "Give the town the story they want to hear."

"And what story is that?" Jessica said, coming out of the bedroom.

"Dustin Fields died trying to save the lives of two high school friends after the lumberyard killer abducted them," Andrea said. "And it was Kyle, who had been stalking Jessica, who brought her here wearing the same white mask in that video because he wanted to frame Dustin."

"But that's not even close to what happened," Billy said.

"No, no, it's not," Andrea said before recalling her boss's words. "But sometimes we have to balance protecting the vulnerable and the public's right to know."

"You really want to make Dustin Fields a hero?" Jessica asked. "I don't know if I can do that. And what about Stacy Brenner? Where's her justice?"

"Same as yours and every other woman he ever hurt," Andrea said. "It will be six feet under, where it belongs."

"She's got a point," Billy said. "I think Stacy wants it all behind her, just like the rest of us."

Andrea looked at Jessica, assessing her. She was battered, blood dried on her bra where she had been stabbed, but also changed by everything that had happened. This wasn't the same girl who tried to stymy Andrea on the porch. This was a woman who was tired of being a victim. She had helped Billy exorcise her greatest demon.

At the same time, Andrea felt sick to her stomach. It was the last thing she wanted to do. Every fiber of her body told her to tell the truth and shame the devil, but she knew this town wasn't ready for Dustin Fields to be the kind of devil that Kyle Brondi had been.

"Who cares," she said, finally. "He's dead. I'd rather protect the living."

Andrea noticed Billy looking down at the two bodies lying lifeless in the recessed living room. She could see it in his eyes. He hated having to take a life, but he couldn't pity either one of them. She couldn't, either.

"We're going to have to get Dustin out of that chair and stage the scene differently," Andrea said. "Do you think we can find more latex gloves like the one Dustin was wearing?"

"I think so," Jessica said. "I'll check the main bedroom and the truck out front."

As she left, Billy put a hand on Andrea's shoulder. She turned to look at him.

"You think this is going to work?" Billy asked.

"There's just as much chaos in here as out there," said Andrea. "With as bad as you two are beat up, they'll expect to see your DNA and fingerprints all over everything, except maybe the weapons. We'll wipe those down and get rid of the gloves. And we'll have to hurry. The flood of emergency calls and storm damage will only delay them so long."

"I don't know, Andrea," Billy said. "If we do this, it's a pretty big secret."

Andrea looked down at the two bodies again. What had District Attorney David Mahoney told her?

"Small towns are built on secrets," she said. "That's why this is going to work."

Andrea picked up her phone. David Mahoney was her next call. This was his chance to bury the Fields story for good and give law enforcement a second chance to shutdown the operation in Nashua.

EPILOGUE

Billy and Jessica were the last two people standing at the grave site of Muriel Michaud as she joined her husband, Edward Michaud, at Maine Veterans' Memorial Cemetery almost six months after the worst wind storm in Maine's history. It was a cool day under partly cloudy skies, with the service lasting a little more than an hour.

"You okay?" Billy asked, putting an arm around her shoulder.

"The whole thing still feels surreal, you know," Jessica said, voice strained from crying. "I mean, leave it to my mom to pick April 1 to die on me. I half expected her to open the coffin and say, 'I'm just like John Partridge. April fools.'"

"I never read that one," Billy said.

"It's okay Billy. It wasn't a book, just a hoax written by Jonathan Swift," Jessica said. "It's a joke only a librarian's daughter can appreciate. Swift was fast and loose with the truth."

"The important thing is you were here for her," Billy said. "We were here for her. You, me, Andrea, Conner, Hope, Derrik, Danny, and everybody, really."

"She loved that best of all, I think. She told me she never felt less lonely since I graduated high school. I wish I would have realized that sooner."

"It's natural to feel that way, Jess," Billy said. "It was like the preacher said when he read that verse. 'We will be as we had never been; because the breath in our nostrils is smoke, and reason is a spark kindled by the breaking of our hearts. Therefore, let us enjoy the good things that exist, and make use of the creation to the full as in youth.'"

"You liked that?"

"I did," said Billy. "It made me think of Autumn."

"He paraphrased the passage, you know," Jessica said. "It also says that when we die, it will be as if we had never been born at all."

"Well, I don't believe that," Billy said, touching his heart. "Your mom will always be with me in here. If she hadn't seen through Dustin's disguise, I would have had no chance of finding you that night."

"Ugh, let's not talk about Dustin Fields today," Jessica said. "The statue his dad put up at Mount Pleasant is too much. I can't even drive by it."

"Sorry, I get it," Billy said. "At least some good came out of the money Dustin wanted to launder. Andrea convinced William Fields to donate it to a women's shelter. If he wants to make amends, he can start there. And now he knows Andrea is watching."

"Small miracles," Jessica said. "I just wish we could do more."

"You already have," Billy said. "Getting Stacy a job at the library was brilliant. And I guess that's my point. Your mom will live on through me, you, and anyone she touched with a love for reading."

Billy tossed the rose he was holding onto the casket. It seemed to float in the air, joining the flowers other guests had brought to honor her.

"That's sweet, Billy," she said. "I appreciate you. I guess I sometimes wish the world knew what she did that night instead of Dustin becoming a hero."

"Andrea was right," he said, kicking at the dirt. "There is a balance in what we did, you know. This story gave us some breathing room to heal and the police a chance to step back. That would have never happened if everything we did was put under a microscope. As long as we know the truth, that's all that matters."

"No, you're right," Jessica said. "I was just thinking of my mom more than anything."

"So what's next for you and Buttons?" Billy asked, changing the subject. "I mean, you were here for your mom. Are you going to head back to New York and scale the corporate ladder again?"

"No, I don't think so. I think I'll stay here for a while. It was nice of Andrea to hook me up with the newspapers, selling advertising. That will work for now."

"See, I told you she was warming up to you."

"Are you kidding? Andrea did that for you," Jessica said. "She hates me."

"Come on, she does not. She's a pit bull in need of her next story. It wasn't easy for her to do what she did, soliciting Mahoney's help. It went against her nature, but she did it for us, and they did it for the town."

"Billy, she blames me for you leaving," Jessica said. "You have to know that."

"She thinks that, but it's not true," said Billy. "If Autumn were still alive, I'd be moving on anyway. It's what Autumn wanted, not much different from you."

"Now you're just being nice," Jessica said. "I was a real bitch. I don't even know why anymore. I had this stupid idea in my head that you'd hold me back."

"You were a kid," Billy said. "So was I."

"Kind of funny. It's a switch. Now I'm the one staying, and you're the one leaving. How's that going, by the way? Do you know where you're going to end up?"

"Not really," said Billy. "I'll visit my folks in Florida and then head west somewhere. Hard to believe I'm making art a full-time job."

"I'm happy for you," said Jessica, her lips pressed thin.

"Funny, you don't look happy," he said.

Billy watched her put her hands in her pockets and look up to the sky. She was thinking of what to say.

"I guess," she said. "Part of me wouldn't have minded us having another go at it, you know?"

Billy bit the inside of his cheek and looked down. It was his turn to slip his hands inside his coat pockets.

"What was it you said to me at the Bear Paw?"

"I don't know," she said. "It feels like that was a lifetime ago."

"What we had was really special," he said. "I don't want to change that."

Billy looked at her, waiting for a reaction. Jessica took a long, slow breath.

"We should probably get going," she said. "People are going to arrive at the house and wonder where the host ran off to."

"You're probably right," he said. "Let's get going."

Billy offered his arm, and Jessica slipped her hand around it. The two of them didn't say another word until they arrived at the Michaud house, content with their redefined friendship. When they arrived, everyone was waiting.

ABOUT THE AUTHOR

Richard R. Becker is the author of the best-selling and award-winning short-story collection *50 States* and the novel *Third Wheel*. Collectively, his first two books have earned eleven literary awards. He is also the author of *Ten Threads*, a companion to *50 States*, which was published as a digital exclusive. *Born on Monday* is his second novel in the *50 States* universe.

When Becker is not writing fiction, he works as the president of Copywrite, Ink., a strategic communication and writing services firm. He has many other interests, including travel, acting, and spending time with family. He is married and has two adult children.

To learn more about Richard R. Becker, visit him at byrichardrbecker.com